Also by Maurice Leonard

Kathleen – The Life of Kathleen Ferrier
Mae West – The Empress of Sex

MARKOV

THE LEGEND

MARKOVA
THE LEGEND

MAURICE LEONARD

Hodder & Stoughton

Copyright © 1995 by Maurice Leonard

The right of Maurice Leonard to be identified as the Author
of this work has been asserted by him in accordance with the
Copyright, Designs and Patents Act 1988.

First published in 1995 by Hodder and Stoughton
A division of Hodder Headline PLC

10 9 8 7 6 5 4 3 2 1

A CIP catalogue record for this title is available
from the British Library

ISBN 0 340 64032 4

Typeset by Palimpsest Book Production Limited,
Polmont, Stirlingshire
Printed and bound in Great Britain by
Mackays of Chatham PLC, Chatham, Kent

Hodder and Stoughton
A division of Hodder Headline PLC
338 Euston Road
London NW1 3BH

Acknowledgments

Before thanking anyone else I must thank Dame Alicia for letting me get to know her a little. Also for the hours of unstinting assistance she gave me, and for allowing me access to her comprehensive library. Without these things the book could never have been written. Her life is history but only she knew the full cast and story. I must also thank her for turning the research into fun. We laughed a lot and I shall miss that.

In addition, special thanks are due to Edna Barnard, Doris Barry, Dawn Bates, Rachel Bond, Ian Brown, Win Couchman, Clement Crisp, Leslie Crowther, Alexandra Danilova, the late Florence Desmond, the late Anton Dolin, William R. Fitts of Hollywood, the late Dame Margot Fonteyn, Freddie Franklin, the late John Gilpin, Malcolm Goddard, Ram Gopal, John Graham, Dame Beryl Grey, Geoffrey Handley-Taylor, Vivienne Haskell, Beryl Kaye, Brian Klein, Nellie and Tony Liddell, David Mason, Angela Rippon, Moira Shearer, Bernard Taylor, Wendy Toye, Dame Ninette de Valois, Rowena Webb and *The Concise Oxford Dictionary of Ballet.*

'. . . the beautiful have no enemy but time.'
W. B. Yeats

'. . . hard work, physical stamina, flawless technique and dramatic flair are not of themselves enough . . . "Giselle" demands the life-blood of an artist and nothing else.' – Alicia Markova

'Not only the best living ballet dancer but probably the best who ever lived.' – John Martin, *New York Times*

'It has been said of Markova that never, under any circumstances or on any occasion, has a hair of her head been discovered out of place. It might be added that never has a leg or an arm departed a quarter of an inch from perfection.' – Carl van Vechten

'Fifty years ago Alicia Markova was acclaimed the greatest of her kind, but who remembers her vividly? Who can recall why she was so outstanding? I can, I saw her repeatedly, I worked beside her . . . I can testify that she was, indeed, the stuff of immortality.' – Agnes de Mille

'As I watch her, Markova – like Duse in Ibsen – seems to be speaking poetry to the company's earnest prose.' – Edwin Denby

'To Helpmann Markova was Pavlova all over again – a creature of magic. Entranced, he relived the hero worship of early adolescence. Markova, like Pavlova, was the embodiment of the classical dancer.' – Elizabeth Salter, author of *Helpmann, the authorized biography*

'With her phenomenal memory of style and step Markova is a balletic treasure house.' – Clement Crisp, *The Times*

'Markova was far above and apart from the rest of us. She was a star. She was unique . . . I never took my eyes off her when she danced.' – Dame Margot Fonteyn, *Autobiography*

'She would have been a star no matter who taught her.' – Dame Ninette de Valois

'She was, indeed, the first British prima ballerina.' – *International Dictionary of Ballet*

'She was ethereal . . . like thistledown.' – Moira Shearer

'She was the complete ballerina.' – Arnold Haskell

'Everyone who sees Markova, that exquisite, ethereal creature, must imagine she lives exclusively on air . . .' – Dame Marie Rambert

'May she stand on a pedestal, among the greats forever.' – Stanislas Idzikowsky

'Historians in the past have been wont to record, "There will never be another Taglioni, another Grisi or another Pavlova," but today there is Markova.' – Vincenzo Celli

'In conversations this writer had with her, Dame Alicia indicated that the hand in that velvet glove was made of durable, if unusually attractive, steel.' – Allen Hughes, *New York Times*

Contents

᪥

List of Illustrations

Alicia and Serge Lifar in Biarritz, 1936.
At Nairobi airport, 1949.
Alicia and Miskovitch, 1954.
Alicia sitting for Tretchikeoff.
Alicia and Dolin in South Africa, 1949.
Alicia and Dolin at Havana, 1950.
Alicia and Dolin waiting to go on stage.
Markova and Dolin in 'Swan Lake', 1950.
Dolin and Alicia in 'The Nutcracker', 1949.
Pas de Quatre: Dolin version.
Doris, Alicia, the Haskells and Vivienne, 1949.
The 'Festival Ballet' on the river.
'The Dying Swan', 1951.

Between pages 242/243

Sugar Plum Fairy on tour in America, 1947.
In Florence being fitted for shoes by Salvatore Ferragamo.
Alicia and Miskovitch in 'Les Sylphides', 1954.
Alicia with Ram Gopal in 'Radha Krishna', spring 1960.
Official Metropolitan Opera House portrait, 1963.
Alicia on stage at The London Palladium, 1959.
The four Marks sisters with Alicia's DBE, 1963.
With Sol Hurok in New York in 1967.
'The Indestructable Markova', 1964.
At the official opening of the Royal Academy of Dancing's premises.
Greeting Sir Frederick Ashton in New York, 1970.
Receiving Doctorate of Music, 1982.
Alicia and Erik Bruhn, 1982.
Alicia on her 80th birthday.
Presenting Dame Ninette de Valois with 'Evening Standard' Ballet Award.
Alicia with 1994 'Evening Standard' Ballet award at the Savoy Hotel, 1995.
Teaching Iohna Loots, of the Balanchine Ballet, 1995.

Foreword

I first met Markova on 31 March 1974. At the time I was working for Thames Television's *This Is Your Life* programme and researching a 'life' on Anton Dolin, Markova's dancing partner. I was about to ask her to come on his show.

They were a distinguished couple whose lives were so intertwined that at times they seemed as one. Many of their fans suspected a romance between them, and hoped for it.

They coursed along brilliantly and sometimes stormily, all their lives, always, in their different ways, caring for each other.

She had met him when she was a child of ten, a professional even then, and billed as 'The Child Pavlova'. He was seven years older and a student. He became a star before her.

I was walking into a potential minefield by asking Markova to appear on Dolin's 'life'. Her own *This Is Your Life* had been broadcast by the BBC in 1959 and Dolin had been conspicuous by his absence. He had refused to have anything to do with it. He had thought he should be the subject and was jealous. Such temperament was nothing new for the great Dolin, his arrogance matched only by his talent. On this occasion he felt affronted.

It would have been inappropriate to have had Dolin as a subject before Markova. By then she was by far the more durable star. Try explaining that to Dolin.

Markova had been curious as to why Dolin had not appeared on her 'life', but she had known him over forty years and, helped by a few hints from colleagues, it did not take long for the penny to drop. I was well aware of this when I called to interview her.

Actually, our first meeting could have been a disaster.

She lives in a big mansion flat in Knightsbridge. I rang the bell and someone showed me into a room and asked me to wait. I was not entirely sure what to expect.

Markova was a legend who had been introduced into my life when I was about ten. At the time my mother had been reading the *Daily Mirror* which carried a picture-story claiming that Markova had to drink a pint of stout a day to keep up her weight.

'Isn't she lovely?' Mother had said as she held up the picture. Markova was wearing a tutu. I had never seen a woman in a tutu and thought it not so much lovely as outlandish. But she was certainly thin.

The fact that my mother knew Markova was an endorsement of her fame. My mother knew only national celebrities like the Royal Family, Lady Docker, Elizabeth Taylor and Prince Monolulu. All were stars. Clearly, so was Markova.

Now I was to meet her. The thin lady in the tutu of all those years ago. I made an idiot of myself.

I was in a pleasant room with neutral walls and two white-wood chairs that had once belonged to Pavlova. The Knightsbridge traffic purred below. A painting of Markova by Richard Banks dominated the room. It was in shades of white, the only relief the brown eyes and raven hair. Matisse had told her she should wear only white. The tiny, unfinished hands tapered into eternity. It had been painted for an exhibition of Balanchine's principal dancers.

I recognized Diaghileff from an autographed photograph in a frame. Several china swans were lying about, gifts from admirers – Fokine had specially choreographed *The Dying Swan* for her. It had become her signature piece. He had originally devised the dance for Pavlova and had rechoreographed it for Alicia.

While I was taking all this in the door opened and in walked an elegant woman with a bouffant hairstyle. She wore a business suit and I presumed she was the secretary.

'I've an appointment with Dame Alicia,' I said.

'Yes, I'm Alicia.'

I leapt to my feet. This was a good start.

'You must excuse me,' I gabbled. 'All my life I've heard of Markova, the legend, and in walks a lady the same age as me.'

I was in my twenties at the time.

'Would you care for a sherry?' she asked, smiling and reaching for the decanter.

I had expected someone older. I took comfort in the fact that I was not the only one to be surprised by how well she looks. When journalist Deborah Ross interviewed her for the *Daily Mail* in 1994 she wrote: 'She is still quite beautiful. She has big, brown eyes, a smiling coral-lipsticked mouth and skin so smooth you imagine that if she ever cried, the tears would roll down it like raindrops on a window pane. As she talks she holds her neck with swan-like poise and her hands flutter gracefully like dancing butterflies. I, a third of her age, but with four times the forehead wrinkles and none of the grace, have never felt less gainly in my life.'

She willingly agreed to come on Dolin's show. Had she decided to play tit for tat I would have been in trouble as we could not have done Dolin's 'life' without Markova. It would have been incomplete. She never mentioned the fact that he had not appeared on hers.

'I'm going on holiday for a while,' she told me as I was about to leave. 'So don't try to ring me. Just send the car on the day and I'll be there.'

After the show, everyone moved to the reception room where the wine flowed.

The reception was lively, and in the midst of it I saw Alicia walk over to where the coats were hanging and put hers on. I went up to her.

'Why are you going? You're the belle of the ball, everyone wants to meet you.'

'I'm going back to hospital,' she said. 'That's why you couldn't ring me. I've not been on holiday at all, but I knew that if I told you I was in hospital you'd have been worried.'

I would have been.

She appeared on several shows for me after that and I broached the idea of writing her life story. We had a tacit agreement that I would do it. We even sat down over a couple of evenings and made notes. I interviewed people.

But she would never tie herself down. She was doing too much for that. One day she'd be off to New York for business at the Met. She'd come back for a few days then go to lecture at a university in Arizona. Another time she was off to Germany. Then the BBC came up with its *Master Class* TV series, and then there were the 'Markova Awards', and so it went on.

The years slipped by and, in the interval, I had six other books published.

But we kept in touch and, sometimes, I would get messages to the effect that she was appearing at such and such a place and would like me to be there. It might be of interest for the book.

Eventually, just after her eighty-third birthday, she agreed.

It's easy to forget nowadays, with today's new heroes, just how much Markova has contributed to Britain's international cultural status, and in a world that was not so easily travelled as it is now.

She flew Britain's flag in balletically uninhabited territory. Before her only foreigners had been ballerinas. No one thought we could do it.

Markova was the first British ballerina to take her own company on provincial tours. Single-handedly she kept the Vic-Wells going through its formative years; she took ballet to South and Central America and many towns in North America where they had never seen it before. She took ballet to the tropics.

Balanchine, Massine, Fokine and Ashton all choreographed for her. She debuted many of their works. She was the first British ballerina to dance *Swan Lake*, *The Nutcracker* and *Giselle*.

Put her in a dressing room and she is happy. Her sitting room resembles a star dressing room with its framed Markova bills, autographed photographs of the greats, bundles of files on her career, and piles of books in which she is mentioned.

Her bedroom is almost spartan with a few feminine exceptions, namely a pink bedspread and pretty pastel carpet. It is scrupulously neat. Nothing is unnecessary and nothing is out of place.

She is still a part of what is happening in the ballet world today, and gives master classes and lectures and appears on television. Although a traditionalist, she is not greatly interested in things of the past. There are no antiques; she doesn't like them, preferring functional furniture.

She is also self-reliant. One day she cancelled an appointment with me. She had just flown in from Paris and had a cold. In addition she had an injured hand. She had been presented with a bouquet the night before and in trimming the flowers had nearly cut off a finger. It was bleeding badly and it was late at night.

She didn't panic. She sat up in bed with the finger upright until the morning when the doctor could come.

She was too ill to go out for a while but was not unhappy about this. 'It's tennis and the Cup Final on the television,' she told me over the phone. 'I shall be all right.' She loves anything involving movement, including military tattoos and marches. As did Balanchine.

While working with her I was also producing a television series starring Michael Barrymore, and she is a fan of his. As I was bundling my notes and cassettes into my bag after one session she cracked, 'Don't get those mixed up with Barrymore. It would be awful if they got into the wrong file.' She always sent him her love.

This book developed over many hours of sitting in her flat. Sometimes I would be working and she would bring me black coffee and smoked salmon sandwiches. The hands, which Epstein so wanted to sculpt and Annigoni to paint, although she never got around to sitting for them, would quietly lay the tray beside me, then there would be a little flourish as she approved of her handiwork. I had the world's most exclusive maid.

Sometimes siren-blaring police cars hurtled by outside. In keeping with ballet, Knightsbridge is also facing the twenty-first century.

Unaffected by the sirens, she would punctuate what she was saying with little asides like 'Talk about luck' or 'I was so naïve'.

I quickly learnt not to chop and change subjects; she likes to stick to one train of thought at a time. Once she mentioned an award she received on television in Rio and added, 'I did lots of experimental TV in New York for NBC.' 'When was that?' I asked. 'That comes later,' she said, 'in the television section.'

What television section? But she had it worked out.

Markova casts a spell. I would chatter to her for hours until her sister Doris, with whom she lives, would come and chase me away. She'd chide me next day for 'exhausting' her. Exhaust her? I doubt a *Tyrannosaurus rex* snapping at her heels would actually exhaust her.

Although she is involved with exhibitions, examinations, performances, academies and students, her story is not of today. It is part of a mystical era when she was introducing an art-form new to much of the world. The characters who move in and out of her tale are fabled – Pavlova, Diaghileff, Spessivtseva, Stravinsky, even a glimpse of Nijinsky. The world was different then. There was no British ballet before Markova.

1

The Dumb Girl of Portici

Lilian Alicia Marks, later known to the world as Dame Alicia Markova, was born on 1 December 1910. Her parents, Eileen and Arthur, lived in a two-room rented flat at 23 Wilberforce Road in north London's Finsbury Park, virtually within throwing distance of Finsbury Park Empire, home of music hall. It was all they could afford. She was given the names of Lilian and Alicia after two great-grandmothers. Her second name was never Alice, as folklore has it, always Alicia.

Coincidentally, that year the ballerina Anna Pavlova, just twenty-nine years old but already a legend, was appearing in London. Not at the Royal Opera House but in music hall at the Palace Theatre with a cast that included Arley's Athletic Dogs. Animal acts were popular – so was Pavlova whose name on the bill was guaranteed to fill any theatre. She was to play a crucial role in Markova's life.

Eileen and Arthur were very much in love. He was a bright, twenty-one-year-old Jewish lad who was a mining engineer. At the time he had no money but was, after his marriage, to make a fortune from his ideas.

His father was in South Africa and his mother was American but no one was sure whether he was born in America or England. Some generations ago his family had originated from Poland. 'It's all a bit vague, they all moved about so much,' says Alicia.

Engineering was in his blood and his ancestors had something to do with both the design of Tower Bridge and devising the glowing electric lights of the Broadway theatres.

Little did anyone suspect that his daughter's name would one

7

day be beaming down from one of those illuminated Broadway marquees.

Eileen was Irish, from Cork, and twenty. She was beautiful. 'She looked like Elizabeth Taylor,' says Doris, Alicia's sister. 'She had the same colouring, the same black hair and the violet eyes.' She had been educated in a Catholic convent, preparing to be a nun.

Eileen and Arthur had married at the Upper Berkeley Street synagogue on 22 February 1910. In order for the marriage to take place Eileen had converted to Judaism. Coming from a strict Catholic background, that was no easy decision for her to take.

As Alicia later told choreographer Agnes de Mille, 'Think of the strength of mind of that woman . . . think of the character. An Irish Catholic yet she abandoned her entire background and accepted for love of her husband a way of living so strange and overwhelming.'

Arthur had met Eileen in Ireland four years before their marriage; he was there, probably for a holiday, after taking his engineering examinations. After the marriage they had honeymooned in Brighton and it was there that Alicia was conceived.

Their marriage remained a love-match and Alicia was to base much of her later interpretation of her most celebrated role, 'Giselle', on the strength of their union. 'Because my parents were childhood sweethearts and each remained everything to the other throughout both their lives, it has not been difficult for me to convey Giselle's single-minded devotion to Albrecht and the fact she cannot picture the world without him.'

Eileen had not realized she was pregnant until quite late on. By that time she had been tossed by a bull when on holiday in Ireland and later, back in London, fainted during a roller-coaster ride at the World's Fair in Earl's Court. It was then that the doctor confirmed her pregnancy.

Alicia's birth was not easy and for a while it was feared that both mother and child might die. 'I was very small,' Alicia recalls, '. . . and what was the word that was used so much then . . . frail? I was delicate and frail.'

Arthur was disappointed when she arrived as he had hoped for a son, but he soon got over this and she became the apple of his eye. He decided that whatever a boy could do his daughter, delicate or not, could do better.

Being an Arsenal fan, he saw no reason why she should not also enjoy a football match, and took her to games, hoisting her on his shoulders for a better view. Alicia has an unusually sharp memory and can still recall those matches when she was lifted above the crowds to cheer. She is still an Arsenal fan and is fond of football in general.

She can remember Arthur taking her to Tower Bridge and explaining how it worked, telling her that it was connected with the family, so to speak. Sometimes he took her to Finsbury Park to hear the band play, and she wanted to conduct it. She still loves brass bands.

Eileen would take her to nearby Clissold Park to see the swans on the lake. Someone has written, clearing thinking of her future association with *The Dying Swan*, that as a child, she knew each swan by name. 'I can't recall that,' she says. But she does recall bringing bits of bread to feed them.

Arthur began to prosper in business. The family were constantly moving to better premises. Before she was four years old they had moved four times, but always in north London. 'I never really had a home, I was like a gipsy, always ready to move, never settled.' She never did settle; that nomad style was to remain a feature of her life.

For one period the family lived with her great-grandfather Abraham in a big boarding house. 'He took charge of me,' Alicia says. 'He was orthodox and while I was with him I was brought up in the orthodox Jewish faith. There were no children, I was the only one. What was I? Two, or three? It's all as though it were yesterday . . .

'I was four when the First World War started. Daddy didn't get called up because he was on special service. He had a factory down in the Caledonian Road somewhere by then where they manufactured his invention, I think it was called "rubberine". It was used on all the armoured cars that had to go to war. By filling the tyres with this they couldn't be punctured.

'Sometimes when he used to go to the Admiralty at Whitehall he would take me with him. I would sit in the car and wait while he went inside. I remember it so well, and one day one of the admirals came out and greeted me. I think it was Admiral Tapper. I know I was very impressed. Apparently Daddy had told him he couldn't stay long because he had his little daughter waiting in the car. I didn't talk but I took it all in and I enjoyed that.'

She didn't talk much at all, just made a few gurgling sounds, and that was worrying, but as she seemed happy enough Eileen and Arthur did not try to make her. They decided to wait and see what happened.

Meanwhile Eileen became pregnant again and gave birth to another daughter, Doris. Alicia can remember being farmed out to neighbours in Barnet during Eileen's confinement. She did not like it; they did things differently there.

She also remembers wandering round to her next door neighbours, the Kurnows. Dorothy Kurnow took care of her sometimes. Alicia couldn't say Dorothy so called her Doff, in the way children do.

When she returned from Barnet she found another new arrival, in addition to Doris. This was Smut, a black kitten – his name was Smudge but she couldn't say that either so he became Smut.

In addition to the neighbours in Barnet, and the Kurnows, she was sometimes, at weekends, sent to Arthur's secretary Muriel and her sister Elsie. 'I was always in strange people's homes, since I can remember,' she says.

After Doris, Eileen and Arthur had two more daughters, Vivienne, who arrived when Alicia was seven, and Berenice, nicknamed Bunny, who came the following year.

After Doris's birth Eileen found it difficult to cope. She was inexperienced, and running a house – they now lived in a house with a garden – and seeing to the children was too much for her. Arthur could see things were getting her down and that she needed someone to take the responsibility from her shoulders and, since he was now earning good money, he hired a home help.

This was the formidable Gladys Hogan, known as Guggy, an Irish spinster who symbolized all that spinsterhood stands for. She came from a military family, had no sense of humour, was incapable of love, and her life was ruled by duty. She was fiercely loyal to the family and to Alicia in particular. She would have killed for her, but could never show affection. She had no time for it.

By the time Guggy arrived the Markses had moved to 17 Cascade Avenue, Muswell Hill. 'Daddy bought that house,' Alicia says, 'because it was just across the road from Alexandra Palace. The British interned German prisoners there. Daddy thought it wouldn't get bombed because the Germans were hardly likely to bomb their own people. He thought we would be as safe there as anywhere.'

On the day Guggy arrived Alicia (who was called Little Lily then) was sitting on the kitchen floor playing with Doris. Not so much playing as eating her sweets. She had been told to give the baby some barley sugar to shut her up, as Doris had started to bawl and that drove Eileen mad. Doris was given a few licks and Alicia ate the rest herself. It was a wicked thing for a little girl to do to her baby sister.

'Mother was sitting in the garden crying,' Alicia recalls. 'Doris was on the floor and also crying and Mummy told me to sit with her. When reporters ask me if I ever did anything naughty as a kid I say "Yes", that was the first time. That's when my sweet tooth developed. I ate the lot and since then I've always loved sweets and chocolates, anything sweet. I can't resist it. Guggy was very capable, she came into the kitchen and took charge at once. I think Mother thought, Thank God, somebody's come to help.'

Within a short time Guggy was running the household.

'Guggy had been there maybe a week,' Alicia goes on, 'and I was in the garden, I loved to be out there with all the flowers. Guggy, Mother and Doris were in the kitchen and suddenly I ran in and said in my funny way – I still wasn't speaking properly – that there was something in the sky. A plane was flying over.

'They rushed out, because planes were still a novelty, and we saw it had crosses on it. All I remember is that Guggy yanked me inside. It was the first daylight bombing raid. I knew what a cross meant because Daddy was always teaching me things, he never talked to me like a child, and he had told me that German planes had crosses on them and that ours had red, white and blue circles.

'After that the bombers used to come at night and we were brought downstairs. There was a heavy oak table in the dining room and mattresses were put on top of this and around it and Doris and I were pushed underneath. It was like a little dug-out and we stayed there until the all-clear went. We didn't have cellars or shelters.'

Alicia is fascinated by all things medical. If she had any childhood dream at all it was to become a doctor; there were no thoughts of ballet.

When she became an adult and underwent various operations she would discuss with the surgeons what was to be done to her and why. She never liked taking medicine. Usually she sleeps like a log and doesn't need sleeping pills, preferring a cup of Ovaltine or Horlicks – a fourteen-hour sleep is not unusual for Alicia. 'That's how I replace my energy,' she says.

If, after an operation, a doctor suggests sleeping pills she will 'bargain' with him. 'I'll say, OK, I'll take your pills if I can't sleep but bring me some Ovaltine first. I'll drink that and, invariably, by the time they return to check me I'll be asleep.'

She was able to put her medical ambition into practice as a child when Doris sliced off the top of her finger while playing with some scissors she had got hold of in the nursery.

When Alicia heard Doris scream she ran to her, saw what had

happened, and placed the tip back on the finger and held it on, yelling for Guggy. She kept it there until Guggy came running in and whisked Doris off to a doctor who managed to save the finger. Thanks to Alicia, Doris now has an unmarred set of fingers. For a five-year-old she displayed a remarkably cool head.

By the time Alicia was getting on for six something was clearly wrong, as she still could not speak. By now Eileen and Arthur were worried. Alicia was happy and took everything in her stride but her silence was unnerving.

She played with her sisters, and would even wander off to neighbours' houses from time to time and mix with them, but she would not speak.

Eileen took her to a doctor who did not seem unduly worried. 'Mother said he told her I was ahead with my brain, advanced for my years, and that I was observant and knew everything that was going on. Perhaps it was laziness on my part. I don't know.

'Anyway, he told her not to send me to school, as I was too sensitive, but to leave me to develop. None of this bothered me, I only knew I was enjoying life. I think I learnt more than at any school, going round visiting people. It was general knowledge, to take one through life.'

This was all very well but she needed educating, otherwise she would become backward, intelligent or not. Guggy gave her lessons. Alicia loved delving into books, particularly those on history. 'I've always loved books.'

But Guggy was not the ideal companion for a child. 'She was very strict,' says Alicia. 'At that time I didn't realize just how strict and, I suppose, I could have turned into a monster. She believed in discipline and acted with the best intentions. I wouldn't say she loved me, though, as there was no affection. I used to be very lonely and Guggy didn't encourage me to have friends. At that period young people were brought up to be seen and not heard. You only spoke if you were spoken to.'

Alicia was eight by the time she eventually went to school and she hated it. The over-protective Guggy had taught her to stand aloof from other children and she was naturally shy and not a good mixer, so it was hard for her to find things in common with her schoolmates.

She spent her playtimes cooped up with her books. It was easier to immerse herself into their world rather than face the reality of a playground.

School became a misery but she was saved from it by a bout

of whooping cough which, at the time, seemed sent straight from heaven. As whooping cough is infectious it meant a lengthy quarantine period, so she was taken away from school. All four sisters had to be quarantined until the household was free of germs. It suited Alicia down to the ground.

By the time she was fit enough to return, so much time had elapsed that Eileen thought it better to send her to another school where she might be happier since she had so loathed her first one.

She hated that too. The lessons were not a problem – Guggy had taught her well, she enjoyed learning and had a talent for mental arithmetic, and her outstanding memory also enabled her to remember all the historical dates she required – but, as before, she had a problem mixing with the other girls.

She did not have to endure it for long. Once again God's messenger came to her, this time in the guise of measles. Measles is as infectious as whooping cough and, again, the girls were confined to home. 'I had everything when I was a child – chickenpox, measles and German measles, the lot. I suppose I really was as delicate as they said.'

By a quirk of fate she never had to attend school again. Alicia thinks that the sum total of her school days amounted to no more than two months.

When Alicia was out of quarantine, Eileen saw that the film *The Dumb Girl of Portici*, starring Pavlova, was on at the local cinema. She decided to take Alicia to see it.

Pavlova was a heroine of Eileen's. She adored ballet and had seen music-hall performances by the great dancer. She had enthused to Alicia about her. When she had been carrying her she had hoped that, if her baby was a girl, she might look like Pavlova and dance a tiny bit as well.

She had told this to Arthur one warm, moonlit night in Egypt, where he had been sent to work on the design of the Aswan Dam. In sight of the pyramids, she had confessed that she would like their child to be a dancer.

So Alicia was a wish come true. She not only became a dancer but physically resembled Pavlova. A glance at any photographs of the two will show that they are strikingly alike.

The Dumb Girl of Portici was special in that Pavlova did not usually appear in films. It was a ninety-minute Hollywood silent with all the panache for which the film capital was already famous.

Alicia sat in the darkened auditorium and watched Pavlova

appear through a swirling mist, dancing to the accompaniment of the cinema pianist. 'I remember it vaguely,' she says. 'I thought she was so beautiful. But it never entered my head that that was what I would wish to be.'

2

Flat Feet

Every summer Arthur would rent a house near the coast, sometimes Bognor and sometimes Littlehampton, and the family would move there for a holiday.

'One summer,' Alicia remembers, 'I was plodding along the sand with the family and Guggy said, "There's something wrong with that child. She's flapping along like a duck."'

The whole family stood to look while Alicia paced the front, carrying her bucket and spade. She was flat-footed which made her pad along, as Guggy had put it, like a duck. She also had knock-knees which made her feet seem flatter. No one had noticed this before.

'When we got back to town Mother took me to Harley Street to see a specialist,' Alicia recalls. 'He was in army uniform, all in khaki with puttees, and I was awed. It was the first time the war was brought home to me. He examined me and then asked Mother if she ever went to the ballet.'

That was an unorthodox question from a Harley Street foot specialist, but he was an unorthodox man. He was interested in ballet from a medical viewpoint, and thought some of the exercises could be beneficial in correcting defects to the legs, notably Alicia's knock-knees and flat feet.

'Mother told him she had seen Pavlova,' Alicia continues. 'She had not seen a full-scale ballet as there were no ballet companies in England then. He told her he thought that was wonderful and they discussed dancing for a while while I was sitting there.

'He told Mother I had a form of weakness in the legs, which was causing my flat feet, and that it emanated from the hips. He was fascinated by the "turnout" used in classical ballet.*

'He asked Mother if she would be willing to undertake an experiment with him. He thought "turnouts" must strengthen the legs and asked her to send me to ballet lessons. He told her if he was wrong, and my legs did not get better, then I would have to wear leg-irons.

'When I heard that I thought, How awful, I'd better try to learn it properly. It had to be better than leg-irons. And that was it, there was no master plan, no sense of vocation, just an attempt to correct my feet.'

Eileen enrolled her for lessons at the Thorne Academy, run by the Misses Dorothy and Madge Thorne, near the Athenaeum Cinema at the top of Muswell Hill. She went every Saturday morning and Doris was sent along too, to keep her company. Guggy took them both. Alicia studied dancing with Miss Dorothy Thorne while Doris studied elocution with Miss Madge.

No one knew Alicia was there for corrective lessons, not even the Misses Thorne. That would have been too humiliating for her.

'I found it fascinating,' she says. 'Although I was there for barre work to strengthen my legs it was all-round training and I was taught old-time dancing as well, particularly The Lancers, and ballroom dancing and skipping with ropes.

'One of the things I did particularly well was working with Indian clubs, like jugglers use. I had to swing them over my head, behind my back and in front, all to music. I did it very well. I was surprising myself as well as my teachers.

'I had such small wrists that people thought I had no strength in them. But my wrists, although delicate-looking, grew strong, thanks, I'm sure, to the clubs. In later life this presented problems for Massine when he was choreographing me because he could never put in an understudy for my roles. I could manage heavy lifts that no other female dancer could handle.

'I got on so well at the Thorne Academy that when it put on a display they gave me a solo. I think it was the spectre of the irons that inspired me.'

Miss Dorothy Thorne was soon aware that she had someone special on her hands. The child was a natural, and easily mastered

---

* One of the basic ballet requirements. Once it is mastered it enables the dancer to move freely in every direction. In order to perfect the 'turnout' it is necessary to study academic exercises over several years.

exercises that baffled many of the other kids, some of them much older than Alicia.

Miss Thorne was so impressed with her that she called on Eileen and tried to persuade her to let Alicia have private lessons. She thought she might even become a professional dancer.

But Eileen's only concern was that Alicia's legs straightened and her feet developed arches. The romantic hopes, whispered at the site of the Sphinx, had evaporated with motherhood. She refused to let her take further lessons. Alicia was too young to be taken seriously.

Nevertheless, she encouraged her at home. It was a way of bringing her out of herself.

Great-grandfather Abraham indulged her. He was a theatrical supplier who provided rich fabrics, embroidery and costume jewellery to Clarkeson's, the famous costumiers. He kept his supplies in the room at the boarding house she had once shared with him.

The house was owned by a family called Crewley, and Alicia was to stay in contact with them for most of her life. 'They were like family,' she says. The Crewleys moved about the country and at various times set up homes in both Brighton and Littlehampton. Later this came in handy at holiday times for Alicia when she had a break from dancing. It was not always easy for the whole family to go away with the three younger girls, but they knew that with the Crewleys Alicia would be properly looked after and get a decent break. So she was sometimes sent off alone.

Alicia loved to roam about in Great-grandfather Abraham's costume room and was fascinated by the sequins and jewels. He gave her remnants of cloth and beads and she made them into dolls' costumes. She was good at sewing and embroidery.

Spurred by Great-grandfather Abraham's donations, she improvised plays in which her sisters could act. 'Sometimes I appeared in them too, but usually I was the organizer. I chose the music for each one. I certainly never danced, I didn't consider myself a dancer then. To me the theatre was magic. Theatrical people tried to create magic then.'

By now she was speaking normally enough, to the relief of the family, although her voice was quiet. It still is. 'I wasn't allowed to raise it then,' she says. 'Somehow people never seemed to want to listen to me, I think that was it. I thought, Why bother? I think I only really started speaking when I stopped dancing, and then I had to.'

The family had a wind-up gramophone, quite a coup, and this

would be moved to the garden, where Arthur had had an area concreted over and made into a little stage for the girls. When they performed he would put on the records. Egyptian themes were popular and Alicia devised a piece to Luigini's *Ballet Egyptien*. 'As far as I remember I directed it and my sisters danced.' Sometimes a few neighbours were invited in to admire the girls.

They also played more normal games. 'We had colourful imaginations and spent hours playing in our make-believe world,' Doris says. 'One of our favourite games was travelling, using the lid of Mother's sewing machine and the upturned nursery table as chariots, magic carpets, or even aeroplanes.'

Other times they would use the table as a bus. 'Vivienne and Bunny were the *hoi polloi*,' says Alicia. 'And Doris was a duchess. She was always a duchess. "I'm a lady," she would say. "I don't know you." I was usually the conductor.'

There was no problem working out the fares. 'She was a wizard at mental arithmetic,' confirms Doris. 'Later, when I used to represent her, she had the financial side of a contract worked out much faster than I did. I would be puzzling it out on paper and she'd have the figures already in her mind. She has an extremely practical side to her nature that not many people know exists. Throughout her career she always looked after her own accounts, no matter how busy she was with rehearsals and performances, and they were always right.'

'I suppose I had to,' says Alicia. 'I didn't have money for accountants when I started. Today it's different. If you become famous you have an accountant and entourage. I think I had those later, in America, but not till then. It wasn't a big thing, I just took care of the budget.'

'When we put on our little shows as children,' Doris continues, 'Alicia would produce, choreograph, design what sets we had, and then teach us what to do, including song, dance and comedy. Alicia and I recited at parties and our favourite piece was the woodland scene from *A Midsummer Night's Dream*, Alicia playing the fairy and I Puck. Alicia still remembers the lines.

'We used to illustrate special programmes which we would sell for the local hospital charity. I've still got one of these. Mother gave it to me, she had kept it all her life.'

Alicia was a fair pianist. She had had lessons since she was two. 'My piano teacher was Miss Nobbs and I stuck with her till I was ten or so. I'd always loved music, the band in the park and marches and our records, but I didn't care for practising scales. I wanted to do more. But Miss Nobbs gave me to understand that I had to practise scales before that could happen. I found that difficult so I started composing. Then I came up with an idea.

'I'd always adored chocolates and there was a cupboard in the room where I practised where Daddy used to put the big boxes he bought from Lyons Corner House.

'I knew they were listening to me outside to make sure I was practising so I'd do a quick scale then make a rush for the cupboard – that spurred me on.

'But when I started dancing and Miss Thorne said I was promising I told Mummy I would have to give up the piano. "You can't dance and play the piano at the same time," I told her. "You can dance and sing at the same time and you may be able to dance and play the flute at the same time but you can't dance and play the piano." So the piano went in favour of the dance. But I was very serious when I went to Miss Nobbs.'

She was very serious full stop. About that time Guggy took her to a wedding, the first to which she had been. 'I was there, taking everything in. It was new and I was enjoying it. Afterwards the priest came to me, a great big man, and he sort of patted me on the head and said, "Why so solemn, little one?" That was me. If you look at early photos of me I'm always solemn. After I was two or three life became terribly serious.'

For special occasions Alicia usually wore her white sailor outfit. That was serious-looking too. She did not like it, and she liked the black sailor suit, which she wore every day, even less. 'They drove me crazy the way they used to dress me. All the other girls had lovely fluffy dresses and there was me in a navy blue sailor suit and sailor's hat with HMS on it and with my Buster Brown hairdo and boots. How I loathed those button boots and the ones with laces. I liked the ankle-strap shoes of the time but I was never allowed them. It took me ages if I went to a party or something to change my shoes. It made me different. Some people enjoy being different and the attention it brings them but I hated it.

'Maybe I didn't have a round, pretty face like my sisters so I was always put in navy blue. It used to make me so sad. I remember being somewhere with Guggy and someone said, "What a sweet little girl you've got, is she French?" This really impressed Guggy and my mother so I was dressed up like a Continental girl. I used to feel like a little boy who's just come off a ship. I'd think, One day, when I can buy my own clothes it will be different . . . The bugbears of childhood.'

When she did come to the stage when she was able to buy her own clothes it wasn't that different. She most often went for black or grey, rarely colours. But by that time they bore designer labels and the fabrics were cashmeres and silks. The sailor hat was exchanged, too, for a variety of huge cartwheel shapes popularized by the mannequins of the 1940s and 1950s.

In the meantime she was about to face her first paying audience. Talent competitions were popular and, upon Miss Thorne's recommendation, Eileen had permitted Alicia to dance at one which was to be held at the Athenaeum Cinema. It would take place between the two films on the programme.

Arthur and Eileen turned up on the night and were, literally, astounded when Alicia made her entrance. They had seen her dance before, at school and in the back garden, but this was the first time they, or anyone else for that matter, had seen her in front of an audience.

What took them aback was not so much her dancing – Miss Thorne had told them that she was talented – but her composure. Their reclusive daughter who had such difficulty in communicating with people was clearly uninhibited by performing in front of a cinema full of people. She had a confidence they had never seen before.

Leaving the stage, to a storm of applause, she was the star of the evening, the undisputed winner. It helped that she was a child. The adults stood little chance competing with a cute girl. But it was not just her childishness, it was the combination of that and her talent.

'The winners were judged on the length of the applause,' recalls Alicia. 'It was the very first time I had heard applause directed at me and, for someone who didn't communicate very much, it could have been frightening. But, I must say, I enjoyed it. I wasn't afraid.'

She won five guineas and a contract to dance at the cinema for a week. But she was too young to be employed so that had to be turned down.

Miss Thorne was proud of her and she became her favourite pupil. The annual performance of the Thorne Academy was coming up once more and Miss Thorne featured her in this. She was cast as a Turkish sultana and received her first press notice: 'Little Lily Marks made a great hit with an Eastern dance.'*

This led to an engagement in the West End, on 1 April 1919, at a charity matinée at the Strand Theatre.

In those days, and it is much the same now, it was the practice of

---

* *North London Sentinel*, 21 February 1919.

producers to audition pupils at schools when children were needed for shows. Miss Thorne was consulted by a producer and had no hesitation in putting Alicia forward.

The matinée was to raise funds for the Italian Red Cross. War had ended in 1918 but its aftermath was still being felt and the Italian Red Cross was in dire straits.

Alicia was billed as a 'danseuse', which was a big description for a little girl, and was placed second on the bill following the Grenadier Guards, 'which I adored listening to. I nearly forgot what I was there for. I've always adored brass bands.' The cast included José Collins, Fay Compton, Beatrice Lillie and Jack Buchanan, the toast of the West End.

This was formidable competition, different to the amateurs at the Athenaeum, but, even so, it was Alicia who took the honours. All those seasoned pros smiled benignly as the moppet stole their thunder and dropped a perfect curtsey.

It was her speed and daintiness which won over the audiences. She came on stage, demure and neat with a serious face, and acknowledged the audience, and her music would start. Then, while maintaining perfect composure, her serious face unchanging, she executed the most complicated movements with the speed of lightning. No wonder the place erupted.

While the baby Markova was taking her first steps into ballet history, the great Nijinsky was taking his last. In Paris, in January 1929, the twenty-nine-year-old phenomenon danced in public for the last time. Only hours before he had started to write a notebook. It was this book,* when examined by Swiss doctors, which prompted his internment in a sanatorium, diagnosed as suffering from paranoid schizophrenia.

Doris was also doing well. She and Alicia formed a pair, whereas Vivienne and Bunny, owing to their younger ages, made another pair. Doris had been chosen to play in a movie version of Dickens's *The Old Curiosity Shop* and the film was about to open. With Alicia dancing in the West End and Doris on the screen, the Marks sisters were certainly making an impression.

When *The Old Curiosity Shop* opened Guggy took Doris and Alicia to see it. Doris was described in the papers as 'England's Baby Mary Pickford'. She was thrilled to see the film but it had no dramatic effect on her. But it had a devastating effect on Alicia. Her powerful imagination made her live through every scene. She was terrified of the evil dwarf Quilp. She couldn't forget him and, that night, as

---

* The unexpurgated books are soon to be released by his daughter Tamara.

the girls were going to bed in their shared bedroom, she looked out of the window and thought Quilp was leering at her from the street and that he was trying to get at her. She screamed and fainted.

This brought home to Eileen and Arthur, again, the measure of Alicia's sensitivity. They already knew she was finely balanced – her difficulties at school, the lateness of her starting to speak and her fear of strangers proved this – but from now on special care had to be taken as to what she could read and see.

The hit West End musical *Chu Chin Chow* was deemed suitable. Set in a fictitious old Arabia, it told the story of a slave girl who thwarts a robber masquerading as a mandarin. Today it would be deemed politically incorrect, but there was no political correctness in those days and it ran for years. Anyone who had not seen *Chu Chin Chow* had not lived.

Alicia loved the show and no screaming fits followed. She set about choreographing Eastern dances in the garden at home. *Chu Chin Chow* was her model.

The Thorne Academy gave another production, this time at the King's Hall in the heart of London. Alicia performed her oriental dance again and took several curtain calls. The 'best individual dance of the afternoon', wrote the *Dancing Times*.

Among the audience was producer George Shurley. He wrote Alicia's name in his notebook for future reference.

Alicia was taken to tea afterwards at Fuller's, famous for its cakes. Some other children who had been in the show were also there with their parents. She noticed them talking about her and pointing.

That was something she would have to get used to.

3

Pavlova

Pavlova was starring in London again, having returned from another sell-out world tour. One of her dances, 'Bacchanale', told of a votary in a state of abandoned lust. If a lesser artist had attempted it, it might have been deemed smutty, but as it was Pavlova it came under the banner of high art. Abandoned lust depicted on a public stage in Edwardian England was demure by today's standards, but there was nothing demure about Pavlova, who lit the stage with her timeless art.

Eileen thought Alicia should see her, as she was showing such promise.

Pavlova in the flesh would have more impact than Pavlova on film. No film managed to capture her glory; she bloomed before films realized their potential.

Arthur agreed to take Alicia. They would travel in style for, by now, he was doing so well that he drove a Rolls-Royce. Not bad progress from two rooms in Wilberforce Road.

In addition to 'Bacchanale', Pavlova danced 'Gavotte', to the music of Hermann Finck. She wore a yellow satin dress with a train. 'Californian Poppy' was also on the bill, and for this she changed into orange-yellow and danced to a Tchaikovsky melody. California was as remote from most Londoners as Mars. The poppy was seen in the splendour of full bloom and, during the dance, it folded its petals. Alicia was most impressed with this. 'Californian Poppy' was such a hit that Woolworth's sold a perfume with the same name.

This time Pavlova's performance had a magnetic effect on Alicia.

Arthur bought her a souvenir programme and, during the interval, she sat engrossed. It was magnificently illustrated. One photograph showed Pavlova reaching out to pet one of the swans that swam on the lake at Ivy House, her country-style home in Golders Green. Her swans must have been as unique as their owner as they are usually spiteful birds, to be admired at a respectful distance. But a woman as remarkable as Pavlova probably charmed swans as easily as she charmed humans.

Alicia was so immersed in her programme she even refused an ice-cream. To Arthur's amazement she asked if she might meet Madame Pavlova after the show.

It was usually torture for Alicia to meet new people and here she was, asking to be introduced to a star. He was not sure what to do. Pavlova was not the most accessible of people. But he did not want to discourage Alicia.

While he thought about this, Alicia added that she thought Madame Pavlova must be kind because she understood flowers and liked swans. 'Kind' was not a word usually applied to Pavlova.

Arthur left Alicia to her programme and did what he could to arrange things. He had no experience of this side of life and did not know how to start.

How do you approach a ballerina? He asked a commissionaire and was referred to a Monsieur Victor D'André, described as Pavlova's husband. This is unconfirmed as no marriage certificate has ever been found.

What is certain is that he was a plump Russian with a moustache, and a landowner and impresario who managed Pavlova's career throughout the world.

M. D'André informed Arthur that Madame saw absolutely no one after a performance. The whole world wanted to see Pavlova. But when Arthur explained that his daughter was a dancer who was in raptures over Madame Pavlova's performance, and that the papers had already taken notice of her, M. D'André relented.

He invited Arthur to bring her to Ivy House at 11.30 the next morning. He was always interested in dancers and frequently needed to flesh out the Pavlova companies with additional performers. Nevertheless, it was a gracious thing for him to do. He was inundated with requests.

Not being versed in the mores of show business, Arthur did not realize what he had accomplished. He returned to the auditorium and found Alicia still in her seat, as good as gold. He told her the news and she sat through the second half with her tummy full of butterflies. Pavlova appeared again and danced to more Tchaikovsky music. Alicia could not believe that she would be meeting her the next morning, just over twelve hours away.

She could not wait that long and, after the show, persuaded Arthur to take her to the stage door so she could see Pavlova leave.

She was not disappointed.

Pavlova's departure was part of her performance. She wore an elegant suit, but attention was focused on her hat, which was enormous with a wafting chiffon veil which floated about her, like a wraith. Alicia caught her breath.

Pavlova did not pause but stepped regally into her waiting limousine which spirited her, as wraith-like as her veil, silently through the night back to Golders Green where, amidst so much else, the swans on the ink-black lake placidly awaited her return. All that was left of her corporeal presence was the faint aroma of her perfume and the still-moving air, ruffled by her veil.

Eileen was in a state of shock when she was told the news. Next morning Alicia was immaculately dressed by Guggy, and her dancing clothes packed in a little case so that she could carry them with her and dance for the great lady.

They took the tube and alighted at Golders Green station and walked up the hill to Ivy House. It was a warm, summer's day.

When recalling this visit, Alicia reached for an old, ornate picture-book of Pavlova, compiled by M. D'André, and pointed out the house. 'It was very open, that's why she liked it. The view reminded her of Russia. Golders Green at that time was quite a way out, well in the suburbs. She loved the trees and the pond. Lots of the Russians who came here settled there as it was like their home.'

A servant ushered the Markses into the spacious hall where they were told to wait. It was jammed with trunks, as Pavlova was about to embark on yet another tour. The trunks were as much a part of her hall furniture as her priceless antiques.

Eventually Pavlova made her entrance, a vision in mauve. She was gracious and expertly put Alicia at her ease. Alicia was so fascinated by her she had no time to be shy. 'I had been told she was the greatest dancer in the world,' she recalls. 'So, naturally, I was impressed. But I just thought, Well, I'd better do my best and dance for her. She will be honest with me, which she was.'

Alicia asked if she should dance right away but Pavlova waved this aside and said she would like to see her perform at the barre.

She showed Alicia into a changing room, just off her studio, and Alicia put on her dancing clothes. When she was ready she went into the studio and Pavlova put her through some exercises, correcting her occasionally – a unique experience.

'There's the studio,' said Alicia, referring to the book again. 'There's where I danced and there's the little room where I changed. There are her chairs,' and she pointed to the two white lattice chairs that had belonged to Pavlova and which now stood in her room. 'Everything was light. She liked light things, like me.'

When Alicia had finished her barre work Pavlova sat her down and told her that one day she could make a fine dancer. She warned her it was hard work and that Alicia must be prepared for this. Alicia was so mesmerized by Pavlova's spell that she would have worn a ball and chain had she asked; she just wanted to be like her.

With that, Pavlova sent Alicia back to the changing room to get back into her day clothes. After a while she joined her.

'Where is your towel?' she asked when she saw Alicia's small case. 'And your cologne?'

Shyness overcame her at these questions, and Alicia admitted that she hadn't brought either of them. She did not possess any cologne and it had never occurred to her, or anyone else, that she might need it. A brisk rub-down had been enough until then. Miss Thorne had no truck with colognes.

Alicia assured Pavlova that she had had a bath that morning so, really, there was no necessity for cologne; she was perfectly clean.

Cleanliness, Pavlova told her, had nothing to do with it. She left the room and returned a moment later with a large towel and a silver and glass bottle of cologne with her monogram, AP, on it. While rubbing the cologne into Alicia she impressed upon her that she must always have a rub-down after every lesson.

She told her to be sure to take care of her teeth. This may seem odd advice from one dancer to another but it does not seem so to Alicia. 'That was more important to her than my barre work. She didn't comment much on that, that was all accepted. But the teeth were the key to health. It's like a little horse, you always look at the teeth. Without good health there could be no career. She knew that.'

Pavlova left the room so that Alicia could finish dressing, leaving the cologne on a shelf. The thought flashed through Alicia's mind that she could steal it and keep it as a souvenir. 'I didn't think anyone would believe I'd been with her, otherwise. No one seemed to listen to me very much and I thought if I had the bottle it would prove it.'

Almost before the idea had formed she dismissed it. If she took it she would be a thief. The bottle remained in the changing room. But as she turned round to check she had everything, it gleamed seductively. She shut the door.

Pavlova was waiting in the hall and saw her off.

The tube took Alicia home but she felt as though she were wafting on clouds. Pavlova had made a little girl very happy. Even legends can, sometimes, have hearts. Pavlova clearly had.

Alicia was obsessed by the cologne bottle and could not rest until she had one of her own. She felt she could no longer continue to dance without such a necessary piece of equipment. How smart and grown-up to have a bottle of cologne!

Indulging her, as he so often did, Arthur stopped at the first suitable shop and took her in to buy some. She chose a bottle with a mauve ribbon. This was Pavlova's colour and from then on it was Alicia's favourite shade.

Alicia saw Pavlova dance again, much later, when she herself was a professional, both in *Giselle* and *Don Quixote*. 'I also saw her when I was a year or so older, and studying with Princess Astafieva. She knew Pavlova and Pavlova came to her studio to choose some dancers for her company. She took lots of Astafieva's pupils. But I was far too inexperienced for her then. The last time I saw her was during Diaghileff's last Paris season, when she was in a box and I was dancing. I didn't meet her but some of the older dancers were her friends and the message came to me that she was so pleased to see me on the stage but she was sorry it wasn't in anything classical. It was all new work and she didn't care for it.'

Alicia was to become identified by the public with Pavlova. Some went so far as to suggest that, after Pavlova's death, Alicia became possessed by her spirit, or believed herself to be. They even said so in print. She emphatically denies it. 'I wasn't that sort of little person. I think I was too practical for that.'

Ninette de Valois, who had seen both dance, as well as Fonteyn, compared all three. She described Pavlova as a 'pure dancer', Fonteyn as 'classical', and Alicia as 'lyrical'.* Alicia was to specialize in lyricism. She was the first British ballerina to dance the big, classical Russian ballets, but at the beginning her speciality was versatility.

But all that was to come.

In the meantime, George Shurley, the producer who had noted her name when she had danced at the King's Hall, was in the

* Interview with Ninette de Valois, 1994.

process of producing *Dick Whittington* to open at the Kennington Theatre on 27 December 1920. He thought Alicia would be just right in this. An engaging tot was required to dance, and they did not come any more engaging than Alicia.

Although Kennington is not in Theatreland today, the Kennington Theatre was a number-one venue in its time and had presented many stars from Lillie Langtry to Mrs Patrick Campbell. Shurley's *Dick Whittington* was to feature the popular Miss Ouida MacDermott as principal boy.

Shurley contacted Arthur and engaged Alicia. She would perform three dances in the show, for two performances a day, six days a week, and receive a salary of £10 a week – excellent money.

Before she could be officially hired, the London County Council had to be approached to grant her a performer's licence. No licences were granted to performers under ten years of age, but Alicia qualified as she had just celebrated her tenth birthday.

There was much nail-biting until the clearance finally came. When it did it meant Alicia was a professional. But the Council stipulated that she would have to have school lessons each week for a minimum of twenty hours. A governess was acceptable. This was to be Guggy. She would also have to undergo the relevent medical examinations. 'I had to go to County Hall for that. Their tutor had to examine me and then I had to go back to see if I'd passed everything.' The LCC also deemed it essential that she had a dressing room to herself, as minors were not allowed to change with adults.

Guggy took Alicia to rehearsals and right from the start was determined that there would be no fraternizing with the other performers. As far as Guggy was concerned Alicia was special and she intended to keep her that way. She was not a music-hall performer. To underline this she dressed Alicia in an ermine-trimmed velvet coat with matching muff. She looked more like a member of the Royal Family than a pantomime performer. 'How I suffered again. All done up in black velvet and ermine and button boots . . . and a muff!'

Guggy was offended by theatrical ways from the outset. The rehearsals were held in a room above a pub in Soho. She was horrified at the thought of taking Alicia into a pub.

They arrived during a break, and Guggy's frozen face did not go down well with the rest of the cast. Alicia did not help either as she was immobilized by shyness and clung to Guggy's hand. They cut unlikely figures in the midst of a panto rehearsal and faced a wall of hostility. Any friendly overture that might have been forthcoming was rebuffed by Guggy.

There were other children there but they were dressed more appropriately, in rehearsal clothes. Alicia stuck out like a sore thumb. Some of the children were eating oranges and looked grubby and the smell of the fruit permeated the place, mixing with the alcohol fumes from below. Guggy was not impressed and neither was Alicia. 'I've never cared much for oranges, and that was all I could smell.'

The cast had already heard about Alicia and were expecting her. Apparently Shurley was giving her special billing on the advertising posters. She was to be 'Little Alicia – The Child Pavlova'. None of the other kids were getting billing.

Before she had been booked, one of the other girls, Jessie Matthews, had been given several speciality dance solos. Shurley now handed these over to Alicia. No one made a move to welcome her.

Jessie, of course, was later to achieve international fame as a theatre and movie star, and on the radio as Mrs Dale of *Mrs Dale's Diary*. But at that time she was just a promising child. 'But very talented,' says Alicia. 'Very talented.'

Rosie Matthews, Jessie's elder sister, was particularly put out. Rather as Guggy took Alicia everywhere, so Rosie was inseparable from Jessie. And she was equally formidable. She resented Alicia and made her feelings plain.

A story was circulating about how Rosie had been rude to Pavlova. Rosie and Jessie had been in Gamba's ballet shop in Soho when Pavlova had come in. Pavlova, normally, had no need to visit Mr Gamba's shop as he was delighted to call on her and bring dozens of pairs of shoes with him from which she could select what she wanted. In acknowledgment of his courtesy, she had signed a large photograph which was hung in the shop.

Rosie had pointed at the photograph while Pavlova was present and loudly remarked: 'My sister's foot is far better than hers.'[*]

Someone pointed out that Pavlova was in earshot. This did not stop Rosie who felt she had a mission to put Pavlova in her place. She continued to Jessie, just as loudly, 'What is more, you'll dance better than she does.'

Pavlova, who had heard that sort of thing before, did not deign to respond.[†]

As soon as Alicia and Guggy entered the rehearsal room the

---

[*] *Jessie Matthews* by Michael Thornton, Mayflower, 1974.
[†] Jessie was not backward in coming forward herself. She once knocked out one of Anton Dolin's teeth in a dispute. Jessie and Alicia later became good friends.

conversation died. The silence was broken by Rosie hissing to Jessie, 'Who's she? How dare they bring in another dancer.'

Alicia heard, as she was meant to, and froze.

Jessie did not say much during the next few days but Rosie made up for her. 'Jessie was like me, we just danced.' The Matthews girls were entitled to feel upset. Things had been going well until George Shurley had hired Alicia. Now all that was left for Jessie, who was an excellent dancer herself, was a sailor's hornpipe. She did not reckon much to it. Neither did she to the news that the playbill, featuring Alicia, was not carrying her name. Jessie was merely one of 'Elise Clerc's Troupe of Cupids'. The said Elise Clerc was responsible for the whole troupe and she was also displeased. She had been grooming Jessie for stardom for two years and thought she had finally got there.

If Jessie tried to be friendly, Rosie would pull her away from the monster who had stolen her dances. On Alicia's side, Guggy made matters worse by leading her to her dressing room and closing the door as soon as her items were finished. She was not allowed to stay to watch the others.

Alicia came to hate that room. When she and Guggy were there, there was no chat, just a heavy silence. Guggy gave Alicia her school books and made her toil over her LCC-stipulated lessons. 'I felt like a prisoner in a cell,' recalls Alicia.

Guggy's over-protection was already beginning to store up problems for Alicia. Rather than encourage her out of her shell, she daily forced her more firmly into it.

During rehearsals another demon came to haunt her. The cast mentioned 'orchestrations' and how different music sounded when played by a band. She had never danced to a band – before she had had piano accompaniment – and she began to have nightmares that she would be unable to follow the rhythm and would make mistakes. She lay rigid with fear at night, conjuring up horror situations.

Then she went down with chickenpox. Eileen thought she might have to withdraw her from the show and, perhaps, Alicia would have been relieved if that had happened.

She recovered and resumed rehearsals. When the band came she found that, rather than cause difficulties, it helped her. 'I was scared but then I enjoyed it. It was wonderful. It was as though I was back in the park with my band. From that moment on and for the rest of my life I enjoyed the orchestra.

'But there was a problem with the chickenpox. It affected my eyes and left them sensitive. I had a veil for the oriental dance and when they put those bright spotlights on me, for the first time, for the first couple of weeks I did it with the veil over my head. I was not accustomed to spotlights then, either. Suddenly I thought, I don't need this and took the veil off.'

Dick Whittington ran until 12 February 1921 and Alicia's three dances went over well. In the first she leapt from behind a cornsheaf dressed as a poppy – shades of Pavlova – and in the second she was a butterfly. She had her solo and Miss Clerc's troupe fluttered behind her. The third was an oriental slave dance similar to the one she had performed when Shurley had first seen her. She ended this dramatically by collapsing on stage with a blood-curdling scream.

She enjoyed the scream. Each time she uttered it she 'gloried' in the reaction of the audience as they gasped with shock. She was taking her first steps in audience manipulation, something in which she was later to excel.

'Little Alicia, whom the programme claimed to be "The Child Pavlova", went far towards emulating her great model.' – *Morning Post*

'Little Alica, "The Child Pavlova", is a very accomplished ballerina in miniature, and even in the trying dance of Salome suggested much of its grim power.' – *Daily Telegraph*

'Little Alicia, described as "The Child Pavlova", more than justifies the title.' – *Sunday Times*

'Little Elise [sic] is perhaps the most wonderful juvenile dancer who has yet appeared on the stage.' – *The People*

'. . . a wonderful youngster, aptly named "The Child Pavlova", who gives solo exhibitions of remarkable grace and beauty for one so young.' – *News of the World*

Once the panto was under way Guggy ran to a regular timetable. She took Alicia on the tube to the theatre then, after the matinée, they had a sandwich, or some soup, before the evening performance. Then she would be confined to her dressing room where she would study her school books. 'Apart from the lessons I had to sleep. She made me sleep between the shows. That's where I formed my very good sleeping habits. I never came out of that dressing room, apart from the performances. Dressing rooms were always my home. Once I went into that room I stayed there till I was finished. Due to my licence I had to be out at a certain time and they used to check. There was a car to take me home.'

In that dressing room sleep became a form of yoga. As she was not tired at that time in the afternoon it was something she learned to do, just as she learnt her lessons from books. She was able to sleep to order and kept this up for the rest of her life, which was useful when travelling long distances. It meant she arrived more refreshed than she might otherwise have been.

She has slept right round the globe. It drives her sister Doris, with whom she now lives, mad with jealousy.

On one of her matinées, and according to Agnes de Mille this was opening day, her performance was attended by a lad of seventeen who was also studying dancing.

He had come to the attention of producers himself and was advised to see 'The Child Pavlova' as he might be teamed with her one day. His name was Sydney Francis Patrick Chippendall Healey-Kay, which he changed firstly to Patrikayev, then to Anton Dolin. When he became an established dancer he claimed to hate his stage name. If anyone, socially, called him Mr Dolin or Anton he would snap, 'My name's Pat.' He was Pat to everyone.

He was so impressed by Alicia that he spent a shilling of his pocket money on a bunch of white chrysanthemums which he anonymously left for her at the stage door.

4

Princess Astafieva

On the last night of the panto, Arthur drove Alicia home in the Rolls. It was a special occasion. She had enjoyed a real success. Unfortunately Eileen never saw her in *Dick Whittington* as she was in hospital having, and then recovering from, an operation. Alicia had been taken by Guggy to visit her in the nursing home during the run. She was upset that her mother had not seen her success.

Arthur was still doing well and investing in other fields. Investment is precarious – just how precarious the family was soon to discover.

But on the last night of *Dick Whittington* all was secure inside the limousine as it rode the bleak winter streets.

Alicia was already booked for her next engagement, which was a charity matinée of *A Midsummer Night's Dream* at the Shaftesbury Theatre, in which she was to play a fairy.

Other dancers also took part in the play and Eileen, who was in the audience this time, was impressed by how good they were. She saw from the programme that they were pupils of Princess Seraphine Astafieva.

When Miss Thorne had asked Eileen to let Alicia have private lessons Eileen had put her off. Now she changed her mind. From what she had heard, and read, of Alicia these last few months she knew that she was exceptional. 'What convinced my parents was the acclaim I had had in the panto. Several people had suggested that I should be trained seriously for the Russian ballet. They suddenly thought maybe there was some truth in it.'

Miss Thorne had been talking sense. Eileen would take Alicia to the Princess. Perhaps she would take Alicia under her wing?

At forty-one Princess Seraphine Astafieva was a haughty beauty and proud of her kinship with Leo Tolstoy, author of the monumental *War and Peace*. She was his grand-niece.

Her dancing pedigree was as impeccable as her bloodline. She was sister-in-law to the Imperial Russian ballerina Mathilde Kschessinska, who had been created *prima ballerina assoluta* of the Marynsky Theatre, St Petersburg, in 1895, the only dancer apart from Pierina Legnani officially to hold this title.*

Other titles Kschessinska had held included mistress to Tsar Nikolai II when he had been the Tsarevich, and she was the morganatic wife of Grand Duke Andrei. She had wielded enormous influence from her palace in St Petersburg, the balcony of which had later been commandeered by Lenin during the Revolution, from where he had addressed the citizens in the newly named Petrograd (formerly, as now, St Petersburg) after his return from exile in 1917.

Not surprisingly, Kschessinska left Russia thereafter and took up residence in the more sympathetic climate of the Côte d'Azur. She gave her last public performance at the age of sixty-four and died in Paris in 1971, at the age of ninety-nine, after a satisfying life.

Princess Astafieva was made of similar stuff. Her own career had also been distinguished. Although too tall to make the perfect ballerina, she was an outstanding mime. She had been a member of the Marynsky Ballet until 1905 and then joined the Diaghileff company where she remained until 1911. Here her greatest triumph had been in Fokine's *Cleopatra*, a performance described as 'an unforgettable impression of burning pride and passion'.†

The Marynsky Ballet had been giving performances at St Petersburg's Marynsky Theatre since 1880, although its lineage can be traced back to the early eighteenth century when a ballet school was founded for the children of the servants of the Tsar.

Its ballets, ballet masters and dancers became world-renowned, and its reputation attracted guest appearances from all the great dancers of the period.

Master choreographer Marius Petipa became solo dancer and

---

* Legnani had been so honoured after electrifying Marynsky audiences in 1893 by an astounding thirty-two *fouettés* in Petipa's *Cinderella*, although she had already performed this athletic feat in London the year before in *Aladdin*. She went on to create the role of Odette/Odile in *Swan Lake* in 1895.
† *Markova: Her Life and Art* by Anton Dolin, W. H. Allen, 1953.

eventually the company director, which led to its Tsarist peak between 1862 and 1903. Petipa, in collaboration with Lev Ivanov and composer, Tchaikovsky, produced *Sleeping Beauty*, *Nutcracker* and *Swan Lake*.

Among the Marynsky's best-known dancers at the turn of the century were Olga Preobrajenska, Mathilde Kschessinska, Vera Trefilova, Nicolai Legat, Tamara Karsavina, Anna Pavlova, and Vaslav Nijinsky.

In 1909 the impresario Serge Diaghileff had taken a troupe of Russian dancers to Paris for what became a series of regular seasons, many of the above taking part, and they caused a sensation.

Diaghileff also introduced Western audiences to the work of choreographer Mikhail Fokine, whose revolutionary new ballets, such as *Cleopatra*, the 'Polovtsian Dances' and *Les Sylphides*, took ballet in a new direction.

The Princess had settled in London in 1916, after fleeing the impending outbreak of the Revolution, and opened a dancing school at 'The Pheasantry' in London's King's Road, Chelsea.

The Pheasantry is now a Grade II listed building of startling architectural interest and is something of a landmark with its distinctive Franco-Grecian entrance arch. It got its name in the mid-nineteenth century when pheasants lived in its garden.

The Princess was the first Russian ballerina to open a studio in London. She was a socialite, as famed for her jewels and extravagant personality as for her artistry. She was the most fashionable ballet teacher in London.

A description of her is given by Dame Margot Fonteyn in her autobiography.* Dame Margot studied with her in the early 1930s.

'Tallish, aged about 60, worldly and elegant with slender legs and an indefinable mixture of the stylish with the slightly grubby that only such an aristocratic personality from Czarist Russia could hope to carry off successfully.

'She always wore a scarf tied turban-wise round her head, and carried a long cigarette holder. She smoked Balkan Sobranies. When she was teaching she wore white cotton stockings and her black, pleated skirt, normally knee length, was tucked into black silk bloomers . . .

'We [Fonteyn and her mother] arrived, apparently, on a day when she was sitting in her dark, inner room in a Russian gloom, both physical and moral. She did not want to accept any more

* *Margot Fonteyn*, W. H. Allen, 1975.

pupils. All her old pupils were ungrateful and neglectful. She was too old to teach any more . . .'

What Fonteyn could not have known at the time was that the Princess was far from well. It was not just Russian temperament which brought on her fits of gloom. By then she was suffering from cancer.

It had not occurred to Eileen to book an appointment with the Princess and she arrived at The Pheasantry unannounced one morning during one of her classes. The Princess would not be interrupted and refused to see them. Eileen had adopted George Shurley's billing of Alicia and had had a batch of cards printed with 'The Child Pavlova' on them. She insisted that one of these be sent in to the Princess.

That did the trick. The Princess revered Pavlova; she was her idol. She abandoned her class, came out at once, and berated both Eileen and her daughter for their presumption. 'The Child Pavlova' quickly learnt the meaning of Russian temperament.

'She was quite right,' says Alicia. 'There was only one Pavlova, how could there be another? I had no right to use her name.'

That was in hindsight. She didn't quite see it that way at the time, and trembled in the presence of this bejewelled virago. 'I think I burst into tears. I was so scared and she towered above me. She was so tall.'

Alicia came to love the Princess, with all her faults. Undoubtedly one of those faults was a hasty streak. She witheringly agreed to see 'The Child Pavlova' dance, but only after she had finished her class. And then she would keep all the pupils back and they could watch. A daunting prospect for Alicia. 'That was the challenge she gave me.'

Tears pricked her eyes. Sitting next to her mother on a bench, she waited silently until the Princess had finished her lesson.

Then, with the other pupils clustered around, the Princess announced that she would like to see what this 'little genius can do'. The words were burned into Alicia's memory.

As soon as the pianist started playing, the awkwardness left her and she danced. Sarcasm disappeared from the Princess's manner as she stepped forward and instructed Alicia to perform steps well in advance of her years.

She danced for half an hour and only stopped when the Princess rushed at her, overcome by enthusiasm, and kissed her resoundingly on the forehead.

'This does not happen every day,' she breathed to Eileen, all aggression gone. 'Take her home and put her in cotton wool. You have a racehorse.'

Alicia was not so much accepted as a pupil as conscripted, and was told to report for class at eleven the next morning. It was the beginning of one of the most remarkable careers in ballet.

It was also the reason for Fonteyn later coming to study with the Princess. By that time Alicia had made a name for herself and Fonteyn's mother wanted her daughter to have the same teacher as Markova.

Had she had no pupils other than Markova and Fonteyn, the Princess would have justified her reputation as a teacher, 'a great teacher,' emphasizes Alicia. Not everyone, however, was convinced by her method.

Dame Ninette de Valois was dismissive: 'She had to do something when she escaped to England so she set herself up as a teacher, but she never had the training to teach. By the time her pupils had finished with her they had to unlearn all they had learned. She was a very good mime artist, but not a teacher. It was Markova's natural facility that carried her through. She would have been a star no matter who taught her.'[*]

The pupil/teacher relationship is a delicate bond. It is a question of who works for whom. For Markova, Astafieva was right.

Alicia burst into tears again when the Princess accepted her, this time for a different reason. 'I was always crying then.' Eileen did not cry but she learnt something about theatrical decorum that day. From then on 'The Child Pavlova' cards were never seen again.

Alicia began the painful process of trying to fit in with the other dancers. The pattern was the same as at Kennington. Guggy took her to rehearsals. They took the bus to Muswell Hill then the tube to Sloane Square and walked down the King's Road to The Pheasantry. Guggy stayed with her during her lessons and as soon as there was a break she took her to one side and discouraged her from mixing.

There is a photograph of Alicia rehearsing with the pupils in Astafieva's class. Guggy is sitting on the piano stool, her eyes locked on Alicia, almost glaring at her. Nearly everyone else is smiling.

Someone who particularly noticed this state of affairs, and thought it a shame, was Anton Dolin, the young man who had sent her the chrysanthemums after *Dick Whittington*. He was another of the Princess's pupils and made a point of being friendly. He was mightily impressed by her work and wrote of her in his biography[†]: 'At the age of 11 she had a technique that

[*] Interview with Ninette de Valois in 1994.
[†] *Markova: Her Life and Art*, W. H. Allen, 1953.

can only be termed fantastic. Madame used her as a demonstration model, to show the others in class, including many professional dancers, how certain steps should be danced. I loved to partner her . . . It was quite simple to make her turn 30 times on one *pointe*, or, having balanced her on one *pointe*, to go out of the room and leave her. Coming back, she would still be there, as motionless as a piece of carved ivory. We used to stand in wonder and watch her. Nothing like this had ever been seen before in one so young.'

Despite her brilliance, he noted that there was a detached quality about what she did. It was as though a clockwork toy had been wound up. There was no heart in it.

She studied with Astafieva for two hours each day for five days a week and, in addition to this, Astafieva arranged for her to have lessons from another of her pupils, Georgina Constable, who later joined the Pavlova company.

All pupils were instructed to arrive on the dot of eleven so as not to keep Astafieva waiting. She herself would stroll in at any time between eleven and one. She wafted the very essence of theatre from her flamboyant entrance to her rapid swings of mood; from her black, gold-tipped cigarettes to her flowing scarves.

Once Astafieva arrived she was an exacting taskmistress. Her method was Russian to the core, incorporating what she had been taught by her masters at the Marynsky ballet school in St Petersburg. Sometimes she would concentrate on just one move for the entire lesson, examined from every aspect; at other times she would demand a whole sequence of exercises.

Alicia was a serious student. So was Dolin, but he thought she needed lightening up. Sometimes, when she was dancing, he would playfully pinch her or pull her hair. She carried on as though nothing had happened.

But she underwent agonies inside, not knowing how to respond. She knew he meant it in fun but did not know how to have fun. It wasn't that she had no sense of humour, for she certainly had that, but it was buried beneath layers of clinical shyness which Guggy did nothing to ease.

Each time she dragged Alicia away from the other pupils she added another layer. Alicia was an extraordinarily obedient child – she had been told to work hard at her lessons and did so. Just as she folded her clothes neatly each night, so she studied ballet. It was what she had been told to do. In her way Alicia was as devoted to duty as Guggy.

Astafieva assessed Alicia as a 'classic' dancer and did not

waste time teaching her skills she thought she would never need. Alicia did not attend the 'character' classes where pupils mimed grotesqueries. She did sit in a few times but the grimacing so upset her that she had nightmares, just as when she had seen Quilp at the cinema. 'That night I dreamt of a whole line of cats grimacing. The mime had had nothing to do with cats but that was how I interpreted it. I had a cat at home and I suppose he got mixed up in it. It was awful.'

After that she was kept away.

5

Diaghileff

There was excitement at The Pheasantry. It was announced that Diaghileff was to bring the first full-length version of *The Sleeping Princess** to London's Alhambra Theatre and the cast would be headed by Russia's finest dancers.

Diaghileff was a phenonemon. Born in Russia in 1872, he became the centre of a circle of St Petersburg-based musicians, painters and writers. He was co-founder of the influential magazine *Mir Iskousstva* (The World of Art) and was appointed Artistic Director of the Marynsky Theatre.

He left the Marynsky after a dispute, but not before he had plucked a young male dancer from its ranks and precipitated him to world fame. Nijinsky was the greatest male dancer of his time and his career became brilliant under Diaghileff's guidance.

They were lovers, living together, but after Nijinsky married Romola de Pulszky, a Polish member of the *corps de ballet*, while on tour, Diaghileff washed his hands of him. Unable to cope without Diaghileff, Nijinsky's career floundered and he slowly went insane. The repercussions of this scandal still echo.

Diaghileff's 1909 Paris season of Russian opera and ballet had scored a unique triumph. Outside Russia, ballet was a Cinderella art; troupes of dancers had mostly to perform in circuses or music hall or provide the *divertissements* in opera. There was nothing else.

Diaghileff later formed the Ballet Russe, conveniently based in

---

* Better known as *The Sleeping Beauty*.

Monte Carlo between the opera houses of Italy and France. From this base he brought about a reformation of European ballet. In effect, he was European ballet.

Initially he was engaged by the Monégasque opera house to provide the ballets for the operas. At this time short ballet runs were followed by longer operatic seasons. All his dancers featured in opera as well as ballet. Owing to his innovative ideas he frequently teetered on the brink of bankruptcy and relied entirely on the financial backing of the aristocracy.

Physically he was stout with a large moustachioed head. He dressed without restraint and lived in great style too, eating in the best restaurants, travelling de luxe and staying in the finest hotels.

Diaghileff, as a friend and former employer of the Princess, was coming to The Pheasantry. Whereas he brought his principal dancers with him, he needed to augment the strength of the company with local dancers.

He arrived in due pomp, accompanied by his faithful *régisseur*, Serge Grigorieff. A former dancer, he had created roles for Diaghileff, including Shar Shaviar in Fokine's *Scheherazade* and the Russian merchant in Massine's *La Boutique Fantasque*. He was now thirty-eight and as prosperous-looking as Diaghileff.

'We were in the midst of class when Diaghileff arrived,' recalls Alicia. 'I'd only been with the Princess a couple of months. While the students Astafieva had in mind danced for him the rest of us made ourselves scarce and quietly sat and watched. I was sitting in the corner with my governess and Diaghileff suddenly asked Astafieva, "Who is that little one? Does she dance?"

'That gave Astafieva the opening. "Yes," she said. "She dances very well. Would you like to see her?" I danced "Valse Caprice", which was in my repertoire. He just looked at me, then called me over, kissed me on the forehead and thanked me. Then he thanked Astafieva and everybody stood up and he left.'

A few days later Alicia learnt that he had been impressed by her. So much so that she had given him the idea of inserting a special variation for her in *The Sleeping Princess*. He would have this choreographed by Bronislava Nijinska, Nijinsky's sister.

Astafieva confided to Alicia that Diaghileff had told her that he could not believe that a child could possess such a dazzling technique. He wanted her dressed entirely in white. The character would be 'The Fairy Dewdrop', the smallest fairy to come to the christening.

Alicia could not believe her luck. *The Sleeping Princess* was the most lavish production of 1921 in London. Diaghileff did nothing by halves. 'His standards were only the best. I was brought up that way.'

Dolin was also chosen, for the *corps de ballet*. Even the *corps de ballet* for Diaghileff meant something. He had to change his name. At that time he was still Patrick Healey-Kay – Anton Dolin didn't emerge for another few years yet – and that was preposterously unsuitable for a ballet dancer. So Diaghileff called him Patrikayev.

Another chosen dancer was Margot Luck, a relative of Astafieva's.

Alicia's role was to be a two-minute solo which occurred in the Prologue. The fact that it came early in the evening had helped when Diaghileff had applied to the LCC for her performer's licence. Alicia was still only ten and the minimum age for a performer had been raised from ten to twelve. He had pulled every string possible to get permission. Being Diaghileff he had achieved it.

There was no doubt that Diaghileff was smitten by her, and remained so for the rest of his life. Ninette de Valois, who joined the Ballet Russe in 1923, remembers: 'He was mad on her. She was small for her age and moved like greased lightning, yet always in perfect control.'[*]

Alicia's excitement was cruelly dashed. Even before rehearsals began she developed diphtheria and was rushed to hospital. Fairy Dewdrop was doomed never to tread the boards. Diaghileff was concerned that even if she recovered in time she might not be strong enough to dance properly. He could not afford to take the chance and, to his regret, cancelled his plans for her.

It was a severe bout of diphtheria and for a while Alicia's life was in the balance. 'In those days it could be fatal or cause paralysis, or affect the heart. It depended what part of the body it hit. So I was forbidden from doing anything strenuous. I was in an isolation hospital but I knew the risks. The matron told me.[†] I was always in tears. Every time they took my temperature it was up, because I was so emotional and wanting to get out. Yet the higher my temperature the longer I had to stay in. I wanted to get to the theatre and see Diaghileff and the performances even if I couldn't dance.'

[*] Interview with Ninette de Valois, 1994.
[†] Years later the matron appeared on Alicia's *This Is Your Life* and told the story.

When she did return to class she was even quieter, if possible, than before. She did not speak of her disappointment until years later, and then she quietly told Dolin that she had wanted to die. Although her body recovered it took longer for the mental wounds to heal. 'It was a terrible disappointment for me – the first of many.'

Meanwhile life continued outside The Pheasantry and *The Sleeping Princess* opened to huge critical acclaim. Unfortunately the public were not as enthusiastic as the critics and the ballet folded, leaving Diaghileff with enormous losses.

Dolin, although appearing in *The Sleeping Princess* under the name of Patrikayev, still studied with Astafieva and persisted in trying to make friends with Alicia. Despite the pinches and hair-tugs, or perhaps because of them, he succeeded, and slowly broke through her barriers.

They started to practise *pas de deux* together and he showed her some of the moves he had copied from the Russian dancers with whom he was appearing. Despite her disappointment at not being in the ballet, she wanted to hear about it, and he told her stories of Lopokova, Nijinska, Tchernicheva, Dubrovska and guest ballerina, the fabled Olga Spessivtseva, one of the most celebrated ballerinas of all time.

For all her early success, Spessivtseva's life was an unmitigated tragedy, only equalled in despair by that of Nijinsky.

Although at the peak of her glory in 1921, she had a mental breakdown in America in 1941 and fluctuated between delusions of grandeur and bouts of religious mania when she imagined she was Christ's emissary and that a burning cross was implanted on her forehead.

After the police had been called to quell several disturbances, she was committed to an asylum. It was then discovered that she, who had been one of the greatest stars in the world, was destitute. Improper management was suspected.

She remained in care until 1963, reliving her roles in her dementia.

In 1963 she was placed in the Tolstoy Farm, New York, where she ended her days in comparative calm, listening to Joan Sutherland and Maria Callas records and telling her many famous visitors that she wished she had been an opera singer.

Dolin helped her tremendously, providing comfort, money and continuous support. Without him God knows what would have become of her. He started off in awe of her, graduated to partnering her, and ended up virtually restoring her sanity. He wrote a book about her.*

'He admired her and was grateful to her, that's why he was so good,' says Alicia. 'Later, she helped him a lot. He had never danced Albrecht until she taught it to him. Naturally he had been in awe of her, who wouldn't be, but later he came to admire her terrifically as well.'

Spessivtseva's cruel fate was not in the offing during the London run of *The Sleeping Princess* and she was still the toast of the ballet world. Alicia loved to hear Dolin talk of her, which he did a great deal. And she could watch her dance.

Although she missed out on the show, Diaghileff did not forget Alicia and arranged for her, and Guggy, to have free seats at the Alhambra whenever they wanted them.

She went many times, as often as she could, to matinées. Evening performances were out; apart from her age, she was still convalescing from her illness.

Sometimes Diaghileff sat with her, explaining what was happening and how certain illusions were created. This was untypical behaviour on his part as he did not like children, and made no secret of it. But the dedicated Alicia was different; she did not know the meaning of mischief. All she wanted to do was work. 'What, maybe, also appealed to him was that I didn't talk. I was very shy, anyway, never a talker and I was just happy to listen to him.'

He recognized her promise and hoped to capitalize on it later, which was why he encouraged her to see so many performances with the different casts. He told her that if she continued to 'work hard with her teacher' he would take her into his company when she was older.

Alicia took it all in and stored up his advice. Later, when she retired from dancing and took an active part in directing, she often remembered the 'wonderful advice' he had given her as a child. Already Diaghileff was assuming god-like proportions in her life.

Although Alicia missed out at the Alhambra she did appear in the West End when she was twelve, and at no less a venue than that historic home of music hall, the London Palladium.

This came about thanks to Nicolai Legat.

Russian-born Legat, then fifty-three, had been one of the Marynsky's star dancers and one of Pavlova's partners. In 1903, he and his brother Sergei had succeeded Petipa as ballet masters

---

* *The Sleeping Ballerina*, Frederick Muller, 1966.

of the Imperial Ballet School, of which he later became Director. He was a renowned professor there.

Legat had fled Russia, like so many others, and eventually came to London. At this point in his vicissitudinous career he had won a contract to provide dancing acts for the Palladium. He was staging a half-hour sequence billed as 'The Russian Art Dancers' which featured his wife, ballerina Nadine Nikolayeva Legat.

He had needed a male dancer to partner her so had consulted Astafieva. He took Dolin, but saw Alicia in class. She still remembers his visit. 'I was around, dancing, and he offered me a contract for the Palladium. He was important to me as a teacher. I had the greatest Russian training since I was twelve. He had observed from Legnani and transferred to Kschessinska whom he had taught and coached. Later she was to coach me. You see how near I am to the roots?

'I was still working with Astafieva when Legat accepted me but she understood that I had to be available to him. So I worked with them both, both Russian trainers.'

At the Palladium she was to dance her variation on *The Dragon Fly* which had been specially arranged for her by Astafieva. 'That was my first appearance at the Palladium. Later I played it many times. Nellie Wallace was topping the bill and she was wonderful to me. Such a nice lady. We were friends till she died.'

Scottish-born Nellie Wallace – 'The Essence of Eccentricity' – was a music-hall star of the highest calibre. Cyril Fletcher once described her as 'a hybrid between the Duke of Wellington and Ken Dodd'. Music-hall historian John Fisher adds: 'Her characterisation was grotesque, but to many a yearning spinster poignantly natural.'* In her act she wore a tartan skirt, Glengarry hat, button boots and a pathetic piece of fur she called 'me bit of vermin'.

At first sight there might not seem to be a lot in common between Alicia Markova and comedienne Nellie Wallace, but there was. Both were able to strike an instant rapport with the audience, although Alicia had yet to develop this skill, and both recognized each other's talent. Alicia learnt a lot from Nellie Wallace, and later incorporated this into her interpretation of the Tango in *Façade*. She even wore 'me bit of vermin'. Miss Wallace also saw a lonely girl who needed friendship.

She was able to help her practically. 'When I did the dragonfly I was very thin and not upholstered at all and very quick so Astafieva arranged a brilliant dance for me full of fireworks. I

* *Funny Way to be a Hero*, Frederick Muller, 1973.

wore an all-in-one outfit with sequined pants and big wings, all very compact so that I could flit around. They were coloured like a dragonfly in pink and blue. It was wonderful. Whenever I did it at charity performances people used to love it. Astafieva and Guggy had made it for me.

'Well, Legat had seen me in class but he hadn't seen the costume so when it came to the Palladium dress rehearsal, and I wore it, he said he couldn't possibly have me going on stage like that. I was a classical dancer and very young, so I had to wear a tutu. The usual, what people would expect from a ballet dancer in Variety. Nothing modern or chic with style.

'He rearranged the variation, too, and took out all the fireworks, all the big things that used to bring applause, and made it much simpler. He said I was doing things beyond my years. He told me I would be injured. Well, you can imagine, I wasn't very happy, Guggy wasn't happy and Astafieva wasn't happy. But, I thought, I must do what I'm told, it wasn't for me to query Legat.

'My dragonfly was followed by the finale which was the second act of *Coppélia*. Legat was Dr Coppelius. He was a famous Dr Coppelius and his wife was Swanhilda. it was very amusing and right for a music-hall audience.

'At the first matinée, I think it was, somebody got mixed up. I was waiting to go on a bit later. I heard music start but nobody was on stage. The girl who was due to dance was nowhere to be seen. I thought, How terrible.

'So I skipped on and improvised. Then I saw Legat and the stage manager in the wings, signalling me to come off, so I fluttered off and the proper girl came on.

'I had to wait for two more numbers before it was my turn.

'Nellie Wallace used to sit in the wings and watch me. I think Guggy had told her something like, "If only you could see her in her proper costume, doing her real dance."

'Before the Saturday night of the last show. Nellie Wallace and Guggy got together and Miss Wallace said, "Why don't you let her do her real dance? They'll go mad." The music was the same and the lighting. It was only the steps that were different and the costume.

'Nellie Wallace knew I wasn't being seen to best advantage. So I got into my outfit with the wings. Nellie came to my dressing room with a huge shawl which she put around me and took me on to the stage so no one could see I wasn't in the tutu.

'She took me to the wings and when it came to the time for me to enter she opened her arms and I shot on and did everything. It brought the house down. I loved dancing it and it was modern, ahead of its time. Poor Legat nearly had a heart attack.

'I was twelve then and it was some time before he spoke to me again – not until I was fifteen and with Diaghileff.

'Nellie Wallace understood what it meant to me.'

Throughout her career Alicia never forgot that her roots were in Variety. She retained an enormous respect for music-hall artistes, something Diaghileff was later to encourage.

As with *Dick Whittington*, Alicia did two shows a night at the Palladium and three shows a day when there was a matinée. Studying with Legat was a bonus. He was one of the world's great teachers and both Moira Shearer and Fonteyn were to study with him.

On 26 June 1923, Astafieva decided to unleash her students to the public and presented her 'Anglo-Russian Dancers' at the Royal Albert Hall. She could not resist the temptation of appearing herself and danced to the music of Gounod's 'Ave Maria'. By now she was forty-seven and did not dance publicly on a regular basis, so the performance was more in the manner of emoting.

Astafieva billed Alicia as 'Little Alicia – The Miniature Pavlova', conveniently forgetting her outrage of a few years ago when Eileen had turned up on her doorstep with cards featuring a similar title.

It was also the first time Anton Dolin was to appear under that name.

Astafieva arranged for Alicia to dance three pieces, *The Dragon Fly*, the *pizzicato* from Delibes's *Sylvia*, and a special arrangement of Pavlova's *The Dying Swan*. The reviews were mixed.

'Little Alicia . . . combined the sang-froid of a prima ballerina with the daintiness and freshness of youth.' – *Daily Mirror*

'Little Alicia is handicapped at the start of her career by programme comparison with the peerless Pavlova, but she danced her way into the affections of the audience.' – *The Star*

'The young child, Alicia, described repeatedly as "The Minia-ture Pavlova", has certainly the makings of a dancer, but I thought she attempted things far too difficult and strenuous for a child of her years.' – *Daily Chronicle*

Suddenly tragedy struck.

Arthur had invested heavily and unwisely in a cork business. He had gone into partnership and did not discover until it was too late that his partner was dishonest. As Alicia put it, 'He was swindled.' The partner was sent to prison and Arthur was financially wiped out.

He fought back, however. 'He went to South Africa where we were to follow him,' says Doris. 'His father and half-brother were out there and he was to go into their line of business – I think it was mining engineering. The house was sold and we took a furnished place in Finsbury Park.

'He came back from South Africa and it was the time when the big Wembley Exhibition was to open, but it was behind schedule. The McAlpine company sent for Daddy to take charge and get things ready on time.

'He took Alicia and me there the day before it was due to open. There was an enormous doll's house which had been sent to the Queen and we helped unpack it.'

'I always loved doll's houses,' says Alicia. 'Daddy made us a doll's house at home, with electric light, and that really was something. I had a doll called Checky Jane, I adored her, she had a big stone head and a checked gingham skirt. She was the housekeeper. I wonder what happened to her.'

'She went down the rubbish chute,' says Doris. 'Years later, when we moved to Prince of Wales Drive. You were with Diaghileff.'

While the Queen's doll's house was being unpacked the big dipper was being tried out. The girls were promised they could have a go. Alicia loved anything to do with the fairground; the more dangerous the rides the better, as far as she was concerned.

But a dreadful accident happened before they could board. One of the workmen jumped on as the dipper was moving and failed to fasten his safety bar. He was thrown off and killed.

'Everyone was shouting for Daddy,' says Alicia. 'Every time I see a big dipper I can hear those shouts for Daddy.'

After the Exhibition opened Arthur was without work again but was not too concerned as the family had plans to move to South Africa. In the end, they never did. Had they done so, the course of British ballet history would have been quite different. Arthur contracted pneumonia and died on 14 September 1924, Eileen's birthday. Alicia was thirteen.

The news was broken to her while she was in Brighton with the Crewleys. Eileen and the other girls were on holiday elsewhere. It was a terrible shock to her. She loved her father and had been particularly close to him. The Crewleys may have been good friends but they were not family. She had to face the shock alone, as she has had to face so much in life.

Suddenly Eileen was an impecunious widow with four daughters to support. 'When I was six we had a Rolls-Royce,' says Alicia. 'By the time I was thirteen, nothing.'

Fortunately the cost of Alicia's training did not add to her problems. Astafieva had not charged fees since the reversal in Arthur's fortunes. She realized there were four daughters and waived all charges. To make Eileen feel better she would tell her she could make it up to her when Alicia became famous, as she surely would.

When Alicia did become famous the Princess still refused to take anything. Her reward was seeing Alicia shape into a ballerina. 'I will always acknowledge the debt I owe her,' says Alicia. She clearly still adores the Princess.

From that time on, and imperceptibly at first, the roles of Eileen and Alicia became reversed. Alicia became the head of the family and Eileen the dependant. 'Somehow I grew up to feel responsible for my mother,' she says.

6

Diaghileff Returns

Despite the losses of *The Sleeping Princess*, the irrepressible Diaghileff returned to London in 1924. His company was appearing as an item in a bill at the Coliseum. As usual, a fanfare of promotion preceded his arrival, but the press were gunning for him.

His company was billed as The Russian Ballet and, indeed, to look at a programme, this might seem to be the case. But those in the know knew better. His ranks had been infiltrated by the British.

As Ninette de Valois recalls: 'Diaghileff liked the English dancers. He took quite a lot of us. He had about six or seven English people when I was with him. We had to change our names. Of course, the press were quick to catch on to that, which irritated him madly.'*

In those days organized British ballet was not taken seriously. As dancer/director Wendy Toye puts it: 'There were no British companies and nowhere for us to work. There are hundreds of dancers around now but there weren't all that many when we started out. And all the people who danced knew each other. It was a very small world.'†

In pre-Revolution Russia the Tsar had supported the Imperial Ballet and the country had become a Mecca for the finest artists in the world. It also produced superb home-grown artists, who had benefited not only from the Russian tradition but also from the

---

* 1994 interview.
† 1994 interview.

a position then Alicia would have to go to Drury Lane. The Theatre Royal was mounting *A Midsummer Night's Dream* and Fokine was choreographing the fairies' ballet. Alicia had already been accepted.

Diaghileff was horrified. 'But she will have to dance every day, eight performances a week,' he protested. 'That would damage her, she is too young.' Astafieva repeated that Alicia had to earn.

This time Alicia did not have to wait for the outcome of their conversation. She was offered a position with the Ballet Russe in Monte Carlo.

Nijinska, who had a daughter of about Alicia's age, told her that she, and Guggy, could lodge with them. The two girls would be company for each other. Diaghileff insisted that Guggy come along. It was essential that Alicia had a chaperone.

After everything had been agreed with everybody, Nijinska accepted another offer and abruptly left the company, partly because Diaghileff had hired an additional choreographer.

This was George Balanchine, another Russian émigré. Alicia now had to audition for him. Buckle writes: '. . . she remembered later, she felt she had been working for 3½ hours.' As she herself put it in *Markova Remembers**: 'Balanchine gave me an exhaustive audition in which I danced everything I knew, and Pat Dolin . . . partnered me in some *pas de deux* I had learnt. Balanchine seemed determined to push me as far as he could, and it was then that he discovered that I was able to perform double *tours en l'air* (which is a step usually performed by men) and multiple *fouettés* as well as acrobatic movement.'

Balanchine, a likeable and boyish twenty-year-old, realized she would be ideal for his new project. Her agility and tiny physique put him in mind of a bird, and he was currently reworking Stravinsky's *Le Rossignol*. She would make the perfect nightingale. At that time he did not speak to her. 'He didn't speak English and I didn't speak – period.'

Later, at a Russian New Year party Astafieva gave, she sat next to him on a piano stool. 'At parties Balanchine always used to find a piano and sit and play. He was a wonderful musician. I loved music and didn't care for parties so I sat on the bench next to him while he played. We didn't speak but he knew I was enjoying his music. Somehow we got along and it was the same later, with his choreography. I think it was the music that forged the link.'

Diaghileff told her, later, to report to Monte Carlo on 1 January

* Hamish Hamilton, 1986.

1925. Her fee would be £2 10s a week. In 1925 many men earned less. In her years with Diaghileff she never once had a contract. There was never even a letter of agreement between them.

She would have received considerably more with Fokine but it was agreed that, if she was serious about ballet, then Diaghileff offered unique prospects. Both Mrs Haskell and Arnold agreed.

Her age, or rather lack of it, presented a problem. The law forbade any child under sixteen from working abroad, although Alicia did not know that at the time. Diaghileff decided to flout the law. If nothing was said then the authorities need never know. With luck.

The difficulty was to make Alicia look sixteen; she actually looked younger than fourteen. The last thing anyone wanted was to draw attention to her as she left the country.

She was about to begin what Agnes de Mille described as '. . . her life's history, which constitutes an awful and impressive story . . . Hers might be the history of a nun or a saint as she was dedicated from youth . . . to a calling much in the style of a maiden given to temple service.'*

Rather than lessen Eileen's financial worries, the Monte Carlo contract increased them. The sum of £2 10s a week might sound substantial but it was not enough to keep Alicia and Guggy while they were away from home, and now that Nijinska had left the company, alternative housing arrangements would have to be made.

Eileen, of course, could not afford to pay Guggy, but Guggy wanted to stay on anyway, without wages. Where else would she go? Her only family was a brother whom she rarely saw. At least now she was a member of a family.

Guggy was a dubious blessing. She had never been abroad, let alone spoke French. A more unworldly companion for a first Continental visit could not be imagined.

And the band of amoral émigré ballet dancers who made up the Ballet Russe might not, necessarily, be ideal companions for a fourteen-year-old either.

Mrs Haskell had no such reservations. When she heard that Alicia had been accepted by Diaghileff she decided to step in. Her son was at Cambridge and would soon be off her hands and she had always wanted a little girl. Now she had one. She kitted out Alicia with dresses, some of which had belonged to her and which she altered, and she bought her a mauve travelling case.

* *Portrait Gallery*, Houghton Mifflin, 1990.

Alicia still did not look sixteen but not much could be done about that.

In addition Mrs Haskell arranged to pay a monthly allowance to Alicia which would cover her pocket money. Another wealthy woman, Mrs Golodetz, paid Eileen an allowance and helped take care of Alicia's sisters.

Doris and Vivienne were at a Masonic boarding school. Arthur had been a Mason and an active charity worker. Now that Eileen needed help the Masons stepped in.

Mrs Golodetz was also an habituée of Astafieva's studios. She was supportive of the young Alicia and, later, had her first tutu made for her. The Golodetzes had been one of Russia's foremost families, having made a fortune from sugar. 'Mrs Golodetz sort of adopted me,' recalls Alicia. 'She and Mrs Haskell decided to provide for me between them. It cut both ways. They had an interest and I had a training.'

With Mrs Haskell and Mrs Golodetz financing her, and Guggy accompanying her, Alicia seemed set for the journey, but still more help was needed. Someone had to steer Guggy and Alicia through the jungle of boats, trains, customs and currency and the many other things required, and it was essential that that someone spoke French. Guggy was just not up to it. That someone would also need to command respect as there could be problems if the authorities challenged Alicia's age and her right to work in a foreign country.

Diaghileff knew just the person. This was one of his dancers who had been with the company since 1923, a formidable Irish woman.

Ninette de Valois, formerly Edris Stannus, was intelligent and tough and believed ballet to be sacred. She was twenty-six, had a Continental gloss, and spoke French. She was told by Serge Grigorieff, Diaghileff's *régisseur*, to present herself at Victoria Station at the appropriate time and escort Alicia and Guggy to France.

Grigorieff recalled his bemusement at Alicia's enrolment in his book, *The Diaghileff Ballet 1909–1929**: 'The last newcomer was for us a somewhat strange one: a little girl of no more than fourteen . . . despite her extreme youth, Madame Astafieva pressed Diaghileff to take her. Diaghileff at first refused but Madame Astafieva was nothing if not insistent and made Diaghileff and myself go and see her protégée at a lesson. The child certainly danced well but was extremely thin and under-developed physically; and though

* Constable, 1953.

we both thought her promising, I could not imagine how we could possibly use her. Nevertheless Diaghileff was in the end persuaded by Madame Astafieva to take her. "We'll give her a chance to grow and study," he said, "and when she has grown and studied a little – then we'll see . . ."'

Grigorieff never got over his surprise at Diaghileff's interest in a child. At times, as he recalls, he was 'not overhelpful'.

Guggy and Alicia arrived at Victoria in a thick and disheartening fog. They saw Grigorieff but almost before they recognized him they heard his voice boom out above the clamour, '*Ou est de Valois!*'

She arrived and seemed none too pleased to see them. 'Is that the brat?' she snapped, jabbing her finger at Alicia.

'I suppose I'll have to look after that little monster, I thought,' Dame Ninette recalls. 'I had not met her but I knew of this child who was at a Russian school in London. We had been told that she was highly promising and that Diaghileff had taken her up.

'But she turned out not to be a monster at all. There never was a sweeter child. She was always good, almost too good. Everything you told her to do she immediately did. She was disciplined. I did everything for them.'*

Alicia was dumbstruck by the chic and sophisticated de Valois and dared not speak to her. She even silenced Guggy.

Alicia and de Valois remembered their first meeting all their lives and both would readily recount the story. In 1994, when Dame Ninette received an award from the *Evening Standard* for services to ballet, she told the anecdote at the ceremony. The award was presented by Alicia, also a Dame by then, who announced, 'I'm the brat.'

Under de Valois's guidance, Guggy and Alicia were soon in their seats on the boat-train.

She guided them to France, dealt with the authorities, who never dreamed of querying her about Alicia, and steered them in and out of Paris hotels and safely to Monte Carlo. The town was smaller and prettier then, perched up in the mountains and overlooking a sun-drenched sea. Alicia had never seen anywhere so lovely. 'It was like a village,' she says.

That was not the only difference from Muswell Hill.

Queen Victoria had developed a fondness for the South of France during the last decade of her life, but had eschewed Monte Carlo which, she was advised, was unsuitable for her august presence.

* 1994 interview.

Its casino, from whose balcony Alicia was shortly to take her lessons and in whose grand rooms she would perform in concerts for the rich, titled, and sometimes debauched, had been the target of an abolition movement in London.

The whole area was louche. Somerset Maugham loved it, calling it 'a sunny place for shady people'. Oscar Wilde had gone further, gleefully describing the accommodating youths of Nice as having 'the same freedom of morals as Neapolitans'. The many lauded brothels of Menton were established and attracted a clientèle from all over the world. They catered for all tastes.

Neither were the mostly Russian members of the Ballet Russe noted for their moral rectitude. Agnes de Mille describes them as a bunch of 'mad and rascally Bohemians'.* Most of them had lived life to the full; they worked with each other, fought with each other, and slept with each other. Their bond was a disdain for convention and a brilliance at dancing.

This was the environment in which Alicia would spend her formative years. Eileen, of course, had no idea about such things. Alicia had never taken so much as a sip of wine or a chaste kiss. She was a child, still on the brink of womanhood, thrust into an extraordinary world. The result was a tolerance for many styles of living that was to last her whole life through.

Agnes de Mille describes her appearance, just a few years later, as 'tiny, dark, compact and as fragile as Venetian glass, her legs and ankles seemed so remarkably slender, her hands so tapering one felt they would snap off with the first jar . . . in keeping with her outwardly effect her expression was demure, the dark lashes rested tranquilly against the wax, pale cheek, a Mona Lisa smile was fixed upon the non-committal lips, until she suddenly glanced up in child-like wickedness and chuckled with a tiny sound like something very valuable breaking . . . always about her there was an aroma of sadness.'†

'That's Agnes,' remarked Alicia, laughing, as she read the description.

Miss de Mille added, '. . . actually, a tennis champion's wrist or a surgeon's was probably a weaker instrument. In those delicate leg bones she had the kick of a stallion . . . she could, in fact, do anything.'

Agnes de Mille described Diaghileff as 'the demon genius who drove them [the Ballet Russe] to world renown.' But Alicia did not

* *Portrait Gallery.*
† *Portrait Gallery.*

encounter his demonic side; instead she found him 'the greatest man on earth'. Miss de Mille considered the Ballet Russe a 'tainted and inflamed group he ruled with such sadistic vigour'. To Alicia they were 'kindly folk, suitable for any Charlotte M. Yonge novel'.

Miss de Mille also states that when Alicia spoke of her years with the Ballet Russe she might have been describing 'nursery teas and how little brother broke his cricket bat, but one is not'.

The dancers were, mostly, kind to her, accepting her with the open-mindedness of show folk. Most of them had suffered in one way or another and went out of their way to protect her. She was a strange, remote and brilliant child – what was one more oddity among so many?

'I was in the most sophisticated company in the world,' says Alicia. 'But they were all protecting me.'

Alicia saw no evil in the shenanigans of her colleagues; all she noticed was that she had much to learn from them artistically.

She was pleased to resume her friendship with Dolin, who was back with the company. He was pleased to see her, too, but he was seven years older and Monte Carlo had attractions for the ambitious twenty-year-old with which Alicia could not compete.

She was the youngest member of the company and this brought her face to face with a loneliness she had never known in London. Guggy, as always, intensified this by not allowing her to mix.

Serge Lifar, at nineteen, was the nearest to her age. But nineteen and fourteen are different universes. He was, in addition, an advanced nineteen-year-old. Despite a technique some have described as unreliable, he knew he was going to be a star. He became one of the brightest, burning with a flame that became nearly as bright as Nijinsky's.

There was some cynicism among the troupe about Alicia's combination of youth and talent. 'I was a child progidy,' she says. 'And everybody said they never lasted, never made it in the end. I think Diaghileff intended to prove that it could be done.'

Devoted to her as he was, though, he was too busy to notice a little thing like her loneliness, which she took pains to disguise anyway. He sometimes gave her a chaste kiss on the forehead and called her his 'new daughter'. He made her grow her hair longer, and swept back, so that the Buster Brown image was replaced by a more ballerina look. He took her to museums and galleries and listened, with her, to contemporary music, explaining the composer's aims. As Ninette de Valois says, 'He was crazy for her.'

So crazy that he insisted that after every performance she erase every vestige of make-up from her face. Nor would he allow her to sit in the sun for fear she would develop an unballetic tan. She was not permitted to walk far or swim as this might develop unsightly muscles.

'The company thought something was seriously wrong with him,' Alicia continues. 'He normally could not be bothered with children and here he was, spending hours talking to me.

'He was formidable to most people, and they shrank in his presence but, and this is the strange thing, I was never afraid of him and never shy with him. Diaghileff and Pavlova were the two greatest people in ballet and they both made me feel at home. I don't know why.

'It couldn't have been easy, when I think back, but all my life has been to reach one thing and then go on to something else or in a different direction. But what an education to have someone like Diaghileff take care of me. People say how terrible he was. Maybe he was to other people, but his kindness to me shows a wonderful side to him which everybody else has missed.

'I used to hear people in the company call him something that sounded like "Sergipops". I was told that this was the Russian way, his name was Serge Pavlovitch, and it was explained they took his first name and then added a bit of his father's name to it. So I always called him "Sergipops".

'He arranged for me to have a French tutor and I would sit on the balcony of the casino, overlooking the sea, trying to learn French. I wish I'd taken greater advantage of the opportunity. The same with Russian. I had every opportunity to learn Russian, nearly all the cast were Russian, but apart from a few words I didn't pick up much.

'I shall be eternally grateful to Diaghileff. My father had died in September and Diaghileff arrived in London in December and opened up the world to me. He was always a father figure; today people would say I had a fixation for him. He took over my life.'

Alicia loved the way he would address the company before a performance, standing centre-stage with his cashmere coat draped over his shoulders and an ornate cane in his hands.

He loved her chastity. It was his aim to protect it and project it on stage.

'He always said that if he had had wealth he would adopt me,' Alicia continues. 'He would become my father. But he said to Mother, "What do I have to give her?" He only had the company and some very rare books which he loved. We had a mutual trust. That's why I never had a contract with him, it wasn't necessary. I loved him very much and knew he was the most important figure in my life. Without him what would I have been?

'Somehow, those sophisticated people seemed to understand me, that's what's odd. It's all crazy. I had no childhood, I never saw anyone of my age. I only saw my sisters when I came home in the summer. I'd stay a bit, then go off to Brighton or Littlehampton or wherever the Crewleys were, to have a holiday, as I would have to go back to work soon. I was always surrounded by much older people.

'The only thing lacking at that time was money, but somehow the people who really understood, like the Haskells, Arnold and his mother, tried to make Mother and me understand that if I was going to be serious then I must forget about money now – that would come later. That was why Mrs Haskell used to help me out.'

Alicia's first role was Red Riding Hood in *Aurora's Wedding*, which was, more or less, a *divertissement* of the last act of *The Sleeping Princess*, bolstered by additional material and based on Diaghileff's 1921 production.

Dolin did not think Red Riding Hood was appropriate for Alicia as it did not show off her individuality. Alicia, however, feels differently. 'It was suitable. I was so tiny I would have looked wrong in a more adult role.'

She was not disappointed with her part but she was with her billing in the programme. As she had joined a Russian company she knew that her name would be changed, but she had not bargained for what she got. 'I was waiting for a wonderful Russian name but when the programme appeared in Monte Carlo for my very first performance I saw myself billed as Alicia Markova. Diaghileff had just removed Lilian, Alicia was already there, and the S was removed from Marks and OVA put on. I had no say in the matter. I knew nothing about it until I saw the programme.'

The Russian spelling of Markova is MAPKOBA, and she had to look for this on the company noticeboard to find out her schedule. 'If MAPKOBA was on the board I knew I was down for a rehearsal. They had to teach me the Russian spelling of my name and of the Russian names of the different ballets I was called for. It was all done by sight.'

She had not been in Monte Carlo more than a few weeks before she was informed by Diaghileff that she would be dancing at the palace. The Royal Family were giving a party and had commissioned him to provide the entertainment. A request from the Royal Family was a command; it was owing to their patronage that Diaghileff was in Monte Carlo.

She danced 'Valse Caprice' and the *pizzicato* from *Sylvia* to Delibes's music. Balanchine rearranged them for her and it was the beginning of their long partnership.

A couple of weeks later she performed in the Casino's Salle Ganne where 'I danced the White Act of *Swan Lake*. I didn't have any tights and Boris Kochno [Diaghileff's assistant] went all over Monte Carlo trying to find a pair small enough for me. Tights, in those days, had to be made to order and there were only two families in Paris who made them. You had to put your order in way ahead and we hadn't done that.

'I remember him coming back and all he could find was a pair of white silk stockings. There were problems with them as I have small feet. But we undid the stocking at the top and tapes were put on them. To keep them up I put coins inside what became the waistband. I used pennies, as they were large, and tied the tape around them so that I made two little anchors. I had two at the front and two at the back. That was how I was fixed up. It was the traditional way to fasten tights in those days.

'The costume they adapted for me had belonged to Trefilova* as she had been tiny, too. You can imagine how proud I was to wear it. I had no feathered crown, just a row of pearls and diamonds. As I was so young, Diaghileff made sure everything was simple. He always kept me simply dressed.'

Alicia's partner was Nicholas Efimoff, chosen mainly because he was the shortest dancer in the company and would not dwarf her. He went on to become *premier danseur* at the Paris Opéra.

Despite the glamour of the performances, Alicia soon came to realize that life in Monte Carlo was going to be drab. There was nothing exciting about it.

Guggy woke her, dressed her, took her to practice or rehearsal and stayed with her all the time. After that it was straight back to the hotel where they shared a cheap room.

Once in the hotel, Guggy allowed no one near her to distract her. She was made to study her school books and Guggy permitted no backsliding. She was put to bed at a sensible hour, fed sensible food, and encouraged to lead a sensible life. When in bed the curtains were drawn and the light switched on.

* Prima ballerina at the Marynsky. She resigned prematurely owing to a series of intrigues waged against her by Kschessinska. She danced the Sleeping Princess in London in 1921. Her third husband was critic Valerian Svetlov.

Her only bedtime reading was the further study of her lessons. There was no conversation at all.

She did not complain, and it was only later that she confessed to Alexandra Danilova, one of the company's leading dancers, how miserable she had been. At the time she just accepted it as a way of life.

They could not afford to eat in restaurants all the time so Guggy converted a corner of their room into a kitchen and bought a saucepan, teapot and spirit stove. These were kept in a hatbox when not in use. Guggy was determined not to worry Eileen with demands for money, and this meant that they could only afford to eat out once a day.

Within the company, Guggy was viewed as a pain in the neck. Alicia could have done with a pinch of excitement, but she did not know it existed. She had embarked on a career as a dancer and this was her life.

There was a respite from her lessons when she was permitted to make her costume headdresses. The wardrobe department would give her, perhaps, a piece of ribbon and some beads and expect her to make something acceptable. This habit stayed with her and, even when she became a star, she nearly always made her own headdresses. Several ballets were premiered with millinery by Markova.

Danilova had noticed Alicia creeping about and felt sorry for her, recognizing her loneliness, and she tried to cheer her up. She thought she might take her out one day.

At twenty-one, Danilova was a lady of the world and even spoke a little English. Trained at the Imperial School in St Petersburg, she had quickly become a ballerina, famous for her sparkling sense of humour, which she was able to inject into her dances, and her outstandingly glorious legs, which had been the talk of St Petersburg and of which she was rightly proud.

After the Revolution she was one of the few Soviet dancers given permission to leave Leningrad and tour Germany, which she had done with Balanchine, his wife, ballerina Tamara Gevergeyeva (later known as Geva), and Efimoff. It was while they were on tour that Diaghileff had invited all four to join him.

Danilova still remembers how Alicia came to her attention. As in all companies rumours were rife and there were several concerning Alicia, making her an object of pity, although she was unaware of it. 'Balanchine told me she was an orphan,' Danilova says.* 'We knew

* Taped interview with Danilova, 1994.

her father had lost all his money and believed he had committed suicide leaving his wife with four little girls to bring up. "She is very charming and very, very talented," Balanchine said.

'"But she is a little girl," I told him. "How will she mix with us?"

'"Well, I will make a special ballet for her," he told me. "*The Nightingale* of Stravinsky." That was how I learnt about her.

'When I spoke to her I found her polite but very quiet, also very observant. I felt sorry for her because not only did she never speak but she looked frightened all the time. So I made a special point of going to see her, to take her out for tea. I thought she might enjoy that and it would get her away from her governess.'

But when Danilova got to Alicia's hotel Guggy was out. She was posting a letter to Eileen. She sent regular reports but forbade Alicia to write to her mother. She took care of that so there was no need for Alicia to take time off from her studies. It never occurred to Guggy that Alicia might want to write.

Guggy had locked Alicia in their room, to ensure that she did not get into mischief, so she could not open the door when Danilova knocked. They exchanged a few words, in Danilova's broken English, through the locked door, but Alicia was clearly frightened of Guggy coming back. It was plain she wanted Danilova to go.

Danilova was so enraged by Guggy's behaviour that she complained to Diaghileff. He took no notice. Alicia might have been special but he was still Diaghileff, not a social worker.

On practice days Guggy got Alicia up at 7.30, gave her her breakfast, cooked on the spirit stove, and took her to her class. She stayed with her throughout the lesson and watched her with an eagle eye. God help her if she was criticized more than usual.

If that happened she withheld Alicia's chocolate ration. Chocolates were one of Alicia's few pleasures and, on good days, Guggy doled her out two each day. Eileen sent her a box now and then and these would be held by Guggy, who rationed her. Other cast members might sometimes casually buy her a box, and these too were taken into Guggy's custody.

Knowing of her sweet tooth, Dolin occasionally took her to tea, to sample the rich cakes in the best hotels. Of course, Guggy had to go as well. They made an unlikely trio, the brash young man, the timid girl, and the hatchet-faced spinster. A real Monte Carlo vignette.

Diaghileff was an idol of Dolin's and he had watched him playfully pop pieces of cake into his ballerinas' mouths. Dolin tried this with Alicia.

Guggy took exception but Dolin silenced her by pointing out that Diaghileff had done it to Lubov Tchernicheva, one of the iciest of ballerinas. Guggy did not approve of fun but Dolin would not, and did not, take too much interference from her.

Alicia started training under Madame Cecchetti, wife of Enrico Cecchetti, who trained the company principals. Italian-born Cecchetti had made his debut in Genoa at the age of five but in 1890, when he was forty, he had become ballet master at the Marynsky. He had taught both Nijinsky and Pavlova and was a master of technique, so much so that in 1922 the Cecchetti Society had been formed in London to preserve his method.

By the time Alicia reached him he was in his seventies and could be irascible. His word was never challenged. He was always referred to as 'Maestro'; no one called him anything else.

Madame Cecchetti's province was the *corps de ballet* and, owing to her age, Alicia trained with them. But Cecchetti walked in one day and caught sight of her practising. He removed her from his wife's class and placed her under his personal supervision. Alicia definitely got her two chocolates that day.

As a principal, Danilova also studied with Cecchetti. She was pleased when Alicia joined her. 'Maestro would always put Alicia in the middle of the class,' she recalls. 'On Mondays we did ensembles and he would be very annoyed if we made mistakes. Alicia always remembered perfectly what we had to do, so before a lesson I would ask her what we had done last lesson. She would show me so that Maestro would not be mad at me because I had forgotten. Cecchetti's classes were difficult for me because he was Italian and I had been brought up in the French school. Alicia's mind was more open.'

Cecchetti had a short fuse and this could blow over any trifle. Sometimes he would throw his cane at an offending dancer. If this happened to Alicia she was made to pick it up and return it to him with a curtsey. No one was offended by Cecchetti's behaviour. As their maestro he had the right to temperament. It was the fault of the dancers for not getting things right.

Danilova also took advantage of Alicia's exceptional memory when they were working with Massine. 'She quickly picked up his choreography and remembered it. Sometimes I would ask her to show me what to do because I had forgotten. She remembered my steps as well as her own. She always helped me. Our friendship worked both ways.'

When the main company was away touring, Cecchetti gave Alicia private lessons. These could last up to three hours without a break, but she was conscious that she was receiving invaluable guidance from one of the world's great masters.

When the company returned, Alicia would be exhausted but she realized that she was technically more advanced. There was no short cut to excellence and sometimes it was not a particularly pleasant road, but it was necessary. Even so, she was relieved when Cecchetti could divert his attention elsewhere.

Alicia sometimes studied with some of Cecchetti's more advanced pupils, not company members but those taking private lessons. Among them was Vincenzo Celli, who was later to play an important role in her life, notably when she was ill in New York and terrified that she might never dance again.

Ruth Page was another private pupil. She later achieved fame as one of the most dynamic personalities of American *avant-garde* dance. She founded the Chicago Ballet and choreographed adaptations of operettas. She had toured with Pavlova in 1918.

Whenever Alicia took part in a performance her ballet shoes were inspected afterwards by Guggy. She had heard that the shoes of a dancer should be as unmarked after a show as they had been when put on. If Alicia's showed signs of wear she was not given her chocolates, irrespective of how well she had danced.

'Guggy would take the shoes to the strong electric light near the make-up mirror,' Alicia recalls. 'If she found so much as a streak, or a spot, on the satin I lost my chocolates, not just for that day but for the entire week.'

Thanks to Danilova, Alicia did not have to do without chocolates entirely. Banquets and formal dinners were frequent in Monte Carlo. Danilova would sneak out some of the petit fours served after the meal and give them to Alicia. When other company members realized what she was doing they, too, jumped on the bandwagon. She was regularly handed little bags of sweets.

Improbable as it seems, Guggy was a fan of the cinema and, if she felt Alicia deserved it, she would take her to see a film once a week. There was an ulterior motive for this. The films were in French and Guggy felt it might improve their knowledge of the language. Alicia had to endure a particular torture at the cinema. 'During the intervals women used to come selling chocolate ice-creams, they were called Eskimo Glaces. We were on such a strict budget that we couldn't afford them and I used to think, Oh, when I have money I'm coming back and I'll be able to buy Eskimo Glaces. Later, in 1938, when I went back to Monte Carlo with the Ballet Russe, I had money. Chura [Danilova] and I went to the cinema and bought them. It was wonderful.'

She buys similar ices in the Knightsbridge shops today.

For her first season in Monte Carlo she wasn't too lonely. Mrs Haskell and Arnold came over – Arnold saw all her early performances – and both Dolin and de Valois were part of the company.

'I don't think she was lonely,' says Ninette de Valois. 'I looked after her. No, she was an intelligent little girl, she could always find something to do and she was still being educated. Diaghileff was very good and saw to that, she had tuition wherever she went, so she had a full day.

'She may have been lonely in the sense she had no one of her own age to mix with, and she was rather young for her age. Today they'd be flying about all on their own, but not in her case. In those days we were very strict.

'We all stayed in the same little hotels so, although she had a room with her governess, and I had my own room, we met up at meal-times and that sort of thing. So she was all right at nights, she had company.'

'She was lonely for spoiling,' says Danilova. 'She was not lonely because she was alone, she was never alone. She was always with her governess or members of the company.'

Alicia was often sent by Diaghileff to dance at charity concerts where she would do 'Valse Caprice' or the *pizzicato* from *Sylvia*.

Opera singers sometimes took part in these concerts and she once appeared on the same bill as handsome Australian baritone John Brownlee, the darling of Dame Nellie Melba. Dame Nellie rarely had time for tenors, whom she viewed as a necessary evil who enabled her to give the audience what it wanted – her performance. But, at her insistence, Brownlee had appeared at her farewell performance at Covent Garden, where they had sung *La Bohème* together.

Alicia's first starring role with the Ballet Russe was *Le Chant du Rossignol*, for which Balanchine had earmarked her when he had first seen her at The Pheasantry. This would be his first major work for the Ballet Russe; in fact, his first major work in the West.

Balanchine had been initially hired by Diaghileff to devise opera ballets, as had his predecessor Nijinska. He was keen to do this as he could try out his ideas in the operas then incorporate those that worked into his full-scale ballets.

Le Chant du Rossignol had quite a history. Diaghileff had produced it in 1920 at the Paris Opéra with Karsavina, Sokolova and Idzikowsky. It had been choreographed by Massine to Stravinsky's music and Matisse's décor. But it had not been a success.

Based on an Andersen fairy tale, it tells the story of a Chinese emperor who bans a live nightingale when he is given a bejewelled clockwork one. When he falls ill the clockwork one breaks down and the real nightingale sings him back to life – the triumph of nature over artifice.

Stravinsky had culled the music from his opera *Le Rossignol* which Diaghileff had produced in 1914. Balanchine had danced in this in a small role so was familiar with the score. He suggested certain alterations to Stravinsky.

Diaghileff and Stravinsky had always believed in the work, although they knew it was not quite right. They now thought the time had come to perfect it.

Balanchine and Alicia began to work closely together. He had limited English and she even less Russian – when she spoke at all. But she was studying French and Balanchine spoke a little of that, so they were able to communicate.

He was easy to work with. He would make suggestions, watch what she did, then nonchalantly make alterations, delighted when things worked out. It was all laid-back.

'He was always very quiet,' says Alicia. 'That was one of the things that worked between us.'

Alicia was virgin territory, as yet untried in a major role. If she was a success then his creation would succeed with her.

In his seemingly unconcerned way Balanchine perceptively assessed her qualities. He stretched her to the limits then pushed further. 'He tested me,' she says in *Markova Remembers*. 'Thinking up steps that he supposed might be beyond me. Yet I managed to produce what he wanted, including a diagonal of *fouettés* across the stage and back, with arm movements as if swimming, which he felt gave the impression of a little bird hopping. In the *pas de deux* with Death [a role taken by Lydia Sokolova] I had to perform double *tours en l'air*.'

At one session she was rehearsing the *pas de deux* with Sokolova when Balanchine suggested she try it on *pointe*. This would be cripplingly difficult but, without protest, she did it. He could not believe what he was seeing.

She inspired him to create even more difficult steps. 'Throughout my career,' she says, 'I have always felt that if a choreographer asks for something, my attitude must always be, "Well, let's try it."'

Agnes de Mille commented in *Portrait Gallery*, 'Throughout her youth she danced hard and correctly, if without expression of any sort . . . Alicia's art, through sheer concentration and focussing of impulse, became transfigured gradually to the beauty and cold endurance of the stars ... choreographers always agreed that she was a delight to rehearse as she did precisely what she was asked and nothing else ... Her memory was legendary, she could remember not only everything she had done but, much more unusual, what she had merely seen. She could compose nothing, not even a school-room series of steps. She had to see and to copy.'

Danilova was also in *Rossignol* and remembers the rehearsals. 'Balanchine demonstrated a new movement to her, a sort of diagonal pirouette with the arms extended sideways, then up, down and sideways again. After *Le Rossignol* was choreographed everyone copied this pirouette and it became very popular – I even saw it later in New York at Radio City – but Balanchine devised the step and Markova was the first to dance it.

'Sometimes her smallness could be a handicap when she was dancing with the company as it made her conspicuous. In certain numbers we had to hide her in the wings at various places then sneak her on again later so that no one would notice how small she was, otherwise she would have spoiled the design of certain groups. We had a lot of fun pushing her backwards and forwards.

'Our company manager, Mr Grigorieff, didn't speak any English so I taught her a few useful phrases in Russian. I taught her to say "Please can I have an advance?" and "Have you any money at all?" It sounded very cute.

'If I had to describe her dancing I would liken it to a desert flower, a cactus with needles. It was always so precise and sharp.

'She was very popular with Balanchine. He used to say that when she would be sixteen he would take her to a night-club and I used to tell her that, when she was sixteen, I would give her a bottle of perfume. She was so young for her years, and locked within herself. We tried to bring her out.'

But she was free when it came to dancing. Because of her compliancy, choreographers were ready to take chances with her and entrust her with experimental works. Sometimes her sheer technical brilliance was an inspiration in itself.

Matisse was the designer for *Le Rossignol* and he created an all-white body stocking for her, adorned with clumps of costume jewellery. He never wanted Alicia in colours. 'Never wear anything but white,' he told her. 'A little impractical when I was travelling,' reflects Alicia.

Although she was clad from head to toe, the effect was of nudity glittering with icy-bright diamonds. Osprey feathers jutted from her head.

The outfit was a surprise to her as, although the costume Karsavina had worn in the opera was unsuitable, she had been expecting something brown and bird-like, rather like the real nightingale. But reality went out of the window. As did any inhibitions she might have had about wearing this daring costume that would not have been out of place in the Folies Bergère. As always, she did what she was told.

Vera Soudeikina made the costume and fitted her. She was a great beauty who, although not a dancer, moved well and had played the Queen in *The Sleeping Princess*. Diaghileff admired her. She later married Stravinsky and Alicia saw a lot of them when she was working in Hollywood.

Soudeikina's studio was in Paris and Guggy took Alicia there, to meet up with Diaghileff, Stravinsky and Matisse, to be fitted.

Arguments in Russian and French burst out all round her as she patiently stood while Soudeikina fitted fabrics and jewels on her. She barely understood a word.

Alicia was put under the musical instruction of Stravinsky. 'Anyone who has had to dance Stravinsky at the age of fourteen has no musical fears after that,' she later told writer Doris Hering. She dismisses any idea that he was temperamental. 'Not with me. He was like a nice, warm uncle. A lovely man, and he stayed that way throughout our relationship. He called me *"petichka"*, which means "little bird", after the nightingale. He taught me all about music.'

He needed to. His music was fearsome, relentlessly changing in rhythm. It was so difficult that no rehearsal pianist could play it and Stravinsky had to record it on to a pianola roll which was used at rehearsals. He told her not to be afraid of it and not to try to count the beats, just to listen and feel the music: 'To learn it.'

Balanchine conceived her entrance in a cage, spectacularly balanced on one leg, held aloft by two men. She left this position and dived gracefully to floor level where she was caught by two more men. Diaghileff was delighted at rehearsals. This was what he had had in mind for her.

Danilova was somewhat overweight at this period and trying to reduce. Earlier, when she had had danced *The Blue Bird* with Dolin, he had quarrelled with her about her weight.

Having endured near-starvation in the Soviet Union, she had made up for lost time. Monte Carlo was full of rich food and she fell on it. The pastries and pâtés went down at an alarming rate.

So much so that Dolin complained that lifting her was like lifting a piano.*

She conceded that she was on the plump side. Never one to do anything by halves, she bought a bottle of pills guaranteed to reduce weight. Not bothering to read the label, she had downed a handful and fainted during practice. Diaghileff banned her from eating sweet things after that and she was gradually resuming her normal weight.

It took some time and she was still on the heavy side when the company later danced in Paris. Pavlova was there at the time, and called afterwards to pay her respects and meet her friend Felia Doubrovska, another member of the Diaghileff company. She sent word to Alicia that she was pleased to see her on stage but was sorry she was not dancing a classic role. Pavlova did not greatly care for modern works.

Doubrovska introduced Danilova to Pavlova and the great lady took them both to dinner at the Atheneum, that splendid hotel where she always stayed. As the waiter served the starters, she asked Danilova how much she weighed. Pavlova could be direct. 'I weighed one hundred twenty pounds,' Danilova recalls. 'I was quite fat and knew it. Pavlova told me I must diet at once and never weight more than one hundred and fifteen pounds.'† She felt every bite was being monitored.

Le Chant du Rossignol opened at the Gaieté Lyrique in Paris on 17 June 1925, with Stravinsky conducting. Sokolova danced Death and Grigorieff was the Emperor.

Picasso was among the audience with his wife, Olga, who had been one of Diaghileff's dancers. Alicia already knew him as he had brought his small son along to rehearsals. 'This jolly little man used to drop by with his son. After a few days I thought, I wonder who he is?, and I asked Chura. She told me it was Picasso and that he had done the décor for *The Three Cornered Hat*.'

In *The Diaghileff Ballet* 1909–1929‡ Grigorieff writes: '. . . the Nightingale was danced by little Markova, whose highly stylized antics greatly diverted the audience.' According to Bernard Taper in his biography of Balanchine,§ 'Markova in the cage looked delicate

---

* *George Balanchine: Ballet Master* by Richard Buckle and John Taras, Hamish Hamilton, 1988.
† Taped conversation with Danilova, 1994.
‡ Constable, 1953.
§ Macmillan, 1960.

and winsome, a wisp of a thing. She may have weighed all of 80 lbs in those days.'

There were three new ballets that season: *Zéphire et Flore*, which had a story by Kochno, choreography by Massine and music by Vladimir Dukelsky, who later went to America and became Vernon Duke; *Les Matelots*, again by Kochno and Massine with music by Auric; and *Le Chant du Rossignol*. By far the most spectacular in terms of cast and orchestral requirements was *Rossignol*.

After that Paris season both Dolin and de Valois left the company for other engagements. The Haskells had also, by now, also left France. Even though Chura Danilova was a friend, Alicia began to feel very much on her own.

7

Alone in Paris

The Ballet Russe regularly gave London seasons in June or July and also, sometimes, in the autumn. Alicia returned to London with the company in 1925. She danced Red Riding Hood in London and also, during a Coliseum season in the autumn, appeared in Fokine's *commedia dell'arte Le Carnaval*. She was Papillon, looking charming in a sort of crinoline with long drawers. She was partnered by the great Nicolai Legat as Pantalon.

When asked if her family were proud of her triumphal return to London she replied: 'I suppose they must have been. I didn't have much time to see them, I was too busy working.' Her sister Vivienne recalls that, occasionally, Diaghileff would let her, and Doris, watch the ballet from the wings. A great treat.

When she did meet her family she stayed with them for a couple of weeks and then, when the season finished, was sent to the Crewleys for a holiday, before her next Monte Carlo season. It was the only chance of a break she would get. Again emotionally she was alone.

Legat joined the company as ballet master in place of Cecchetti who had now taken up a position with La Scala in Milan. According to Grigorieff, Diaghileff and Legat did not see eye to eye, notably about Serge Lifar whom Diaghileff did not feel was progressing sufficiently quickly under Legat. Legat did not stay long. But long enough for Alicia to resume her studies under him and continue her unbroken Russian ballet tuition.

Alicia toured widely with the Ballet Russe. For two years she travelled across Europe dancing in the world's greatest theatres, among them La Scala, Milan, the Paris Opéra and the auditoriums of Germany, Spain, Belgium, Hungary, Austria, and Czechoslovakia. It was an unrivalled education for a teenager.

Among the London appearances was one, on 3 December 1926, at the Lyceum Theatre in *The Triumph of Neptune*, a 'pantomime' in twelve scenes with libretto by Sacheverell Sitwell.

The Sitwells, being self-consciously devoted to the arts, courted Diaghileff. It was assumed that Edith Sitwell, the poetess, would be deeply moved by ballet; in fact it bored her stiff. As her biographer Victoria Glendinning states, 'she was moved hardly at all by ballet'.

But her brothers Osbert and Sacheverell loved it and Sacheverell wrote an 'English' ballet for Diaghileff. Edith's indifference to the art did not prevent her from attending the first night, escorted by artist Alvaro Guevara with whom she was then smitten.

The music was by Lord Berners and Balanchine had choreographed it. The décor was by Prince Shervashidze. Among the principals were Danilova, Tchernicheva, Serge Lifar (who did a hornpipe), Lydia Sokolova, and Balanchine himself, who played the Negro. The orchestra was conducted by Henri Defosse, a talented ballet conductor who, according to Grigorieff, was the only conductor with whom Diaghileff never quarrelled over tempi.

This was an occasion when Alicia's diminutive stature stood her in good stead. She and Vera Savina played fairies and, as such, had to fly across the stage.

That great innovator in stage flying, Mr Kirby of Kirby Wire fame, was consulted to train the girls. Flying is not easy, and to avoid disaster it is imperative to learn how to land, take off, and to steer a positive course. 'You've got to keep your wits about you,' as Alicia says.

She loved flying and was a 'natural'. But she nearly came to grief on one occasion. 'It was during the transformation scene, in a snow storm [The Frozen Forest],' she recalls. 'We had wands and the tops of these were wooden balls, they were solid, but painted and glittering, and as we flew we waved them. It looked beautiful.

'Vera used to start on one side and I the other and we crossed in mid-air. This one performance, as we crossed, I got a crash on the head and it nearly knocked me out. Oh, I thought, Vera, watch what you're doing.

'After the scene was over and the curtain came down I walked to the middle of the stage and I said, "Vera, please be a little more careful with your wand, you nearly knocked me out." She said, "What are you talking about? You did that to me." I said, "I never touched you." She said, "I'm very sorry, you hit me on the head." So there we were, these two fairies, with this altercation going on and Grigorieff came on and said, "What is the matter? You have a quick change for the next scene."

'At that moment one of the crew came rushing on stage and explained what had happened. The scenery was held by planks of wood which were netted to keep them in position. Apparently one of our wires had sliced the netting as we crossed and a strip of wood had come adrift and smacked us both on our heads as we passed. You can imagine the roars of laughter when everyone heard about it. But we just carried on with the next scene. Remember, there were no unions then.'

Both Grigorieff and Dolin remark that, at times, there was a certain amount of jealousy in the company brought on by Diaghileff's closeness to Alicia and the fact that one so young should be given plum roles. If there was, she refuses to acknowledge that it bothered her. 'If there had ever been any jealousy aimed at me I wasn't aware of it. Maybe there was, I never noticed. It didn't matter. It was more important to me that Diaghileff had replaced my father. He was always strict with me but a definite father figure. I felt I could trust him and he me. That was all that mattered, jealousy was unimportant.'

Back in Monte Carlo Alicia resumed Guggy's strict routine. She was still packed off to bed early with her school books, the daylight was blacked out, and Guggy sat and knitted. The only sound was the clicking of her needles.

'I was getting on for sixteen and developing a definite inferiority complex,' she says. She never shook it off despite receiving cheers that shook the rafters.

It gradually became clear to Alicia that Guggy was not well, although she had not complained to Eileen or Alicia. A doctor was sent for who ordered her to bed.

So Alicia was no longer seen at tea with her or the other English dancers. The English at tea had amused Danilova, and the other Russians, who called them 'The English Colony'. To them it was a symptom of eccentricity – although for the Russians to call the English eccentric was the pot calling the kettle black.

Alicia was dancing on the evening of the day Guggy was confined to bed and, for the first time in her life, she would have to get ready alone, as Guggy could not go with her. She had no idea what to do. She had never packed her make-up case before and Guggy had always put on her make-up. 'I'd done absolutely nothing.'

From her bed Guggy told her what to pack. Lydia Sokolova was also dancing that night and Guggy told Alicia to contact her as soon as she got to the theatre. She would help her with her make-up.

Alicia knocked on Sokolova's door and explained the situation. It was a busy time for Sokolova as she, too, had to get ready for the performance. They were in *Le Carnaval* together and Sokolova was Columbine. She told Alicia to bring her make-up to her room and she would give her a hand. Alicia fetched her case then sat on a chair waiting for Sokolova to do her face.

Sokolova was appalled. She was even more so when she discovered that Alicia needed to be dressed as well. She told her she should be ashamed of herself. 'The dressing-down she gave me, I was in tears. I was always in tears then. I thought I'd never get on the stage. I can't dance the way I feel. It was terrible.'

When Alicia's cue came Sokolova shoved her out of her room and told her to dance, adding witheringly, 'if you can manage that without help!'

'Oh, that Sokolova!' says Alicia. 'But from that day on it was independence. From then on! She also asked me, "How do you think you can accept the responsibility when Diaghileff makes you our ballerina if you can't even make up? How will you get to the stage alone? I am ashamed of you." She wasn't one to mince matters.'

After curtain-down Alicia apologized to Sokolova who, now that she had given her performance, was more relaxed. She brushed Alicia's apology aside.

But Alicia's face burned with shame. She learned a valuable lesson that day. She knew she had to stand on her own two feet.

It was as well she was a quick learner. Guggy was seriously ill. Alicia realized she was in deep trouble when Guggy started complaining to the doctor that she could not sleep at night as she was being bitten by mosquitoes. She usually slept like a log and Alicia had had no trouble with mosquitoes. Guggy was losing her mind.

Suddenly Alicia was solely in charge of a dying woman. As always in emergencies, she coped. *Le Carnaval* was the last ballet in the Monte Carlo season and she was scheduled to travel with the company for rehearsals and performances in Paris.

The company left but Alicia did not go with them as she would not leave Guggy alone. She felt she could not do it. She had known her companion since she was four years old and had done little without her. She had become dependent on Guggy.

But Diaghileff could not hold up the Paris season for a dying old lady and a young dancer. He sent Alicia a peremptory telegram.

'Unless you rejoin the company within 2 days consider yourself no longer a member – Serge Diaghileff.' 'That was from the man I'd thought of as my dear papa,' recalls Alicia. She did not know what to do.

Without the company, Alicia now had to eat in the restaurant alone. Another English lady lived in the hotel, a Miss Barnes, and seeing poor adolescent Alicia sitting at her lonely table, she suggested they eat together. She knew Alicia was with Diaghileff's company. Alicia poured out her problems to Miss Barnes.

'She told me, "You have to go to Paris, this is your life." She told me she would look after Guggy and she helped me pack. She put me on the train with a basket and some sandwiches. She put my money in a little sock and pinned that inside my clothes, telling me I wasn't to go to sleep and must sit up, awake, all night.

'I was terrified. I'd always travelled in a carriage full of my colleagues before. Talk about shock! You have to envisage what trains were like in those days, and it was the end of May and quite hot. They were steam trains and people opened the windows and the smut came hurtling in. I looked like a chimney sweep by the time I got there.

'I'll always remember arriving at the Gare du Nord and suddenly realizing I was alone. No one had given me an address to contact. I had no guidance and had never done a thing for myself. Can you imagine arriving in Paris, of all places, alone as a child? Thinking back on it I think I survived because I was so naïve. That's probably what protected me.

'I suddenly remembered the Haskells used to stay at the Hôtel Majestic, Mrs Haskell's mother used to live there, so I went to a porter and asked him to get me a taxi. I'd started to learn French by that time. It was somewhere to go. Better to be lost in the Majestic than on the station.

'I got there and, looking as I did, having travelled all night, I went to the concierge. I said every prayer I ever knew, then asked him for Madame Haskell. I waited with baited breath. The concierge picked up the phone and asked for her. "In the name of who?" he asked me. I nearly fainted with relief, they were there. He told me to please wait.

'A lady's maid came down and got me. Mrs Haskell was there, visiting her mother. As soon as I saw the Haskells I burst into floods of tears and they thought something terrible had happened. They gave me a bath, cleaned me up and gave me breakfast. I showed them Diaghileff's telegram threatening to fire me if I didn't arrive.

So they found out where the company was rehearsing and their maid took me there.'

There was a stunned silence when Alicia walked into the rehearsal. The company was amazed when she told them that she had made the journey from Monte Carlo alone. So was Alicia.

Ninette de Valois sorted her out. She was back guesting with the company. In an amazingly lucky coincidence for Alicia, Sokolova had been taken ill and de Valois was dancing some of her roles.

'Once again Grigorieff shouted, "*Où est de Valois*,"' Alicia continues. 'And there was the brat standing before her again. I thought to myself, I'm the little brat and I'm staying by her side. She got me a room in her hotel and showed me how to fend for myself.

'She taught me how to buy things in shops as I'd never been shopping alone in a big city. In Monte Carlo it was all right, it was a village, and all the shopkeepers knew me. They called out "*bonjour*" when they saw me and I would call "*bonjour*" back. I never had to worry about walking there, but Paris was different.'

De Valois remembers Alicia's arrival in Paris. 'I had a terrible time. I became a sort of foster mother to her, I suppose. The company had no one to look after anyone and I, being British, naturally had to take her over. So I had not only my own job to do but to look after this little girl.

'I remember, I had a friend in the British Embassy and he took me out for a drink in the hotel one afternoon. When it came to six o'clock I said to him, "I'm afraid I've got to go upstairs now and look after my little girl who's here." He asked about her and I told him she'd been left alone and that her governess was ill and that I'd had to take her over for Diaghileff.

'He stopped me and said, "Don't tell me any more or I shall have to put your precious Diaghileff in prison for leaving an unchaperoned little girl alone in the middle of Paris."'

Later, Diaghileff was to send Alicia for lessons with Lubov Egorova, otherwise Princess Nikita Troubetzkoy by marriage. Known for her grand manner, Egorova, a former Marynsky ballerina, had founded a ballet school in Paris in 1923.

From Paris the company moved to London for a season at the Coliseum, where Eileen was waiting for Alicia. The Haskells were on holiday and loaned them their house.

When Guggy was well enough to travel, Miss Barnes put her on the train and she returned to London. Then her brother took her to his home and eventually she was put into a hospital where her condition deteriorated, both physically and mentally. She ended her days in a state of bewilderment, not recognizing anyone. There were few visitors anyway. A governess's job was thankless and most died alone.

It was clear that Alicia would need another chaperone. This time Eileen stepped into the breach. Her other daughters were looked after by Mrs Haskell and Mrs Golodetz between them; Doris and Vivienne were at the Masonic boarding school anyway.

Alicia rejoined the company after her annual holiday. The company travelled to Berlin, for a two-week season, before returning to Monte Carlo.

The company was a disaster in Berlin and it played to nearly empty houses. As Grigorieff puts it, 'In view of our almost invariable success elsewhere this was extremely puzzling. But there it was.'

Business was so poor that the German impresario could not afford to pay Diaghileff who had to get to Paris as quickly as possible and raise funds, as usual, otherwise he would have been unable to transport the company back to Monte Carlo. It was the Christmas season and this was difficult. But, being Diaghileff, he succeeded.

One of the reasons for the company's failure may have been the high French content of the repertoire. At that time hostility to France was common in Germany.

Eileen, with her bright personality, was less restrictive company for Alicia who thrived on her new-found independence. 'I found I ended up looking after Mother,' she says. 'She was a lovely, caring and sweet person but I had to learn for myself that when you're out in the world alone it's competitive. There have been times when I've needed help in my life but I've not always had it. People have been there but I end up helping them. It's because they think I'm so efficient. I think it comes from starting out so early as a performer. I've never had time to get the vapours, I just got on with it. But Mother enjoyed the change and her new life.'

8

Promotion

Alicia knew that Diaghileff was pleased with her, and she looked forward to being promoted to weightier parts on a regular basis.

She was disappointed.

Diaghileff sent for her one morning and, sitting in the theatre with the house lights up, talked to her about her future. 'He kissed me on the forehead and called me "*dushka*", which means "little darling",' she recalls.

But the little darling was dismayed by what he had to say. Diaghileff had to speak in English, a language in which he was never at his best. Haltingly, he dropped a bombshell, as he explained he was cutting her out of all featured roles in the future apart from Red Riding Hood.

He told her he felt she was missing out on her basic training and this could only be put to rights if she now danced with the *corps* and learnt everything from the beginning up. She was a little taller now so would fit in with the line.

'I was demoted to the *corps de ballet*,' Alicia recalls unemotionally. 'Diaghileff put me there because he thought I would last and grow that way. He wanted me to work my way through the ranks so that no one could say I had got to the top solely through his influence.

'Once he explained this to me, I accepted it, and I've been grateful to him ever since. It gave me experience which was to come in useful later on. When you run companies, as I did, it helps when you've been through every stage yourself. It's like being in the army, you don't enlist as a general.'

She stayed uncomplainingly in the *corps* for an entire season. Many would have felt humiliated, but as it was Diaghileff's wish she accepted it.

After this he allowed her to dance solos again. One of these was *Le Carnaval*, which she had already danced in her first season. He took a special interest in her flowing costume for this and, as her legs were still on the thin side ('People were not always kind to me about this,' she remembers), put her in organdie pantalettes so as not to draw attention to them.

Alicia grew up in the next couple of years. The Continental tours were interesting, and certainly more pleasant with Eileen, and although she did not get much time to explore, she enjoyed what she saw.

Diaghileff arranged for Kschessinska to coach her in *Swan Lake*, although she did not dance this publicly yet. But he had plans for her. Alicia found her kind and helpful. 'I never had any trouble with the greats,' she says. 'Kschessinska had taken over from Pierina Legnani who created the role of Odette/Odile at the Marynsky in 1895. She had partnered Legat, who had also coached me, and Legat had danced in the first British production of *Swan Lake*. So I couldn't get closer to its origins.'

In 1927 Alicia came to London with the Ballet Russe in the hopes of repeating her success with *Le Chant du Rossignol*. This would be the first time London had seen the production.

Her costume had to be modified. What went in Paris did not go in London. 'I could not appear to be naked in London. The Lord Chamberlain would not have allowed it. So, Matisse had to dash off some chiffon pants and a tunic to go over the body tights to make me decent.'

This time the reviews were universally excellent.

'A miniature duet between Death (Mme Sokolova) and the Nightingale (Mlle Markova) was nothing short of marvellous.' – *Daily Mail*

'Alicia Markova is brilliant in the role of the Nightingale . . . she is able to overcome the innumerable technical difficulties without any apparent effort.' – Arnold Haskell, *Some Studies in Ballet*

Another success was Balanchine's *La Chatte* to music by the young French composer Henri Sauguet.

La Chatte is a fable about a young man who falls in love with a cat. He prays to Aphrodite to transform her into a woman. She does so, but when a mouse appears the woman abandons the man to chase it. She is changed back into a cat and her lover dies.

Its set was 'constructivist' and contained lots of celluloid, as did the costumes, and scaffolding structures. The poses were 'sculptural'. In Grigorieff's opinion it was the best work Balanchine had yet done.

Balanchine created the ballet for Lifar and Spessivtseva and they had premiered it in Monte Carlo on 30 April 1927. It proved a huge success, particularly for Lifar.

From Monte Carlo the company travelled to Marseilles and Barcelona, then Paris. Unfortunately, Spessivtseva injured a foot in Paris and was unable to dance. Grigorieff says Alicia still looked 'too much of a little girl' to dance her role then.

On Lifar's recommendation Spessivtseva's role was taken by Alice Nikitina, who had been a member of the company, joining the year before Alicia. She left, but was a close friend of Lord Rothermere's, who was sponsoring the Ballet Russe. Consequently she returned from time to time as a guest artist.

She was an extraordinary person who, in 1938, switched to singing and became a coloratura soprano. In 1949 she reverted to ballet and opened a school in Paris. In Grigorieff's words, she had an 'instantaneous success' with *La Chatte*.

During the autumn mid-European tour of Germany, Austria, Czechoslavakia, Hungary and Switzerland, Diaghileff gave *La Chatte* to Alicia. Grigorieff says she did 'extremely well'. Lifar was also pleased with her, as she was so light for him to lift.

Almost as soon as Alicia had joined the Ballet Russe she had appeared in the ballet sections of operas. She loves opera and always enjoyed this. In Monte Carlo, she had been in Massenet's *Thaïs* as a handmaiden. This was the historic, not to say notorious, production in which soprano Fanny Heldy appeared topless.

When this scene was about to occur, Grigorieff would beckon Alicia off stage from the wings, until Madame Heldy had replaced her garments. He considered her too young to see such things. The stage was covered in flowers for *Thaïs* and, after the curtain had come down, Alicia would gather them up and take them home to Eileen.

She also played an angel in *Faust* for which she received extra payment from the opera house as she had to fly on a Kirby wire. Dressed in a golden wig and white gown, Alicia, and a sister angel, were to lead Marguerite up to heaven, all on Kirby wires. 'I used to be paid danger money for flying. Sometimes I'd make as much from that as Diaghileff was paying me. It really is an art. People would say it was easier for me as I was light but that didn't make any difference. A man works with you to counterbalance you. He used to say to me, "Are you ready?", then off I'd go. The skill is in the knees, the *demi-plié.*'

Marguerite and her accompanying angels were supposed to rise slowly and gracefully until they disappeared from view. During rehearsals it was clear this was not going to happen; nothing would stop the wires from twisting and the trio with them. By the time they got to the flies the audience was looking at their backs.

This crisis was overcome by a cord, invisible to the audience, which was attached to the fingers of the two angels and became taut when they rose. Marguerite could balance against this as her feet left the ground and remain facing the audience.

The first opera in which Alicia had appeared, at the age of fifteen, had been Ravel's *L'Enfant et les Sortilèges.*

'I was always considered suitable for roles which required a fairy-tale illusion. In the first scene I had to enter from the fireplace as Smoke, wreathing and floating on *pointe*. In the second I was a squirrel. Even now, if I see a squirrel in the park I compare its movements to the impression I tried to make.'

Balanchine choreographed her and featured her unique speed and agility. He had noted when he had auditioned her in London how rapid and light her *chaînés* were and had specially choreographed a display of them in *Le Rossignol*. Many critics, particularly those in Berlin and Paris, had marvelled at them. Most dancers found it difficult to *chaîner* in a straight line but Alicia had performed a rapid sequence in a circle. Because of the arm movements Balanchine created to go with them, this gave the illusion that she was flying. He had utilized simliar rapid movements for Smoke.

Ravel conducted the performance himself and Alicia still remembers his slim and handsome figure as he came on stage during dress rehearsals.

Another opera in which she appeared, when she was about sixteen, was *Samson and Delilah*. 'This was Balanchine's version, and I wasn't allowed in the Bacchanale as I was too young. Grigorieff wouldn't permit it. But then someone was ill and they had to have a replacement. So I was put in the orgy scene.

'They knew I knew everything as I used to watch all the operas. So, without further warning I was told at lunchtime that I would be in the orgy that night. They taught me the steps and we were in flimsy scarves, not a lot of clothes, naturally.

'What they didn't tell me was about the collapse of the temple.

I was following everybody around and they told me to listen for Samson's shout. Well, he made the shout but they hadn't told me to get down-stage when he made it. The orgy people were all down by the footlights out of the range of what was about to come crashing down.

'I saw everyone rush downstage and I thought, Oh, I'd better go, but I was a little late. Suddenly everything crashed down and there was this awful dust everywhere and all those bricks. They were made of solid canvas and I got hit on the head.

'I wasn't told to dive on the floor and cover my head to avoid the dust and bricks. There I was, I couldn't breathe. Bits of wood were everywhere and these blessed bricks. When the curtain came down I was in a terrible mess and Grigorieff came rushing on and dragged me off.

'Another opera I was in was *Quo Vadis*, it's hardly ever given now. The singers used to love it because it had fabulous roles. In those days we used to keep the special effects a surprise until the night.

'Diaghileff had made me grow my hair so it was long. I was dragged on by this at the end of the act. I was a Christian about to be thrown to the lions.

'I was dragged to centre-stage and a bass was singing. He was a priest battling to save the Christians. I clung round his legs, it was a super mime but not a dance, those were the things you had to do then. I had make-up bruises all over me as if I had been ill treated.

'The priest was singing his last aria and then the Romans came. I had been told to look up at the priest as he was my saviour. Then the Romans would stab him. Inside his robe was a pouch of prop blood. Out this blood spurted, all over me. Surprise, surprise.

'But when the curtain came down, what a triumph! It had been so realistic.'

Later, during the 1929 Ballet Russe season, she was to dance in Janáček's *Judith*.

Because Monte Carlo is situated between La Scala and the Paris Opéra, many singers gave performances there *en route* from one big opera house to the other. Alicia was privileged to be on the same stage with many of the great singers of the day.

During the late 1920s Alicia went down with 'double pneumonia, pleurisy and congestion of both lungs'. It was serious and, once again, for a while her life was in the balance.

Although she had worked so prodigiously she was still delicate and the illness was too severe for her to be moved to the American Hospital, the nearest big hospital on the outskirts of Nice. The doctor had to tend her in the hotel, in the single room she and Eileen shared, a large, elegant room with marble floors, filled with antiques.

The doctor saved her life utilizing a practice that is now outlawed. She could not breathe owing to the congestion of her lungs. In order to relieve this he turned her on her tummy and heated several small glass jars by burning cotton wool in them. He then cut incisions in her back and applied the glasses to them. The suction removed the fluid from her lungs.

Clearly she could not dance until her strength came back. This placed Diaghileff in a difficult position as *Le Chant du Rossignol* was a favourite ballet of Princess Charlotte of Monaco and she had requested it as a command performance. She would not hear of a cancellation.

Alicia knew the younger princesses as they had come, with their nanny, to watch her as she had practised with Maestro Cecchetti during her first season.

No one could dance Alicia's part except the man who had taught her, Balanchine. Alicia had been described as 'delicate and winsome, a wisp of a thing'. Balanchine weighed in at least four stones heavier.

Bernard Taper writes in *Balanchine*: 'Clad in an improvised nightingale's costume, sewn together in haste backstage, he just barely managed to squeeze into the cage. Pressed against the bars, with his muscles rippling and bulging, he looked – one witness recalls – more like an ape in a cage than a nightingale, a white faced ape with a beak. Tchelitchev, who happened to be present, thought he looked like a stuffed rabbit.

'As soon as the maidens of the Emperor's court glimpsed this apparition, they began to titter. Grigorieff, the company's stage director and disciplinarian, was playing the dying Emperor. "Shut up, girls," he threatened under his breath . . . But then, opening his eyes, he caught sight of the caged Balanchine and choked with laughter himself . . . Diaghileff all the while was rolling about in his box with mirth at the sight.

'Had it been Paris rather than Monte Carlo Diaghileff would have cancelled the performance rather than substitute a man for Markova . . . The Princess, it is said, witnessed the whole per-formance gravely. Afterwards she is supposed to have remarked judiciously that Mr Balanchine was very good but she still pre-ferred the little Markova girl.'

While Alicia was recovering there was a knock on the door one afternoon and Eileen was staggered to see Mathilde Kschessinska standing there, the picture of elegance. She was always elegant, as befitted a *prima ballerina assoluta*, and wore an exquisite summer dress with pearls.

In her late fifties, Kschessinska was now a Grand Duchess. Standing behind her was an older man, her husband, the Grand Duke Andrei. Alicia liked the Grand Duke; he was always easy-going and spoke English beautifully.

Kschessinska was there because she had bumped into Diaghileff in Paris, where the company was fulfilling its obligations. He had told her that Alicia was ill.

She wanted to know if she could do anything to help. It was a charming gesture from a great ballerina to a promising dancer. 'That was how things happened in those days,' recalls Alicia. 'At every performance the senior dancer would always send flowers to the ballerina, and vice versa. The women would receive baskets of flowers often bigger than they were and the men would get a laurel wreath or wonderful fruit.'

The Grand Duke was carrying an enormous basket of flowers for Alicia that day.

No matter where they were, Diaghileff would not permit Alicia to have boyfriends. It was pointed out that, however personable her partners were, they were not to be thought of as objects of desire. They were dancing partners and that was all. She must not try to forge deeper links.

Nevertheless, she received a proposal when she was seventeen from a young musician, an assistant to Sir Thomas Beecham. It happened in Edinburgh during the provincial tour.

Sometimes Sir Thomas would conduct the orchestra as guest conductor. This was the case in Edinburgh, and he had brought his assistant with him.

Sir Thomas had returned home but his assistant had stayed on and invited Alicia and Eileen to dinner. 'Mother was with me when he proposed. He got on very well with her so I thought that was good, it might divert him from me. He'd watched me dance, I suppose, but I just wasn't interested. I think I laughed, I must have been awful.

'I knew Diaghileff had fabulous things in mind for me, and that he was training and educating me. I was always made to understand from Diaghileff not to look for love in any direction. Perhaps "respond to love" would be a better way of putting it, because I wasn't looking for it. I didn't want it. It was *The Red*

Shoes in reverse. I didn't want love, I didn't want it to interfere with what Diaghileff was giving me.

'I needed his support. Diaghileff was my only security. I'd always been moved around alone.

'Diaghileff never found out about the proposal and I never told him. I didn't want anything to interfere with his plans. People look at me now as though I had leprosy or something. They don't understand what life was like.'

Later, when away from Diaghileff, she claimed that as a young woman she did fall in love, quite easily and lightly, and she just as easily fell out. 'I suppose I did fall in love,' she says. 'But I can't remember now. It wasn't important.'

The company was obliged to be as economical as possible while on tour so, whereas Diaghileff and the principals travelled first class, the rest of the cast, among them Alicia and Eileen, travelled second, eight to a compartment. Which was pretty tight.

Once the train arrived at its destination, Diaghileff and his coterie would get taxis to their five-star hotel. The company had to fend for itself and people usually teamed up in groups.

Alicia and Eileen were taken under the wings of the Hoyer brothers, two Polish character dancers who were married to girls in the company. They often included Vera Savina in their group. 'The Anglo-Chankies' they were affectionately called.

The British-born Savina needed friends. She had been the first of Massine's three wives and had toured South America with him. They divorced in 1924 but both came back to Diaghileff. Unfortunately for Vera, Massine came back with a new love which made things awkward for her. Neither did she enjoy a similar relationship with Diaghileff to Alicia's. He never totally forgave her for taking Massine away in the first place.

Vera teamed up with Alicia and Eileen. She and Alicia often danced together as they were both small. 'She knew I admired her as a dancer,' says Alicia. 'She had the most fabulous jump which, at that time, wasn't common in a woman. Things were not always easy for Vera.'

As soon as the train stopped at the station the Hoyer boys would supervise the removal of the hand luggage. Alicia's hatbox was among this, still carrying their portable kitchen. The girls would be left to guard the bags, Alicia usually perched on top of the pile, while the boys went into town and sorted out digs.

At the digs immediate needs were unpacked. Then it was a short rest, if they were lucky, then off to the theatre.

Once they were in the theatre, Grigorieff always knew where to find Alicia. If she was not in her dressing room then she was in the canteen. 'All those opera houses had wonderful canteens for the orchestra, crew and artists. You can imagine what they were like in Germany, with all those sausages and wonderful potato salads. I could never put on weight so I would be there. If I wasn't on stage I'd sit there, it would be quiet during a performance. It suited me down to the ground.'

Once, during a tour of Budapest, Alicia had unwelcome visitors.

'We had just left Vienna which I had loved, a wonderful city with wonderful audiences, and I imagined that Budapest would be wonderful too. In my mind I could see the glamorous blue Danube.

'Then a terrible thing happened. We all had bed bugs and were covered in bites. Mother and I were in an old four-poster and I think our bugs came out of the wood. But there must have been a plague of them in the city because no one was exempt, not even Diaghileff in his luxury hotel. All the performers had blotches and we looked terrible and tried to cover them with make-up.

'I couldn't sleep at nights because of the thought of them but Mother told me, "You go to sleep and I'll stay awake." She rubbed the bed with a cake of soap then sat up all night with a magazine swatting the bugs when they appeared. I usually slept like a log so I was all right once I knew she was guarding me.'

In 1928 the company were in Britain again on a tour of several major cities which included Edinburgh and Manchester. Among the dancers were Leon Woizikovsky, Lifar, Doubrovska, Danilova, Balanchine, who was dancing as well as choreographing, Tchernicheva, and Alicia.

In a photograph of the company, taken in Edinburgh, they look a louche bunch. The ladies wear heels, furs and cloches and the men double-breasted suits and trilbies, similar to outfits sported by Al Capone. Alicia is the most demure and has leggings, buttoned to her feet, beneath her coat. She looks pretty. Their nationalities are indeterminate, a truly cosmopolitan bunch. 'I don't think Diaghileff ever looked upon me as English,' says Alicia.

Grigorieff tells us, 'During this season Diaghileff, who was always eager to promote young talent, first gave Alicia Markova the opportunity of distinguishing herself in two classical *pas de deux* – one in *Cimarosiana* and the other the famous *Blue Bird*.'

She danced her first *Blue Bird* in Manchester and Diaghileff had a new costume made for her. According to Dolin, this caused jealousy to flare. Most costumes were cleaned and shared, but

Alicia was so small this was not practical. She had more new costumes than anyone else.

Vera Savina was nearest to her size, and she danced *Blue Bird* too, but she was a different shape to Alicia.

Her costume, in any case, might have been deemed unlucky by some for, although it had been cleaned, there was a slight discoloration on it, invisible to the audience but visible to the wearer. This was blood.

It had happened when Vera had been dancing *Blue Bird* partnered by Massine, who did not normally dance it then. But someone had been indisposed and he had gone on. During the dance the gems on the sleeve of his costume caught Vera's arm an unlucky blow and sliced a vein. She bled profusely but managed to finish the dance before collapsing in the wings.

Alicia remembered her being brought home 'all bound up'. The company divided into factions; those who supported Vera blamed Massine.

On the morning of her first *Blue Bird* there was a dress rehearsal where Diaghileff exploded. Although Alicia had a new costume she still wore Savina's ostrich-feathered headdress. She looked like a child in her mother's clothes.

'Diaghileff was always making chewing movements with his mouth,' Alicia recalls. 'Someone said he was chewing the cud. He came on stage and said, "I don't like that headdress – out!" I, naturally, just stood and listened. "They are not for you," he said. "Ostrich feathers are vulgar." They weren't vulgar on Vera, they were right for her, she was blonde and curvaceous, but I was a different type. "Get bird of paradise feathers," he said. "Blue!"

'That was Diaghileff's genius, how to get the best from a person. Bird of paradise feathers were brilliant but not towering. Vera wore ostrich feathers and pearls and I wore blue bird of paradise feathers and diamonds.'

But first they had to be bought. 'Diaghileff said to my mother, "You go shopping." Everyone thought, Manchester on a Monday morning? Bird of paradise feathers? Blue? But that was Diaghileff. Mother said she was willing to go but what about the money? Bird of paradise feathers were about the most expensive thing you could buy, if you could find them.

'Diaghileff put his hand in his pocket, he was always putting his hand in his pocket for me, and took out several of the old five-pound notes. It was the same when I first got to Monte Carlo and was coughing. I had no money to buy the big bottles of cologne necessary and he paid for those for me.'

Eileen had to search long and hard to get the feathers but she succeeded. Alicia wore them that night. She received a warm reception and believed the feathers had brought her luck. She still has them. *Cimarosiana* had started life as a *divertissement* in Cimarosa's opera *Le Astuzie Femminili*, which Diaghileff had earlier presented at the Paris Opéra.

Dolin saw her dance this and commented: 'She was completely oblivious of any difficulty in the *pas de deux* . . . one of the most difficult of Massine's *pas de deux*. Alicia sailed through with effortless ease. I have seen many ballerinas who only just made the difficult unsupported two inside pirouettes . . . and I have seen others who failed. Alicia never missed them.'*

On 27 December 1928, when the company was at the Paris Opéra where Karsavina had returned as a guest to dance *Petrushka* with Serge Lifar (as the Blackamoor), Alicia glimpsed one of the most charismatic names in ballet – Nijinsky. He had created *Petrushka*, under Diaghileff's direction, in 1911, with Karsavina as his partner.

Nijinsky could no longer dance in public, he had long been far too ill for that, but he came to see the ballet at the invitation of Diaghileff.

Nijinsky was by now advanced in his insanity and had been institutionalized for years but was allowed out under supervision.

Diaghileff had occasionally made contact with him since their split, but had never forgiven him for his marriage.

Petrushka had been a favourite ballet of Nijinsky's and Karsavina was an old friend. They had both studied in St Petersburg and danced together at the Marynsky. Diaghileff hoped that by resuming contact with Karsavina and watching *Petrushka*, something might gel in Nijinsky's brain, some memory perhaps stir.

Nijinsky was taken to the Opéra before the performance and, Grigorieff recalls, '. . . very gently, as if he were some precious object that might easily be broken, he was escorted by Diaghileff across the stage to a box . . . Diaghileff told me afterwards that Nijinsky watched the performance with great attention, but made no sound and would not answer when spoken to, and that when the ballet was over he did not want to leave. During the interval Diaghileff led him on stage and, bringing him up to me, said, "Don't you remember, Vasya? This is Grigorieff." I put out my hand, which he took very slowly without saying anything, he just

* *Markova: Her Life and Art.*

smiled but quite vacantly . . . This, then, was our final farewell to Nijinsky.'

Alicia was standing on the stage while this was taking place. She was dancing *La Chatte* that season, and recalls Nijinsky's spectre-like appearance. 'He didn't know where he was. He had a nurse with him. He was a sick man, very sick indeed.'

There was no flicker of recognition when Nijinsky met Karsavina, either. She tried everything, but whatever she said he remained impassive. No memories came back.

Later Diaghileff took Lifar to meet Nijinsky. Whatever hurt Nijinsky had given Diaghileff, he had his revenge that day as his feeble ex-lover looked up at the new favourite. But Nijinsky was too ill to be a victim.*

Lifar wrote of the occasion in his autobiography *Ma Vie*: 'His [Nijinsky's] nervousness showed only by the movements of his hands. At one moment he would scratch them until they bled while at another moment he would make affected gestures with them.'

According to writer Peter Oswald, neither was Diaghileff well at that time. He had diabetes and refused to take the prescribed insulin. Alicia saw no sign of ill-health: 'He used to eat and drink like mad.'

Alicia was soon back in Monte Carlo to dance in a charity gala at the Hôtel de Paris, where she was partnered by Lifar in the *pas de deux* from *Cimarosiana*, which she had first danced earlier on the British tour.

They made a striking couple, he with his superb physique and she contrastingly delicate, in a costume designed by José Maria Sert. Diaghileff loved to see them together on stage. They were both his favourites in different ways.

After she had danced she changed into her street clothes and was about to go back to the hotel when Grigorieff knocked at the door. He told her that Diaghileff wanted to see her right away at his table in the ballroom. She protested that she was in her street clothes; she couldn't walk into the ballroom dressed like that, in Monte Carlo of all places. Grigorieff told her that was unimportant, she must come at once. She wondered what she had done wrong.

Diaghileff was sitting in state, surrounded by Tchernicheva, Danilova, Balanchine and Lifar. The men were in white ties and the women ballgowns. Alicia was distinctly out of place, as she knew she would be.

* Account taken from *Vaslav Nijinsky: A Leap into Madness* by Peter Oswald, Robson Books, 1920.

Diaghileff did not mind, and she had done nothing wrong. As she stood respectfully in front of him he asked her how old she was. She told him she was nearly eighteen and he told her that now she was almost of age she must have a glass of champagne. 'It was the first time I'd drunk champagne.' They all toasted her. For a 'sadistic genius' Diaghileff could be kind. 'To me,' adds Alicia pointedly.

Things continued to improve for Alicia. Now she was over eighteen, Diaghileff allowed her to go to some of the functions to which the company were invited. In order that she might do this is a manner befitting her station, Mrs Haskell bought her an evening dress and a pair of silver high-heeled shoes, her first pair of stilts.

High heels suit ballerinas. They were to become one of Alicia's trademarks; she adored them. Sometimes she did walk-throughs in them, to the consternation of impresarios who had never seen the like.

She presented a cool image, but this was as illusory as the bejewelled nightingale she portrayed. She was, after all, in the business of perpetrating illusions. Diaghileff still did not permit admirers and she was not allowed to accept gifts, not even chocolates.

Even chocolates from such a well-connected man as Lord Rothermere (who tried to meet her) were sent back by Diaghileff. The only exception he allowed was a box from the great bass Chaliapin.

Chaliapin was an old friend of Diaghileff's. He had brought him to Paris in 1907 when he had electrified audiences with a series of Russian concerts. The following year he had launched him at the Paris Opéra in *Boris Godunov*. Until 1909 opera had taken up most of Diaghileff's energy. Ballet had appeared for the most part within his operas.

Apart from a desire to protect Alicia from the seamy side of life to which, clearly, Diaghileff felt the acceptance of a box of chocolates might lead, he was adamant that the dignity of the company be upheld. A tradition Alicia was to adopt herself. Diaghileff ballets were synonymous with quality. He intended to keep things that way. Respectability was the keynote, or as much respectability as could be mustered when in control of a large company of volatile artists. Pavlova had run her company under much the same rules.

While appearing at La Scala, Alicia was able to hear the Lancashire soprano Eva Turner in *Turandot*. Her 'In Questa Reggia' sent shivers down Alicia's spine as the mighty silver voice filled the auditorium.

Not surprisingly, their paths regularly crossed during the years. Alicia was the first British artist in her field to win international acclaim and a similar claim could be made for Dame Eva, as she later became.

On Eva's ninetieth birthday a party was held for her at Covent Garden and her peers from the opera world were on stage to pay tribute. Alicia had also been invited, and had prepared a little speech.

Unfortunately, on the day, she was afflicted with laryngitis. Sir John Tooley, then manager of Covent Garden, had to make a speech apologizing for her absence. 'If anyone had told me I would come on to the Opera House stage and apologize to the audience for the absence of a prima ballerina because she's lost her voice, I would never had believed them,' he told Alicia afterwards. 'How Eva and I laughed about that,' she recalls. Even now, if she has a lot of public speaking to do, she will point at her feet and say, 'These have been trained, the voice hasn't.'

In 1929 the Ballet Russe was back at Covent Garden. The most exciting news was that Spessivtseva, as guest artist, was heading a cast that included – in addition to Alicia – Karsavina, Danilova, Sokolova, Lifar, Woizikovsky, and Dolin.

Alicia and Dolin were dancing the *Blue Bird*. It was the first time they had publicly danced together and the first time two British dancers had appeared together in major roles at Covent Garden.

Agnes de Mille was in the audience and noted in *Portrait Gallery*: 'She seemed like any string bean adolescent in a diamanté bandeau, like a little girl dressed up in her mother's party clothes. I think she must have weighed 60 lbs. She had all the voluptuousness of a grasshopper, but she hit the stage like a veteran, for all her youth she *was* a veteran.'

'We only gave the White Act of *Swan Lake*,' says Alicia. 'Diaghileff had got Spessivtseva. She was the top of the tree so the rest of us all had to slide down a grade. Danilova had been dancing *Swan Lake*, it was her ballet, but now she took a lesser part. Can you imagine how high our standards were?

'Spessivtseva was partnered by Lifar. Dolin was now part of the *pas de trois* with Danilova. Savina and I had been doing the *pas de trois* with Idzikowsky so we were now part of the four cygnets. We also danced the two swans with the *corps*. With Diaghileff everyone accepted the situation.'

She was already a ballerina in that she carried two ballets, *Le*

Rossignol and *La Chatte*. But while they were in London, Diaghileff told her he planned to raise her status next season to prima ballerina. Among her roles, in addition to the Balanchine ballets, would be *Swan Lake*, *The Firebird*, and *Les Biches*, and he wanted her to partner Lifar in a new ballet about which he was already in discussion with composer Paul Hindemith. She would also dance *Giselle*, alternating the role with Spessivtseva.

Diaghileff now insisted, for the first time, that Alicia must have a contract. 'You're going to work for yourself,' Alicia remembers him telling her. 'From fourteen to eighteen you worked for me. Not any longer, you must now work for yourself. You must have a contract.'

Giselle is among the most romantic of ballets. It was first performed in 1841 at the Paris Opéra with Carlotta Grisi in the title role. A year later she repeated her success with it in London. She, too, had been undecided as to whether to concentrate on singing or dancing for a career. Her success with *Giselle* decided the issue.

It is a role to which all classical ballerinas aspire and requires a great range in that Giselle is a peasant in the first act and, in the second, is transformed into a spectre. It ideally suited Spessivtseva's special qualities. Diaghileff had revived it for her. Now he wanted Alicia to dance the part. To be put on the same level as Spessivtseva was praise indeed.

Diaghileff told Alicia of his plans as they stood in the wings of Covent Garden. He had made no secret of them and had said as much to the press. In 1928 the *Manchester Guardian* stated '. . . he intends to make a ballerina of the English girl Alicia Markova.'

After the Covent Garden season the company moved to Vichy for further performances. Chaliapin was also there and he came to every performance, applauding wildly. Included among the repertoire were *Cimarosiana*, *Le Tricorne* and *La Boutique Fantasque*.

The curtain finally came down for Diaghileff's Ballet Russe in Vichy on 4 August 1929.

9

Without Diaghileff

Alicia took a holiday in Littlehampton after Vichy, where she stayed with the Crewleys. It was a long, hot summer and she relaxed.

On the late afternoon of 19 August 1929, a date she was never to forget, she walked to the end of the garden to collect the evening paper. The paper boy always left it there. Glancing at it, she was jerked out of her serenity by the shrieking headline, 'DIAGHILEFF DEAD'.

She collapsed on to a nearby garden seat. As she put it, the news 'struck me like a fierce blow'. Her stomach convulsed with the shock. Diaghileff was not just her inspiration, she was devoted to him, and she doubted her ability to cope without him. She was not sure she wanted to cope without him. It was a nightmare.

He, too, had gone on holiday, to Venice in the company of his handsome secretary, Boris Kochno, and Lifar. Within a couple of days he had run up a temperature and, after falling into a diabetic coma, had died. Just before his death he had visited Hindemith to discuss Alicia's new ballet with him. He was buried where he had died, in Venice.

In deep shock, Alicia packed her case and went home to her mother. It seemed the only thing to do. By now Eileen and her daughters were living in a two-room flat in St Quintin Avenue, just off Ladbroke Grove.

The flat would be cramped but Alicia had nowhere else to go.

She could not have afforded a place of her own even if she had wanted it.

The shock of Diaghileff's death was compounded on 14 September when she received a letter from Grigorieff laying the facts on the line. 'I must inform you that I have received a letter from the judicial administrator of Serge de Diaghileff's successors, in which he declares that Serge de Diaghileff's enterprise has come to an end and begs me to inform all the artistes of the company about it.'

That was that.

Pavlova contacted her. 'She sent a message', says Alicia, 'that there was a place for me in her company. She knew what Diaghileff's plans were for me.'

Alicia did not fancy being an anonymous company member once again. Diaghileff had built up her hopes and she was loath to relinquish them.

After so much had been promised, so much effort put in and so much achieved, she was now an out-of-work dancer.

Things did not get better as autumn grew chillier. Alicia fell into a depression that made her physically ill. She did nothing and had no energy. At eighteen she felt her life was over.

She was a stranger in England, just another country to which she had travelled to dance. 'My real country was with the Diaghileff company, wherever they were. But his death had over-ridden that and I could never go back there.'

Then an offer came from Grigorieff. He had secured a contract to provide ballets for the Monte Carlo opera, just as Diaghileff had done. He was enlisting a few of the old Ballet Russe dancers and wanted her. This was the tonic she needed and she pulled herself together.

But Monte Carlo was not the same without Diaghileff. Neither were the ballets inspiring. The only thing that interested her was a *pas de trois* from Petroff's *A Night in Venice* which she danced with Tchernicheva and Danilova.

It was good to see Danilova again and she, like Alicia, was only too painfully aware of the void in their world. At least they could commiserate together. At the end of their contract they parted dismally and Alicia came home as depressed as when she had left.

No further offers came from Monte Carlo. Grigorieff was not Diaghileff.

For a year, what British dancing there was took place without her. For want of something to do Alicia applied herself to a few domestic chores.

She had had quite a triumph baking a cake a few years previously. She had decided to make an elaborate cake for Eileen's birthday as a surprise treat. At that time the family had been living in a flat in Prince of Wales Drive, Battersea, borrowed from Madame Lilitchka, a friend of Astafieva's.

No one had taught Alicia how to bake so she had obtained a recipe book and set about it. It took several days of preparation and she had to hide the mixture in a hatbox on top of the wardrobe when Eileen was there. She concocted excuses for Bunny and Doris to take Eileen to Battersea Park, across the road, while she got on with the baking. In the end she produced a magnificent iced affair.

There had been one dramatic incident when a mouse ran across the floor during the making. Alicia, who is not overly bothered by insects, is terrified of mice and wanted to move. But a borrowed cat put the situation to rights.

She did not make cakes in St Quintin Avenue, Eileen's cake had been 'my first and last effort', but she did embroider. Arnold Haskell's grandmother had taught her and she made some guest towels which are still in use in Knightsbridge.

She also made a dress. Eileen had a sewing machine and she set about mastering that. This was prompted by Arnold Haskell who, at that time, worked for Heinemann, the publishers, and invited her to a garden party. She could not afford to buy a new dress so bought a pattern and some material and made her own and, according to accounts, looked fetching in it.

Haskell stayed in touch with the Marks sisters all his life. People thought that, at one time, he and Alicia might marry. She never thought this and says that he regarded her more in the manner of a sister. But, in later life, his second wife was Alicia's sister Vivienne. Many were surprised, including Doris, but it turned out to be a highly successful partnership. They were devoted to each other. 'I always looked upon you as the sister I never had,' he told Alicia. 'Now I can truthfully say you are my sister-in-law.' Alicia is aghast at the idea that people thought she and Haskell might marry. Their relationship was never of that order.

Meanwhile, things started happening in the ballet world. There was a feeling among British dancers that they had something to offer of their own. Why import foreigners to dance and invent dances? The British had the talent and it was time they asserted themselves. Nationalism was stirring.

As a result, the Camargo Society* was formed in 1930, largely due to the efforts of Philip Richardson, editor of the *Dancing Times*, and Arnold Haskell.

The purpose of the Camargo Society was to encourage British ballet. It did a fine job and many new works by British choreographers, performed by British dancers, took place under its banner.

One of the leading lights of the new movement was Frederick Ashton, then a twenty-six-year-old choreographer and dancer. He had seen Alicia with the Diaghileff Ballet Russe at the Prince's Theatre in *Le Rossignol*. He had been in the gods and had been astounded by her unique double turns in the air.

When Ashton learnt she was in London, and felt he had the right vehicle for her, he wrote, saying he was devising a ballet for the Lyric Theatre, Hammersmith. This was to be a sequence in a drama, Dryden's *Marriage à la Mode*, starring Angela Baddeley, Athene Seyler, Glen Byam Shaw, and Adele Dixon. The producer was Sir Nigel Playfair. Ashton would dance in this and wanted Alicia to be his partner. They would be backed by four *corps* dancers.

After the prestigious dances in which she had taken part for the Ballet Russe, Alicia might have thought Ashton's work small fry. But when you are doing absolutely nothing there is no such thing as small fry.

She arranged to meet him at Hammersmith tube station; he would then take her to Sir Nigel's office to discuss the details.

Ashton was already a force with whom to be reckoned. He had gone to Massine for training but Massine had been unable to accept him, as he was going away, and had passed him on to Marie Rambert.

He had just returned from a tour with the Ida Rubinstein Company. Miss Rubinstein was an exotic Russian dancer who had started with Diaghileff but now ran her own company. Fokine had choreographed *Salome* for her but she had danced it just once before it was banned on grounds of indecency. She could fill houses wherever she went.

She later achieved success with Bronislava Nijinska's *Bolero* at the Paris Opéra, performing on a table-top to Ravel's erotic music. The décor was by Benois.

---

* Marie Camargo had been a pioneer ballerina who among other things had introduced shorter ballet skirts to enable greater freedom of movement. Such was her fame that chefs vied with each other to name dishes after her, hence Bombe Camargo, Filet de Boeuf Camargo and Soufflé Camargo.

Ashton and Alicia did not have much space to work in at the Lyric, as actors were on stage at the same time, and they had to confine the action to a small area.

She was to be costumed in a wig and long dress, neither of which she, or Ashton, liked. 'It was a period Nell Gwyn red wig and Fred wanted me with my own black hair. "Do you think you can do it in the style?" he asked. We had all learnt to do things like that with Diaghileff so that was not difficult. I lost the wig. All the photographs of me were with my own hair.' She also raised the hem of the dress.

She and Ashton received a fee of £10 each a week, which she negotiated with Sir Nigel: 'I'd only just met Fred but soon learnt he could never negotiate for himself. He said, "Will you see about my money, too?" So I fixed it up.'

The production later transferred to the Royalty (the old Royalty in Soho, not the later theatre).

Ninette de Valois then invited her to premiere her ballet *Cephalus and Procris*, to music by André Grétry, for the Camargo Society on 25 January 1931, at the Apollo Theatre.

Choreography was now de Valois's passion and she had already had *Danse Sacrée et Danse Profane*, to Debussy's music, performed by the Camargo Society. She was to continue to work with the Society and went on to create *La Création du Monde*, music by Milhaud, and *Job*, music by Vaughan Williams.

Two days before the premiere, on 23 January, devastating news hit the ballet world. Pavlova had died while on tour in The Hague. She was not yet fifty. For many, Pavlova *was* ballet. Her death, coupled with Diaghileff's, shattered the foundations of Alicia's world.

She reflected on what might have happened had she accepted Pavlova's offer to join her company. 'I had thought at the time that maybe I had been wrong to turn down her offer, but I had already had ballets created for me and was not thinking in that direction. My decision had been right. Had I gone with her my life would have been in turmoil once again and delayed everything that was to happen to me in British ballet. I had been honoured by her offer but I had been right to turn it down.'

It was also right that the Camargo Society pay tribute to Pavlova.

On the opening night of *Cephalus and Procris*, before the performance started, the audience stood in tribute while a single light played on an empty stage. The orchestra then performed Saint-Saëns's 'The Swan', the meltingly beautiful music to which she had performed *The Dying Swan*. The very essence of classic dancing.

It was the end of an era.

Alicia now saw de Valois frequently. Seeing how hard-up Alicia was (she was not going to get rich with the Camargo Society), de Valois took her to the pictures once a week, followed by a meal in Soho. De Valois was not wealthy herself and most of the money she made was ploughed straight back into ballet.

Alicia was embarrassed as she could not reciprocate, but de Valois, with typical aplomb, dismissed this. Looking after Alicia was now a part of her life, she said.

At that time de Valois was courting her husband-to-be. She had been ill and fallen in love with her doctor. Alicia would accompany her and her doctor on some of their outings. They would go across to the pub for a sherry after rehearsals, then on to dinner.

The doctor and de Valois married in 1935. They lived in the country and de Valois would cook roast Sunday lunches which Alicia sometimes attended. It was a happy marriage and lasted until the doctor's death.

De Valois was still dancing herself at the time of her courtship. 'She was a very experienced and professional dancer,' says Alicia. 'She had brilliant footwork and that came out in her choreography . . . and administration – she got that from her father. He was in the army, it was a military family. He knew all about strategy and so did she. It rubbed off on me. I used to listen to her. She had to make ways to deal with things. It was a great help to me later, when I was dealing with companies.'

As Alicia could not afford a regular teacher she worked out at home, using the towel rack in the bathroom as a barre.

She was knitting Eileen a bed jacket for a Christmas present – she had knitted all her life; Guggy had taught her – when the idea came to her to knit a pair of tights. 'When I was with the Diaghileff company I noticed that the Russian dancers used to wear thick black woollen tights, to try to lose weight. Danilova always had them on.

'My problem was the reverse, I had legs like sticks, as some people used to unkindly say (but I learnt to live with that). I wanted to put on weight. I was meditating on this as I was knitting Mother's present. I was using those big wooden needles, they were called Bimbos, when I suddenly thought I could make some tights on these and put them on over my silk tights. That way they would keep me warm and my legs could breathe. I wouldn't perspire.

'So I went to the Scotch Wool shop next day and bought some

flesh-coloured wool. I've still got the last pair I was making somewhere half done.'

She turned up for rehearsals in them and started a mini-fashion. Nowadays knitted tights are regularly worn by dancers, but they were not before Alicia introduced them.

'Later both Harold Turner and Bobby Helpmann asked me to knit them some, but in bright blue.'

Occasionally she would go to The Pheasantry to see Astafieva and take a lesson from her. She wore her tights there.

As well as belonging to the Camargo Society, Ashton was also a member of the Ballet Club, which was affiliated to an organization founded by Arnold Haskell, Marie Rambert and her husband, Ashley Dukes, which eventually, and through various incarnations, became the Ballet Rambert. The Club gave Sunday-evening performances in a little church hall in Notting Hill Gate. It had sprung up largely thanks to Alicia's success at Hammersmith and with the Camargo Society.

Its stage measured just eighteen square feet, but this did not stop the equally diminutive, but intrepid, Madame Rambert from grandiloquently naming it the Mercury Theatre. She ran it with as much discipline as though it were the Royal Albert Hall.

Like the Camargo Society, the Ballet Club's aim was to promote British ballet. Madame Rambert ran a dancing school and this was used as a recruitment centre. By now a few of the younger dancers were confident enough to retain their English names.

Alicia's name was Russian and she was Russian-trained but she danced at the inaugural performance of the Ballet Club on 16 February 1931, partnering Ashton in his new ballet *La Péri* to music by Dukas. According to Agnes de Mille, Ashton was Alicia's 'artistic mentor and coach' by now.

London was undergoing a Persian phase at the time, inspired by an exhibition of Persian art at the Royal Academy. It was the biggest thing in London.

'That was why he did *La Peri*,' says Alicia. She, Ashton and Billy Chappell, a dancer who also designed, had gone to the exhibition to study the make-up, style and colours before starting work. Inspired by the paintings, Alicia painted her eyebrows straight across her forehead, with no curve, and her fingernails purple, something previously unseen.

Alicia's fee was 10s 6d. She had been offered 6s 6d but by the time she had paid for her shoes and other accessories, plus her taxi fare, she was four shillings out of pocket, so Madame Rambert made up the difference.

Not before she made it painfully clear to Alicia that this was coming from finite funds. She had needed considerable persuading to part with the extra four shillings. She did not approve of Alicia taking taxis and made it plain she expected her to travel by bus. But the No. 52, which stopped nearby, only ran until 11 p.m. Alicia could hardly be expected to tramp the length of Notting Hill Gate with her costume and make-up over her arm at past midnight. Madame Rambert was not fully convinced. Alicia was. 'There was no argument. I just said, "I need 10s 6d because 6s 6d goes on the shoes and it's four shillings for a cab home. I don't get a penny, I'm giving the performance for nothing."'

As with Hammersmith, Alicia did the deal and Ashton received the same as her. She was the bigger name but he was the choreographer. It worked out evenly.

Agnes de Mille believed that the four-shilling salary difference was important to Alicia as it made a division between her and the other dancers and endorsed her status. She and Ashton were the only company members to receive such a lofty salary.

She had never before danced on such a small stage. She was used to top theatres, including the Palladium, Coliseum, Covent Garden and Europe's top opera houses such as La Scala and the Paris Opéra. Although space had been restricted at the Lyric, the stage itself had been large. Now, however, she was consigned to an area that she described as 'like a postage stamp'. Consequently she had to scale down her performance. 'I've always been adaptable so I thought if this is it then I'll have to get on with it.'

'Those first Sunday nights at the Mercury were magical,' she says in *Markova Remembers*. There was a spirit of adventure in the air and she thrived on being part of an eager young group.

Her talent, honed by Diaghileff to fit into an international company, was now being used to promote a home industry. Things happened at the Ballet Club; it was both an artistic and a social arena.

It caught on with the public, or rather that artistic portion of it that thrives on exploring new frontiers. Some of the wealthier ladies would donate clothing which could be cut up and made into costumes. Even Madame Rambert supplied an evening dress which was used to make Ashton's costume for *La Péri*. She had been reluctant to part with this at first, as it was her only decent evening frock, but Ashton had set his heart on it. He more or less tore it from her back.

Many of the designs and costumes were created by Billy Chappell, a valuable member.

Among other dancers who later appeared at the Ballet Club was Agnes de Mille, niece of the film director Cecil B. de Mille. Miss de Mille became a life-long friend of Alicia's.

In 1990 Agnes de Mille wrote her book *Portrait Gallery* and described Alicia's appearance at the time she was performing with the Ballet Club:

'She had inordinately long arms and legs and a small head. Her body line, therefore, had the pure luxury of ease and melting continuity that made for delicious phrasing. Her arabesque was more fragile, aerial and brilliant than anyone else's. Possibly because of the almost double-jointedness of her hip and back. It invariably brought the shock of delight one inevitably experiences from the high E of a great coloratura . . . Her foot was long . . . but very slender, strongly arched and as delicate as a bird's claw. On the end of this delicate parenthesis she alighted and hung poised like the crescent moon, a stillness of the movement of time . . .

'Her technique was prodigious, her technique was bolts of light-ning and steel. However, it took a professional eye to recognize this, she seemed to laymen to float in a mist and they remained wonderstruck . . .

'Always about her there was an aroma of sadness. A hint of death in the moment of consummated effort. This was her Jewish heritage, as it was Anna Pavlova's who made her world-wide reputation with a dance of death, *The Dying Swan*.

'On reflection, I realize that Markova seemed, for all her delicate beauty, unphysical, even unsexed. Admittedly no great ballet dancer is physically sensual, preferably she is the instrument of sensuous release – but she, more than anyone else (with the possible exception of Margot Fonteyn), suggested romance while preserving always the chaste austerity of classical discipline. It could almost be said that the passion of her discipline, like all great restraints, was in itself a kind of sensuality.

'Although English . . . she was in face and body astonishingly like the Russian Pavlova – the same black and white beauty, the same serene brow, the dark burning eyes, the precise, patient mouth, the swan-like neck. Indeed, Markova was well aware of the likeness and was often accused of modelling her style closely on her great predecessor's. She did not have Pavlova's gift of hypnotising her audience but she did have the same ethereal quality to her dancing. For quite a period she even claimed that the spirit of the Russian inhabited her body . . .'

The last sentence was fantasy on Miss de Mille's part. When Alicia was questioned on this her head was shaking in denial even before the question was finished. 'We looked alike and we had certain things in common, but she had a different temperament. Anyone who had seen us both knew we were quite different people.'

Working at the Mercury provided a different satisfaction to that of performing with Diaghileff. The glamour with which the Ballet Russe had been suffused was replaced by earnestness. Her associates were not international names but young hopefuls. None of them had had her experience.

Working in such cramped conditions (she could have touched the audience), she presented her face as an implacable mask so that attention was focused on her movements. 'I'd been trained never to show any effort and that's where it stood me in good stead, and breath control was important.'

This grew into another facet of her legend. In later years, some performers and audience members were convinced that her dancing was without exertion, that she had come in from the street, donned her costume, and effortlessly performed, never having practised. Beryl Grey, who danced in performances with her many times, was struck by her composure. 'We would come off-stage after we had danced, hot, sweaty and breathless, and Alicia would be standing there waiting for her entrance, cool and serene. She would then go on, execute the most intricate steps and bring the house to its feet, and then make her exit as coolly as she had gone on, not a hair out of place. I don't know how she did it.'*

She was introduced to a variety of new works through Ashton, most of which he choreographed and co-danced with her.

Among these was Walton's *Façade*, premiered on 26 April 1931, by the Camargo Society, at the Cambridge Theatre.

Adapted from music written to provide settings to poems by Edith Sitwell, the original *Façade* had had a tempestuous history. Before Ashton developed it into a ballet it had had its first performance at the Aeolian Hall. The reception had been anything but adulatory. As Dame Edith puts it, 'Never, I should think, was a larger and more imposing shower of brickbats hurled at any new work . . . Indeed, the attitude of certain of the audience was so threatening that I was warned to stay on the platform, hidden by the curtain, until they got tired of waiting for me and went home.'†

---

* Interview with Dame Beryl Grey, 1994.
† *Edith Sitwell: A Biography* by Geoffrey Elborn, Sheldon Press, 1981.

The cause of the uproar was the originality of the piece. The backdrop depicted a head with a gaping mouth through which a megaphone protruded and through which poems were declaimed. These varied widely in pace and pitch, to the accompaniment of four instrumentalists.

The ballet, however, created no such unrest, although there was initial incredulity. Alicia danced the 'Polka'. It was her first comedy role and audiences were unprepared for this most controlled of dancers showing her knickers, which is what she did.

She was discovered on stage, gracefully standing on *pointe*. Once this had been registered, she whipped off her skirt, revealing showy knickers, and completed the dance in a boater.

At first there was a shocked gasp, for which she was 'prepared', then the audience erupted. 'People went into shock. They were expecting a very lovely delicate *pizzicato*. I was willing to dare anything if it was new and going forward. There was no prettiness about it, it was a send-up of music hall.

The piece was so successful she repeated it, and that became her practice whenever she danced it.

Façade became a regular item in the Ballet Club's repertoire and later Alicia also danced the 'Tarantella' and the 'Tango'. The Sunday Pictorial commented:

> 'The best of the post-Diaghileff ballets has much virtue in addition to the fact it is new fashioned . . . the lovely Markova is, again, the best of all. She is one of the absolute dancers.'*

'I enjoy comedy,' says Alicia. 'I can make an audience laugh as easily as I can make them cry. Ashton knew that but the "Polka" was a shock to the audience. It was the first ballet striptease.

'That opening night at the Cambridge when I walked out of my skirt the cast gasped, as well as the audience, because I hadn't done it at rehearsals. I wanted to keep it as a surprise. I wore a pair of knickers because we had no money for anything more elaborate.

'I put in all the things I'd learned from Nellie Wallace including her fall-over step, which all the comedians used. Fred and I adored

---

* It is not always possible to date the reviews. Archives of defunct newspapers no longer exist. I have verified and traced what I can and articles that cannot be specifically dated are left undated. In the American section there are various out of print publications that I cannot trace. ML

music hall and jazz and those sort of things, so it was a little joke that we had. I was a classical dancer and people were expecting a beautiful ballet from Ashton – on *pointe* – they were shocked.'

She and Ashton enjoyed their jokes together until a rift separated them. It was not until they were middle-aged that they resumed their friendship. He would then complain to her that he looked ancient whereas she stayed young. She would recommend potions. 'I've bought you some cream from Harvey Nichols,' she would say, giving him a little present.

After two performances with the Camargo Society, *Façade* went into the Ballet Club's repertoire.

'There I took on the "Tango" as well – Lopokova had danced that previously – that happened when Fred came over and asked me, "What about the Tango?" I said, "Yes and no." "That's a funny answer," he said. "What's 'yes and no'?" "Yes," I said. "If I can do it my way but I couldn't copy Lopokova. I couldn't do what she did, she was wonderful, but entirely different to me. It's up to you," I said. "If you let me do it my way then I'll do it." Well, he let me.

'I wore a deliberately silly costume with a mangy bit of marabou and high heels, and all the wrong colours. She had everything wrong, the jacket was ill fitting and made from cheap material. It was designed like that – but that wasn't my invention. Lopokova had worn that, too – she was a deb but she was a country bumpkin. Every step she took was new to her. He threw me up in the air and I landed all over the place, it was hilarious. I learnt a lot of what I did from Nellie Wallace.

'We had a very funny time and the audience learned to think of me as something more than a classical dancer.'

Alicia and Nellie Wallace remained friends until Miss Wallace's death. Alicia never forgot the debt she owed her, and her kindness to her when they had appeared at the Palladium together and Miss Wallace had smuggled her to the stage under her shawl for Alicia to dance her dragonfly variation. Alicia loved Miss Wallace's act and for 'Tango' wore her bit of marabou as a tribute to her dead friend.

Within a short time she appeared in two more of Ashton's new works.

Rio Grande is a one-acter in which she played a Creole prostitute, 'very daring in those days. Mother never knew what I was coming home as next.' This had music by Constant Lambert, who had assisted Walton in the composition of *Façade*, but whose activities as a composer were eclipsed by his wider interests in conducting and performing. He had declaimed some of the poems in *Façade*'s pre-balletic existence with stunning dexterity.

The jazz-influenced *Rio Grande* is scored for chorus, piano and orchestra. The large cast makes it expensive to mount, one reason why it is rarely done now. The music does sometimes pop up in concerts and Alicia once introduced it, years later, at the Festival Hall. She did a whole series of introductions to orchestral works with which she had been associated.

Dolin saw her in *Rio Grande*. He was impressed by the extension of her range but did not care for the ballet. 'It did not call for ballet dancing,' he wrote in *Markova: Her Life and Art*. 'Pat always preferred me in classics,' says Alicia. 'In this I had fuzzy black hair, high-heeled silver shoes and black fishnet stockings and I did a tap dance. Of course he didn't like it.'

Less than three weeks later, on 15 December 1931, at the Carlton Theatre, Haymarket, she premiered *The Lord of Burleigh*, another one-acter, to music by Mendelssohn.

These ventures kept her in front of the public, but it was an élite public, and there was no money in such activities. Often she did not even cover her expenses, although she was by now getting two guineas a performance from the Camargo Society. 'It was better than 10s 6d. I kept trying to push it up.' Apart from being broke herself she could see how hard pressed Eileen and the girls were. She was twenty-one and her sisters were all teenagers, just the age when they wanted money to spend.

Doris was still bitten by the show-business bug and keen to go on the stage as a revue artist, and the youngest, Bunny, was already set to become a ballet dancer. She took lessons and almost worshipped Alicia. Vivienne was the only sister not interested in show business. She fancied working in an office.

Ashton knew how hard-up Alicia was. He was just as pressed himself with a mother and sister to take care of, but came to her rescue again.

In those days West End cinemas had a stage show between films; the programme consisted of a feature, a B film and a show. Ashton had a contract with the Regal Cinema, Marble Arch, to stage its shows. He recommended Alicia to the management and she was offered a fee of £20 a week to dance between the movies three times a day. It was more than she had ever earned in her life and she grabbed it.

Her engagement started during the run of *Outward Bound*, a successful Warner Brothers film starring Leslie Howard and Douglas Fairbanks Junior as ghosts on a ship bound for Purgatory.

Ashton had her fronting a group of thirty-two dancers, and she made her entrance descending from the flies in a crescent moon, after which she performed the 'Dance of the Hours' to Ponchielli's music, played by full orchestra. 'The producer was American and he'd worked at the Roxy in New York and they had done things that way over there. That was the way he wanted it and I was prepared to listen.'

To the audience she was something from fairyland. There was invariably an 'aaah' of admiration when she appeared. She danced a classical *pas de deux*, in which she was partnered by Billy Chappell, and this was followed by a variation coda.

She was so successful that her contract was extended for a new show, again choreographed by Ashton. This time she appeared as a fox in a hunting scene. In furry ears, bushy tail and paws, she was pursued by the other dancers who were dressed as hounds. She fled the pack by spinning like a top across the stage.

Doris, who was helping her backstage, was standing by with the sticking plaster and witch-hazel.

'I remember she had to be padded under her tights to protect her from getting hurt in the "kill",' Doris says. 'I can see her now dashing into her dressing room after the show, stripping off her all-over tights, tail and ears, then grabbing her tutu and rushing away to a theatre to serenely dance a ballet.

'Next day she'd be back at the cinema again. It was the only way she could afford to keep dancing in ballet. But it was by dancing in the cinema that Alicia became loved by the man in the street. She built up a public and it came to see her when she joined Sadler's Wells. She sowed the seeds of appreciation among ordinary people.'

'Yes,' says Alicia. 'They weren't afraid to come. They didn't feel it was above them. All my life I've tried to appeal to ordinary people. I've never brought my art down. I've always taken them up.'

Engagement after engagement followed at the Regal. Alicia was able to repay Ashton the debt she owed him by insisting, as each show changed, that he be re-engaged as choreographer. By this time Alicia was, in addition to her other engagements, dancing for Sadler's Wells as a guest artist. By now, she was dancing a great deal.

'I would do my first two shows at the Regal, then I'd go to the Wells and open the programme with the White Act from *Swan Lake*. I'd come back to the Regal to do my 9 p.m. show then I would go to the Mercury Theatre and do their last item on the programme, perhaps *Façade*. It all had to be done.'

She travelled across London by taxi; in those days traffic was easily negotiable. She had to pay the fares herself, of course, but by now her financial hardship was lessened by the Regal. In addition she received £5 a performance from Sadler's Wells and 10s 6d from Marie Rambert for the Mercury Theatre performance.

Another of Ashton's extravaganzas at the Regal was built around the Faust legend. It started with the dancers slowly rising from below floor level, then Alicia herself arose, a sea of white froth. 'It was all white, the girls were in long white dresses and I was in a classic short tutu. There were white gauzes everywhere. With the *Faust* music, it was beautiful.'

The audiences loved it, and this was a big, packed-out West End cinema, not a tiny specialist theatre. As the Regal management quickly realized, she was a great draw.

Ninette de Valois realized it too.

10

Queen of Sadler's Wells

Alicia's big breakthrough in British ballet came on 30 January 1932, when Ninette de Valois invited her to dance in two of her own ballets, *Cephalus and Procris*, which Alicia had already premiered, and *Narcissus and Echo*. Both were in the same programme which she danced at both Sadler's Wells and the Old Vic. The theatres were owned by Lilian Baylis who wanted to see how Alicia would go down with her audiences. The ballets displayed Alicia's range.

Cephalus and Procris was classical in style and danced on *pointe*, the type of thing people expected from Alicia.

In contrast, *Narcissus and Echo*, in which she was partnered by Stanley Judson, was modern. The music, which had a vocal arrangement, was by Bliss who, whenever he met Alicia later in life, always remembered her performance. 'There were only four of us on stage,' says Alicia. 'Narcissus and Echo and two nymphs. Narcissus was in a white tunic and sandals and Echo was bare foot in a chiffon shift, very plain and very modern. There was no décor, no one had a cent, and it was done against a black background. Ninette knew I was capable of it. Like most choreographers, she'd throw everything at me.'

According to Dolin the ballets were neither here nor there as far as the audience was concerned. It was Markova they loved. As he put it, 'She was so frail, so different and danced so delightfully . . .' Later, in 1953, he noted, 'No one can ever estimate how much the company [Sadler's Wells] owes to Markova. Had it not been for her, I doubt whether the Sadler's Wells Ballet would exist today.

She, and she alone, put that company firmly on its feet.' Sadler's Wells became the Royal Ballet.

Sadler's Wells was the result of an amalgamation between Ninette de Valois and Lilian Baylis. Baylis was running two London theatres: the Old Vic in Waterloo and Sadler's Wells in Islington. The Old Vic specialized in Shakespeare, and Sadler's Wells, a new theatre built in 1931, in opera. Both theatres were run erratically, but successfully, by Miss Baylis, who was a tough champion of the arts. It was only a matter of time before osmosis brought Baylis and de Valois together.

De Valois had founded the Academy of Choreographic Art and, in 1928, Baylis commissioned her to choreograph and cast a ballet for an Old Vic production of *Hansel and Gretel*. She then invited her to house her school at Sadler's Wells.

In 1931, de Valois went to see Baylis with a specific project in mind. 'I asked to see her because I couldn't see any other way of starting a company,' Dame Ninette remembers. 'No one was very interested in putting ballets on and the West End was too expensive to rent a theatre.

'Lilian Baylis was a wonderful lady and the Royal Ballet wouldn't be here today but for her. She was determined we should have a state ballet company and theatre, so she went to the other side of the river, very unfashionable then, took over the Old Vic and Sadler's Wells and built up everything we know as state theatre today. We owe everything to Lilian Baylis, she had tremendous foresight. I certainly owe everything to her. She actually sat and listened to me, which no one else would do. And she was very practical.

'I remember she had a lot of letters piled at the side of her desk and at the end of our conversation she pushed these to one side, I can still see her doing it, and she said, "I think you know more than any of these and have had more experience and I like your face." She was a great character. I don't think much would have happened if she hadn't liked my face, but still, she did.'*

In order to gauge public interest in ballet, de Valois had presented an evening of her own works at the Old Vic on 5 May 1931. These included *Les Petits Riens, Danse Sacrée et Danse Profane, Hommage aux Belles Viennoises, The Jackdaw and the Pigeons,* and *The Faun.* She danced in some of these herself.

The theatre sold out. She gave more evenings, sometimes at

* Interview with Ninette de Valois, 1994.

With her mother, Eileen, aged 2.

BELOW LEFT. Alicia and Doris with Guggy.

BELOW. Already on pointe. Guggy made her wear the bow in her hair. She detested it: "When I started panto, I was able to get rid of it. Thank God".

"Giselle" with Markova-
Dolin Company, 1935.

"Waterlily", 1935.
Choreographed by Dolin
to Lizst's Third
Consolation, Markova-
Dolin Ballet. (© Theatre
Museum, V&A)

"The Blue Bird" wearing the Bird of Paradise feathers Eileen bought in Manchester. "Ballet Russe de Monte Carlo", 1938. (© Maurice Seymour)

"Les Masques" 1933. Choreographed by Ashton to Poulenc's music. Premiered "The Ballet Club" 5 March 1933. Alicia is making the most of the tiny stage.

"The Polka" from "Facade". Choreographed by Ashton to Walton's music. There was a gasp, people expected her to be wearing a tutu. Premiered 26th April, 1931 at Cambridge Theatre, for "Camargo Society".

Alicia and Dolin
warming up,
Markova-Dolin
Company, 1935.
(© The Yorkshire
Post)

Members of the
"Ballet Russe de
Monte Carlo",
1938. Bottom
upwards:
Tarakanova,
Krassovska,
Alicia, Freddie
Franklin (with
hand on
shoulder),
Delarova
(Massine's second
wife), Jeanette
Lauret (sitting on
pillar), Roland
Guerard (blonde)
and Mischa
Panieff (dark).

"The Sky" from "Seventh Symphony", 1938. Choreographed by Massine to
Beethoven. Costume by Christian Berard. The original head-dress was mysteriously
missing for the Monte Carlo premiere. Alicia's head-dress (here) was cut out of
paper by Berard immediately before the performance.

the Old Vic and sometimes at Sadler's Wells. Dolin danced one evening, which Alicia attended, to show his support.

While de Valois was attempting to build a national ballet company, pioneering was also taking place in other directions, namely television. Television was unknown to most of the British public in 1932, and the idea that every house might one day possess a set existed only in the minds of science-fiction writers.

But John Logie Baird was making his first test transmissions and a few of the privileged had rudimentary sets, although the receiving area was limited.

Realizing the interest television would create, Selfridges in Oxford Street placed a set prominently in their store and advertised that performances would be transmitted at 4 p.m. so that the public could view them. Such was the excitement whipped up by this new science that advertisements were taken along the sides of buses stating when programmes could be seen.

Baird invited Alicia to take part in a transmission and she reported to his studio in Portland Place. This was a tiny room, twelve feet square, even smaller than the stage of the Mercury Theatre, and it had a floor of black and white squares and a single camera which emitted stroboscopic lighting – very eerie, like something from *Metropolis*.

Baird explained that, in order to get a sharp picture, her costume would have to be edged with black tape. Her make-up was terrifying; she was used to the fantastic make-up sported by some of the ballet characters but this outdid even them. Her face was painted an unrelieved white and her lips black. Her eyebrows had to be purple. She looked like a 1990s punk.

She had to choose a repertoire that did not require moving about, as the camera could not follow her. So she danced 'Moods', a piece Balanchine had devised for her to perform in music hall, and the Polka from *Façade*.

She danced to piano accompaniment and, after the performance, had to exit, out of vision, by crawling under the piano as it could not move.

She enjoyed the experience and, later, did another transmission. Few were aware of the full potential of television then. It was a novelty.

Ninette de Valois did not respond to the novelty but she did see Alicia at the Ballet Club and noted the excitement her appearance caused. Afterwards she told Alicia it was 'about time' she performed with the Sadler's Wells company she had now founded.

'She came into the Sadler's Wells Ballet and became a great name with us, and we helped her to achieve that, but she would have been a star wherever she appeared. She had a natural facility, an easy, flowing technique.'*

In March 1932, at de Valois's request, Alicia staged, and danced, *Les Sylphides* at Sadler's Wells.

That same year de Valois was engaged upon an even more adventurous undertaking. In co-operation with Dame Adeline Genée she was assembling a group of dancers to appear at the Royal Theatre, Copenhagen, in the presence of members of the Danish Royal Family and the Prince of Wales, later Edward VIII, who was in Denmark to promote British interests. It was the first group of solely British dancers to appear abroad. Alicia was to be the featured ballerina.

Genée was Danish by birth and had made her debut in 1888 in Oslo at ten years old. From then on it had been straight to the top, her most famous role being Swanhilda in *Coppélia*. At the turn of the century she had been resident dancer at London's Empire Theatre, after which she embarked on the first of her many world tours.

She gave her official farewell performance in 1917 after which she regularly danced for charity. She was President of the London Association of Operatic Dancing, a founder member of the Camargo Society and, in 1931, had inaugurated the Adeline Genée Gold Medal, the highest award given to a dancer by the Royal Academy of Dancing.

The repertoire for Copenhagen included *La Création du Monde*, *Chopin Ballade* and *Job*. Alicia was to dance a purely classical repertoire including the variation from the last act of *Swan Lake*, *Les Sylphides* and *The Lord of Burleigh*. Although the latter was a modern work it was 'classical' in style.

Wendy Toye, later famed as a director and choreographer, was a junior member of the company, and she recalls: 'After *La Création du Monde* there was a terrible silence in the house. It was very *avant-garde* and we all thought the audience had hated it. But then the Danish Ballet came crashing through and said how wonderful it was. They told us that no one applauded at the end of a performance when the Danish Royal Family was present. No one had bothered to tell us.

'Alicia used to invite me to breakfast in the hotel with her. I was absolutely in awe and always have been. To me she was on a pedestal, the successor to Pavlova. She was very quiet, but I think

* Interview with Ninette de Valois, 1994.

she enjoyed my company. I suppose she wouldn't have invited me otherwise.'*

Alicia had first met Wendy when she (Wendy) had been about eleven. It was after Diaghileff's death and Wendy's teacher had invited Alicia to give some lessons. The venue had been a large room above a pub opposite Holloway Prison.

Back in London, in June 1932, the Vic-Wells and Ballet Club united to offer a season at the Savoy Theatre under the auspices of the Camargo Society. The pivot of this was the return to London of Spessivtseva who, as guest artist, was to dance the White Act of *Swan Lake* and her *pièce de résistance*, *Giselle*. Dolin was to be her partner.

Alicia was engaged for several items, including de Valois's *Origin of Design*, *The Lord of Burleigh*, and the jazz ballet *High Yellow*, in which she danced a black girl, there being no black ballerinas then. For this she received coaching in jazz dancing by Ashton's American collaborator, Buddy Bradley, a number-one dance director who had been brought over to mount the celebrated C. B. Cochran's revues. By the time he'd finished with her she was an expert on 'The Snake Hips'. '. . . and not just "The Snake Hips". He taught me jazz dance.'

Alicia never missed a move of all Spessivtseva's performances and, at Spessivtseva's suggestion, sat in the wings through-out *Giselle* – watching and learning. She barely breathed while Spessivtseva gave her performance. Posterity acknowledges her excellence and she has gone down in history as one of *Giselle*'s outstanding interpreters.

As soon as Spessivtseva started to rehearse *Giselle* she gave up *Swan Lake*. She would only work on one ballet at a time. 'She thought the difference in styles conflicted,' recalls Alicia. 'So I took over *Swan Lake* with Dolin. It was a bit complicated in that I was still in *High Yellow* so I had to get completely blacked up after *Swan Lake*.'

The production was not lavish. The Camargo Society was short of money and the scenery and most of the costumes for the *corps de ballet* were borrowed from the last production of *Giselle* which had been danced by Pavlova. Victor D'André had kindly lent them. As Alicia says, 'It was Spessivtseva herself who spread a magic over the whole.'

The magic had caught Alicia unawares. She had intended to watch Spessivtseva's performance from an analytical angle. 'But

* Interview with Wendy Toye, 1994.

a strange thing happened,' she writes in *Giselle and I*.* 'Before I had got far with my analysis, there would be a lapse, a suspension of time for me; the curtain would come down to frantic applause upon the death scene at the end of Act One, and I would be sitting in the wings with a lump in my throat and tears streaming down my face. Here was a "fourth dimension" in the world of ballet. I had not been schooled in this.'

Until that time she had believed that 'technique must dominate emotions'. She now had to rethink that. Spessivtseva had 'so thrilled and moved me, revealing wonders of which I had never dreamed,' she continues.

Up to that time several had noted, Dolin and de Mille among them, that her work was cold. This could be an advantage when executing ice-brittle choreography such as required by *Le Rossignol* or *La Chatte*, but not when applied to a romantic ballet.

Spessivtseva had not done well in *La Chatte*. Her art had taken her past a display of technical brilliance. Alicia, as a child, had succeeded. It was all she had to offer.

But now, as an adult, after seeing Spessivtseva's *Giselle*, she realized that more was needed. Spessivtseva had brought her to a turning point. From then on technique was not enough. It was a foundation upon which to build.

She was also in love with *Giselle*. They were linked for her entire life. She sacrificed health, money and livelihood for her. To know *Giselle* became a quest.

Each evening, as soon as Spessivtseva came off stage, Alicia would wait in the wings then wrap her in a shawl and take her to her dressing room. They did not speak; Spessivtseva was still absorbed in her part.

On Spessivtseva's last night, however, Alicia clearly remembers her saying to her: 'I hope that you have watched closely. This is a ballet that will be good for you.' Diaghileff had said the same thing. Alicia now wanted to dance it more than anything in the world.

She wrote in *Markova Remembers* of the Spessivtseva performances: 'I knew that I was seeing "the dance", pure and illuminated by the most ardent feeling. When we worked in company class with the Diaghileff Ballet, we learnt that there existed certain absolute standards which we must strive to achieve if we possibly could. These were what Spessivtseva showed, never merely academically correct, but touched with soul and poetry.'

She was able to do some practical work on the part. She had made

* Barrie and Rockliff, 1960.

a friend of Cyril Beaumont, ballet historian, critic and owner of the ballet bookshop in Charing Cross Road, which he ran for fifty-five years until his retirement in 1965.

He had a marvellous ballet library consisting of hundreds of books and prints. Most of these lay behind a closed door, away from the main area. That door led to a magic grotto over which Mr Beaumont presided.

There, in a little office, warmed in the cold weather by a spluttering gas fire, he wrote at a small desk. Manuscripts and lithographs were everywhere, chronicling the history of ballet from its origins to the current time. Privileged people, such as Alicia, were admitted to this sanctum and could browse at length. She pored over hand-coloured lithographs which, now, would be worth a fortune but were then considered curiosities.

Author Geoffrey Handley-Taylor knew Beaumont. 'The last time I saw him,' he relates, 'he was looking at me from the back of his shop. He'd a curious sort of bristling fringe of hair at the front of his head, rather like it was part of a busy yard-brush and just as sturdy. If his head had been on top of a pole that fringe would have swept the toughest ceiling of cobwebs. What a formidable critic he was, and his store of ballet history seemed to be without compare.'

Alicia spent hours with Mr Beaumont and his tomes, researching *Giselle* and studying prints of Carlotta Grisi who had created the role.

In addition to the times when he conducted the orchestra for the Ballet Russe, Alicia worked with Sir Thomas Beecham on several occasions, and each time it was uncomfortably memorable.

The first was in 1932 when the Camargo Society mounted Ninette de Valois's *Origin of Design*. The ballet was set to Handel's music which Beecham had arranged and conducted. In a tableau scene Alicia was lifted by two male dancers, and held in attitude for a few seconds while the music was suspended. As it started again she was lowered to the ground.

On one evening when she was lifted the music did not start again. As she was held by the men she noticed, in alarm, that their arms began shaking with the strain. If the music did not recommence soon she would surely be dropped. She whispered to them to lower her. It was not until she was safely on the ground that the music started again.

Afterwards Beecham casually commented to Alicia and de Valois that he had been so taken by the pose that he thought the audience might enjoy it for a little longer than usual. He had deliberately withheld the music. He trusted that had caused no inconvenience?

She also worked with him on the last night of the Camargo Society's last season when she danced the Polka from *Façade*. He had not studied the score in detail but had seen Alicia in the Polka and, doubtless, made notes. He had also been briefed by the resident conductor, Constant Lambert.

As Alicia came to the Savoy for the performance, Lambert told her that Sir Thomas had asked to conduct the item. There had been no rehearsal. 'I wish you luck,' Lambert said to Alicia.

She needed it. During the reprise Beecham went faster and faster. The piece drew to its conclusion with a circle of intricate double pirouettes on *pointe* and ended on a double *tour en l'air*. Owing to the relentless tempo she was hard pressed to keep up. She is not the panicky sort, but had she been she might well have had an attack then.

There was gratifyingly thrilled applause afterwards, although she had not intended to be quite that breathtaking, and she saw Beecham grinning up at her from the pit.

After the dancers took their applause, Sir Thomas came on stage himself for his bow and the curtain came down. Ashton and de Valois instantly appeared on stage too. What had happened?

'I wanted to know how fast you could go,' he told Alicia. 'So I went for it and, good girl, you kept up with me. Oh, that was exciting.'

'He enjoyed himself,' said Alicia. 'He never worried about me, he knew I'd follow whatever tempo he set. I would go along with him. It was like working with Stravinsky on *Le Rossignol*. I was just told to feel the music.

'Later, in New York, when I danced [Antony] Tudor's Juliet to Delius's music, it was the reverse situation. Those *legatos*, he went slower and slower. The management used to go mad because they would be into overtime, but I used to love it. I'd be in heaven.'

De Valois and Baylis realized that Alicia was bringing in hundreds of patrons to Sadler's Wells each time she appeared there. Up to 2,000 people turned up for a Markova evening. She took up to fifteen curtain calls a night and left the stage surrounded by flowers to repeated calls of 'Markova! Markova!' Sometimes her curtain calls would last over fifteen minutes. It was not just the fans who roared but the critics as well; they could not praise her highly enough. She put Sadler's Wells on the map and made herself a star at the same time.

Her fees did not rise accordingly. Baylis wrote offering engagements for the new season and ended her letter: 'We would offer you £5 a performance as before. I want you to do lots of well-paid work but hope you'll manage to come to us in between the good engagements.'

She accepted and her name was splattered all over the Sadler's Wells publicity, ensuring full houses. It was not just a question of ballet becoming popular. Dolin himself acknowledged that on evenings when Alicia was not dancing the company played to half-empty houses.

While Alicia was wooing them at Sadler's Wells, she gained a rich admirer. This was Reginald Wright, a married businessman. Dolin states that the admiration was platonic. Alicia says: 'When he was younger he had seen Pavlova and adored her. He was a true balletomane and he and his wife came to the ballet every evening I was on. If his wife was ill, and she suffered from delicate health, then he came alone. He did send me baskets of fabulous flowers.

'He had a house in Biarritz, as well as a place in England, and, when Pat and I were doing a concert at the Casino there, we stayed with them. It was a beautiful house. He had it built specially near the lake. He loved dancers.'

According to Dolin, when Wright was in London he would sweep Alicia off after a performance in his Rolls to a dinner that was even more costly than his flowers.

Sometimes he got a kiss on the cheek for his attentions, but that was all, and she never invited him in for a nightcap when he dropped her at home. Dolin says this was not so much a desire to keep him at arm's length as self-consciousness about the drabness of the flat. It was not the sort of place where people expected the star of the Wells to live.

'I was conscious that I'd been with Diaghileff and all the great people in Monte Carlo. Suddenly it was the other side of the coin. I had been out of work a lot and we were living in tiny furnished rooms. I felt, and maybe it was a little bit to do with what I was trying to create, that I didn't want to disillusion people. In the theatre I had to foster illusion, that was what Diaghileff had trained me to do. Pat understood me and, may I say, it was exactly the same with him.'

Dolin sometimes took her out for a meal, when she drank only milk with her food. She enjoyed the occasional glass of wine, champagne even, when it was available, but with Dolin she plumped for milk. Like her, he was one of the world's workers, and she did not want to bankrupt him. They never went to cheap places. Dolin liked to be seen at the best restaurants.

'It was always the Savoy Grill,' says Alicia. 'That was because of our association with Diaghileff. He always stayed at the Savoy.

Much later Sol Hurok stayed there, and he represented me for years in America.'

On 9 October 1932 Alicia played the Ballerina in Ashton's *Foyer de Danse*, music by Lord Berners, at the Mercury Theatre. Ashton had been inspired to do this ballet by the paintings of Degas. She played comedy again, an over-the-top dancer consumed by vanity.

The set took up the entire stage. Behind this was the staircase that led up to the single dressing room shared by all the girls. It was a corridor in which they sat side by side. Alicia often sat next to Diana Gould who was a prominent soloist and had created roles in Ashton's *Leda and the Swan* and *Capriol Suite*. She later married Yehudi Menuhin.

The staircase formed part of the set, and once a dancer was in the dressing room she was marooned there until her stage entrance. If she was not in that particular ballet she was isolated until it was finished. If there were special stage lighting effects then no electric lighting was allowed in the dressing room, so the girls had to sit by the light of a candle.

The dressing room had a window at the far end which overlooked the street. This came in useful at times, particularly at the end of the evening when Alicia and Ashton wanted to make a quick getaway before being button-holed by Madame Rambert, who would discuss the performance until dawn if not stopped.

Ashton would surreptitiously leave the theatre and walk round until he was below the window. Alicia would then steal out of this on to his shoulders and he would lower her to the ground. It was not unknown, if someone was needed on stage and stranded upstairs, for them to be helped out of the window in this way, then creep round to the front of the house and get to the wings through the auditorium.

There is a fragment of film in existence of Alicia in *Foyer de Danse*, shot on a single camera.

She and Ashton worked closely when he was concocting a ballet. As with Balanchine, she inspired him. They would try out steps as they went along and he wrote scenes that specifically displayed her talent. It was a profitable partnership. Their fame grew equally.

That year she created Marina in Antony Tudor's new ballet *Lysistrata*, music by Prokofiev, in which Walter Gore partnered her. Tudor was studying with Rambert at that time, but he was also in charge of the box office and the stage lighting. 'He used to get shouted out a bit by Fred and me,' Alicia remembers. 'We'd be standing in costume and he would be doing the lights. "You've got that wrong, Antony," we'd say. He was learning then and everybody had to do everything. We did it for love, there was no money at all.'

In *Lysistrata* she danced a *pas de deux* with Gore. It was really a *pas de trois* as she danced with a baby (really a doll) in her arms which had to be put down from time to time then picked up again.

In November 1932 she was at the Alhambra to appear in the musical *A Kiss in Spring*, which starred the Danish Eric Bertner. It was a lavish production in which she and Manchester-born Harold Turner appeared only in the last act, in a *divertissement* called 'Ballet of Spring', devised by Ashton. The show was a disaster but the critics loved Alicia and Turner.

'As I can find little that is good to say about *A Kiss in Spring* . . . let me at least begin pleasantly by congratulating the British *corps de ballet*, with Alicia Markova and Harold Turner at their head they were the success of the evening . . . we had to wait long for their coming. Not till a dull show had dragged its slow length along for nearly three hours did they appear. But when they did they aroused their audience to a pitch of enthusiasm that had at one time seemed impossible.' – *Daily Telegraph*, 29 November 1932

'. . . For two acts then this spring drags wearily on, disappointing us in the theatre as it so often disappoints us in reality, but suddenly on the stage comes Alicia Markova with Harold Turner and a *corps de ballet*. Then we sit erect – entranced. Markova is now that miracle of art, a great dancer in her prime . . .' – *Sun Pictorial*, November 1932

'. . . When at last the play became a leg show it did so with taste and dash. Alicia Markova and Harold Turner leading the ballet with a lively beauty . . . the discreet will visit the Alhambra after a very late dinner . . . near the end of the second act. They will possess themselves of patience during the opening of Act Three and be abundantly rewarded when the ballet, led by Madame Markova and Harold Turner, comes into its own in the penultimate scene. All else in this lamentable tale . . . is unspeakably dull. But the ballet is genuine ballet, not the grotesque acrobatics that are sometimes substitutes for it, and it is a pleasure to watch . . . not that among ballets this one is a masterpiece . . . but within its limitations it is a thing of minor beauty. Decorative, charming and well performed. Madame Markova and Harold Turner bring the evening suddenly to life . . .' – *Observer*, 2 December 1932

'The show will run if the first two acts can be brightened up, but I would not have missed the dancing of Alicia Markova and Harold Turner in the final scene. It was a return to the best of the old Alhambra tradition.' – *Daily Herald*, 29 November 1932

'I went again to see this piece at one of the matinées. The concluding ten minutes when Markova is dancing with the ballet are lovely. I state regretfully that the remainder is dull. What Sir Oswald wants to do is engage a first rate comic, and I don't mind how red-nosed he is.' – *Sunday Referee*, 28 November 1932

'. . . the admirable troupe, led so superbly by Mme Markova . . . lifts the piece at once into a higher realm of art. They come too late in the action and should have been used in the first scene.' – *Pictorial*, November 1932

In another edition, the *Pictorial* carried a large photograph of Alicia in cartwheel hat, captioned 'Alicia Markova – A Poem of Grace'. The copy read, 'She bears an extraordinary resemblance to the great Pavlova who said to her that if she had had a daughter she would probably not be as nearly like her as Alicia.'

Pavlova had told her that when she had auditioned her.

That November the *Daily Sketch* carried an interview with her – Alicia rarely refuses interviews. 'According to Alicia Markova . . . our audiences no longer look on ballet as highbrow nonsense but as an important item of popular entertainment and what was once of interest to a few intellectual snobs has now become the delight of the ordinary theatre goer. "British ballet has had to work hard but I think we have come through," Miss Markova told the *Daily Sketch*. "It is becoming so popular in theatres and cinema houses that thousands of British girls are going into training. Soon we shall be able to leave off our Russian names – be just plain Jones and Smith," laughs Miss Markova.'

Unfortunately the ballet was not enough to sustain *A Kiss in Spring* and it soon closed.

On 5 March 1933 Alicia was back to the restricted dimensions of the Mercury Theatre in *Les Masques*, another Ashton ballet set to music from a Poulenc trio. It was designed by Sophie Fedorovitch and costumed entirely in black and white.

Ashton partnered her as a diplomat while she played his mistress, a daring theme for the time. Walter Gore was with her again, and he played the diplomat's wife's lover who was supposed to be black – revolutionary then.

'At the beginning I entered masked with Ashton, and Walter was with the diplomat's wife, Pearl Argyle, who was our beauty. Suddenly the diplomat and his wife found each other and the mistress went off with the wife's friend.' The ballet ended happily as Alicia danced off with Gore to a jazz routine. There was lots of jazz about in the 1930s; it was the craze of Europe, helped in its popularity by the success of cabaret star Josephine Baker.

In June 1933 the Camargo Society closed down. It had served its purpose and British ballet was now established. To mark the occasion it gave two gala performances at the Royal Opera House, one of which was to be given in the presence of Queen Mary and the Duke and Duchess of York. The occasion was to honour the delegates to the World Economic Conference. Alicia was to be presented to Queen Mary after her performance.

She was to dance the second act of *Swan Lake* with Dolin. She wanted a new tutu for this but was told she would have to pay for it herself. The Camargo Society was non-profit-making and, since the occasion was for charity, no one was getting a fee.

Having one professionally made was out of the question, so Eileen bought a roll of tarlatan, the transparent muslin from which tutus are made, and with her daughters' help made the dress at home in her bedroom. They worked until virtually the last minute. Alicia went to bed at 4 a.m. on the morning of the performance. She had been sewing until then.

That evening as she was being sewn into her new tutu* in her dressing room there was a knock at the door.

It was an equerry from Queen Mary. Plans had been changed. Her Majesty would now see her before the performance, right now if it was convenient. Alicia could hardly unpick the stitching, so she had to go half sewn into her tutu with the needle tucked in behind. More embarrassing was that she was dusted in white powder to create the swan-like effect.

She quickly grabbed her new white kid gloves which had taken the last of her savings. She had been told that even if she was in costume it was essential she wear white kid gloves when meeting the Queen. 'There I was, going up to see the Queen, covered in white powder, dressed for *Swan Lake* with a crown of white feathers, the needle tucked into the back of my costume, and white gloves. People said I never seemed nervous but they should have seen me then.'

Her Majesty complimented her on her costume, which was

---

* Customary practice. Hooks and eyes could be lethal for a partner.

beautiful and covered with tiny, hand-sewn-on sequins, and Alicia explained that she had helped make it herself. Queen Mary was vastly interested in needlework and asked Alicia to turn round so she could see the back of the tutu. It was a command. Alicia's face glowed with embarrassment as she thought of the needle still tucked into the back.

The press commented on the performance:

'With the Queen present last night at Covent Garden at a gala performance . . . British ballet may be said to have taken its greatest forward step . . . to conclude there was an abbreviated version of Tchaikovsky's *Le Lac des Cygnes* in which Alicia Markova performed the principal part with exquisite grace and lightness. This was dancing in the best classic tradition of the old St Petersburg school.' – A. E. Wilson, *Star*, 28 June 1933

'Alicia Markova, perfectly partnered by Anton Dolin, was as enchanting a Swan Princess as I have ever seen. The standard is a high one but this young English dancer does not lower it. Her performance was excellent . . .' – *Observer*, 2 July 1933

'Dolin was the perfect dream prince to Markova's princess's exquisite and appealing fragility.' – *Evening News*, 28 June 1933

'All Europe and more – the world – was represented there last night at the gala which the Queen and the Duke and Duchess of York attended . . . the exquisitely graceful and accomplished Alicia Markova . . . proved that although Imperial Petersburg may be no more, the noble style is a living and cherished tradition.' – *Daily Telegraph*, 28 June 1933

A short while later other publications carried a series of photos of Alicia and Dolin in swimming costumes on the beach at Hythe, where they were appearing at the open-air theatre, 'discovered perfectly expressing the poetry of pose just for the joy of it'.

That August a magazine called *Modern* featured a picture of Alicia in peignoir, ballet slippers and huge hat, captioned 'Alicia Markova, the lovely Russian dancer, gives us an idea of what we might be wearing in 1943. Well, if we had legs half as shapely as hers we wouldn't do so badly.'

It was a far cry from her first days with the Ballet Russe when she wore pantalettes on stage to hide the thinness of her legs.

11

Giselle

Alicia opened the 1933 Sadler's Wells season with *Le Spectre de la Rose*, which had been choreographed by Fokine in 1911 for Diaghileff as a vehicle for Nijinsky and Karsavina. Alicia's partner was the Polish Stanislas Idzikowsky, with whom, later in the season, she danced *Le Carnaval*.

Elsewhere in the programme they performed the *Blue Bird pas de deux*. She had seen Idzikowsky dance this in Diaghileff's *The Sleeping Princess*, in which illness had prevented her from taking part.

It was still clear to de Valois that the only way she could be certain of a full house was to book Alicia. It was by no means sure that Sadler's Wells Ballet would be a long-term success, and Arnold Haskell had written only recently that he feared de Valois had bitten off more than she could chew. Robert Helpmann had joined the company by then and he echoed Dolin's sentiments in his biography – unless Alicia was dancing, the house was half empty.

On 5 December 1933 she took part in another of Ashton's premieres for Sadler's Wells, *Les Rendezvous*, to music by Daniel Auber. Constant Lambert had found and arranged the music as he did so often for the Vic-Wells company.

The ballet was designed principally for Idzikowsky, 'our famous, wonderful guest artiste' as Alicia described him. He had deputized many times for Nijinsky when the Russian had been unable to dance and had created roles in *Good Humoured Ladies*, *La Boutique Fantasque* and *Pulcinella*, but his most famous part was the Blue Bird. The *Daily Telegraph* commented: 'The choreography is by Frederick Ashton who, knowing that to Alicia Markova nothing is difficult, has given her some difficult steps to do which she does with such ease that only experts know the high merit of her performances.'

Ninette de Valois also appeared in *Les Rendezvous*, as did Robert Helpmann, whom she had just promoted from the *corps de ballet*.

Meanwhile the former members of the Ballet Russe who were in London held a reunion dinner which Alicia attended. According to an unidentified press cutting: 'There must be members of the Diaghileff Russian ballet in every capital in Europe . . . but London keeps a few of her favourites. No fewer than nine were at the reunion dinner at the Faculty of Arts. The list included that gracious lady Madame Karsavina who made one of her wonderful after dinner speeches. There is grey in her hair now but youth stays in her face and figure and I thought how pretty she looked when I saw her leaving in a little astrakhan pork pie cap and a beautiful sable coat . . . there was a last minute surprise guest in the appearance of Danilova, whom everyone thought to be in Paris. Danilova is even prettier off stage than on – big, expressive blue eyes, small features – there was much excitement among her friends over her engagement to Mr Giuseppe Masera.'

Danilova's dramatic late entry clearly upstaged Alicia as much as had Karsavina's pork-pie hat.

That year Alicia and Dolin also appeared at the Coliseum in Ashton's period *pas de deux, Rondo*, to Rameau's music, and *The Nightingale and the Rose*. She was also at Sadler's Wells in de Valois's *The Foolish Virgins*.

Lilian Baylis upped her fees to £10 per performance. Even she realized she could no longer expect her star to continue to learn new ballets and bring in the crowds for £5 a show.

But for that extra £5 she expected Alicia to lend her services as a choreographer. She regularly worked with Ashton and it was a fine line where his influence ended and hers began. 'Sometimes', says Alicia, 'he'd have an idea and I would try to implement it. Sometimes I'd say, "No, I don't think you can do that, try it this way." We understood each other.'

Miss Baylis did not want to tie Alicia to an exclusive contract. Quite the reverse, she wanted her to take as much well-paid extra work as she could, but she insisted that a printed recognition of Alicia's commitment to Sadler's Wells be printed in each programme when she appeared elsewhere, thus furthering the company's fame. Alicia was 'delighted' to comply.

Miss Baylis got a lot for her £10 and not many impresarios could have done better.

Alicia sacrificed a great deal for Sadler's Wells. She had been invited to join Massine's Monte Carlo ballet but turned it down. Arnold Haskell was incredulous. 'I had to make the decision and I wanted to stand by Ninette and what she was trying to achieve,' Alicia says. She also turned down offers from Alexandre Levitoff to dance in Egypt and from Serge Lifar to partner him in America.

De Valois offered something in return. 'We served each other. Ninette gave me the classics. She knew I wanted to dance them. She also knew that if she wanted to establish a company she had to do it with the classics. They are the training ground for dancers, just as Shakespeare is for actors.'

They decided that, in addition to the new ballets, Alicia would dance the Russian masterpieces. Enterprising as the new works were, it was the classics which the general public loved. The combination of a 'classic' and Markova would be a sure-fire success.

Alicia and de Valois had no difficulty in deciding which to choose first – *Giselle*. Audiences had responded well when Spessivtseva had danced it at the Savoy.

Giselle had been premiered in 1841 by Carlotta Grisi and Lucien Petipa, brother of choreographer Marius Petipa, who had worked with Tchaikovsky on both *Swan Lake* and *The Nutcracker*. It had been an instant success, since when it has been danced in every country in the world which has a ballet tradition. It received its first London performance in 1842.

But *Giselle* had had a long, low dip to its fortunes. New styles had come along and, by the turn of the century, it was considered out of date. For many years it was performed only in Russia.

Diaghileff revived it and brought it to Europe in 1911. He had had two Giselles, Pavlova and Karsavina, who had alternated with each other then, just as he had wanted Alicia to alternate with Spessivtseva. Nijinsky had been Albrecht. The part of Giselle's mother, usually played by a man, had been taken by Enrico Cecchetti.

The story is in two acts.

In Act One a peasant girl, Giselle, is in love with Albrecht who is a count but has passed himself off as a peasant. Unknown to her he is engaged to the Princess Bathilde. The gamekeeper, Hilarion, is in love with Giselle and jealous of Albrecht, so he tells her Albrecht's true identity. The shock drives her insane and kills her. This provides a mad scene which can be a stunning virtuoso piece for the ballerina.

In the second act Giselle has become a Wili. These are ghosts of brides who have died before their wedding day. Their fate is to lure male travellers whom they dance to death. They start their ghostly rites at midnight, when they rise from their graves led by their queen, Myrtha.

After Giselle's death Albrecht goes to her grave to beg forgiveness. Myrtha forces Giselle to lead Albrecht in a dance until he dies. But Giselle cannot bring herself to kill him and she continues to dance until dawn when she has to return to her grave. By doing that she saves Albrecht's life.

Alicia's interpretation has developed through years of dancing the role and studying it with experts. It is full of subtleties.

'The way Pat and I did it, it was not as though Albrecht had behaved badly. Today they make him out a cad or a playboy but we didn't see it like that. He was a count who had dignity and bearing.

'The décor explained his, and Giselle's, situation. Here was Giselle's mama's cottage and on the other side was another cottage. Way up on the hill you saw the castle where the other folk lived.

'To me it was always so simple and I think, when I did it, audiences understood it. What you saw was Giselle's whole life; she'd never been further than that area. She wasn't simple but this was her world. She didn't know anything else. That was how I portrayed it.

'Albrecht must have seen her. He was bored in the castle. He wasn't a cad, he was betrothed to Bathilde, he knew that, she knew that, everybody knew that. He decided, with his valet, to put on peasant clothes and see what it was like among the peasants.

'They came together, as happens. She was very shy and he was more worldly and understood that. He treated her tenderly and this was the awful tragedy. The public knew that something was bound to happen.

'At the end of the act, as I've always done it, after the mad scene, when she collapses, he comes to her and he is distraught.

'As he comes towards her she leaves her mother and, with those last big chords, she turns and, for a moment, she recognizes him. Certain things have to be done to certain music. She gets enough strength and she mimes "I", and he waits, then she mimes "You", then drops dead. It is a shock to everyone. No one ever knew what Giselle was going to say.

'That's why, in the next act, he comes with the lilies to her grave in remorse. He doesn't know if she was going to say "I love you," or "I forgive you," or what. It never happened. I always stopped in mid-breath. It was too late.

'It all made perfect sense.'

When Alicia had been a child she had once seen Pavlova dance Giselle; Arnold Haskell's mother had taken her to a matinée at Covent Garden. It had had no effect on her; she had been too young. 'To be truthful the memory is not sharp enough, though I did sense the dramatic power in the performance.'*

It had taken time for her deep feelings for the ballet to develop. In 1929, when Diaghileff had first mentioned the prospect of her dancing Giselle, she had experienced no dedication. As Alicia says, 'The thought should have overwhelmed me and, in one sense, I suppose it did. But still it seemed oddly remote, and I cannot pretend that, at that time, I felt any romantic longing to dance the role.'

The trend then was for 'modern' ballet and she was caught up with Balanchine's contemporary creations. She had delighted in providing the fireworks for which the modern works called.

It was not until 1932, when Spessivtseva had danced Giselle, that Alicia awoke to its possibilities. As she wrote, 'she opened new worlds to me.'

One new world was soon to take shape. Within a short time she was being schooled by Nicholas Sergeyev in an intensive six-week rehearsal period.

Sergeyev was something of a legend himself. By then he was getting on for sixty. He had been born in St Petersburg in 1876 and became *Régisseur-Général* of the Marynsky in 1914 where he remained until after the Revolution. Then he was accused by Soviet historians of having been guilty of running a dictatorial routine contrary to the Party spirit.

He fled Russia in 1918 but took with him no less than twenty-one Stepanov ballet notation books on Marynsky productions. These were ledger-like tomes containing choreology and production notes on the Imperial Ballet's repertoire. It was these books which were to be his salvation. Nowadays there is bitterness expressed towards him in Russia for the theft of what amounts to a national treasure. The books eventually came into the possession of ballerina Mona Inglesby who sold them to Harvard Library. According to the Oxford Dictionary of Ballet 'there can be no doubt that he laid the foundations of Western knowledge of the Marynsky classics.'

Ballet teacher Stepanov had studied anatomy and developed a system of dance notation which became incorporated into the syllabus of the Imperial Ballet. Among the notations in Sergeyev's

* *Giselle and I.*

Stepanov books was the choreology of the Imperial Ballet's original production of *Giselle*.

By applying these to Alicia, Sergeyev ensured that her interpretation was as near to the original as could be. Being in possession of the notes, and one of the few who could decipher them, made him a unique source of information.

The reverence in which he was held had done nothing to sweeten his disposition and, like all old ballet maestros, he could be a tyrant. Dancers today will never experience the like, be that a good thing or a bad. If Alicia closed her eyes she could, at times, have imagined she was back rehearsing with Cecchetti in Monte Carlo. All it needed to complete the picture was Guggy standing on the sidelines refusing to give her any chocolate.

Sergeyev had produced *The Sleeping Princess* for Diaghileff in 1921 and also *Giselle* for Spessivtseva during the Camargo Savoy season. Since then his fortunes had waned.

Lydia Lopokova had brought Sergeyev to de Valois's attention. 'I got the Russian over from France,' de Valois recalls. 'He was a choreologist and knew how to write down choreography but when I wrote to him he was a refugee with no work. Lopokova told me, "For goodness' sake get hold of him, he'll put on all the classics for you, at the present moment he's starving in Paris." I soon got hold of him. He was a quiet old gentleman with me, on the whole, but rather obstinate.'*

Alicia took the bus to Sadler's Wells and rehearsed with 'the quiet old gentleman' in the mornings in the boardroom, then, in the afternoon after a sandwich lunch, she joined the company for a further four hours' ensemble work. She worked until six and then got the bus home. So much for those who say Markova never practised.

When she started working with Sergeyev it seemed to her that he would never get down to the actual dancing. He spent hours lecturing her on the part, in broken English, which she had to put together as best she could, and when she dared remark that she had seen Spessivtseva in it and had read, in Beaumont's bookshop, accounts of other ballerinas who had danced the role, he flew into a rage.

He stamped his foot and yelled then she must forget all she had learned and approach the role afresh. He informed her, in no uncertain terms, that she would otherwise be 'just a copy'.

His lessons could be as dry as a bone. He stuck to his notebooks

---

* 1994 interview.

and seemed devoid of theatrical flair. If she questioned anything no answer was forthcoming until he had consulted the notebook. But, as Alicia says, 'His notations were the essential scaffolding on which I built the role . . . looking back, I see a kind of wisdom in his deliberate policy of not interpreting the role for me . . . my work was learning the choreography of the Marynsky production.'

She accepted that he knew best and started working, herself, on the psychology of the part, building up the character and trying to understand Giselle's motivation.

She realized that the first-act variation, now a standard part of the role, had not been in the original but was an invention of Spessivtseva's. It fitted so well that nearly every ballerina who danced it after her included it, as did Alicia.

'It wasn't in the original production and musically it doesn't belong in the score. It was separate. But when he was teaching me the coda at the end, I was given a choice. I had seen Spessivtseva's Giselle by then and I took it for granted, I liked it very much. But he also offered me the alternative that Karsavina had done. I preferred Spessivtseva's version because it moved across the stage. Karsavina's was more in one place. He showed me both. That's how I gained knowledge and that was the same way we later worked on *Swan Lake* together.'

There was excitement at the thought of her forthcoming *Giselle*. The *Dancing Times* of January 1934 reflected the anticipation:

'The presentation of that world famous ballet *Giselle* at the Old Vic . . . is not only the biggest undertaking yet attempted by the company but it will afford Alicia Markova the most important role she has yet filled. There is no English dancer more worthy than Miss Markova to play the part.'

Opening night was 1 January 1934 at the Old Vic. She had gone to bed early the night before but need not have bothered. It was New Year's Eve and the house in which the Markses had their flat had been shaken by the other tenants's merry-making till dawn. She could not sleep at all.

The first day of the new year dawned cold and damp, just the sort of day when most people would want to turn over and go back to sleep. 'Another delightful factor was the fog,' she says. 'A throat-tightening, all-obscuring pea-souper.'

People would have difficulty getting to the theatre. That was most encouraging. By four in the afternoon it was so dark it could have been midnight. She remembered that a fog had nearly obliterated Victoria Station when she had first left to join the Ballet Russe in Monte Carlo. Here it was again. It seemed symbolic. 'Real Markova weather,' she says.

As she could not get a taxi she took a tube to Waterloo. She arrived early, as she always does, and started her implacable routine of getting herself ready.

She had always disliked the stage at the Old Vic. 'I preferred the Wells because it was flat whereas the Old Vic had a terrible rake. The rake never bothered me if I was working on it all the time, but I only went there for single performances and, by then, I'd got accustomed to the flatness of the Wells.'

There was to be a curtain-raiser before *Giselle*. Ashton's *Pomona*, to music by Constant Lambert, danced by Robert Helpmann, who was also Hilarion in *Giselle*. Alicia peeped through the curtain to see the size of the house. There were several empty seats. This was heart-breaking as it had been sold out well in advance.

Attendance, however, picked up. She was further cheered by an opening-night present from Marie Rambert, who was in the audience, fog or not. It was the bodice worn by Karsavina in Act Two of *Giselle* when she had danced it for Diaghileff. Madame Rambert thought it might bring her luck.

Agnes de Mille was with Madame R and noted in *Portrait Gallery*, 'People were very proud of Alicia. She was a home town girl doing nicely.'

And the people responded nicely. The press commented:

'Technically flawless, Markova has at last been given the opportuntiy to show that her range of mime runs from gaiety to poignancy and includes both . . . she was the perfect instrument through which the tragic tale was transmitted.'
– *Time and Tide*

'Though eminently Victorian in style, pace and sentiment, this professional old ballet is all alive. It has its longueurs, of course, for the days of its youth were leisurely. The action is sometimes slower than the musical and choreography contents seem to justify, but it does pay for dancing. If the principal dancer has youth, grace and charm so much the better but if she has also a good ear, acting ability, extreme virtuosity and the kind of stamina that could carry her, still breathing, up Mont Blanc – if, in short, she is less gifted than Markova then *Giselle* had better be left to moulder . . . Giselle is a role that demands all a dancer's arts but gives her abundant opportunity to dare, dazzle and dumbfound . . . these are feats that defy mere twinklers but Markova performed them beautifully. She is a star – light, graceful, clear – who never gives one the fear that she may wane in transit; that one clean arabesque may be less brilliantly achieved, held, resigned, than its predecessor or that the edges of a perfectly executed phrase may be blurred by careless finger-tips or toes. She dances like a well-tempered clavichord; her line is as clean as Ingres . . . the Vic-Wells ballet may be very warmly congratulated . . . all who enjoy the art of ballet should flock tomorrow when *Giselle* will be danced again.' – *Observer*, 7 January 1934

'. . . it gives Alicia Markova an opportunity to show that she is an actress as well as a delicious dancer. In her mad scene, with its grim conclusion, she held the packed house with her tragic mime and later, when in the second act she returns as a spirit, her ethereal grace attained a truly poignant beauty . . .' – *Daily Telegraph*, 2, January 1934

After the performance Dolin gave a curtain speech paying tribute to Alicia as the first British ballerina to dance Giselle. Madame Rambert and Agnes de Mille came round to the dressing room and the faithful Miss de Mille recorded the occasion in *Portrait Gallery*. 'I was there when [Marie Rambert] gently took Alicia's head between her hands and kissed her. "You have come of age," she whispered.' Lydia Lopokova was also there, with her English husband, the economist Professor (Lord) Maynard Keynes.

Dolin was to dance Albrecht many times in the future. He came to know Alicia's Giselle better than anyone, and whereas he acknowledges that she was good that night, he felt her performance developed with time. As he put it: 'No one could hope to dance Giselle to perfection the very first time, it . . . requires many performances before it can reach an ideal interpretation. But Alicia gave an unforgettable performance . . . It was truly great dancing. I think it ranks with Melba's Mimi and Chaliapin's Boris Godunov as one of the greatest artistic creations of the century.'*

For all the applause and reviews, Alicia was far from satisfied. Not that she has much memory of the night; it all seems a blur. She felt she had taken a rung up the interpretative ladder but it was still a long climb to the top. She wrote in *Giselle and I*, 'I have been gifted from childhood with such a facility in the technique of ballet that the

* *Markova: Her Life and Art.*

32 *fouettés* were nothing to me, a mere exercise to be tossed off . . . Perhaps this gift had put up a barrier against emotional expression . . . I must own that in this first performance I explored only the fringes of my new world. It was, however, a beginning.'

Markova is a professional being separate from Alicia. When questioned about her life she will reel off the facts of Markova's career like a computer, but when asked a personal question she stops and ponders. 'I've got to think about that,' she says. 'That was me, not Markova.'

When practising she rarely looks in a mirror. 'I don't need to. If I look then my body's not right.

'I was always very critical of myself. Today there are videos and it's easy to watch a performance but I never looked at myself much. Not even in studios. To me it was always the feel of the thing. I could go into the studio with the mirror and look, but then what happens when I go to dance it? I come out on stage and I just want to go. It's the feel. I can't remember what I saw in the mirror.

'In the studios when I'm giving a master class, I'll often turn the dancers round and won't let them face the mirror. Otherwise the placing as we were taught is wrong. There are rules and different choreographers' rules.

'Nowadays with new works nobody has to sustain anything and carry it with responsibility. You'll have a boy who has a wonderful balance, he'll come bounding on, he'll do huge leaps, and then he'll do something and run off. Then you'll get another one doing the same thing from the other side and he runs off. Then you'll have one who'll come on and do a few turns around and he runs off.

'But if you have to come on and hold for two minutes with every eye glued on you, it's different. Then you have to be able to sustain, then you find yourself. I'm always saying to everybody, "You're individuals, I want to see you." That's why I never demonstrate because I don't want them copying me. They've got to use their own minds. I will show them after I've explained what I want.'

She was getting better-paid bookings and the family were able to move out of the cramped flat and into a bigger apartment near Marble Arch. Property was not as ferociously expensive then.

Doris was now able to contribute towards expenses. She was nineteen and had realized her show-business ambitions by becoming a dancer herself, not a ballet dancer but a *soubrette* at London's famous Windmill, the city's leading revue theatre. Prior to this she had been at the Gaiety in *The Love Race* and had already agreed to appear in *Casanova* at the Coliseum. Then the offer came for her to appear in *Revudeville* at the Windmill which she took in preference.

She had taken her mother's surname and was now Doris Barry. Like Alicia, Doris never married.

Alicia had noted that her first performance of *Giselle* was 'a beginning'. It was a beginning that was soon subject to change. Dolin went down with flu and was unable to dance the second performance.

At the time she was rehearsing *The Nutcracker*, her next 'classic' production with Sadler's Wells, with Stanley Judson. He had never danced Albrecht but had immediately to step into Dolin's shoes.

He was the leading male dancer at the Wells, Dolin being a guest artist, who was never a member of the company. Judson was a former member of the Pavlova company, and his experience showed that night. He proved his mettle and became a regular partner of Alicia's as Dolin often had bookings elsewhere.

At that particular time Dolin was appearing in revue with Jack Buchanan. He danced when he could with the Vic-Wells but his contribution to the company was not on a par with Alicia's.

He was unable to partner her in *Giselle* the following season and Robert Helpmann replaced Judson as Albrecht.

That year, 1934, Alicia was at the Royal Opera House in Rossini's opera *La Cenerentola*. This marked the opera-house debut of the great Spanish singer Conchita Supervia, an artist of unique charm and beauty, possessed of one of the most vibrant voices of her generation. As a coloratura mezzo she was able to sing the Rossini roles in their original keys without transposing.

This was a Beecham season and it had been an achievement on his part to get Supervia. Previous plans had twice been thwarted, once because of dissension between management and the artist and on another occasion because of the indisposition of Dino Borgioli, the Prince Charming of her choice. Borgioli was a superb tenor and a big man. A heftier example of Prince Charming could not be imagined.

Beecham was sure that Alicia's presence would be the icing on a glamorous cake. She believes that de Valois was also instrumental in getting her the engagement. As it was, de Valois provided the choreography.

'There is no ballet music in *Cenerentola*,' says Alicia. 'But Sir Thomas asked Ninette to choreograph a dance for me. Beecham was not conducting himself but brought Gino Marinuzzi, the great expert on Rossini, over from La Scala and between them they found a fabulous variation from another Rossini opera and put it in.

'Bobby Helpmann and I led the dancing at the ball. I think we started with a gavotte and I was on *pointe* the whole time. Everything was in period. I had a high white wig and a paniered skirt.

'Ezio Pinza was Don Magnifico and I later got to know him better in New York when he was doing *South Pacific* and I was on Broadway in *The Merry Widow*. We met in a bar. I'd just finished rehearsals and he had done a matinée, and he introduced me to the drink, Fernet-Brianca. "You must try this," he told me. "It cures butterflies in the tummy if you're nervous before going on. It settles you wonderfully."

'I had the next dressing room to Supervia and she was a darling, married to an Englishman then and living in Surrey. They used to grow orchids and she used to come into my dressing room, before I arrived, and arrange the most beautiful orchids for me.'

Supervia, with her shining red hair and vivacity, was just as outstanding on stage. She made her entrance to the palace in a gilt coach pulled by four miniature ponies. Her 'success was beyond all question', wrote critic Edwin Evans.

After this Alicia and Dolin went on a music-hall tour, starting with London theatres. *Stage* magazine covered this and the reporter noted, '. . . if my campaign were in full swing Markova would find herself being rammed down the throats of the public with a persistence that might help her to achieve more rapidly the position to which she is entitled.'

They started off with a week at Golders Green Hippodrome followed by two weeks at the prestigious Alhambra in Leicester Square. The *Evening News* commented:

'Not for a long time has the West End seen a better Variety show than is provided at the Alhambra this week, it is Variety in the true sense of the word, bearing the stamp of quality . . . old time songs are delightfully recorded by Olive Goff and Thorpe Bates in "Romance in Harmony" and peeps into ballets of quality were provided by Anton Dolin and Alicia Markova.'

From Leicester Square they went to the Chiswick Empire and then on to the Streatham Hill Theatre followed by a provincial tour including dates at the Manchester Hippodrome, then on its last legs as a theatre and about to be converted into a cinema. Said the *Manchester Evening News*:

'The bill is graced with the presence of Anton Dolin and Alicia Markova . . . There is one brief moment when Markova and Dolin appear as though they are going to devote the rest of their dancing act to hot jazz but, after a modern tremor or two, they return to more graceful activities.'

12

Farewell to the Vic-Wells

'Markova stayed with me at Sadler's Wells four to five years. She grew up there, really, and developed while she was with us. When she had been with Diaghileff she had done modern ballet but with us, through Sergeyev, she learnt all the classics, she learnt the lot while she was with us.'*

On 7 February 1934 Alicia was on television again in a transmission advertised as being by the Baird Process. The music was simultaneously broadcast on the radio. The show was at 11 p.m. and she was part of a programme that included singers Thea Philips and Gavin Gordon. The *Evening News* wrote:

'Alicia Markova, who recently danced the name part in the French ballet *Giselle*, will be televised from London tonight at 11 p.m. She would be worth seeing – if you had a television receiver . . . It seems a pity to me that so much talent should be wasted on the television programmes. If only we all had the necessary television apparatus. As it is, I doubt whether more than a score or two lookers in will see her. But everyone can hear her . . . She will also dance with Anton Dolin in a forthcoming production of *Elijah* at the Albert Hall.'

The *Elijah* production was lavish. Presented by Harold Holt, it was to run consecutively twice nightly from 12 to 24 February, and was advertised as having 1,000 performers – mostly the vast chorus.

* Interview with Ninette de Valois, 1994.

The climax of the piece was Elijah ascending to heaven in a fiery chariot. Every episode in Elijah's career was covered except for his feeding by the ravens. There were even angels and seraphims, one a staggering forty feet tall.

The producer was that noted showman T. C. Fairbairn, who had had a prior success at the Albert Hall with Coleridge-Taylor's *Hiawatha's Wedding Feast*.

Eric Coates was conducting the orchestra, and tenor Harold Williams was Elijah. The cast also included contralto Gladys Ripley and the substantial Madame Stiles Allen, about whom one of her pupils had irreverently commented: 'once around the gasworks, twice around Stiles Allen.' Mme Stiles Allen had been in *Hiawatha* and a critic had written that he had had difficulty telling her apart from the wigwams.

The price of admission was 2s 6d for the best seats, and there was a lavishly produced souvenir programme with a cover coloured in the shades of the desert. It was a classy affair – the to-ing and fro-ing in the boxes during the interval was more reminiscent of a cocktail party than an oratorio. That was what Mr Fairbairn had wanted and the public flocked to it.

There is no ballet music in *Elijah* so a special arrangement of Mendelssohn's 'Spring Song' was commissioned for Alicia (by kind permission of Lilian Baylis) and Dolin to dance to.

> 'Back in London I found the fog in charge once again. It did not deprive us of seeing Alicia Markova using nearly the whole of the Albert Hall arena in her dainty feather-weight dancing in one of the ballets of the *Elijah* performance.' – *Evening News*, 13 February 1934

She had first appeared at the Royal Albert Hall as a child as part of Astafieva's troupe, when the Princess herself had been on the bill.

The Princess had gloried in Alicia's success, but this was to be one of the last of Alicia's triumphs she would see. She died that year of cancer.

Alicia, and her other pupils, now realized why Astafieva had so often been late for appointments, and sometimes had not turned up at all. It was not solely temperament; the Princess had been ailing. Her bravado when she did arrive, flaunting her black cigarettes and trailing scarves, was partly to disguise the extent of her illness.

1934 was an important year at the Wells for Alicia. On 30 January she appeared in the Vic-Wells production of *The Nutcracker*. It was performed in two acts; this was the first London production of the complete ballet. To undertake full-scale versions of both *Giselle* and *The Nutcracker* in one month caused something of a furore in the ballet world. Alicia danced the Sugar Plum Fairy and, once again, had the pleasure of learning the role with Sergeyev. He had proven his value to de Valois since she had found him 'starving' in Paris.

The reviews were enthusiastic:

'. . . There is no dancer, now dancing, male or female, to hold a candle to her. She is as classical as Mozart and as vertebrate in her liveliness as Scarlatti, achieving irresistible freedom without ever betraying the fundamental formalities. No one should miss her in *Casse-Noisette* – for her miming, which is superb – see *Giselle*. But where may Markova be seen? My dear sir (or Madame), at the Vic or the Wells, in the Vic-Wells Ballet. And what pray is the Vic-Wells Ballet? My dear sir (or Madame), go and see for yourself and don't waste so much time over fifth-rate stars in sixth-rate talkies.' – *Evening News*

'Her dancing in the last scene was as fine as I have ever seen – highly traditional, highly individual, immaculately severe, profoundly delicate, responsive, controlled, strict, free, perfect. Here is supreme art – the one really great experience on our stage at the moment . . . if Markova is not filmed for posterity the future will have a black mark against 1934.' – Herbert Farjeon

Two other members of the cast became illustrious with time. Elsa Lanchester, who was in the 'Danse Arabe', became the Bride of Frankenstein the following year in the Hollywood film of that name.

She was married to Charles Laughton, who was starring in a recently released film. During this he gave a 'funny little whistle' which had caught on with the public. He was in the audience that night, and as Alicia finished her dance he let rip with the whistle. 'I don't know how I contained myself,' she says. 'It happened immediately I stopped dancing and preceded a crash of applause.'

Robert Helpmann co-performed the 'Danse Chinoise'. He became a world star, long-time partner of Fonteyn, a choreographer, director and character actor to boot.

Alicia was still regularly performing at the Ballet Club. In October 1933 the *Dancing Times* had covered her performance there in

Ashton's *Les Masques*, referring to her as 'this most brilliant of our young British dancers'. Now it noted: 'It is quite impossible to refer to the work of "The Ballet Club" without mentioning Alicia Markova. Miss Markova is not a product of the "Ballet Club" but has been on its stage for a long time now. She has been given the opportunity of ripening her art, increasing her already considerable repertoire and making her name a household word among the ballet loving public of Britain.'

On 3 April she returned to modern ballet with Ninette de Valois's *The Haunted Ballroom*, music by Geoffrey Toye. The story concerned an aristocrat who is doomed to dance himself to death in a gallery in his house which is hung with portraits of ancestors who have already met their ends in a like manner. One critic commented:

'Miss Markova . . . is meteoric. Her dark piquancy was admirably expressed by the white dress she wore and for her last exhibition she looked like a sparkling gem in her scintillating shoulder straps and sparkling head-dress, as she pirouetted on toes . . . She received great applause and I'm confident many felt as I did and could have watched her dance and dance and dance far into the night.'

The Haunted Ballroom had been designed primarily as a vehicle for Helpmann about whom de Valois was becoming more and more enthusiastic. It was his first starring role with the Vic-Wells.

Her character, Alicia, was named after her in a similar fashion to those of the other two central female characters, Ursula (Moreton) and Beatrice (Appleyard).

Ninette de Valois, in press releases, had announced that there were no stars at the Wells; she believed in company unity. She was, however, commercially minded enough to recognize the public draw of a star. Alicia was always advertised, and Helpmann too from then on.

In May Alicia went to Blackpool to adjudicate at the Blackpool Dance Festival.

'The audiences at the Blackpool Dance Festival were almost as interested in Mlle Alicia Markova, who was at the adjudicator's table, as they were in the young people on stage . . . although Mlle Markova is olive skinned and has dark eyes and black hair she is really English. "This is my first visit to Blackpool and I have been looking forward to it" . . . she was wearing a simple grey tweed suit and dark hat.' – *Lancashire Evening News*, 2 May 1934

A fellow adjudicator was Grace Cone. This was their first meeting. Later Miss Cone was to become closely associated with the Arts Educational Schools of which Alicia is today President. Miss Cone's pupils were also later to form the body of the Festival Ballet, which Alicia co-founded in the early 1950s.

She was to return many times to Blackpool, a town of which she grew inordinately fond. 'I always found it bracing.'

On 15 May Alicia was at the Mercury Theatre with Ashton in the Ballet Rambert premiere of de Valois's *Bar aux Folies-Bergère* which was set to Chabrier's music for 'Dix Pièces Pittoresques'.

Alicia was La Goulue, a celebrated can-can dancer. For the sake of veracity de Valois recommended that they visit a little street just behind the stage door of the Hippodrome Theatre, where the prostitutes plied their trade, and study how the ladies moved. There was not much they would not do for their art.

'We often used to rehearse on a Saturday morning at the Wells,' recalls Alicia. 'Then Ninette would say, "Let's go to Soho for lunch." We used to go to Gennaro's, it was famous, and Gennaro, a delightful old gentleman, always greeted me with a rose. I'd known it for years. All the Diaghileff company had gone there when they were in London. Cecchetti loved it, he was always in Soho.

'After lunch Ninette said, "Come along, we'll take a look and you can see what's happening." So we looked at the ladies and I took it in and she said to me, "You see that little walk they do, with the handbag, I want you to do that on *pointe*."'

Bar aux Folies-Bergère was the only ballet de Valois created for Rambert.

On Saturday afternoons de Valois and Alicia would usually go to the cinema. The Empire Cinema was just round the corner from Soho. 'That was our day of leisure.'

Alicia and Ashton were back at the Mercury on 13 June in *Mephisto Valse*, a new Ashton ballet to music by Liszt. Walter Gore was Faust, Ashton Mephisto.

Alicia's salary was raised to £15 a week for the forthcoming Vic-Wells season plus £5 for any additional performances she might fit in. Miss Baylis had tried to get her for £12 but Alicia had baulked at this and, with no agent to help her, had written that she might have to give better-paid engagements priority if her demand – which, after all, was reasonable – was not met. Miss Baylis knew when she was beaten. 'We just feel we would hate to lose you . . .' she wrote to Alicia on 16 May 1934.

Helpmann opened the season with *The Haunted Ballroom* in which Alicia danced her namesake.

Playing the role of the young lord was a fifteen-year-old girl in a Fauntleroy suit. She was not really ready for the part and had only been given it because she was small and the girl who usually danced it had left the company. It was a mime role, requiring no dancing, but it was important in that it both opened and closed the show.

This was Peggy Hookham's first appearance in a featured role, although she had previously made a student appearance as a snowflake in *The Nutcracker* in which Alicia had been the Sugar Plum Fairy.

In Peggy's own evaluation, her elevation was 'poor', pirouettes 'mundane', and she had a 'low arabesque'.* She also feared that her face was wrong for a dancer as her hair grew too low on her forehead and her chin was hefty. She decided to continue with her career, nevertheless, but changed her name to Margot Fonteyn.

In later years, when she was a ballerina, the press sometimes suggested that there was enmity between Fonteyn and Alicia. Alicia insists that this was never the case, and so did Fonteyn. The facts speak for themselves. In her autobiography, Fonteyn wrote:

'Markova was far above and apart from the rest of us. She was a star. She was unique. Not only did she have the essential physical qualifications for a ballerina – black hair, an oval face, a long neck and beautiful feet – she also had the lightness of a bird and possessed a strong stage presence. I never took my eyes off her when she danced. She combined extraordinary speed and ease, and this she accomplished without ever being seen to attend a practice class. Somehow she just appeared on stage a few minutes before curtain time, pointed her toes once or twice, and then proceeded to dance in the most scintillating manner, making difficulties look utterly effortless. If one had occasion to touch her hands during a ballet they were ice cold. It was as though none of the usual rules applied to Markova; other dancers were hot and out of breath but she only became cool and light as the sylph she so often portrayed.'*

Towards the end of their careers – Fonteyn was nine years younger than Alicia – the ladies sometimes stood in for each other at various meetings and committees.

Alicia had coached Fonteyn in romantic roles, and had even given her the occasional lesson at The Pheasantry: 'One day something

* *Margot Fonteyn.*

happened and Astafieva could not take her,' says Alicia. 'I remember I took Margot.' Fonteyn also had the advantage of watching Alicia rehearse and in performance.

Alicia's sister Bunny entered the Vic-Wells school at more or less the same time as Fonteyn, and they became friends. Dame Beryl Grey remembers Bunny as a 'bright' dancer. She eventually graduated to dancing the lead in pantomime before giving it up for marriage. Alicia knew what it was like to be a child in an adult company and went out of her way to be nice to both girls.

Bunny clearly adored Alicia; she was her heroine. She bought a 'Whopper Scrapbook' in which to paste Alicia's press cuttings. She wrote across the cover 'First edition of a book on the famous ballerina Alicia Markova. Copyright 1934 by Berenice Barry.' She, too, took Barry as her professional name.

Bunny's book is a unique research tool as Alicia did not keep her cuttings – she was travelling so much she was unaware of many of them – and most of the publications in which they came out are long defunct and the archives destroyed. Unfortunately Bunny did not list the dates and names of the publications which makes tracing the original date difficult and, occasionally, impossible.

That year Alicia received a letter from a Madame Manya (a costumier of consummate skill who had made Pavlova's costumes, travelled with her and lived with her as her companion until the great lady's death) offering to make costumes for her. Madame Manya is credited with inventing the lightweight whalebone hoop used in the construction of tutus so that they do not wilt in the heat of the tropics. This may not seem much but it is a great deal to a dancer in the tropics – Madame Manya has been blessed on many a tropical tour.

When Pavlova died Manya, who was devoted to her, announced that she was hanging up her needle and thread and would never make another costume. Seeing Alicia dance changed her mind.

Madame Manya not only made Alicia's costumes but, later, her personal clothes as well. For Manya, making a costume meant seeing the whole ensemble through. She hand-painted designs, hand-sewed immaculately, cut, sprayed and dried.

Alicia's costumes were frequently jewelled and had to be covered with a mesh, invisible to the audience. During the lifts the costumes took some rough handling and if a bead became dislodged and fell on to the floor and she or her partner, or a member of the *corps*, trod on it, it could throw them on to their backs.

Manya stayed with Alicia for the next five years and would, in all probability, have stayed longer except for the intervention of the war which separated them.

Manya had an extraordinary life. She was Russian and had left her homeland and joined Pavlova in 1922. She could never return to Russia and never saw any of her family again. Pavlova took her on and assumed responsibility for her.

She and Alicia were both bombed out during the war and lost touch with each other. Alicia had been in America for years but when she returned she searched high and low for Manya without success. Eventually someone mentioned, casually, that Manya was working as a seamstress for Berman's, the theatrical costumiers. No one knew who she was. Alicia checked this out and found her.

She was living in a single room in Hampstead. Since her grasp of English was limited she was frightened because her documentation was not in order. She had never learnt to write in English. There had been no one with whom she could discuss her problems.

By then Alicia's sister Vivienne was working for the Civil Service and, at Alicia's request, she sorted out Manya's visa and passport problems.

Alicia stayed closely in touch with her till she died. Manya left her several pieces of Pavlova's furniture, which had been willed to her. She'd stored them lovingly in her one little room.

Alicia kept two white-wood chairs for herself, which are in her sitting room, usually piled high with papers and books, much, in all likelihood, as they would have been with their original owner. The rest are on permanent loan to the Royal Ballet School. 'I wanted them where they could be seen by students – Arnold Haskell advised me to do it.'

Meanwhile, at the Vic-Wells, the young Fonteyn learnt her craft, studying her elders. As she progressed Bunny took over the mime role in *The Haunted Ballroom* from her.

The star of the Vic-Wells prepared herself for *Swan Lake* in which she would be partnered by Robert Helpmann, who had just started spelling his name with two Ns, 'in order to make it seem more foreign'.

Opening on 20 November 1934 as a gala performance in aid of Queen Charlotte's Hospital, this was to be the first full-length, four-act, Western production of the ballet. Alicia had previously danced just the second act. There had been earlier, truncated versions but these had been rare and, hard as it is to believe now, it had been fourteen years since London had seen any version at all.

The first London production of the second act had been given in 1910 at the Hippodrome when Odette/Odile had been danced by

Olga Preobrajenska. Preobrajenska had dominated Russian ballet for the first twenty years of the century and had undertaken several world tours before, finally, settling in Paris as a teacher, becoming among the most celebrated.

'I used to see her when I was in Paris,' says Alicia. 'I never studied under her but there were times when I had to visit her. Naturally I always took her flowers. I would sit and watch while she taught. I had studied in Paris with Kschessinska, Trefilova and Egorova, so I couldn't study with her. But she was always nice.'

Sergeyev was again producing and they adopted the same rehearsal schedule as for *Giselle*. Alicia spent her mornings in seclusion with him before joining the cast for ensemble work. He had Kschessinska's choreology in his Marynsky notebooks. Again Alicia was taught choreography as near to the original as possible.

In her search for authenticity she took private lessons on the third act with Nicolai Legat. The original Marynsky production, using Petipa choreography, had been given in 1895 with Legnani as Odette/Odile. Legat claimed she had disclosed to him the secret of her famed *fouettés*. He now entrusted this to Alicia.

'I'd worked with Legat at the Palladium when I was twelve,' she says. 'Then, again, at the Ballet Russe. I called him again, he had a studio in Baron's Court. "Maestro," I said, "I need some help," which, of course, he understood. I went without a new dress to pay for those lessons. I knew my whole career could rest on it. The money I would have spent on the dress I gave to Legat and he prepared me for the Ballroom Act.

'You took every minute from those people you could – we all felt like that then, you listened to them – gained from their experience and the experiences of the great teachers they had had.

'In the White Act of *Swan Lake* I had been coached by Kschessinska, in Monte Carlo. Now, ten years later, I was with Legat for the Ballroom Act. The first person to dance *Swan Lake* after Legnani had been Kschessinska. Legat had also known Legnani and learnt the *fouettés* from her and then coached Kschessinska. That's how fortunate I was in that he was in London at that time. That's the man I went to.'

Dancing with Alicia was a thrill for Helpmann. As his biographer, Elizabeth Salter, puts it: 'To Helpmann, Markova was Pavlova all over again . . . As the doomed Odile, fluttering among her swans, embracing her lover with the sinuous elusiveness of a half human, she was real and unreal, a manifestation of Tchaikovsky's melodic torment, a creature of magic. Entranced he relived the hero worship of early adolescence. Markova, like Pavlova, was the embodiment of the classical dancer . . . The artist in Helpmann responded to an experience compared with which revue was an empty thing.'

'Last night the role of the Swan Queen was danced with surpassing grace and beauty by Markova. It is to be doubted if it has ever been done more perfectly.' – *Daily Telegraph*, 21 November 1934

Within a year, Alicia had introduced three classic ballets to the British – *Swan Lake*, *The Nutcracker* and the trailblazing *Giselle*.

When dancing Giselle she was protective of the wings she wore when she became transformed into a Wili, and took them home with her after a performance in a case. If they had been lost she would have been in trouble. One night she left them by mistake in a taxi. As she walked up the steps to her flat the driver bounded after her. 'You've left your wings,' he shouted, waving them.

Alicia's early success inspired other impresarios who now unleashed a stream of 'Baby Ballerinas' on the world. Colonel Vassily de Basil arrived in London that season with the company he had formed with René Blum.

The great René Blum was another of ballet's tragedies. 'I never heard anyone say a detrimental word against him,' says Alicia. He lived for his art and is described in the *Oxford Dictionary of Ballet* as 'a man of exceptional culture and immaculate taste. It is partly due to him that so much of the Diaghileff heritage has been conserved so faithfully.' He had been part of the Ballet Russe when Massine had tried to persuade Alicia to join him.

He was Jewish and, during the war, was deported to the concentration camp at Auschwitz and killed.

Among the Colonel's dancers were fifteen-year-old Irina Baronova, who was born in Petrograd and was a Preobrajenska pupil in Paris. After creating roles in several Massine ballets, she went on to become a ballerina of the Ballet Theatre in America and appeared in several films.

Moscow-born Tatiana Riabouchinska was seventeen and had studied with Kschessinska and created roles for Balanchine. She eventually married David Lichine and they opened a successful ballet school in Los Angeles.

Tamara Toumanova was born on a train somewhere near Shanghai and was also seventeen when she appeared with the de Basil company. She created numerous roles, some for Balanchine, and became a movie star, appearing in, among other films, Hitchcock's

Torn Curtain, Invitation to the Dance with Gene Kelly, and Billy Wilder's *The Private Life of Sherlock Holmes*.

This Hollywood career was not hampered by her marriage to screenwriter Casey Robinson. 'They all wanted to be in movies,' recalls Alicia. 'Hollywood had arrived and there was the glamour and the big money. There was never any big money to be made in ballet.'

The yearning for money was not surprising. The girls could not return to Russia and wanted as much security as possible.

All these glowing careers were inspired by Markova. It is doubtful if any company would have offered the public juvenile dancers in leading roles had she not blazed the trail. She was the first 'Baby Ballerina', although Diaghileff had had too much style to use the term. 'It gave me rather a strange position in life,' she says.

Colonel de Basil himself was wildly charismatic, the like of whom could only be found in ballet. Born in Kaunas in 1888 he claimed to have been a Cossack officer, and may well have been, before changing careers to become assistant to Prince Zeretelli, who was organizing the London and Paris seasons of Russian opera. In 1932 he had launched his 'Baby Ballerinas' on the world with all the panoply of a ringmaster.

They returned to Covent Garden in the summer of 1934. Yet, for all de Basil's flair, he could not dethrone Markova:

'If you want to see a packed theatre and an audience beside itself, go to Sadler's Wells on any ballet night when . . . the prima ballerina is Alicia Markova. Last night was typical. Markova had been on the stage for only a minute or two . . . when the audience went mad. They had good reason. There may be, and there may have been, better dancers than Markova, but I for one don't believe it.' – *Evening News*, 27 March 1935

The following item by Adrian Stokes also appeared in the press at that time:

'Alicia Markova is dancing at Sadler's Wells and the Old Vic throughout the winter . . . This English girl is a ballerina of the first rank . . . Her performances possess that ease in execution to which the adjective "consummate" may be willingly applied. Such an ease in dancing may be obtained only by a dancer possessing great pertinacity, experience and, at the same time, youth. Markova is still very young although her training and achievements are extensive . . . Markova possesses beautiful feet and beautiful legs, the comparison of these respects with Pavlova is constantly made and with good reason.

'Markova's physical virtues are emphasised, it is true, at Sadler's Wells . . . I believe that Markova's technique today, and she is dancing this year even better than last, outshines that of the Russian ballerinas whom we saw at Covent Garden this summer . . .

'The babes Toumanova and Baronova cannot yet produce an equal fluency. It is as if the very forms of their bodies and the disposition of their weight were not yet fully settled. Riabouchinska alone inspires a confidence similar to that one we owe to Markova.

'For these reasons a visit to Sadler's Wells to see Markova is strongly recommended.'

It seemed, too, that a visit to the cinema would also soon be recommended for the same reasons. Journalist John W. Newnham reported:

'HOLLYWOOD WANTS MARKOVA

'I hear that she has received offers from two of the biggest studios over there and there is an extreme likelihood that she will accept one of these offers if the tests are satisfactory. At the time of writing, however, nothing definite has been fixed and the whole matter is somewhat in the air. Her name has been mentioned in connection with the role of Pavlova in the film to be made of Pavlova's life and this, I fancy, was one of the offers she received. It would be difficult to find anyone more suitable for the part in looks or ability. But it is not likely that the offer will be accepted. I don't know the real reason why not but I can hazard a guess that Markova would not be keen on portraying such a world famed figure as Pavlova. I think she would be wise not to do so. If she has a film career in mind this wouldn't help much. The screen Pavlova will be a one picture star. It's nearly always the way in these cases. Markova would certainly be a noteworthy edition to the roster of screen stars.'

Alicia never became part of the roster of screen stars although she was to make a film in Hollywood. But her name was added to the roster of ballet biographies written by Cyril Beaumont, the critic in whose bookshop she had studied. He had published a selection of ballet biographies but she was the first English dancer he favoured. The book cost 3s 6d – and in those days that was a fair price. The cost of seats in Sadler's Wells varied from 6d to 6s, and dinner at the Savoy cost 6s.

A feature film of Pavlova's life has never been made, despite numerous plans. Alicia was offered the part and turned it down. Firstly she was too busy dancing and, secondly, because: 'I thought it was too early to pay homage to her. When Fokine eventually choreographed *The Dying Swan* for me I had said, "No, no, no, no." Then Sol Hurok tried to persuade me, too. When I did agree to dance it, it was only on the condition that every programme carried a printed notice that it was done in memory of Pavlova.'

The thought of acting on the screen did not worry Alicia. As she says, she acted in ballet all the time. Cyril Beaumont, among others, had praised her for it: 'With *Giselle* you have to act while dancing and dance while acting.'

'That was how I felt,' she says. 'Either a role appealed to me or it didn't. The first question I would ask when a new ballet was discussed was, "What's the role?" I never wanted to be me, I always enjoyed interpreting someone, or something, entirely different.

'I know I became typecast towards romantic ballets, which I adored, but I also loved things like *Bar aux Folies-Bergère* and *Façade*. As long as I could interpret what the choreographer had in mind, I was happy.

'I think that was one of the reasons why I decided to retire when I did. I had danced most characters I felt I wanted to. There were two ballets, maybe three, that were discussed and which I never did but would have liked to have done but we never got around to doing.

'One idea I discussed with Roland Petit was *Wuthering Heights*, which he wanted to do for me and Hugh Laing. That appealed tremendously but it never came about because I retired. Then there was *Pelléas et Mélisande*. Maggie Teyte, who was a good friend, saw me in *Romeo and Juliet* at the Met and said to Antony Tudor, "Why don't you give a thought to Alicia as Mélisande?" We started to discuss it but then I left the company and other things took over.'

By 1935 Doris was still in *Revudeville* at the Windmill and, naturally, the whole company knew she was Markova's sister. She urged Vivian Van Damm, the Windmill's manager, to see Alicia in *Swan Lake* at Sadler's Wells.

Van Damm was a man of great entrepreneurial experience but was unacquainted with ballet. Alicia was his first experience. She

151

knocked him out cold. He described it as 'an evening in fairyland
. . . every ballet fan will know how I felt at witnessing, almost for
the first time, such crystallised perfection of music and drama.'*

He was also impressed by the mighty applause she received and
suggested she tour for him, forming a company of which she would
be a leading part, the body made up of Vic-Wells dancers. He was
keen not to compete with the Wells but to 'link up with them for
a brief season; and – more important still – we should bring ballet
to the great provincial cities.'* He proposed they devise a first-class
company which, before touring, would provide a short West End
season.

Van Damm wrote in his memoirs: 'Before we parted company
that night I was in the grip of a great enthusiasm. I am not the sort
of showman who can enthuse entirely about petty matters, and here
was a nation-wide plan – something worth achieving, surely?' Later
he added, 'The true purpose of our plan would be defeated if the
ballet company taken out throughout Britain was not the best that
Britain herself could provide.'*

There was enthusiasm for his idea among the dancers as the
season was coming to a close and it would provide work. Sadler's
Wells usually remained dark between seasons. Apart from the mice,
that is, who moved in in droves. When the dancers moved back, it
was a trial of strength to see who would win the territory. The mice
nibbled their way through most things, costumes included. Alicia
was terrified of them. Big dippers she found enjoyable, spiders,
even tropical ones, she will easily dispose of with a glass and a
card, but she was petrified by mice.

Van Damm set about finding a backer. He did not have to
look far. The Windmill was owned by Mrs Laura Henderson, a
wealthy, eccentric widow who happened to love ballet. She agreed
to finance the project. But things did not work out that simply. As
Alicia says:

'He asked me if I would like a company of my own but, at first, I
said I was happy with what we were doing at the Wells with Lilian
Baylis and Ninette. The star thing did not appeal to me, although
I knew the value of my own work. I needed the settings that the
Wells could provide.

'But what always bothered me was when the season closed, the
gap between May and September. People had to get jobs where they
could and you just hoped they'd be able to come back for the new
season. Sometimes they couldn't.

* *Tonight and Every Night* by Vivian Van Damm, Stanley Paul, 1952.

'I told Van Damm he would have to speak to Lilian Baylis and Ninette to see if he could take the company out with me and fill up that gap. All the business side of things took place between him and Miss Baylis. It wasn't just that he saw me and arranged things, it wasn't as easy as that.

'Once he knew we would be available he got on to Moss Empires and the Howard Wyndham group who owned the theatres around the country. I knew he would be very good at that, that was his business. I just danced and left people who knew what they were doing to get on with the rest.'

Van Damm had seen Helpmann with Alicia and wanted to enlist him as principal male dancer but was thwarted by Helpmann's decision to enter the Hassard Short revue, *Stop Press*, at the Adelphi. If this did well he expected to tour America with it. Hassard Short was later to present Alicia in *The Merry Widow* on Broadway.

Van Damm acknowledges that it was Alicia who suggested Dolin to him as a substitute. It was a lucky break for Van Damm who also acknowledges the enormous support Dolin gave him both in front of the footlights and behind. But for that, he felt, there would have been no touring company.

Lilian Baylis was not difficult to persuade. She and Mrs Henderson, two formidable theatrical ladies, understood each other at once. Van Damm was relieved at the outcome. 'I was frankly apprehensive and expected fireworks,' he writes.* Miss Baylis made her usual condition that the Vic-Wells be recognized in all publicity and Mrs Henderson was happy to accede.

'Good luck to you,' Van Damm recalls Miss Baylis saying when the details had been ironed out. 'I think you will do much good for British ballet but you will lose a fortune.'* She was right on both counts.

Ninette de Valois had not been so easy to convince. For her own reasons she did not want the Vic-Wells to tour at that time; possibly she was worried that standards might drop for the touring company would be performing eight times a week. Fortunately she did not have the last word as Lilian Baylis overruled her. De Valois accepted the situation and was not unhelpful.

She was actually unwell at the time and, shortly afterwards, repaired to hospital for a serious operation.

Mrs Henderson agreed to underwrite an extended season at Sadler's Wells, which would continue the scheduled season, and after that a week's season at the old Shaftesbury Theatre, during

---

* *Tonight and Every Night.*

which they could run-in the tour repertoire, followed by a five-week tour of the provinces playing major theatres on the Howard and Wyndham circuit. The Vic-Wells would not run any financial risk as Mrs Henderson guaranteed the expenses. The new development was under the aegis of 'Van Damm Productions', the nucleus of which was Mrs Henderson, Van Damm and Alicia.

Alicia was keen that Constant Lambert travel with them. He was, after all, the Musical Director of the Vic-Wells and played a large part in its artistic output. He agreed to conduct the orchestra and Van Damm set up a dinner party to discuss details. The guests included Dolin and Mrs Henderson. Mrs Henderson was described by dancer Keith Lester as 'a little old lady who owned a theatre in London and a repulsive Pekinese dog and had a deep love of dancing'. She was also, according to Van Damm, a Tartar who would sometimes take against one of the Windmill girls for seemingly no reason. When this happened the girl's life could be made a misery. She was also shrewd and not unsympathetic to a good cause, provided she was not being taken for a ride.

At the coffee stage, when the finances were being mooted, Lambert, engrossed in the project, lit up a cigar. The meeting nearly closed prematurely. Van Damm recalls: 'To the general astonishment and my horror, up bounced Mrs Henderson. "I never sit at table with anybody who smokes cigars," she burst out. Constant Lambert was obviously taken aback, and most distressed. "I'm so sorry, Mrs Henderson, I had no idea—" he began. "Well, that's all right then," she said, and promptly sat down again.'*

During the extended Wells season Alicia premiered another de Valois ballet which had been timed for Van Damm's tour. *The Rake's Progress*, music by Gavin Gordon and décor by Rex Whistler, opened on 20 May 1935 to a capacity audience with over 400 standing. Ninette de Valois had been inspired by a collection of Hogarth's paintings she had seen in Sir John Soane's Museum.

She had to be consulted during rehearsals and, as she was still in hospital, would receive company members, and Van Damm, propped up in bed surrounded by flowers.

De Valois had conceived the role of the Rake for Helpmann but as he was still in revue Walter Gore took over and was given just two days to prepare for it. To help things along, fate decreed he had to have a painful wisdom tooth extracted at this time. 'I was afraid he would collapse at any moment,' recalls Alicia. *The Rake* turned out to be one of de Valois's most successful ballets. The *Daily Sketch*

* *Tonight and Every Night.*

commented on 22 May 1935: 'Markova, as the Betrayed Girl, was her exquisite self – a delight . . .'

Van Damm had issued Alicia with a year's contract which allowed her to dance also at the Wells.

Immediately after the Shaftesbury season, which was a sell-out, she was joined by Dolin and they toured Britain, including the cities of Blackpool, Manchester, Glasgow, Edinburgh, and Bournemouth. 'Together, Markova and Dolin were superb,' writes Van Damm.

In Bournemouth there were a few difficulties backstage and Van Damm noted: '[there were] disputes which showed me for the first time that ballet people must be handled with kid gloves, and not even chastened with a feather duster.'

He recalled that Dolin had warned him: 'Don't run away with the idea that all ballet dancers are nice, charming, human people, out to help their fellow artists. They're not.'

The tour was a risk. Ballet was still largely unknown outside London. Mrs Henderson could have lost a fortune. It took nerve also on the parts of Alicia and Dolin; they could have played to empty houses. No one knew what the audience reaction would be.

When the company hit the road every theatre on the circuit was packed out. The Vic-Wells was the first ballet company to perform in the provinces since Diaghileff, and the first British company ever. Audiences gave them standing ovations every night. Alicia's performances in the classics were compared in the press to 'moonlight on a rippling stream'.

The success of the tour brought home to Dolin and Alicia the fact that they could fill theatres on their names alone.

Van Damm also realized this and it caused trouble. Alicia was under contract to Van Damm, and wanted to work with him, but de Valois was once again ensconced at Sadler's Wells and waiting for Alicia to lead the new season.

Dolin, too, was under contract to Van Damm and was able to stay with him. But without Alicia he was in the lurch. A splendid dancer, he had been a star before Alicia but she had now eclipsed him. On his own admission, it was Alicia the public came to see.

Helpmann had developed, literally, in leaps and bounds. De Valois felt optimistic about his future with the Vic-Wells. He had returned with his tail between his legs after his revue had ingloriously folded. There had been no American trip and no West End success. He was banging on de Valois's door and she was only too eager to let him in. With Helpmann in the company de Valois would have to relinquish Dolin's services as she could not afford two premier male dancers.

Alicia was obviously keen to dance with Dolin, and de Valois felt, perhaps, it was time to cut the cord that artistically bound them and release her. Alicia had been paramount in helping to establish the company; now it was only fair she should be allowed to go her own way. De Valois would build Fonteyn into her prima ballerina.

After much deliberation, harsh letters, tears and threats of litigation between nearly everyone involved, the situation was eventually defused.

Fonteyn had been part of the Vic-Wells tour. As they had been performing eight times a week, Alicia could not dance everything, and had already taught Fonteyn *The Haunted Ballroom* and *Rendezvous*. De Valois was philosophical about losing Markova and Dolin:

'She and Dolin thought they were old enough to go out on their own,' she says. 'And I had people like Helpmann and Fonteyn coming up, so it was a natural change-over. They were getting famous and they wanted to get on with their own lives. There was a perfectly good friendship between us, there always has been, and there was no trouble.'*

Alicia was under contract to Van Damm and not the Vic-Wells. She decided to part from the Vic-Wells and take part in the formation of a new company.

While this was taking place both Dolin and Alicia slipped away for holidays. Van Damm had told them it would be best to go now as it would be all systems go when the new company came into being. Before leaving, Dolin took an engagement at the Grosvenor House Hotel with C. B. Cochran's revue where, to the accompaniment of Larry Adler's mouth organ, he danced his celebrated 'Bolero'.

'Bolero' had caused controversy. Van Damm had wanted to include it in the Shaftesbury season but certain experts considered it too 'music hall'. He had removed it and inserted it in the following tour. It invariably brought the house down.

When they returned, Dolin and Alicia helped Van Damm select dancers for the new company. Among those they chose were Wendy Toye, Keith Lester, Frederic Franklin, Stanley Judson, and Molly Lake – all dancers with nowhere else to dance now that the season had ended.

The repertoire was to be a mixture of new works and classical including *Swan Lake* and *The Nutcracker*, produced for them by

* Interview with Ninette de Valois, 1994.

Sergeyev; *Giselle* in an adaptation staged after the Sergeyev version; Fokine's *Le Carnaval* and *Les Sylphides*. This time the company was to bear their names – 'The Markova-Dolin Company'. Dolin was a co-director with Alicia.

13

The Markova-Dolin Company

☙❦❧

It was not all celebration. When Ashton heard of Alicia's alliance with Dolin he felt hurt. He did not speak to her for some time. He had always treasured their association and could not bring himself gladly to accept the new company.

Then, one day, he rang Alicia out of the blue. He told her he thought he had been silent for 'long enough'. She was delighted to hear from him. From then on they resumed their friendship.

As stars of the new company, both Alicia and Dolin each received a salary of £40 a week, but out of this they had to pay for their living expenses, including meals and hotels. But as most hotels were well under £1 a night she would be comfortable enough.

The Markova-Dolin Company was to feature a front cloth by Jacob Epstein. Epstein was fascinated by Alicia all his life, particularly her hands, which he wanted to sculpt. She, however, was always too busy to sit for him.

Among the modern works to be performed by the Markova-Dolin Company were *Aucassin and Nicolette* and *Show Folk*. It also premiered new dances by Keith Lester.

Lester was a former pupil of Astafieva, Fokine and Legat and had studied with Dolin. He had danced with Karsavina, Spessivtseva and Ida Rubinstein and was now keen to choreograph. In this capacity he had created an abstract ballet for Alicia to Bach's music, and two other ballets for the company, *David* and *Death in Adagio*.

David was a vehicle for Dolin. The music was by Maurice Jacobson who, a few years later in 1937, was to feature in another musical first. He was adjudicating at a competition in Carlisle when a beautiful young contralto sang Quilter's 'To Daisies'. She had only entered to win a bet and ended up winning the competition. Her name was Kathleen Ferrier and she became one of Britain's most beloved singers.

Death in Adagio is set to Scarlatti's music and was written specially for Alicia. It tells the modern tale of a blonde homicidal typist who murders her victims with the aid of a poisoned typewriter ribbon. As Alicia says, 'It made a change from *Giselle*.'

These were *avant-garde* works, new enough to challenge London audiences, but they were aimed at the provinces.

Freddie Franklin was a member of the Markova-Dolin Company. He had already toured the provinces, as part of an act with Dolin and Wendy Toye, some years previously. He and Dolin were among the first male dancers to appear in music hall and he still carries painful memories, not to say scars, of those days:

'Pat was twenty-eight, Wendy was fifteen and I was eighteen. We managed to get a job on a number-two northern touring show called *King Follie*. It included Leeds, Newcastle, and Glasgow.

'We used to follow a comedian called Billy Dennis, who was billed "Almost a Gentleman", who told lewd stories. Then we'd come on dancing the Cucaracha. There was a band of musicians behind us with accordions – a bunch of cut-throats. They were all glowering. It was terrifying.

'I got the bird every night. I would stand in the wings, terrified, waiting to go on. At the weekends the audience was always drunk. I opened the act with a piece entitled "Ballet Mécanique" wearing all-over white tights decorated with nails.

"Look at him!" they'd shout. "Here, you've got your knickers on, mate!" I'd be doing my big *jetés* around the stage – oh, terrified. We used to dread it. They'd never seen ballet before let alone a man in tights. Believe me, it was a different era.

'Wendy and Pat would be standing in the wings, knowing they had to come on. Wendy and I did a garden scene together, then she would run and look for Pat who entered with his back to the audience.

'You'd hear them shout, "He's over here, missus!" We got it all. Pat came off swearing every night.

'We were followed by a lady snake charmer and Wendy had to share the dressing room with her. The snake was in a box, and Wendy would be changing with this huge python curled up next to her. The room had to be kept very hot for the snake.

'Things were a bit better in London but it was only revue or cabaret. Sometimes we did five shows a day, changing in taxis as we moved from one venue to the next. One night I remember doing the Grosvenor House Follies, the Garrick and the New Theatre, where we danced to an organ. The theatre was so big we danced to the echo, it was all we could hear.

'It was impossible to get work in ballet. I'd tour the agents and they were very nice but there was no ballet in Britain. In the end I had to go to Paris where I saw a job advertised at the Casino de Paris. Josephine Baker was the star.

'I was amazed when I got there to see that Harold Turner had also applied. He was a brilliant virtuoso, especially in character roles, and I knew him from the *Dancing Times*, a marvellous dancer. He got dressed to perform and this lady came to him and said, "Oh, Mr Turner, there's nothing for you." I was mortified. If he had no job, what chance was there for me?

'She then asked me if I did tap and I said yes. I was so poor I had no practice clothes and I had to dance in what I wore. She demonstrated a step and asked me to do it, so I did, then she showed me some more and I did them. She asked me where I had learnt the steps and I said, "From you, you've just showed me." "You've never done them before?" she asked. "No," I said. "What you show me, I do." I got a job at the end of the line.

'I joined the Markova-Dolin Company because Pat took me to one side one day, you know how domineering he was, and told me it was time I took my career "seriously". I said, "Yes, Mr Dolin." "Right," he said. "Alicia and I are forming a company and you're in it." I said, "Thank you, Mr Dolin."

'That was it. It was very much forelock-pulling time, it was very much Mr Dolin and Miss Markova.'

Alicia's absence was felt deeply at the Vic-Wells. The company experienced something close to panic when she left. Although it gave Fonteyn her big break, and forced her forward, she was far from confident at the time.

'Markova was both my inspiration and my despair,' she later wrote. 'From the point of view of her career I can see why Markova decided to leave the Vic-Wells in 1935 and form her own company with Anton Dolin. She was too far ahead of our company, and she could not afford to wait for us.

'In England Marie Rambert, the Camargo Society and Lilian Baylis furnished the only opportunities, but none of them could provide an adequate home for a fully fledged ballerina. It is one of my greatest pieces of good fortune that I was exactly the right age to be able to develop coincidentally with the Vic-Wells Ballet. I was like a surfer riding a particularly long wave and it was Markova's departure that launched me . . .

'The news of Markova's impending departure threw me into despair. "Whatever will happen to us without Markova? . . ." Many people thought, as I did, that the company was finished.'*

The Markova-Dolin Company opened to a tremendous reception in Newcastle on 11 November 1935. Freddie Franklin was there and, to his surprise, was promoted to soloist, partnering Markova in *Carnaval*.

'I made my debut as a soloist on the opening night of the Markova-Dolin Company dancing Harlequin with Markova as Columbine. Suddenly, there I am on stage with Markova. I was terrified to touch her. I really didn't partner her, but I lifted her or supported one arm.

'She was a piece of steel. The body was so worked it was like iron. When I touched her, or took her hand, it wasn't a little, limp thing, it was a HAND.

'After the curtain came down Mr Dolin called me back to his dressing room and I thought this is it. It's all been a disaster and they're shipping me back to London. When I got there Mr Van Damm was also there with Alicia. He said to me, "After tonight's performance we've all decided you will be Mr Dolin's understudy, you will dance with Miss Markova when required and your salary will go up by £5 a week." I said, "Thank you, Mr Van Damm."

'Alicia never said much to me then, she was very quiet, but when she did speak it meant something and you had to do it. She would say, "I suggest you do this, or that . . . ," it was all about dance. We were not on a friendly level at that time, that developed later.

'But she was very friendly with Wendy Toye and would stand up for her. When certain roles came up she would say, "Wendy must do this," and she did.

'Markova was streets ahead of the rest of us, there was no question of it. She was England's only ballerina. It came from all that training with Diaghileff. I first saw her dance, in Liverpool, with the Diaghileff Ballet when I was fourteen. It played to standing houses. The audience for the Ballet Russe was quite different to the audiences I had played to in music hall. But whatever aura she had then was not so definite, that built up through the years.

'Later on the tour, as I came to know Alicia, I would say to her, "We're the pioneers of ballet, like the early settlers. We're the covered wagons."'

* *Margot Fonteyn.*

*   *   *

'As a dancer, Miss Markova approaches nearer to the thistledown lightness of Pavlova than any other I have seen . . . her exquisite performance in *Les Sylphides* was a good approximation to that ethereal defiance of the laws of gravity.' (The *Spectator*)

Apart from Markova and Dolin there were two reasons for the company's success. Firstly it was British, and promoted this. Secondly the choice of repertoire was popular. The new works highlighted the particular skills of the dancers, such as Dolin's 'Water Lily', a solo he had choreographed for Alicia which displayed her romantic expressiveness.

While on tour Alicia and Dolin met up with Adeline Genée and, over dinner, she regaled them with stories of her heyday. Censorship had forbidden her from dancing with a man when she had been at the Empire, she told them, and she had had to partner a female in male attire. Male dancers were considered effeminate. Dolin replied that he had put an end to that sort of thing by presenting such a masculine figure on stage.

About this time Alicia acquired a permanent dresser. Previously she and Dolin had shared a married couple, but the constant travelling was too much for them. Her new dresser was Silva Mortimer, formerly an actress in silent films.

Morty, as everyone called her, became a dresser quite suddenly. It had happened when she had been walking down Charing Cross Road one day and met a Mr Lestocq, a producer friend who was now manager of the Windmill. Morty confessed 'talkies' had ruined her career. She had no work.

Lestocq told her that the Windmill needed a wardrobe mistress. She took the job. At the Windmill Doris told Morty that Alicia needed a dresser on tour. Morty joined Alicia on the road and her daughter Edna, a former Tiller Girl, took over from her at the Windmill.

Morty stayed until she retired, and then Edna took over and remained with Alicia for the rest of her dancing career. She still helps if Alicia has a special function. 'I feel I've never left her,' she says.

The first thing that strikes the eye when visiting Edna's flat is a large painting of Alicia as the Dying Swan. 'Markova was the greatest ballerina this country has ever produced,' she says. There can be no argument. 'People tell me I'm biased but I'm not.

'We've never had a cross word although I knew her moods. If she wanted to be quiet I kept quiet and if she wanted to chat I chatted. Once she was in her dressing room she was dedicated to what was coming up. *Giselle* always took it out of her, she lived that ballet.'

Doris and Vivienne could vouch for that. Alicia's placid equilibrium might be strained on the day she was to dance *Giselle*. 'We called it "D Day",' says Doris.

'She was never one to complain,' Edna continues. 'But she insisted on taking a sleep in the afternoon if she was dancing that evening. Remember, she danced five full ballets a week then and *divertissements* on Saturdays, because of packing up. She never had a night off no matter if she had a cold or felt ill. Ballerinas today don't know they're living, doing just one performance for thousands of pounds.

'Markova had a marvellous stage presence. I remember once we were appearing at the State Cinema, Kilburn, an enormous place. It was a matinée and there were lots of kids in the audience. Dolin was dancing "Bolero", which did go on a bit, and there was some giggling among the kids. He wasn't best pleased. "Can't someone keep these children quiet," he snapped as he came off.

'Markova was in the wings waiting to go on and when she started to dance you could hear a pin drop. It was a wonderful moment. I told her so when she came off and she just gave a little smile. She took it all in her stride.

'Like the time I was with her in Paris when she was dancing *Giselle*. French stage hands are a pretty hard lot, a law unto themselves, they've no souls. But when she was dancing I saw one of them crying into his handkerchief. That was something to see, this hard man crying at her dancing. I told her that when she came off but, again, she just smiled.

'She had a wonderful sense of music. In those days musicians used to put in deputies if they had engagements elsewhere. I used to live in the same house as an oboist and he told me one day that he'd see me at Covent Garden that night as he was "depping" for another musician.

'As soon as she came off stage that night, Markova knew something was different with the oboe. I told her what had happened. She was fine then, she was just curious. She was the same with the lighting, and spoke up at once if anyone altered the pattern just a fraction. No wonder she became a marvellous director herself. There's nothing about the stage she doesn't know.'

Once Alicia was in her dressing room she was dedicated to the performance, nothing else existed. Organization was the keynote.

Firstly she would select which shoes she would wear. There were always half a dozen new pairs waiting for her and she would try them on. Once she chose a pair she would sew on the securing ribbons herself.

When this was done she would take off her street clothes, put on a dressing gown, and start to make up. Her make-up would be applied with military precision; she was, after all, going into battle. She never overdid the facial effects as can some dancers.

When her make-up was done she would warm up for fifteen minutes then fit her headdress. This was a specialized manoeuvre as it had to be secured with no visible means of support, yet had to remain stable throughout the most energetic movements. Fitting her headdress was a skill that relied on years of experience. As Dolin put it, 'A garland of roses knocked over one eye is enough to kill any romantic ballet.'

Finally she would put on her costume. Once this was done she had to remain standing or it would crease. The whole transformation took about two hours.

In plenty of time she would walk to the wings and await her cue. 'Sometimes my stomach was knotted with nerves,' Alicia says. 'But I never let it show. No one knew.' To the cast and crew she was inscrutable. No one knew of the inferno blazing beneath the tulle.

She was secure in what she was doing. She did not worry about what was to come, just made her mind a blank, then 'went for it. Sometimes I might get in an extra pirouette in a difficult movement. I would sometimes see other dancers working on pieces before they went on and they might topple over. I thought, Why bother?, by that time there's nothing you can do. I just hoped for the best.'

Alicia had been taught about lighting by Diaghileff. She had often sat in empty theatres with him while he explained sequences, and she was meticulous about her own lighting.

During one performance the lighting had not been up to scratch. An effect had been ruined by wrong cues. She was furious as she stood centre-stage afterwards, surrounded by flowers, a bouquet of white orchids in her arms, and took several curtain calls.

When the curtain came down for the final time the stage hands carried her bouquets to her room, while she still held the orchids. She carefully laid these on the floor, and walked to the electrician.

He watched her coming.

No one knew what passed between them since, as always, her voice was not raised. 'He listened to what I had to say,' she says. 'Then quietly told me, "I accept all you say, madame, I know it's right, but what do you expect for 7s 6d a night?" It stopped me in my tracks. He had a point when you think of what I was earning. They didn't get much, I know, but, even so, I told him he should get it right.'

Among the dancers recruited by the Markova-Dolin Company was Beryl Kaye. In *Giselle* she was one of the Wilis, a phantom in filmy drapes. At one point in the ballet, while Alicia was dancing, she was stationed near the gravestone.

'I had a cold during one performance,' Miss Kaye recalls. 'And it left me with a hacking cough. I did my best to stifle it but it was hard work and once or twice I couldn't help letting go, it sounded as though I might be in the grave next. No one in the audience seemed to notice it, thank God, but Alicia heard. The next day she came in waving a bottle of cough mixture. "Who's the girl with the cough?" she asked. "Tell her to take this."'

Alicia was regularly sought out if medical attention was needed. 'I carried the first-aid kit,' she remembers, 'so it would make sense that I'd come in with cough mixture. People were always coming to me if something was wrong. I tried to take care of myself so I carried medication. If there were any emergencies people came banging on my door.'

She was not just called on for medical emergencies, either. She could be handy with a screwdriver, prepared to have a go at any rate. She was called upon to sort out faulty bathroom plumbing and other practical difficulties. Even now, if something goes wrong in the flat, Doris will shout for Alicia to sort it out.

While dancing *Giselle* with Dolin in Birmingham she found that the stage was slippery. 'I had to make an entrance carrying a bunch of lilies,' she says. 'I would leap up and throw them to Albrecht. Just as I took off, my foot slipped and I landed on my back. I was still holding two lilies in the air. Dolin came leaping up and nearly landed on top of me. "Are you all right, duckie?" he asked. I couldn't stop laughing, it was probably hysteria, so I muttered, "Just help me up."'

The audience had been as shocked as she, and there had been a stunned silence.

She had given her head a harder thump than she realized. That night, at one in the morning, she awoke with toothache. It ached the rest of the night. She could not sleep and she was giving a matinée that afternoon.

She went to a dentist in the morning and was told she had shattered a tooth when her head had hit the stage. An immediate extraction was performed. This was done under anaesthetic and, by the time she left the surgery, it was time to go to the theatre.

She was still partially under the effects of the gas while she danced. It was strange dancing a spectre while feeling not of this world herself.

In the new year the company returned to London where Alicia danced *Giselle* in a twelve-week season at the Duke of York's in a new production with new costumes.

For the first act she wore her hair in ringlets, which were put in by a hairdresser with tongs heated in a portable stove. But by the end of the mad scene her hair had straightened out which was convenient for the second act where a more sober style was required. Spessivtseva had dipped her head in a bucket of water to get the right effect.

The Duke of York season was followed by yet another tour. It was suggested by her fellow directors, Dolin among them, that *Giselle* be dropped. It was not box-office like the other classics. Alicia was outvoted three to one.

At a further meeting, in Leeds, it was again voted that *Giselle* be dropped. Alicia, again, pleaded for it to stay but the others would not hear of it.

Everyone was in her dressing room, which had a balcony, at the time. She threatened that if *Giselle* were not reinstated she would jump off. She ran to the balcony and opened the door to show she meant business. It was a long way to the ground.

Van Damm nearly had a heart attack.

Giselle stayed.

It is doubtful, in the cold light of day, that anyone could have believed she would jump, but the shock tactic worked. Everyone was aware that the tour would have had a very unhappy ballerina on its hands if *Giselle* had gone, and no one wanted that. Goodwill was essential.

It would have been educative for American writer Carl van Vechten to have seen her balcony scene. He wrote: 'It has been said of Markova that never, under any circumstances or on any occasion, has a hair of her head been discovered out of place.'

'People are always saying that about me,' she says. 'I never thought about it.' A few hairs were out of place that day.

Freddie Franklin was part of the new tour as Dolin's understudy. He soon discovered this meant that he was never sure of what he was dancing until he arrived at the theatre.

'I remember one day in Brighton I walked into the dressing room I shared with the boys and saw a Blue Bird costume lying there. I thought Wardrobe had laid out the wrong clothes as I didn't dance the Blue Bird.

'Then there was a knock at the door and Mr Dolin walked in. "Freddie, dear," he said. "You're on tonight in *The Blue Bird*." "What, Mr Dolin?" I asked. "There's the costume," he said. "Now go down to the stage and do a couple of pirouettes with Markova." Well, the boys looked at me and I looked at them. "Get into the costume," he said.

'So I went down and Alicia was wonderful. "Now Freddie, dear," she said. "We're just going to do a couple of pirouettes." We did one, two and three. "Fine," she said. I hadn't lifted her, I hadn't put her on my shoulder, I hadn't done a thing.

'The entire company was in the wings when we went on. Well, she didn't end up in the pit and I didn't drop her and I did my solo. When I finished Pat said, "Freddie, dear, the end was wonderful." And that's about all he said. The whole thing was incredible. She thanked me and I thanked her and we both went to our dressing rooms and got ready for the next bit.

'If you let nerves get the better of you then half your energy's gone and you need that energy. Danilova used to say, "Ice cold here," tapping her head. "Warm heart and lots of personality."

'*Aucassin and Nicolette* was usually danced by Dolin and Alicia, and I was one of the boys. One Friday, Dolin told me I was doing his part in the Saturday matinée, so I rehearsed it. He watched me, then he said, "We're playing tennis on Saturday morning at ten, be there." "Oh, Mr Dolin," I said, "I don't think I can, I'm dancing that day." "You're playing tennis at ten," he said. So I arrived and thought, What am I doing playing tennis when I've got to dance with Markova this afternoon? He did it on purpose to wear me out. He was a terrible man, but I loved him.

'I never really rehearsed with Alicia. I was thrown on. The only exception had been *Carnaval*, I did rehearse that, but normally I was in the throwing-on department. But Alicia copes with that, she's had to do it herself. She's been thrown on in certain things, too. She always wanted me to know what the pitfalls were and what the difficulties would be before we started, but that was all. These days people do weeks of preparations but we were often thrown on.'

One evening, back in London, Dolin had a few friends round to his flat and one of them commented on a framed lithograph on his wall which depicted four historic ballerinas – Taglioni, Cerrito, Grisi and Grahn. It was entitled 'Pas de Quatre'.

Someone suggested he devise a ballet with four ballerinas impersonating the styles of the dancers in the lithograph. Keith Lester choreographed the piece and the music was based on a composition by the nineteenth-century Italian composer Cesare Pugni.

Dolin told Alicia he wanted her to dance Taglioni, that great exponent of *pointe* ballet. Unfortunately, when the ballet was premiered, in Manchester in May 1936, Alicia was committed to other works and the role was danced by Cornish dancer Molly Lake, whom both Dolin and Alicia had known for years as she, too, had been an Astafieva pupil.

London was awash with ballet that summer. Colonel de Basil and his Baby Ballerinas were at Covent Garden. Mikhail Fokine, Diaghileff's right-hand man until they had quarrelled about Nijinsky, was at the Alhambra with the Blum company in *Don Juan*, and the Markova-Dolin company was at a vast cinema in Streatham.

Many in the audience still believed Markova was Russian. At the end of a performance Dolin would sometimes make a curtain speech. 'We'd take the bow and Pat would lead me to the front. Then he would address the audience. He loved speaking in public and he did it very well. I used to stand with my flowers, I wouldn't have dreamed of speaking, I just danced my way through the evening, it was all I wanted to do. Apparently one night my mother was in the audience and she heard the people in front say, "Isn't it wonderful the way he always gives the speech because she doesn't speak a word of English."'

That Christmas, when the company disbanded, Alicia and Dolin were in *Mother Goose* at the London Hippodrome where, to Tchaikovsky's music, they danced a Petipa *pas de deux* arranged by Nijinska, who had joined the Markova-Dolin Company in 1936. This was a de luxe panto with a cast that included star dame George Lacy and the queen of revue, Florence Desmond.

In a recent season at the Palladium, Miss Desmond had brought audiences to their feet with her wicked impression of the superb French Follies artist Mistinguett. Mistinguett, Maurice Chevalier's mistress, was famous for her wondrous legs. She glittered on stage but, off stage, her dourness was matched only by her stinginess. When informed of Miss Desmond's irreverent aping she was not thrilled.

Miss Desmond, 'Desi' to everyone, was conscious of *le coup de grâce* in having Alicia on the bill, and took full credit for booking her. The ladies remained friends all their lives. In the 1970s, when Thames Television transmitted Dolin's *This Is Your Life*, Desi and Alicia were joint guests – a *Mother Goose* reunion.

After Alicia and Pat had danced their *pas de deux*, George Lacy, as Mother Goose, performed a parody ballet in a tutu, by the magic lake. By this time Alicia was in her dressing gown and she stood in the wings every night to watch him, applauding out of sight of the audience when he had finished.

They performed two shows a day, and as the show was strenuous, the cast seldom left the theatre between performances, unless there was a press call or an opening ceremony. They would take turns to entertain each other at tea, which was quite a hearty affair as they all needed to keep up their strength. Champagne would flow in George Lacy and Desi's rooms. He would also have oysters while Alicia preferred smoked salmon sandwiches. 'No one dieted then,' says Alicia. 'We didn't need to, we all worked too hard.'

People are sometimes nonplussed that Alicia is so at home in music hall. This was a result of Diaghileff's training; he taught her to respect all branches of theatre. During their Coliseum seasons they had appeared on the same bill as many music-hall acts, including the superb Nervo and Knox.

She recalled, shortly after joining Diaghileff, being wonder-struck by the talent of a troupe of Chinese acrobats. The whole family went everywhere together. To keep the children quiet backstage, family members were practising balancing plates on sticks; even children as young as three were doing it. 'I always enjoy whatever I'm doing at the time,' is her standard reply when her broad taste is questioned.

Not everyone was so egalitarian. An editorial in the *Manchester Guardian* expressed outrage at Markova appearing in *Mother Goose*. Dolin rose swiftly to her defence and took up his pen.

'This snobbism appals me,' he wrote in a published reply to the *Manchester Guardian*. 'Did Pavlova imperil her art because she appeared at the Palace Music Hall or danced in a bull-ring? Was the Russian ballet any less great when, in 1924 and 1925, it was presented as part of a Music-Hall programme at the London Coliseum? . . . When Markova and I appeared in *Mother Goose* . . . we gave the audience a strictly classical Tchaikovsky *'pas de deux'* based as nearly as possible on the original Petipa steps . . . the only criticism from the audience . . . was that they would have liked to have seen more . . . it takes a very great artist to be a complete success outside the atmosphere and entourage of the ballet . . . it must be said that both Markova and I have appeared on many occasions without this help and atmosphere and always received at the hands of the audience our full measure of success.'

This was a theme to which both Markova and Dolin would regularly return. 'Neither Dame Ninette nor I started off in ballet,' says Alicia. 'Maybe that's why we understood each other. We used all the elements of the theatre.'

By now it was well known that, critically successful though the Markova-Dolin Company was, it was expensive to run. Rumour was rife as to its deficit. Mrs Henderson made a press announcement. She was, she stated, continuing to sponsor the 'Markova-Dolin ballet because it is British, and I am a firm believer in all things British and British dancers in particular . . .'

In the spring of 1937 the Markova-Dolin Company reconvened for a season at the King's Theatre, Hammersmith. Two Nijinska ballets were on the programme, *House Party* and *The Beloved*.

Older than Alicia, Nijinska, too, had studied under Cecchetti, but in pre-Revolution Russia. She had toured as a dancer with her brother, Vaslav Nijinsky, then returned to Russia at the outbreak of war, where she remained throughout the Revolution. In 1921 she had joined the 'Ballet Russe de Diaghileff'.

Her fame had increased meteorically. 'Though she was, perhaps, the most revolutionary and modern choreographer then working,' says Alicia, 'she had a deep respect for tradition.'

She had worked closely with Stravinsky, having choreographed both *Les Noces* and *Le Renard*, and her output included Milhaud's *Le Train Bleu*, in which she had danced and in which Dolin had partnered her. It had been one of his greatest successes.

There were others which had broken new ground in their day. She had created the wildly successful *Bolero* for Ida Rubinstein and *Le Baiser de la Fée* in which Fonteyn had made her first major appearance at Sadler's Wells.

The Beloved, set to music by Liszt and Schubert, tells the story of a poet (Dolin) who reminisces at the piano about the loves of his life. Alicia was his Muse. Ida Rubinstein had commissioned the ballet and had presented it at the Paris Opéra in 1928.

House Party, to music by Poulenc and originally entitled *Les Biches*, had been staged by Diaghileff in 1924 when Vera Nemchinova had created the role of the Girl in Blue. It contained themes of sexual ambiguity.

Although impractical in the extreme when it came to business matters, Nijinska's artistic input was a terrific asset to the company. Another asset was Wendy Toye, who had been with the company since its inception, when she had been nineteen. She had already choreographed a complete ballet for Markova and Dolin, *Aucassin and Nicolette*.

Although Alicia had not been aware of it, Wendy had not received much encouragement in this from Mrs Henderson, who had to be consulted as she would finance the new work. Van Damm championed the ballet and Mrs Henderson was 'openly indignant', he says. She refused to attend any rehearsals or look at any of Wendy's notes. The more Van Damm tried to convince her of the ballet's worth the more she took against it. 'I gently closed the door so that nobody would hear Laura Henderson in full blast,' says Van Damm in *Tonight and Every Night*.

Mrs Henderson finally gave in and washed her hands of it. It was an outstanding success and stayed in the repertoire for two years.

If Mrs Henderson was hostile, Alicia was not, although it was an unorthodox work in some ways.

'It was the first ballet Alicia had not done on *pointe*,' Miss Toye remembers. 'Everyone said to me, "You can't have Markova not on *pointe*," but I said, "I don't want her on *pointe*. I want her to be much more contemporary." She was terrifically supportive about the whole thing.'

'I didn't want to be on *pointe*,' says Alicia. 'I had so much work. I said to Pat, "I must have something not on *pointe*. I can't do it for two hours." It's like a singer, you can't hit high Cs all evening.'

'I was still very much in awe of her,' continues Wendy, 'as were most of the company. She was never unfriendly but there was an aloofness there which I think was deliberate, not shyness. She was well aware she represented a tradition. She had an untouchable quality, like Garbo.

'In her gentle way Alicia has that strength that makes you a star, and when you have the blazing talent she had you don't need to be so forceful. What you do speaks for itself.

'I've never seen her cross in her life. I've seen her get upset and turn sulky but I've never seen her lose her temper. But you jolly well knew by her manner when she was unhappy. It was generally Dolin, the naughty boy.

'The extraordinary thing about her is that not one of us has ever seen her practise. I've seen her rehearse many times, which is a different matter, but no one that I know of has seen her practise. She used to come down to the stage and do a tiny bit of warming up, whereas other people were going at it like crazy, but she knew exactly what was right for her muscles. She's remarkable.'

'I never enjoyed class with a big group,' says Alicia. 'I don't think I ever did company class except when I started with Diaghileff. I was with Madame Cecchetti, and that was company class, but Maestro moved me on and put me with the principals after three weeks. You didn't say who you wanted to work with, you had to wait for them to approach you.

'I used to share lessons at times. Danilova and I would take a lesson together. Balanchine used to give the two of us private lessons in Paris, I must have been about fifteen or sixteen then. Other times we went to Madame Egorova.

'All those great dancers, who were then teaching, didn't teach you for nothing, I might say. We were told how much it would be and then it was up to us – I was the baby so I didn't have any say. There were four of us, Madame Danilova, Dubrovska and someone else. They knew I wanted to work and they wanted me to work. They just told me, "It will be so much."

'On the low salaries we were getting it seemed a lot but it didn't matter, we'd go without things – anything – we just had to have those lessons from this great person.

'Arnold Haskell and his mother helped me. They would say, "You can have an early birthday present," or something like that. I've had wonderful friends.'

'Dolin would take the company practice lessons when we were on tour,' resumes Wendy. 'He used to do battle with everybody. Alicia never appeared for these.

'She always looked immaculate. We all used to put on old jerseys and things, not quite as slovenly as they are today but ultra-casual, but Alicia never did. She always looked a star and there must have been times when she didn't have a great deal of money. But she was always smart, and with wonderful carriage. She was dignified.'

14

America

For all the new and contemporary works, the highlight of the 1937 season, at the King's Theatre, Hammersmith, was Alicia's *Giselle*.

During the run, with a final two weeks to go, she was scheduled to appear at a charity event, the Nijinsky Matinée at His Majesty's. One night she badly injured her foot during a performance. She felt she might collapse but forced herself to carry on.

For the finale she was to make a joint entrance with Dolin. He knew she was in trouble, she could not walk let alone dance, so he carried her on his shoulders while she gestured, smiling to disguise the pain. He gently put her down on her good leg and she dipped her curtsey.

The next day her doctor diagnosed synovitis, brought on by continuous overwork. She could not appear at the charity or continue to dance at the King's. Rest was essential or she could do herself permanent harm. She must not dance for weeks.

Markova, of course, had no understudy, and if the season was to continue, another dancer had to be found immediately. Fortunately, between them, Nijinska, Alicia and Dolin knew plenty.

After a flurry of telephone calls, Vera Nemchinova was tracked down in Paris. She had danced in the *House Party* premiere and Dolin had partnered her before, notably in *The Nightingale and the Rose* which he had choreographed for her. More importantly, she knew *Swan Lake* which had been widely advertised as part of the Hammersmith season. Fortunately she was not only free but, once the situation had been explained, happy to come to London. Van Damm arranged her labour permit.

It was announced that Markova would not be dancing on the Monday and that Nemchinova was dancing *Swan Lake* on Tuesday. She saved the day. The Markova-Dolin Company – now minus Markova – was lucky to have found her.

Prudence Hyman took over Markova's role in *The Beloved* for which Nijinska coached her on the day she danced.

There were disappointments at the box office when it was learned that Markova was not dancing but these were smoothed over and the show did not have to close with the financial loss that would otherwise have ensued.

Actually, if people had craned their necks on the last night they could have seen Markova. She was in a box. Although she could not dance she was able to get about with the help of a stick.

Massine was with her. He was in London attached to Colonel de Basil's Ballet, which was again at Covent Garden. It was no secret that Massine was not getting on with the Colonel, and that he wanted to break away. He was to join Sol Hurok and become artistic director, choreographer and dancer with a new American company. Sol Hurok was the impresario who had introduced Pavlova to America.

Massine wanted Dolin and Alicia to join him. Alicia remembers him telling her, 'You have done all you can for British ballet, you must become international now.'

She had not danced abroad for eight years. This had been a deliberate policy – she had had offers from abroad but had rejected them in order to concentrate on building up a home audience. 'If people wanted to see me dance they had to come to Britain,' she says. For the previous two years she had put in eight performances a week, which was why her foot had given out.

Massine had been trying to persuade her to join him since 1932. He had told her they belonged together, she should 'come home'. She had responded, 'I felt then my home was with young British ballet, at the Mercury Theatre, at the Vic-Wells and with the Camargo Society.'

She felt that if she accepted Massine's offer she would be a deserter, leaving a ship that was still not yet properly afloat.

Freddie Franklin, too, had been contacted by a busy Massine.

'It was a wonderful season,' he recalls. 'All the de Basil Company were in the audience. Danilova was there and Massine and Alicia were in one box and Colonel de Basil in another.

'After the performance I got a note to see Massine at nine the next morning. I went round, terrified, but he was wonderful. I adored Massine. I took one look at those big brown eyes and signed a contract as *premier danseur* with his company for four years. It was frightening as I was still under contract to the Markova-Dolin Company.'

The big brown eyes could have been his downfall. Signing the contract could have landed him in court.

Alicia did not know what to do about Massine's offer. In her heart she wanted to pick up the American gauntlet. To succeed there would be marvellous. On the other hand she did not want to desert the Markova-Dolin Company.

Mrs Henderson made up her mind for her. Her purse was not bottomless and she felt she had subsidized ballet for long enough. There was no government support and she had had to cover every deficit. The company could not carry on without her and had to be dissolved. But, as Vivian Van Damm says, 'It is Laura Henderson who must receive the largest part of the credit for making it possible for a top rank ballet company to tour Britain.'*

No one had been prepared for the cost of running the Markova-Dolin Company. It had played to full houses, enjoyed critical acclaim and been run economically. Alicia prided herself on how frugally she had conducted things. But no company could make a profit out of touring versions of full-scale ballets. Diaghileff had known that, which was why he courted the rich all his life and had little in the way of financial resources himself. He had not adopted Alicia because he had nothing to give her.

Provincial theatre managements would not put up the prices of their seats for the ballet, despite its enormous running costs. They were right not to do so; audiences might well have been put off if they had. But at an average top seat price of 5s 9d the audiences were charity recipients.

The company ran up a deficit of £1,600 a month. This included the costs of maintaining the full company, including the orchestra, at a weekly output of eight performances. Each performance lost £50.

'It was an artistic success but a financial failure,' said Van Damm when he wrote his memoirs in 1952. 'By the time Mrs Henderson and I ended our nationwide experiment about £30,000 had been lost. But it was counted as money well spent . . . I think that even now ballet is reaping the benefit of what we did.'*

The ballet world did not always see things that way. Van Damm adds: 'There was a suspicion among the ultra-highbrow ballet fans that we were "a dreadful company out to make money".'

Alicia signed a three-year contract to go to America with Massine

* *Tonight and Every Night.*

and Hurok, and resumed touring after the Hammersmith season had ended. By now her foot had mended.

Dolin was not going with Massine. He had been eager to sign until he learned that Massine had engaged Serge Lifar as guest artist and commissioned him to restage *Giselle*. Dolin was so furious at this double slight that he signed with Colonel de Basil to go to Australia. The Colonel and Massine were bitter enemies by now.

The Markova-Dolin Company finished its tour in the autumn of 1937. By now Alicia was exhausted. The continuous grind had drained her. But she was relieved that she had signed the contract and was actually looking forward to 'another adventure'. Dolin, too, was not sorry the company was winding up.

'I felt an enormous weight had been taken off my shoulders when the curtain fell for that last time . . . I knew it was the only alternative . . . I knew it would not be possible without other stars or name dancers to take some of the tremendous weight off our two shoulders.'*

Alicia went to France for a holiday, which restored her health, then Freddie Franklin contacted her. 'I rang Alicia,' he says, 'and we arranged to meet. She looked absolutely wonderful and was nut brown. She asked me if I'd signed for Massine and I told her I had. She said, "So have I."

'The way it resolved our contractual difficulties was bizarre, because Alicia, too, would still have been under contract to the Markova-Dolin Company had it not been dissolved. I then told Pat I had signed and he was unhappy with me and he was unhappy with Alicia, too.

'There was also some trouble with the rest of the company. We were ostracized a bit so Alicia and I were thrown together. We were both leaving and both culprits so it was difficult. In the end I had it out with Pat, I said to him, "Look what you did to Diaghileff. You were in and out of his company all the time, and the same with the Vic-Wells. You were all over the place." It was difficult for a while but we survived.

'Alicia and Pat had a turbulent relationship. Both had wills of iron and both knew exactly what they wanted. Although both could exist without the other their relationship was built on mutual need.

'She needed his flair for organization and publicity and he was the most reliable and best partner she ever danced with. He also supported her emotionally. Taking the knocks and fielding off

---

* *Markova: Her Life and Art.*

"The Nutcracker", The Snow Queen with Eglevsky, America 1940. "Ballet Russe de Monte Carlo". The first "Nutcracker" to be seen in the USA.

"Rouge et Noir": Choreographed by Massine to music by Shostakovitch. Costume by Matisse, Chicago 1940. Matisse drew this costume over Markova's body. The appliques were then sewn onto allover tights. (© Maurice Seymour)

Alicia and Dolin in South Africa, 1949. (© Steve Mornay)

Alicia and Dolin relaxing on the beach at Havana, 1950. That day they had lunched with Hemmingway.

Alicia and Dolin waiting to go on stage just before curtain up. Alicia's niece, Susie, copying Auntie Alicia, 1949. (© Keystone Press Agency)

BELOW Markova and Dolin in "Swan Lake", 1950. Giving a gala performance. The company eventually became the "Festival Ballet". (© Houston Rogers)

Dolin and Alicia in "The Nutcracker". Gala performance, 1949. (© Houston Rogers)

Pas de Quatre: Dolin version. Alicia foreground. Paula Hinton (left) Rossana and Krassovska. (© Paul Wilson)

Doris, Alicia, Mrs Haskell, Arnold Haskell and Vivienne, 1949. (© G.B.L. Wilson)

The "Festival Ballet" on the river. Miskovitch, Benn Toff (far left), Danilova, Alicia, Robert Zeller, Krassovska, Mr and Mrs Braunsweg and another. (© C. Loral Andrews)

"The Dying Swan", 1951. (© Gilbert Adams)

things that might be hurtful. He protected her. If people wanted to get to Markova they had to go through Dolin first.'

Freddie thought that she was in love with him.

'There were spats between them, and I used to think, They're such lovely people, why do they fight? But I would look at her and think she was very much in love with him, that's why they fought. I still do. Really in love. I thought that when I was eighteen years old and first saw them together. That love grew into a great friendship and mutual responsibility. But I don't know if they could have married. It would certainly have been tempestuous.'

Alicia marrying Dolin is not a preposterous idea. Plenty of marriages are unorthodox and work well enough. When asked if she was in love with Dolin she did not dismiss the possibility. She paused and thought about it. 'Perhaps like a brother and sister,' she said eventually. But that was only part of it. Dolin twice asked her to marry him and she twice refused.

In public they often behaved like a married couple. He would stand centre-stage in a drawing room, or her dressing room, and absorb all the praise while she would sit quietly, as though she had nothing to do with it. Agnes de Mille was present on one of these occasions in Chicago and said she felt like hitting him.

He was scrupulously polite when discussing Alicia with the company and insisted on according her the full dignity of a leading lady. She was 'Madame Markova' to the other dancers. He was besotted by her. She knew his wiles but, eventually, forgave him everything. They were together for years, and closer than many marriage partners. They also worked in conditions that would have tried any relationship.

Alicia says she nearly married several times but Doris is inclined to dismiss this. 'You were in love with dancing,' she tells her, but Alicia will deny this.

'I could have married several times,' she says. 'When we were in Denmark with the Prince of Wales, the leading Danish dancer asked me to marry him. He came to England to see me and Mother knew him. Later there were two or three millionaires. They're dead now. Perhaps Doris feels I should have accepted and got the money. I never ruled marriage out if the right person should come along. But it would be unfair to him to ask him to share my life. Looking back, too, I can now see that if anyone did become too interested in me Pat would see that it never bloomed. Maybe the right person just didn't come along.

'When I was younger, maybe, I felt I shouldn't disillusion people by getting married. It was part of my training. I portrayed fragile people on stage. Massine always saw me as fragile – he knew I was reliable, but fragile.

'The last time I saw him, not too long before he died, we were both attending a performance at Covent Garden. His legs were bothering him and he was having difficulty with the stairs. I came out of the crush bar and suddenly he was there. We were so happy to see each other. We'd written but hadn't seen each other for a while. "Alicia," he said. "I've one regret, you're not fragile any more."

'I was no longer dancing and I had matured. I was always fragile in the wonderful ballets he created for me.

'Then, I can remember Pat saying to me once, when I was depressed about something, "You know, you don't realize how strong you are." I'd always thought of him as the strong one. Now, with the years, I understand. I'd had to be strong. I had been trundling around the world, alone, since I was a teenager.'

For three months after the Markova-Dolin Company folded Alicia did not dance publicly. After her holiday she stayed in London and studied with Anna Pruzina. Every day she exercised, taking herself back to basics, which was something she had previously been unable to do with the constant touring. Before leaving for America, Massine was giving performances in Monte Carlo and London. She knew the publicity would be extensive and wanted to be in immaculate condition.

'I studied with Pruzina because Massine had told me he wanted me for his new "Symphony" ballets, much of which were based more on the Duncan style. He knew I would be interested. Pruzina was wonderful in that area. I knew she would prepare me. I knew from what I'd seen already that it was much freer and more plastic. I had the time to study before I went to Monte Carlo in the April.'

Her friends all agreed she had made the right decision in going with Massine. De Valois told her that America was where her future lay. She had taken the consequences of forming her own company; now she must take the consequences of America.

Arnold Haskell who by now was writing for the *Daily Telegraph* agreed with de Valois.

Even so, she spent Christmas praying she had made the right decision.

In Monte Carlo, in the spring of 1938, things looked brighter. The place was as pretty as ever and several of her old friends were now members of Massine's company, among them Danilova, with whom she would be sharing roles. Freddie Franklin was also there.

'It was wonderful seeing Alicia and Danilova together again, back in a company with Massine. He must have been forty-three then, and still dancing all his ballets. He put me in *Gaité Parisienne*, his big, new ballet of that season. I learnt everything from him.

'There was one wonderful moment when all the lords and ladies who were giving their money came to Monte Carlo. He introduced me to them as his new "*jeune premier*". He said to me, "Well, Frederic, which part do you think you would like to dance?" I said, "Mr Massine, that's entirely up to you." "I think the Baron's your part," he said. I created the Baron for him. He was a genius, no doubt about that, and what he did for Alicia was phenomenal. He created things that suited her.'

While in Monte Carlo she took lessons from Julia Sedova, a former Marynsky dancer who had a studio in Nice and who had coached many eminent ballerinas.

Alicia was due to dance in several ballets in Monte Carlo before the company left for Paris, where they would be joined by Serge Lifar, now Director of Ballet at the Paris Opéra; they would then travel to London where they were due at Drury Lane.

First among these was Massine's *Seventh Symphony*, choreographed to Beethoven's Seventh Symphony. Massine was keen on symphonic composers and had already set works to music by Tchaikovsky, Berlioz and Brahms. This was going against fashion somewhat as the new wave of choreographers tended to favour the more contemporary sounds of Ravel or Stravinsky.

The free-styling Isadora Duncan had performed a dance entitled 'Seventh Symphony', to the same music, in New York as long ago as 1909, about which Carl van Vechten had written, 'It is quite within the province of the recorder of musical affairs to protest against this perverted use of the Seventh Symphony, a purpose which Beethoven certainly never had in mind when he wrote it. Because Wagner dubbed it the "apotheosis of the dance" is not sufficient reason why it should be danced to.' In 1938 no one minded anyone dancing to Beethoven's music.

Seventh Symphony has an abstract theme, in four movements – The Creation, The Earth, The Sky and Bacchanale – which symbolize the birth and destruction of the earth. In the first act Alicia was 'The Sky' and in the third act the 'Goddess of the Air'. Her costumes were designed by Christian Berard. As 'The Sky' she wore 'A ravishing costume of all over white silk tights', she writes in *Markova Remembers*, '[and] over them, a sensational chiffon skirt which was cut 'on the cross' with invisible white horse-hair woven into it so that the fabric moved like clouds. The silk chiffon of the skirt was a clear sky blue with faintest pink clouds appliquéd on to it. It fastened at the waist with a pink and blue band, and a cloud was also appliquéd to my breast, covering one shoulder. The costume was a work of art, easy to dance in, and of exquisite beauty – such creations have largely disappeared from ballet today.'

She was also dancing two Fokine ballets – *Les Elfes* to Mendelssohn's music from *A Midsummer Night's Dream* and his Violin Concerto, and *L'Epreuve d'Amour*, a folk story, premiered two years earlier, based on a Chinese fairy tale and danced to music attributed to Mozart. The designer was the respected André Derain, who had worked for Diaghileff and designed Massine's *La Boutique Fantasque*.

These three ballets had to be learnt and, in addition, Alicia was dancing *Le Spectre de la Rose*, *Les Sylphides* and the White Act of *Swan Lake*.

Her partner for *Seventh Symphony* was Igor Youskevitch, a former Olympic sprinter and swimmer who had given up athletics to dance. He had studied with Preobrajenska and Nijinska. Alicia thought him 'wonderful'.

On the evening of the premiere Alicia was in her dressing room waiting for her costume. It had been returned earlier to costumier Barbara Karinska for last-minute alterations so she was not unduly worried. But when the ten-minute call came and it had not reappeared she became jittery.

Finally just the skirt arrived, altered as required, but with no top or headdress. By now Alicia was in a flap and demanded the rest of the costume. No one knew where it was and Madame Karinska could not be found. The temperature rose rapidly in the little room. As 'The Sky' Alicia was due on stage right at the beginning of the ballet.

Then the designer, Christian Berard, rushed in, hearing of the panic. He found his ballerina in a skirt and no top and clearly distressed about it. Berard's eye alighted on Alicia's evening frock, which she planned to wear for the party afterwards. It was behind the door, on a hanger. It had a pale blue chiffon scarf; he snatched this and fitted it to her bodice. He then yelled for someone to bring him some white paper which was thrust into his hands. He drew two wings, cut them out, and pinned them to her hair. After the weeks of preparation, that was how *Seventh Symphony* was premiered.

That was not the end of the costume problems. There was a quick change in the third movement and the headdress was still missing.

Once again Alicia's after-show ensemble was raided. She had bought a costume tiara that afternoon, which she had intended to wear with her now denuded evening frock. She fastened it to her hair and made her entrance.

The headdress never turned up. The next morning she bought some artificial flowers from a stall and made another. She asked Berard what he had in mind and he told her to buy 'rainbow' flowers to match her costume. She kept the headdress for years and then gave it as a present to critic Clement Crisp.

There was much excitement in London about Alicia's *Giselle*. This was the new production Massine had commissioned from Serge Lifar, who was also dancing Albrecht.

He had danced Albrecht many times in Paris. But his interpretation was different to that given by Dolin. This was his production and, in his view, Albrecht was the dominant personality. He built up the part accordingly. This suited his athletic build, handsome face, and the way he could leap, and it also suited the Parisians who came to see him in droves. He had become a star of the Opéra where he could do no wrong.

Marlene Dietrich and her daughter, Maria Riva, were among the thousands in Paris who flocked to see him. In her biography of her mother,* Miss Riva writes: 'Serge Lifar, Nijinsky's heir, was rapturously exclaimed over as he sprung and pirouetted in the air, all muscles, both front and back, rippling under white tights. In our darkened opera box my mother turned to my father and whispered: "Has he got Kotex stuffed in there or is that all him?" . . . I looked through my precious opera glasses to see what my mother was interested in.'

Lifar's Albrecht conflicted with Alicia's Giselle. Their styles were incompatible. She wrote, '. . . his views, which stressed the importance of Albrecht, and mine, which were the result of my work with Nicholas Sergeyev and with Spessivtseva, were very different. I knew my version was correct within the traditions of the Imperial Russian Ballet – which had saved *Giselle* itself from oblivion.'

Lifar was not bothered by tradition, Sergeyev or the Russian ballet for that matter. He was all for Albrecht.

Rehearsals progressed uneasily. Neither side gave way. Alicia danced *Giselle* as she thought fit and Lifar likewise.

The décor for the production was by Alexandre Benois and there were new costumes to match it. Alicia had had fittings for these but

---

* *Marlene Dietrich* by Maria Riva, Bloomsbury, 1992.

had not seen them when show-day approached. She was assured everything was in order. The finished costumes would be in her dressing room in time. But she was uneasy.

She was right to worry. It seemed that skulduggery was afoot. In his biography of Sol Hurok,* Harlow Robinson writes:

'Not everyone in the company was pleased with Markova's arrival and obvious status. The costume shop was staffed by long time friends and admirers of Toumanova. They had always made costumes only for her and refused to produce any for Markova.'

On *Giselle* morning, Alicia went to Drury Lane to clarify the situation. Wardrobe assured her the costumes would be in her dressing room well before time.

She came back home and worried all through her steak lunch. Then she remembered the Bakst costumes she had worn previously, which were in London. She telephoned Manya, her costumier, to get them to the theatre. It was an insurance.

When she returned to the theatre that evening, at her customary two hours before curtain up, she was gratified to see a queue for tickets stretching along Drury Lane.

But there were no costumes in her room. Wardrobe was locked up; no one had arrived yet.

When Morty came, Alicia sent her to Wardrobe with orders not to return without the costumes. She chose her shoes and set about her make-up.

Morty came back with Wardrobe in tow, carrying the costume for the first act. The relief flooded through Alicia as she tried it on.

It hung like a sack. Wardrobe confessed it had been made for Tamara Toumanova who, they had been told, would be dancing. Toumanova was a friend of Lifar's and had danced the part with him before. Lifar had made it known that he had wanted Toumanova rather than Alicia.

Alicia sent for Massine. She told him she was not wearing the new costume. He must make an announcement to the audience, and she was explicit as to what he must say, telling them she was ready to dance but that her costumes had been made for Toumanova and, therefore, Toumanova would dance. On no account must he suggest she was ill.

London was, of course, Alicia's home territory; most of the audience were supporters. There would be terrible disappointment.

Massine refused to make the speech, and who can blame him?

* *The Last Impresario*, Viking, 1994.

By now the performance was late and the auditorium was alive with rumours as to what was happening.

Then Alicia remembered the Bakst costumes. She would wear them.

Lifar was told and charged into her room shouting that in no way could she wear the old costumes in his new production; it would ruin it.

Suddenly her room was full of people. She burst into tears. Danilova, who was dancing the Queen of the Wilis, comforted her and reminded everyone that Alicia had a performance to give.

Sol Hurok then made his stately entrance. These was a respectful silence for the impresario. Hurok informed everyone that, as the new costumes did not fit, Alicia could wear the old ones. Alicia sobbed that she was not going to dance at all, she was too upset.

Baron, the photographer, was there. It was his first commission and he had arrived feeling rather nervous. Suddenly he was in the middle of this *scandale*, as the Russians termed such situations. He rushed to get Alicia a glass of brandy.

She took a few sips between sobs and Danilova started putting her make-up to rights.

When Alicia finally made her appearance the audience burst into applause. But there were more dramas to come.

Alicia's *Giselle* was a favourite among London's balletomanes and Drury Lane was packed with them. She gave her customary 'imperial' performance while Lifar danced spectacularly in the way his Paris audiences so admired.

London was not Paris and Alicia was among fans. Lifar was booed and Alicia was cheered.

When she took her solo curtseys at curtain time the audience erupted. Dolin was in the audience, and wrote: 'she was greeted by a roar of applause which was almost terrifying.'

Alice wrote of that night in *Markova Remembers*: 'I imagine that Serge . . . could not appreciate that, for the London public, I was coming home. Alas he had to be physically restrained by two stage hands in order that the theatre might be calmed down, while I received the public's thanks and showed mine.'

It was true. Lifar had to be restrained. He was so incensed while she took her calls that he had tried to run on stage and drag her off. The press commented:

'Serge Lifar, imported from Paris, seemed more intent upon advertising himself than Markova. Her dancing last night was so diamond bright and her acting so restrained that

185

she emphasised what London audiences already know, that there is no finer classical dancer in the world. She did this against the heavy handicap of a partner whose intensive efforts at feats of elevation and display made anything but a satisfactory background. The performance ended with a campaign waged relentlessly by the gallery to separate Markova from her partner and give her her belated due. After 10 ferocious minutes they succeeded.' – *News Chronicle*

'There was not a single moment's doubt last night of her ability to carry the whole weight of this long ballet. Her miming has gained enormous conviction . . .' – *The Times*

'She received a wonderful ovation, the gallery demanding with irresistible insistence that she should appear alone before the curtain to receive a huge roar of applause. In this the audience showed good sense, as they did in their protest in the curtain going up nearly 20 minutes late.' – *Daily Telegraph*

'There are rare coloratura singers who create the illusion that their florid convention is a natural mode of expression. That is what Markova does with the classic convention on the *pointes* – so successfully that when she descends from them it seems a condescension.' – *Time and Tide*

'Alicia Markova has a special place in the heart of her London public. Her swift, neat movements, her lightness, and her great gift of making the air her own particular element combine to make her the supreme classical exponent of her day.' – *Punch*

Alicia did not bear Lifar any lasting animosity. In 1994, when reflecting on the *Giselle* situation, she stated: 'His attitude then can be summed up in one word – jealousy. We had never had any trouble before and he had always been kind and helpful to me when we had been together with Diaghileff. It was just too much for him.'

Lifar was in London in 1984 selling part of his collection of paintings at Sotheby's. He and Alicia got together, at Sotheby's suggestion, and posed arm in arm under a portrait of Lifar in his prime when he looked every inch the star in swimming trunks and a sailor hat, such as he had worn in *Les Matelots*, during which he had so won Diaghileff's admiration.

'We went out to dinner afterwards.' Alicia says. 'It was like old times. Serge was staying at Claridges and I went back to have a nightcap with him. We were sitting in the foyer when he got up, told me to stay where I was, and ran upstairs.

'He came down with a piece of paper. It was a copy of a memo from him to the directors of the Paris Opéra. He had asked them to book Pat and me for a season and he wanted me to see it, so that I would know he had borne no animosity.

'It couldn't be done, but he wanted me to see he had asked for me. The ballet world could never understand why Pat and I hadn't appeared at the Paris Opéra. He wanted to explain it to me and had brought the letter specially to London for me to see. Little did I know it was the last time we'd see each other. Bless his heart.'

In 1938, however, her troubles with Lifar were far from over. The Ballet Russe was due to appear at Covent Garden in the autumn and while Alicia and Lifar were rehearsing for this he put her down awkwardly and she sprained her ankle. She was told that if she wanted to open the Metropolitan Opera House season in October, as Hurok had planned, she must rest. She could not take part in the Covent Garden season.

While she was recuperating she worried about the Lifar situation. She would be dancing *Giselle* with him in New York and did not want there to be any more problems. Dolin had told her he thought Lifar was behind everything that had gone wrong, but she found this hard to believe.

Sol Hurok was in London, at the Savoy where he always stayed, and asked Alicia and Eileen to tea there. She confessed her worries to him and he told her that things would level out.

She also told him that she did not think she would be a success in America. 'In my mind the successful people had all been blonde, with long eyelashes, and glamorous. I felt I wasn't that type at all. Even so, I knew I was opening in *Giselle* and was prepared. We made a bargain. He persuaded me to go ahead and open at the Met. I was contracted to follow this with a long tour, but he said that if I wasn't happy after I'd opened then he would release me and I could come back to London. That was the beginning of our long relationship. Later, of course, I came to think that I'd never get back to London. It was one contract after another.'

Hurok, a worldy man who had brought both Pavlova and the Ballet Russe to America, continued to placate her. She had a burning ambition to dance *Giselle* in America, but she needed reassurance.

Alicia was to open at the Met on 12 October. Lifar resented her even more by now, blaming his hostile reception at Drury Lane on her. Once again he tried to persuade Massine to replace her with Toumanova. Once again neither Massine nor Hurok would hear of it.

It was hardly surprising that Lifar was jealous. Hurok clearly thought Alicia was wonderful. In a letter to his friend, Irving Deakin, he wrote, 'I believed I worked a miracle here . . . Alicia Markova will be *the* sensation. To me she is the only classical dancer since Pavlova; in fact, I believe she's even better than Pavlova in *Giselle*.'*

There was great interest in *Giselle* in New York. It had not been seen there in its entirety for fourteen years since Pavlova had danced it. There had also been a twenty-minute version given by the Mordkin Ballet at Radio City but that had not been a success.

Rehearsals were held at the Met. The day before the scheduled performance Toumanova's father barged in. He strode up to Massine and demanded to know if his daughter was dancing the following evening.

When Massine told him she was not, he knocked him to the ground. He was escorted from the premises.

Alicia had seen the whole thing.

After rehearsal she waited at the stage door, with Danilova, for a taxi to take them to their hotel. The rush-hour crowds surged by. Someone shoved a note into her hand and disappeared before she could see who it was. It read, 'Don't dance Giselle tomorrow night or . . .'

Her knees buckled.

Back at the hotel Danilova rang Hurok. He warned Alicia not to spend the evening alone.

She took his advice and went with Danilova, Freddie Franklin and the muscular Youskevitch to Madison Square Garden to watch a rodeo. 'Can you imagine it? A rodeo? Before the opening of *Giselle*?'

Nothing sinister happened but she spent the night with Danilova to be on the safe side. Next day, she told Hurok she did not want to dance that night. Let Toumanova dance. He refused to let her off.

Nevertheless he implemented a full-scale security alert and altered some of the staging, avoiding, as much as he could, anything that could be dangerous. Alicia had been due to make one exit through a trapdoor but this was now cancelled. Security guards were posted in the wings.

Act One went well but in Act Two Lifar appeared with a bunch of real lilies as opposed to props. Some of these were dropped as he

* Quoted in *The Last Impresario*.

made his way to Giselle's tomb. If trodden on they could be lethal. Alicia managed to avoid them as she was moving, but some of the *corps* could not break their lines and took a tumble.

At another point in the ballet Giselle picks some lilies from the ground then, mid-leap, throws one to Albrecht. It always drew a gasp from the audience whenever Alicia did it.

On this particular evening, as she went to pick a lily, she found it nailed to the ground. She gave a pull but it would not budge; she tried another and that would not move either. She wrenched with all her might and eventually managed to pull one up. Because of the time this took she was late with her moves. But she took her leap, throwing the bloom to Albrecht while in mid-air, to the usual gasp from the audience.

She suspected dirty work again but the reverse was the case. The stage hands had been alerted to watch out for subterfuge and in order to ensure that the lilies stayed in place they had nailed them to the floor. Everything was nailed down that night.

There was another lethal factor to avoid. The actual stage was hazardous. The Met was not designed for ballet and the stage had a central trapdoor with a furrow round it. As Freddie Franklin put it: 'If you got on that it was Goodbye, Charlie, the pirouettes were gone. You just had to cope with it.'

Sol Hurok wrote of that evening in his memoirs, *Impresario*: 'Markova triumphed that night in *Giselle* as she had in London. It was also a vindication. She had made her great name only in her own country, and her countrymen might have been forgiven if their appreciation of her gifts had been a little inflated by pride in a native ballerina. For New Yorkers there was no such patriotic association. On the stage of the Metropolitan that night, she stood strictly on her own merits. She met the ordeal, and New York lay beside London at her feet.'

Agnes de Mille also recalls it. 'That night, everything she did provoked an ovation, an eventuality that her partner, Serge Lifar, had not foreseen. He became upset . . .'

On the second night, in Act One, as Giselle sat on Albrecht's knee, Lifar slipped. She fell to the floor and he, caught off balance, rolled on top of her, crushing her foot which was still weak from the London sinovitis. A bone fractured.

Alicia says this was an accident but some of the New York papers thought differently. She finished the act in agony then fainted as soon as she left the stage. There was no possibility of her finishing the ballet.

'I continued the whole solo variation,' Alicia later told Agnes de

Mille. 'Little hops on *pointe* and all. Think of it, right across this stage on one toe on a fractured foot. In the mad scene I began to feel something was wrong and, it seemed, in the end I passed out.'

Fortunately the glamorous, red-headed Mia Slavenska* was a member of the company and able to deputize. She was a former member of the Zagreb Opera Ballet, and Alicia had taught her the role as she, and Toumanova, were to alternate with her on the tour.

Slavenska took over the performance but no one had informed the audience of the substitution. People were amazed as Giselle appeared out of the grave a striking redhead. As Alicia says. 'She died blue-black and emerged red.' It looked at though she had spent the interval at the hairdresser's.

Lifar's bad feeling spread to other company members. After a performance of *Swan Lake*, he objected to the warm applause accorded Roland Guerard. He wanted his variation removed. Massine refused and Lifar challenged him to a duel (which never took place). Hurok told him to 'take a headache pill'.

The press got hold of the story and carried columns about the high passion at the Met. Hurok was not displeased with the attention this focused on the box office. The house sold out nightly with receipts of $3,000. The gross takings for the New York run alone were $83,000.

After this Lifar tendered his resignation which was accepted.

This took place while Alicia was nursing her bad foot. She could not dance for nine days and the classics had to be abandoned. New York had to wait for the following spring before it saw her in them.

A few days after she fractured her foot she woke up one night with terrible toothache. She was staying in the Astor Hotel, on Times Square, and went to a dentist across the road. An extraction was necessary and the dentist packed the gap where the tooth had been.

This was still in place when she resumed dancing. She was able to perform *Seventh Symphony*, which was lyrical but did not require *pointe* work, and was partnered by Youskevitch.

In the third act she was turned upside down. She had told no one of her visit to the dentist and had thought no more of it herself. 'As the boys held me upside down I realized the packing in my tooth

---

* She can be seen in the 1938 film *La Mort du Cygne* and later created Blanche du Bois in Valerie Bettis's TV ballet *A Streetcar Named Desire*. She was a pioneer of television ballet.

had come loose. I kept my mouth closed and got through with Igor. We had to do three big jumps to get off. As soon as I leapt into the wings out flew the plug and blood gushed everywhere.

'This was my entrance to America. I started the tour with a little splint in my shoe and packing in my mouth.'

Youskevitch remained her partner throughout the tour. From New York they moved towards Boston, the first leg. They travelled by train. Alicia did most of her sight-seeing through windows as they did not spend long in the towns. Sometimes she no sooner arrived than she was in a dressing room getting ready for a performance. As soon as that was over it was back to the station and the next stop – the famous one-night stands.

'We did one hundred and ten cities in six months on that first tour,' Freddie Franklin remembers. 'And we danced on anything. Some of the stages were in a terrible condition. My salary was seventy-five dollars a week, but you could have breakfast for fifty cents and if you paid two dollars for your dinner it was de luxe. The hotels might be two dollars fifty a night.' Alicia was getting $150 a week.

Freddie was a principal dancer so fared better than the *corps de ballet* who had a rough time of it. In those pre-union days they were worked to death and badly paid and could only survive by cheating the hotels. They operated a system that Alicia called 'The Army Game'. One would check in, then six others would sneak in and use the room, bribing the maid for extra towels. They slept wherever they could. They toured like that for months on end.

They played the Opera House in Boston. For the first time since the accident Alicia was now able, with Hurok's persuasion, to dance *Giselle*. Massine had told her that if she felt she had to alter it a bit, to accommodate her bad foot, to feel free to do so.

Now that Lifar was in Paris, Alicia hoped that her *Giselle* might go more smoothly. But clearly there was still someone who wished her ill. When she was changing into her Wili's outfit in the interval she found that the skirt had been hacked out; only the bodice and a layer of tulle remained.

The dresser was adamant that it had been intact when the ballet had started. Someone had gone to her dressing room while she was on stage and sabotaged her costume. It was a chilling thought.

Before leaving London there had been a discussion about the sinister happenings connected with *Giselle* and she had thought it prudent to bring her Bakst costume. This was now in a trunk backstage. It was hastily pressed during an extended interval.

The ripped-out skirt was discovered screwed up in a ball and stuffed in a corner of the ladies' toilet.

Nonetheless, her performance attracted positive comment.

'All that they say about Alicia Markova's *Giselle* is deserved. Her characterization of one of the great characters of ballet has, if anything, been under-praised . . . Last night, with . . . the exquisite dancing and miming of Markova, *Giselle* came to life as compellingly as the name-character arises in the second act of the tale.' – *Boston Evening Transcript*

Unpleasant incidents continued to dog her throughout the tour. She would have left but for her loyalty to Massine. She could not abandon him. She never found out who was gunning for her.

Her morale was not boosted by her injured foot which still needed attention.

From Boston the company proceeded through Ohio and on to Illinois, spending Christmas in Chicago. While there, Hurok conducted a survey which showed, unsurprisingly, that works such as *Les Sylphides*, *Le Beau Danube* and *Prince Igor* were far more popular with audiences than Massine's more experimental works, such as *Seventh Symphony* and *Bogatyri*. *Bogatyri*, set to Borodin's symphonic music, told of the legendary knights of Old Russia during the reign of Vladimir I. Danilova and Freddie Franklin had premiered it at the Met on 20 October 1938. Alicia should have been in it as well but her accident had prevented it. As it happened, the ballet was never a success.

By the new year they were in Los Angeles and, once again, Alicia's unseen enemy struck in *Giselle*. She felt the impact during the second act – at the point where the Wili queen touches her and Giselle spins off stage to return a few seconds later.

As she spun off stage she felt a painful stabbing in her thigh. Massine was in the wings and removed a viciously long needle lodged in the folds of the costume. As she says, 'it certainly made an effective goad.'

Massine was always in the wings at that time, wrapped up, as he was due to go on in *Gaité Parisienne*. The evenings would usually start with *Giselle*, given in two acts, and end with *Gaité Parisenne*, the first tragic, the second frivolous.

In Los Angeles many movie stars attended the performance. 'There was a big party after the show, it was arranged by the management, I think. We were all in long dresses and the men in dinner jackets. I didn't have an escort but they told me I would need one, I couldn't go in alone. They'd fixed me up with somebody, I think I said, "Thank you very much."'

Had Dolin been with her he would automatically have taken his place at her side. As it was she didn't do badly.

'When my escort turned up it was Ramon Novarro. He was such a nice, dear person and I'd seen all his films.'

Novarro was hot box office, a handsome Mexican star who had been a serious screen rival to Valentino, although they were friends off screen. In 1925 he had played the title role in *Ben Hur*, the American silent screen's biggest epic.

Tragically, sound ended his career and, even more tragically, he was killed in 1968 when two men broke into his house and tortured him to death, destroying his home and mementoes in the process. They found a gift from Valentino which they rammed down his throat for kicks. A disgusting end to a thoroughly decent man.

From Los Angeles the Ballet Russe moved to San Francisco and, eventually, Texas. On a one-night stand there Alicia was dancing *Coppélia*. 'The stage had a deep rake. I was wheeled on in a chair, with my book in my hands, it was in the second act when Swanhilda is changed into the doll. Suddenly I saw that I was moving very slowly downstage with the rake towards the conductor. He'd also noticed. I thought "Oh, my God!"

'Everyone in the wings could see the situation. I tried to point it out on stage but I couldn't be that loud. Nicholas Beriozoff was Dr Coppelius and he was standing next to me, studying his magic books. He caught me just in time and moved me back. It was very funny to the audience, they roared with laughter. He let me go and I said, "No, I'll go again."

'Freddie Franklin was in the wings and I heard him say, "Turn her round." That was the only way they could stop me, by moving me round so I was looking into the wings. I said, "Let me get off this damn thing as quickly as possible."

'After that Youskevitch asked me, "What are we going to do about the last act *adagio* on this rake?" It had some terrific balances in it. So we had to turn again. It wasn't like Chicago or New York where they knew every move, so we got away with it.'

Nicholas Beriozoff was a ballet master and renowned character dancer, one of the best in the business. He was the father of ballerina Svetlana Beriosova whom Alicia had known for years. Her mother had been a costumier and made tutus. When she had fitted Alicia for the Ballet Russe, baby Svetlana had come with her.

While they were in San Diego Youskevitch sprained his ankle. He and André Eglevsky loved to go fishing when they could. It relaxed them after the turmoil of constant performances. They had rushed off to fish one day and only just made it back in time for the matinée.

There was not enough time for Youskevitch to properly warm up and, as he was hurrying through his exercises, his ankle gave way. Roland Guerard had to deputize at short notice.

It was in San Diego, too, that the scenery nearly came down on top of them all. The opening ballet, *Carnaval* that night, was in progress and Alicia and Massine, and others, were behind the scenery warming up.

They used the scenery supports as a barre. Suddenly, to their horror, they felt the scenery toppling towards them. Their weight had dislodged it. The stage hands came rushing forward and, together with the dancers, hurled their weight against it to keep it upright. Everything had to be done in total silence as *Carnaval* was being performed just the other side.

After that a directive was issued to the effect that all warm-ups were to be done without the use of the scenery. Only permanent fixtures were to be used as barres.

During the tour Alicia appeared in Cincinnati, Ohio, a city that was later to feature prominently in her life.

The company returned to the Met in early spring for the season, where Alicia was able to dance the classics that injury had prevented her from performing the previous autumn. During this run they performed at a special gala in honour of Sol Hurok's Silver Jubilee.

The Ballet Russe was due back in Monte Carlo in the May of 1939. 'The Ballet Russe de Monte Carlo', the title Massine had inherited for the company, and which Hurok so valued, had to appear regularly in Monte Carlo to justify its prestigious name and patronage.

The company crossed the Atlantic on the SS *Rex* and docked, by special arrangement, at Cannes, from where they would travel on by land to Monte Carlo.

The *Rex* was bound for Genoa after Nice and had to keep to schedule. There had been some unpleasantness at the dock due to the length of time it took to unload all the scenery and costumes.

As the ship was too big to get into the harbour, launches had to be sent out to bring the cast, costumes and scenery to land. Time was progressing and the captain was concerned for his schedule. Suddenly he announced he could wait no longer. Certain effects had been unloaded but the rest, he said, would have to go on to Genoa, from where it could be brought back to Monte Carlo.

In the ensuing confusion an entire load of scenery and costumes was accidentally dropped into the ocean. 'It's still at the bottom of the sea at Cannes,' says Alicia. 'Among it was Fokine's *L'Epreuve d'Amour*. As soon as I saw what happened I knew I'd never dance that again with Ballet Russe and I never did. It was a beautiful ballet, with décor by Derain. Recently there was an exhibition of Derain's work and someone asked why *L'Epreuve* was never revived and did anyone know where the costumes were? They are at the bottom of Cannes harbour.'

Despite this, the company opened two days later, on schedule, although there were necessary alterations to the repertoire. But the precious contract was honoured.

In Monte Carlo the new production in hand was Massine's *Le Rouge et le Noir*.

Freddie Franklin was present when Massine selected Alicia for her role. 'There were four ballerinas all running around hoping to be chosen – Slavenska, Danilova, Markova and someone else. Massine just pointed to Alicia and said, "I give to you," and that was that. It was wonderful for her.

'She did so much modern stuff before the war. I wish the Americans had seen it but they loved her in classical roles. No one in America has seen her do what we all saw her do in Britain, things like the blues in *High Yellow* for instance, *Façade* with the boater, *The Haunted Ballroom* and all those other ballets that she made famous. Massine gave her the opportunity to do modern things but she tended to veer towards the *Giselles*. Markova was such a versatile artist, her range was incredible. Towards the end she specialized in one particular thing, which she was superb at, but I just wish the Americans had seen what we all saw.'

Le Rouge et le Noir (its name was later changed to *L'Etrange Farandole* just for the following Paris season) had décor and costumes by Matisse and is set to music from Shostakovitch's First Symphony. 'We were the first company outside Russia to use his music,' says Alicia. 'When I did something modern, believe me, it was really way out.'

It is an abstract work depicting the struggle of Man and Woman against the world. Alicia's costume consisted of all-over white tights with material appliquéd to them. In order to get the right shapes Matisse would draw on her body exactly what he wanted.

Opening night was 11 May 1939 in Monte Carlo. Alicia was partnered by Youskevitch and the cast included Nathalie Krassovska, daughter of Lydia Krassovska. Nathalie had recently toured South America with Lifar.

From Monte Carlo the company moved to Paris for a season at the Palais de Chaillot.

That July Alicia came to London where she was due to open the Covent Garden season with *Le Rouge et le Noir*. Before that she appeared in a big charity gala at the Albert Hall. The celebrated tenor Alfred Piccaver was starring in a mammoth production of *Faust*; a special ballet segment was inserted for her. She had danced in *Faust* before leaving for America, when Ashton had arranged her variation.

She also appeared at the Westminster Theatre as Marie Camargo, after whom the Camargo Society had been named, in a fund-raising evening on behalf of the Royal Academy of Dancing.

Then there was another television appearance. She had made several by now. Television had improved considerably since her debut in 1932. Now, instead of the white and black make-up that used to be essential, the improved cameras required her face be coloured brick-red with a substance called 'panchromatic' which had been developed in the mid-thirties. Make-up, too, was improving all the time.

The BBC studios had moved to the more spacious surroundings of Alexandra Palace, near where she had lived as a child. The first transmissions from there had started in November 1936 when all receivers had had to be within a twenty-mile radius.

In those days a television set cost about about £125, £5 cheaper that an Austin Seven and, more or less, what a cheap one costs today. What sets there were had bulky cabinets standing nearly five feet high and almost as wide, with a nine-inch screen. In 1937 HMV had introduced its Model 902 with a screen magnifier. It wasn't until 1939 that Cossor offered a fourteen-inch screen at the knock-down price of forty-eight guineas.

Despite these technical improvements. Alicia was still obliged to confine herself to a small area. But there was a breakthrough in that an orchestra could now be accommodated. On previous transmissions she had danced to a piano, usually played by Paul Hambourg.

The orchestra could not be housed in the same studio as Alicia, as there would have been no room for her to dance, so it was in a studio nearby.

A floor assistant had to run between studios to inform the conductor, Eric Robinson, 'my good friend', when she was ready to dance. The transmission was live and if she made a mistake she had to carry on, no matter what it looked like.

Morty was with her, and as she was carrying Alicia's costume to the car after the performance a gust of wind caught the tulle and inflated it like a parachute. The costume nearly took off and Morty with it.

While in London Alicia and Dolin went to the Aldwych to see Indian dancer Ram Gopal. He had set out to popularize classical Indian dance. He was an expert in 'Mudras', the Indian hand language which, it is claimed, has over four thousand movements. He had also mastered the four schools of Indian technique – 'Bharata Natyam', 'Kathakali', 'Kathak' and 'Manipuri', each having its own particular dance characteristics to rhythmic and musical accompaniment.

Gopal's costumes consisted of lavish decorations, often in gold, draped over a perfectly formed body, climaxing in an elaborate headdress. For some dances he extended his fingers with tapering gold attachments several inches long. He assumed the guises of a god, a bird, a prince or a legendary being. Britain had never seen anything like him. He had attracted great attention, had been painted by fashionable artists and photographed by the top photographers. His sell-out season at the Aldwych was part of one of his many world tours.

Filled with admiration, Alicia and Dolin called round to his dressing room afterwards to pay their respects. Gopal told Alicia she reminded him of Pavlova, who had flirted with Indian dance, and that he would like to dance with her some day.

She had seen nothing to equal this exotic creature who put her in mind of a sophisticated bird of paradise and replied that she would be honoured.

Later that year she went on a music-hall tour with Wendy Toye and Dolin. Dolin was keen to re-establish himself with British audiences as he had been in Australia and New Zealand working for Colonel de Basil.

They appeared in, among other places, Harrogate, Brighton and Folkestone. In Folkestone they gave three performances at the Leas Cliff Hall (a matinée and two evening performances) on 16 and 17 August. A local paper covered an unusual incident that occurred during the evening performance on the 17th.

'During a performance by Markova and Dolin . . . last night the lights failed and the body of the hall was plunged into darkness. The musical director called out "Sorry we can't go on" and Markova brought her dance to a close. The people in the hall whiled away the last half-hour before the lights came on in singing songs. The municipal orchestra played tunes and waitresses supplied refreshments carrying lighted candles on their trays.'

The lights had been extinguished as a security precaution. War was imminent and a surprise attack feared.

The lights of Britain were soon to be turned out for a long time to come. On 4 September, war was officially declared between Germany and Britain.

The performance of *Le Rouge et le Noir* scheduled for Covent Garden was cancelled. All theatres were closed and Alicia's performance was just another casualty of war. 'War was declared on Sunday and we were due to open on Monday. We had all been all prepared.'

15

South America

Alicia and Danilova, who was in London on the expectation of dancing the now cancelled *Le Rouge et le Noir*, volunteered for war work.

'We used our brains. Chura had been through revolution in Russia and she said, "They need nurses for the fighters," so we volunteered as midwives, we thought that might release the nurses for other work. So we reported to a hall somewhere near Maida Vale – everyone was trying to organize themselves – and the first thing we found ourselves doing was washing up in a big enamel bowl. Chura washed and I dried. But we only went there once. We were recognized and told they would rather we didn't come again as it disturbed all the other people. Meanwhile, Sol Hurok was trying to get us to New York for the Met season.'

Alicia felt she should stay in Britain. 'I really didn't want to go to America, I made all kinds of excuses. I wanted to stay here with the family and everybody else.' But Hurok reminded her she was under contract to appear at the Met in the forthcoming season with Massine's Ballet Russe de Monte Carlo.

Her appearance had been widely advertised in New York. War did not alter the facts, and if she did not turn up he would serve an injunction on her preventing her from appearing anywhere. In effect she would have been unable to earn her living. She consulted her solicitor but he told her she could not get out of the American contract. She had signed for three years. She had to go.

'If I had stayed I suppose I could have been a paratrooper,' she says. 'I always wanted to jump with a parachute.'

Alicia believes there is a possibility that Hurok was particularly insistent as he had heard a 'whisper' that she might be working for the great C. B. Cochran in a West End show.

'Cochran thought Pat and I would be here and wanted us to star in his new revue. We went to lunch with him at the Ecu de France in Jermyn Street. I had never believed Cochran would give me a thought as he always had to have glamorous blondes and people like that.

'The previous year, when I'd been in Paris with the Ballet Russe, I had a lovely silk suit made to be photographed in, it was special, I'd worn it in America and thought it would be right for Cochran, the great showman. Pat hadn't seen it. I had my hair done and wore a jaunty little hat. It was as though I was dressed for another ballet, a new role.

'For once Pat paid me a compliment. Afterwards he said to me, "That was wise wearing what you did." Usually it was things like, "Your hair looks terrible," or "Why are you wearing that?"'

She was unable to accept the revue, anyway, due to her Hurok contract.

She was accused by some of using her privileged position to escape the war. 'I had to smile,' she writes in *Markova Remembers*. 'It was my bank which obliged me to leave my country, where I could not work, in order to find a livelihood where I might use the gifts I had been given.'

It was one thing for Hurok to insist she return to America but another for her to get there. The shipping lines were over-booked and panicking passengers jammed every office.

Most of the would-be passengers, however, did not have Hurok as a representative and, through his influence, Alicia was accommodated on the SS *Manhattan*, the last American boat to sail to New York before hostilities started.

Choreographer Antony Tudor and dancer Hugh Laing were also on board as were singer Paul Robeson and pianist Artur Rubinstein. So, too, were Danilova and Dolin. Danilova was also contracted to Massine, and Dolin was booked for a further Australian tour.

He was touring, for de Basil, with former Baby Ballerina Irina Baronova, also on board with her husband. Now aged twenty, the Baby had grown into a fully fledged star who had created roles in *Les Présages*, *Jeux d'Enfants* and *Paganini*.

Because of the shortage of space Alicia and Danilova shared a cabin with four Irish women, all from the same family, a great-grandmother, grandmother, mother and baby. As Alicia says, 'it was rather like the Marx Brothers' cabin in *A Night at the Opera*.'

Farewells were difficult. No one knew what the future held. Alicia could only hope for the best. She expected to be back shortly after Christmas.

In fact, she stayed for eight years and during that time undertook coast-to-coast tours and travelled to parts of the world of which she had not previously heard.

She arrived in New York with little money. War restrictions forbade money to be taken out of the country. What had been allowed had been used up on the trip. She was not unduly worried as she knew her contract would guarantee her $150 a week.

Hurok's representative advanced her $20 out of her wages to tide her over. There would be no high living for a while. She felt bitter about her hardship. 'I found it ironic that a singer or an actress with a public comparable to mine could earn thousands of dollars a week. But for us in the ballet the rewards were artistic rather than financial.'*

She had a consultation about her finances with Massine's wife who recommended a single room in a hotel for $3 a day, $1 for breakfast, $2 for lunch, and $3 for dinner. That totalled $9. So, Mrs Massine told her, if she allowed $10 a day she would be comfortable. Alicia reckoned she could manage on $100 a week which would enable her to send money home to Eileen. She had been helping to support her mother since her first permanent contract with the Wells in 1934. She continued to send money home until Eileen's death.

Although Massine's company was billed as the 'Ballet Russe de Monte Carlo', the only members of the original company were Alicia and Danilova and, of course, himself. The rest had been stranded in war-torn Europe. He had to recruit other dancers where he could and was lucky to get Moscow-born André Eglevsky, who happened to be in America at the time and who had been with the American Ballet working for Balanchine.

Much later, Eglevsky gave her a kitten, which was not the smartest thing to do, as she was embroiled in tours by then. But the poor little thing would have been abandoned had she not taken it, and she always loved cats.

'We were rehearsing at the School of American Ballet on Madison Avenue then. There was a drugstore downstairs which was won-derful for us. André, who was partnering me in *Nutcracker* at the time, went down to get some sandwiches and came back with this little weeny kitten, all black but for white socks and shirt and the

* *Markova Remembers.*

most enormous whiskers. He had to grow into them so I called him
Whiskers. So I was saddled with Whiskers. I took him back to the
Windsor Hotel and looked after him but as soon as we finished the
season I had to find him a good home.' There was no shortage of
takers for Markova's moggy.

Eventually other Ballet Russe dancers managed to join them by
one means or another, but the cast was still thin by opening day.
Massine was saved on the very morning of their first performance
when a boat, the *Rotterdam*, arrived from France carrying several
of his dancers, including Freddie Franklin. Hurok met them at the
dock. 'Get going,' he greeted them. 'Tonight you perform.'*

They were on that night, sea legs or not, although there was
some confusion backstage as no one was sure who was dancing
what. 'We had rehearsed and prepared our opening programme
on dancers that were already there so, on opening night, there were
two companies.'

But Alicia was certain of her repertoire. She was to open by
giving the American premiere of *Le Rouge et le Noir*.

John Martin in the *New York Times* commented:

'It reveals Alicia Markova in an entirely new light, and shows
that, if she is exquisite as the wistful Giselles and Odettes of the
romantic repertory, she is also moving and beautiful in the stark and
distorted medium of abstraction and what is sometimes known as
modernism.'

She danced in just a single performance of *Giselle* that season as
Massine was keen for her to appear in modern works.

Many remembered her from the previous season and she became
a New York celebrity. According to Dolin this presented her with a
new problem, or rather, the resurfacing of an old problem. She had
never overcome her shyness.

This was variously interpreted as aloofness – which went with
her stage persona – 'English reserve' or unfriendliness. Rarely was
shyness diagnosed. How could a creature who shimmered on stage
be shy?

Sometimes she sat in a corner, while Dolin posed centre-stage
and gestured with his cigarette, convulsing all with his caustic
wit. A popular man, he dominated any gathering. As the laughter
ricocheted off the walls there were times when she wished she
was elsewhere. She would have been, too, had Dolin not dragged
her along.

His intentions were honourable enough. Naturally he basked in

* *The Last Impresario.*

her glory but he also wanted to show her off, and for her to enjoy her fame.

She often wished she was in her hotel with a book. As it took nerve to leave a room full of sparkling people she just sat. 'I'm not a party person,' she says.

Someone who did manage to get through to her was British actress Constance Collier. Then in her mid-sixties, she had made a career in Hollywood by playing aristocrats. When not working in Hollywood she preferred to base herself in the more sophisticated climate of New York. An actress of great flamboyance, she would seem an unlikely companion for Alicia.

Dolin, however, adored her and took the, at first, reluctant Alicia to tea with her. The two hit it off and had several cheerful tea parties after that. Miss Collier had seen her dance and was a genuine admirer. She decided to act as her champion and with Constance Collier behind her Alicia gained confidence.

'She tried to help me find myself,' she says. 'It was difficult for me in America, nearly all the time I was on stage so how would I meet anybody? I'd always enjoyed reading in my room and it wasn't really fair to me, to take me to those parties, although I didn't realize it at the time.

'With Diaghileff I'd felt secure. I knew I could discuss anything professionally. Somehow, beyond that, no one ever wanted to listen to me. Daddy listened, that was why I missed him so much, and Diaghileff replaced him which was where I was so lucky. Also with Ninette and Danilova, they were very good friends to me. Although I had travelled and met lots of people I probably felt a little strange in America.

'But Constance would ask me questions, ask my opinion. Frankly, I don't think anyone had ever bothered before then. That was the first thing she did for me. "I'm not going to teach you to speak," she told me. "You must just say what you feel, be yourself." I felt like saying, "Who is myself? I don't know."

'We got along very well. She would invite me round for lunch or tea. I was at the Windsor Hotel on 58th Street and she was on 57th Street, so she was only the next block. She was someone who understood if I was rehearsing, there was no explaining to be done. She was understanding, that was the wonderful thing.

'She had a companion, Phyllis. She would get on the phone and say, "Miss Collier wants to know if you're free about five this afternoon. If you'd like to come round she's got a couple of friends coming too." I would arrive and it would be Vivien Leigh and Larry Olivier, they were in New York for the *Cleopatra* season. We met each other as people. I admired them no end and, apparently, they'd seen me. Without Constance we would never have have met in a relaxed atmosphere.'

Later, in California, Miss Collier introduced her to her old friend Charlie Chaplin. They had first met when Miss Collier had arrived in America to appear opposite Sir Herbert Tree in a silent film of *Macbeth*, and had imperiously beckoned Chaplin to her table in a restaurant.

He had gone like an obedient dog and had remained her slave ever since. He remembered watching her from the gods in London, where he was born. She had helped him improve his elocution and did the same for his wife of the time, film star Paulette Goddard. Unfortunately Miss Goddard was not as grateful as Chaplin.

Chaplin took to Alicia. As a mime artist he appreciated her skill. When the great comic W. C. Fields had been forced to sit through a Chaplin film he had exclaimed, 'The son of a bitch is a ballet dancer!' Realizing he could not compete on that footing, the hefty Fields continued, 'He's the best ballet dancer that ever lived and if I get a good chance I'll strangle him with my bare hands.'

Chaplin loved to tell these anecdotes and others. Alicia was a good listener and sat in rapt attention while he unfolded his triumphs.

Dolin did not continue to Australia – the war had also affected de Basil's plans. He accepted an offer from the New York-based Ballet Theatre to be leading male dancer and choreographer.

He remained in New York but Alicia, after her Met season, had to start her tour.

In the spring of 1940 she was back at the Met for another season. She again danced *Giselle* on 3 May. Critic John Martin was again in the audience:

'Alicia Markova . . . gave such a performance as balletomanes dream about seeing in some distant realm of perfection, but never really expect to see. If this role is the Hamlet of the ballerina, as is frequently said of it, because of the great demands it makes upon its player, Markova has assuredly proved her mastery of it, and never more eloquently than on this occasion. Not only does she dance it with exquisite precision and incredible lightness, but she plays it with such imagination and style that, stilted and old-fashioned as it is dramatically, it becomes both believable and moving. Truly, here is the first ballerina of her time . . . it is not a new role for her to be sure, but in this, her first performance of it in the spring season, she danced it as she has never danced it hereabouts before . . .' – *New York Times*

Youskevitch was now her regular Albrecht. His quiet sense of humour matched her own. Technically he was an excellent partner. His swimming training had made his arms and shoulders powerful and he could effortlessly lift her.

But, earlier in the season, Hurok arranged that Dolin reunite with her for a single guest appearance in *Giselle* at the Met. Dolin had mounted a successful 'rival' version for Ballet Theatre at New York's Centre Theater.

Such was the interest in the Dolin/Markova performance that an adapted version was broadcast on radio on 25 April. Melodies from the ballet were played on the piano by a Madame Demidoff and Dolin and Alicia gave explanations as to what was happening.

It was an innovation in several ways, not least because Adolphe Adam's original score was so rare. Madame Demidoff had had to borrow Alicia's precious copy. Nowadays, when the music is readily available on CD, it is hard to appreciate that it was virtually unknown then. Few copies of the score existed outside Russia. It was the first time it had been heard on American radio.

The Ballet Russe had been scheduled to move to Paris from New York for appearances at the Théâtre Palais de Chaillot, but the war prevented this. France had been defeated and Hitler's troops occupied the capital. Hurok quickly arranged a tour of South America instead.

They were booked for appearances in Rio, São Paulo, Buenos Aires, Rosario and Montevideo. They were to travel to Rio, via Trinidad, by boat.

Before leaving for South America the cast had to be inoculated against tropical diseases. As female dancers' arms are often exposed during performances, and their legs covered by tights, it was thought wiser to inject in the legs. Unsightly blotches would be covered. No one, however, had taken the swelling into account.

The trip to Rio took three weeks from New York. The nearer they came to South America the hotter the weather became. Alicia went down with a fever and her injected leg swelled to twice its normal size. She could barely move.

She lay on deck trying to get what breeze there was, chatting to Rubinstein and the tenor Jan Kiepura, who were also on the tour.

Rubinstein was a great asset. After dinner, they would gather over a few drinks in the lounge, and he would regale them with anecdotes that had them roaring with laughter. Danilova, too, liked to hold court. Alicia was content to sit back and listen. There was, actually, some apprehension in the air as, although they were assured the waters were safe, they were not absolutely certain.

Rio was shortly to explode upon the movie scene as the centre of musical romance with the screen arrival of 'Brazilian Bombshell' Carmen Miranda who, at that very time, was shooting her American film debut. Her follow-up, *That Night in Rio*, was to open the floodgates for Rio as a tourist centre.

But Alicia arrived before Carmen Miranda's movies. As she eased her improving leg into mobility to disembark, everyone was warned not to drink from glasses or cups in restaurants as they risked getting syphilis of the mouth. That would have looked pretty in *Giselle*. The girls, too, were warned about going out alone as they ran the risk of being abducted by the white slave traders. Another comforting thought.

According to Danilova there were complications with Alicia's name as they were disembarking. 'It was a time when passports were always being checked. There was a call on the boat. "Danilova, Eglevsky, Slavenska and Marks." She didn't budge and I said, "Alicia, that's you!" She said, "What do you mean?" I said, "Marks, that's you." "Oh my goodness," she said. "So it is, that's right, it's me." She often forgot her real name. We had a lot of fun about it.'*

Danilova, too, sometimes forgot her name, notably during the period when she was married to an Italian and her passport was altered accordingly.

Alicia, even with her painful leg and fever, was faring better than other members of the cast, many of whom were doubled up with diarrhoea, dysentery and other illnesses.

She opened with *Swan Lake*. *Giselle* was on the second night. This was due to be followed by the 'Polovtsian Dances' from Borodin's *Prince Igor* which featured Freddie Franklin as The Warrior.

During the morning rehearsal Hurok called a meeting of the principals. There was a crisis; so many of the *corps de ballet* were ill that there were not enough left to make up the full complement of the chorus. If he cancelled he would not be paid so would be unable to unable to pay the cast. The only way the ballet could go on would be if the principals doubled up as members of the chorus. Their identities would be protected.

* Taped interview with Danilova, 1994.

They agreed, provided Massine, too, joined them. Massine thought it best not to tell Freddie, who was not present at the time.

The audience that night saw a unique *Prince Igor* consisting of the most expensive *corps de ballet* in the world, but not the best rehearsed. There were monumental gaffes, particularly by Massine who, at one point, turned left when the rest of the chorus turned right. Freddie could not believe his eyes; it was as though he were in some nightmare.

'There, on the back row, were Massine, Eglevsky and Youskevitch. None of them knew the ballet so there was a free-for-all going on back there. Then Eglevsky and I did a *tour de rôle* and I was at the back. I knew it all, of course, and Massine said, "Well, Freddie, get us through this."

'Igor was hopeless and so was Massine. They'd never been in the *corps de ballet* and it was alien to them. They didn't know anything. I don't know if Massine ever danced The Warrior but he certainly didn't know the ballet.

'Because so many people were ill we had to double up in all sorts of things. I remember Alicia doing one of the statues in *Bacchanale*, to the *Tannhäuser* music, and that was after she'd danced *Giselle*. Danilova was a fish. Everybody was on, we all had to do it.'

While in Rio there was a programme change and Alicia danced *Giselle* followed by *The Blue Bird*. Normally she did not dance anything after *Giselle* but Massine pleaded with her. She completed the programme then fainted in the wings.

On their one day off in Rio, Alicia and Freddie went to the movies. The Pathé News came up. There was news of a German victory and the whole cinema stood and applauded. Freddie clutched Alicia and said, 'If you want to get out of here alive, you'd better stand up.' They took care not to speak to each other during the film.

Everyone thought, naturally, that Alicia was Russian, but the American Ambassador knew her nationality. He offered to make her an American citizen there and then but she said no. She was several times offered American nationality and always refused.

The humidity in Rio was so intense, with no air conditioning, that the company were forced to sleep on wooden slats as mattresses would have been impractical.

They limped on to São Paulo, the next venue. After her performance Alicia was presented with a huge basket containing five hundred white gardenias.

She was accustomed to getting bouquets of orchids larger than she was, but the gardenia basket was bigger than anything anyone had seen before. The entire cast took bunches and her room still looked like a flower shop, heady with the overwhelming perfume. Gardenias are her favourite flower and, later, in Mexico, Dolin bought her a whole pillowcase-full to sleep on. She had told him it was one of her fantasies and he fulfilled it for her.

From São Paulo they moved on to Santos. The trip was rushed and exhausting. They gave matinée and evening performances and then returned to the dock to await the boat that would take them to their next port. All Alicia recalled of Santos was the overall smell of coffee and orchids and a famous snake farm they all rushed round.

There was no time to rest and, given the distances covered, there were vast changes in temperature and climate. They played in mountain regions, where there were near-winter conditions, and on the plains where the temperature hovered around 120 degrees Fahrenheit. Buenos Aires was like England in November, damp and foggy. It was also fiercely pro-German.

Today, such a tour would amount to exploitation, and would not be permitted by the unions. But trades unions were not properly organized then.

As it was, expenses were so high that Hurok lost $22,000 on the venture.

Back in New York, in the autumn of 1940, the Ballet Russe appeared at the 51st Street Theater, as the Met was out of commission being renovated. It was the only theatre Hurok could get. Such was the popularity of Alicia's *Giselle* that the programme was changed to accommodate an extra performance. John Martin wrote in the *New York Times*:

'. . . Miss Markova last night caused its familiar technical vocabulary fairly to glow; and when the large audience burst into spontaneous cheering, it was not because she had been performing difficult acrobatics, but rather because she had transformed the basic material with which she was working into the stuff of sheer emotion.

'For all her superb technical power, it is her habit to understress virtuosity, and to discover beneath the surface of even the showiest passages, the essential idealism of the medium. Her style is thus supremely simple and pure, with never a false nuance or a superfluous ornament. It is perhaps this that enables her to find the link so often missed in *Giselle*, between the dramatically difficult first act and the technically brilliant second act.'

That season, partnered by Eglevsky, Alicia gave the Americans the first *Nutcracker* ever performed in America. Like *Giselle* it was a performance in two acts.

Various Balanchine ballets were also revived and she danced in *Poker Game*, to Stravinsky's music.

Olga Spessivtseva was living in a hotel in New York at the time, with her friend Leonard Brown. Although Spessivtseva had retired she had not yet become sufficiently unwell to be committed to an asylum. But she did not want to see, or mix, with people.

Alicia was an exception because she associated her with pleasant times. Alicia had taken a studio at Carnegie Hall where she could practise quite alone, without even a pianist. She coaxed Spessivtseva to come with her, as she thought it would be good to get her out of her room.

There in Carnegie Hall the great lady would watch Alicia work and take note of all she did, commenting when she thought it necessary. She knew Alicia was serious in her work and this pleased her.

Alicia barely had time to unpack before repacking for another tour. This time they were to travel across America from the East to the West Coast taking in numerous towns and cities.

In many of these places the dancers were regarded as awesome curiosities, rather like icons. Some of the people had travelled, literally, hundreds of miles for the performance. For many Americans she was their introduction to ballet and, for some, the only example they ever saw.

They gave just a single performance in some towns. Alicia would arrive in the afternoon, dance in the evening, then return to the station for a journey that could involve hundreds of miles. If she was lucky she was in a sleeper; if not she had to sit up and doze as best she could.

The coaches in which they travelled were hired and attached to scheduled trains. Because they were not in everyday use they were often run-down, even broken-down, dilapidated and with damaged springs. Sometimes Alicia would leave the theatre without eating and, if there was no buffet car on the station, she stayed hungry.

She travelled well and could sleep better than most.

'I had an inflatable pillow I used to blow up. I'd put it against the window and rest my head on it and off I'd go. That pillow was most important to me. I rarely dropped off before two in the morning and often there was a 6.30 a.m. call. We were shaken from one station to the next.'

Other times she fared better.

'As soon as we got in the carriage, the boys would take our bags and coats and build up a bed on the floor for us. We'd pull the shades down, all get on it and lie flat out. If there was no early call we'd sleep till lunchtime. The carriage would be shunted into a station and we'd sleep on. No one questioned things, and we just worked out the best way to survive. I was given a place on the bed because I was dancing big parts. Most of the men sat up all night and played poker.

'On some long trips we weren't told we had to change trains. We'd arrive at a station in the small hours and someone would shout, "All change!" We had to get out and drag our baggage across a bridge to another station.

'It was things like that that started the need for unions. I was voted union representative, they chose me instead of a Russian as they might get excited. I was one of the first to explain the problems to management, particularly those of the *corps* as there was no one to speak up for them. They were getting about thirty dollars a week. I don't know how they managed to keep themselves on it.'

Fortunately she never needed to take sleeping pills to nod off, as some other company members did. There had been occasions when the effects had not worn off in time for the performance.

If a train was late arriving at a town then the performance would be late starting. The curtain came down correspondingly late and the cast would find themselves still in make-up rushing neck and neck with the audience to the station.

Massine tried to rotate the soloists as much as possible so that a dancer who performed a taxing role one night could take a lesser one the next.

Danilova and Alicia looked after each other during those arduous tours. The company contracts stipulated that certain stars must appear at each booking and they were able to deputize for each other if one was unwell.

'Once my toe went septic,' Alicia recalls. 'We were on the train and suddenly it swelled up. I'd had to wear coloured tights for a performance and the dye had got in. Perhaps I was overtired which made it worse.

'I couldn't get my shoe on and the doctor said, "She'll just have to stay off for a couple of days." The whole repertoire had to be changed, which affected everyone. Danilova said to me, "You can't dance like that. If it's OK with the management I'll dance for you." So, immediately I had to get Libby, our manager, and tell him Chura would dance for me and ask him to check with the local management that this was acceptable. As it was Madame Danilova, it was alright.

'We deputized for each other several times. Whenever we got anywhere where there was snow she used to get bronchitis. Once she got a temperature and I asked, "What are you dancing tonight?" She told me and I said, "Well, it'll be me. It's all right. I can manage it."

'I got on to Libby and said, "Chura has a temperature and she's no voice left. I think if she stays in bed tonight and has room service and sleeps she'll be OK.. It's too risky for her to dance tonight." We were leaving on a train for somewhere else the next morning.

'He agreed and got on to the local management right away. As it was me that was acceptable. I would be on twice instead of once but that was all right. This was the way we had to work. It could happen to anyone.'

Alicia was rostered to alternate with Slavenska but Slavenska became ill and could not dance for three weeks so Alicia had to take over her roles in addition to her own.

When they reached Los Angeles they were able to settle into a hotel for a while as they were giving several performances. She and Danilova shared a room and they found the hotel crowded with a convention of vine growers.

'One evening, when we had gone to bed, there was a knock on the door,' Danilova remembers. 'A waiter came in with two baskets of fruit, chocolates and wine. Oh, I thought. How nice of the management. So we sat up in bed and ate the fruit and chocolates and drank the wine.

'Next morning two old gentlemen knocked at the door and asked to take us to dinner. It might have been fun but neither of us could oblige as, as we explained, we were dancing that evening. The men were not as forward as it might appear as they had assumed that we, like them, were vine growers. We could not return the food as we'd devoured it all. The gentlemen were delightful and apologized for their mistake. We laughed so much when they had gone.'*

In New Orleans they were unable to get accommodation as

* 1994 taped interview.

an important football match was on and the city was full of
supporters.

From New Orleans they moved north to Canada. While in
Toronto, dancing *Giselle*, Alicia was horrified, in the interval, to
find a female dancer, who had been undergoing an unhappy love
affair, blind drunk in her dressing-room toilet. It was not a question
of the girl having had a few drinks; she was unable to stand.

But she could still shout and was doing so at the top of her voice,
carrying through to the auditorium. Alicia tried to sober her up
with coffee and smelling salts. The second act was delayed while
she changed and hoped the shouts would not spoil the ethereal
atmosphere.

That Toronto *Giselle* was fated. On another occasion the stage
was so oily, greased, with the best of intentions, to look good for
the ballet company, that several members took tumbles although
Alicia managed to stay upright. 'We used to take bets to see who
would go down each night.'

Eventually the stage was swept and dusted down during one
interval, and the dust made her sneeze and she could not stop. As
she says, 'A sneezing phantom was out of the question.' She could
not continue until a doctor gave her medication.

Once again the interval was prolonged.

Alicia's and Dolin's paths did cross from time to time as he
toured with Ballet Theatre and they met up in Chicago in the late
autumn of 1940.

Alicia felt the cold in the Windy City and went to a store to buy
some gloves. The only ones that fitted were children's. She chose
a Shirley Temple pair.

Miss Temple was eleven and at the height of her fame. Her latest
film, *The Little Princess*, was doing her usual excellent business.
Merchandizing was at its peak, hence the Shirley Temple gloves.

Much later, Alicia was to meet another soon-to-be-great star
in Chicago – Liberace. He was about to make his debut at the
Empire Room of the Palmer House Hotel. Alicia remembers their
meeting.

'It was his very first engagement in Chicago. He used to come
to our performances in the opera houses – he liked ballet – and, I
think, he had probably met Dolin first and got to know him.

'He told us that this was his very first engagement in Chicago and
that he was going "commercial". He'd thought out his programme
and he said it would help him if we'd be his guests.

'We went to his opening night. It was very simple, just a grand
piano with the candelabra on it. He played beautiful Chopin which

he dedicated to me as he had seen me in *Les Sylphides*. He told the audience that he had seen Dolin and me dance and that we honoured him by being there. He was very sweet.

'From then on whenever we were in the same city we'd ring each other. His mother would often be there – he was into his family, his mother and brother George were often with him.'

Alicia's three-year contract with the Ballet Russe was coming to an end and Dolin did not think she should renew it. He wanted her to sign for Ballet Theatre where she could be his partner again.

Another inducement was that Hurok was switching allegiance to Ballet Theatre, and she would have the opportunity of working with Fokine (Massine was to join a year later).

The Ballet Russe did not want her to go and asked her to name her price if she would stay. But she had made up her mind and signed with Ballet Theatre at $400 a week, at that time the highest salary ever paid to a ballet dancer but less than she would have received had she stayed with Ballet Russe.

'Alicia was the one who made the breakthrough with salaries,' remembers Freddie Franklin. 'When she joined Ballet Theatre she went to Lucia Chase, who had founded it and was in charge of things, and said, "I want X amount of dollars." It went through the grapevine and we all heard how much she was getting. It filtered through.

'I was earning a hundred and twenty-five dollars a week by then and I went to the management and asked for more. They said we'll give you two hundred and fifty a week but you'll have to sign for another three years. By now I was on a nine-year contract or something like that, it was ridiculous. But the management eventually changed and the structure changed with it and then contracts became more realistic.

'But Alicia was the one who challenged them. She had the courage to say no. She's very aware, everywhere, of what's going on. She doesn't always say much but she takes it all in. She's aware of herself and the things around her, that's what made her so good.'

16

Romeo and Juliet

Before starting with Ballet Theatre Alicia and Dolin ran a summer school and festival for three months at dancer Ted Shawn's farm, 'Jacob's Pillow'.

They were backed financially in this by her wealthy fan Reginald Wright, who used to take her out to dinner in London, and who took out the lease on the farm for them. He had always told Alicia that he would back the right platform for her and he considered 'Jacob's Pillow' to be right.

Situated in the beautiful Massachusetts countryside, 'Jacob's Pillow' had been converted into a dance studio and each summer it held a festival that attracted enthusiasts from all over the world.

Shawn, an international star in his own right, had appeared in one of the first dance films, *Dance of the Ages*, and had married dancer/choreographer Ruth St Denis who had designed some of the spectacular dances for D. W. Griffith's monumental film *Intolerance* in 1916. One of Miss St Denis's aims was to render music visible by the abstract nature of her dances. Her motivation was oriental dancing although, as *The Concise Oxford Dictionary of Ballet* puts it, 'she had a rather imprecise idea of the various oriental dance styles.'

The Shawn marriage did not last and, after parting from Miss St Denis, Shawn pioneered the cause of male dancers. In 1933 he formed the All-Male Dancers Group which toured widely, fighting what Shawn considered to be prejudices against male dancers. Dolin was with him all the way there.

Shawn had bought 'Jacob's Pillow' in 1933 but by 1941 he was in financial difficulties and needed the festivals to survive.

Alicia and Dolin decided to accommodate the entire Ballet Theatre company at 'Jacob's Pillow'. They had the support of Sol Hurok in this. The company had no work for three months and the dancers were out of contract. In the normal course of events the various members would have accepted what work they could get elsewhere, and there was no guarantee they would all be free when Ballet Theatre was due to start a Mexican season after the summer.

In return for their accommodation they had to help in running the festival and contribute what they could towards their keep. Everyone had an area of responsibility.

The dancers, and some of the students they accepted, received an unemployment benefit of $10 a week. Out of this they contributed $7 for their food – $1 a day – and kept $3 spending money.

Alicia was responsible for the catering.

Students sometimes arrived with their families, and they were roped in. The mothers acted as waitresses or worked in the box office. It was like Tolstoy's idea of a socialist community, everyone working according to their abilities.

Performances were given, which the public could attend, and these were economically costed with the best seats costing $1.50. Tea was thrown in, served in the grounds. Since it was summer the weather was warm.

According to Agnes de Mille, who came one weekend to dance, Alicia had seconded a girl 'acolyte' who ran errands and generally looked after her. Alicia sometimes 'adopted' such a student. 'Markova always talked in front of her as though she were not there with regal imperviousness to human criticism,' recalls Miss de Mille. '. . . for her payment she would watch a genius rehearse every day.'

When the 'Jacob's Pillow' deal was finalized it was decided that the students and other artists would be billeted in the many cabins situated in the grounds. Alicia alone would be in the house and take possession of Shawn's master bedroom, an upstairs room of palatial proportions which contained a vast four-poster. It had a little terrace outside the bedroom window where Shawn liked to sun himself. There was no rail and an unwary person could have fallen to his death.

Alicia decided to make it more cosy.

'I loved that room and made it like a country cottage. When I knew I was going to be there for three months I went off to New York and bought some lovely flowered curtains and a large pink rug because there were only polished bare boards. I also bought a little dressing table and a great pink eiderdown for the four-poster. There I was in this huge grandmother bed, all in pink. It lifted my spirits. I'd moved in. I had my practice tutus hanging all round the walls.

'Pat and I barely saw each other. We were both going from nine in the morning till gone midnight. At eight in the morning there would be a tap at the door and there was Kapp with my breakfast tray. As I was in charge of catering it was fortunate we had a good chef. Kapp had been in the army and he used to come up to me each day to go through the menus.

'Lying in my pink four-poster I'd ask, "Good morning, Kapp, what do you suggest today?" There was always the question of expense. Everything was rationed and we had two meatless days a week – and dancers used to live on meat then.

'Pat would never help, he would say, "That's your department, you sort that out." And likewise I would let him get on with his department.

'We didn't work on Sundays and always had a Sunday lunch. I would say, "Kapp, we must have the big ribs of beef, Yorkshire pudding, vegetables and apple pie." That was the day everyone used to descend on us, all the tourists and families of the dancers. It was open house. I used to go crazy because I never knew how many were going to arrive and we had to cater for them.

'Anyone who had a car, and gasoline, which was rationed, used to arrive. All the photographers from *Vogue, Harper's* and the rest used to come. I knew them all, they would come to photograph me.

'I remember getting up at seven one morning because one of them wanted to catch a certain light to photograph me through the trees dancing *Les Sylphides*. I'm not an early riser and it was agony.

'When Kapp went I had to get myself up. There was no bathroom but I had a place like a little cupboard with a tap and, I think, a sink and a lavatory. Ted and his men used to jump into a nearby stream. They were hardy.

'When I first saw the toilet arrangements I thought, Well, this is it, what am I going to do? But when things are primitive one gets accustomed to it as I've done in many different countries.

'I went to New York, to a camping shop, and asked what they could suggest. They were experts. I got myself a camping bath, all in rubber and folded up in a zipper bag. It wasn't too heavy and you could open it up. I could stand in it and fill it with water and get my sponge and do what I could. There was no hot water and no running water.

'The problem was getting the water pumped up. The pump was

in the yard and the area where it was was covered with beautiful mint – everyone had mint juleps. I got one of the boys to pump the water for me. Then I used to have a rub-down with alcohol. All dancers rub down with alcohol as Pavlova had taught me.

'When I first moved in I was very much alone at nights as I was the only one sleeping in the house. One night a terrible din woke me and I thought, I'd better stay in bed and pretend to be asleep. It carried on and, eventually, I dropped off again, I was so tired.

'When I woke up it was daylight, it must have been about seven. I thought, Thank goodness I've come through the night. Then the noise started again. Such a racket. I thought, Kapp will be up at eight and I'll get him to see what it is. So I lay there until he came.

'Do you know what it was? The roof was corrugated and chipmunks were rolling nuts down it. I thought, Oh my God, what animals are these? I was unacquainted with the country and Americans have a different set of animals to us. Once I knew what it was I didn't mind. But the noise.'

Highlights of the festival were performances by Alicia and Dolin, plus other artists such as Baronova and Agnes de Mille, and pieces performed individually and together by Shawn and Ruth St Denis. Although separated, they still worked together. Miss St Denis opened the festival with a study entitled 'Incense'.

She was not resident, purely a guest artist, but Ted Shawn stayed the whole course, dancing, advising and teaching. He performed 'Cosmic Dances of Shiva' in front of a magnificent hand-carved altar which still exists and is occasionally paraded out for exhibitions.

As Alicia had commandeered his quarters he was domiciled nearby at Mother Derby's, as were Baronova and her husband, and Antony Tudor and Hugh Laing.

Mother Derby was the proprietress of a huge converted barn virtually on the doorstep. That, too, was primitive in that it had no bathrooms, electricity or running water. Nevertheless she housed and cooked for her guests in a fulsome way. She'd been there for years. 'It was always country cooking,' recalls Alicia, 'and she used to give me enormous portions because she used to think I needed fattening up. She usually had her gun nearby to shoot something for the pot. You were in a different world.

'When the guests started to arrive at the station there was no transport to bring them to us. Some of the students were only ten years old, and teenagers, and we were responsible for them all. Kapp told Pat we needed a second-hand station wagon. I left that to Pat. "I'm doing the catering," I said. "You can see to that."

'He made a deal somewhere and we got the station wagon. Kapp would pile the students into it and drive them to the town where they would collect their unemployment benefit which they had to bring back to me. I received the dollar a day to feed them. I asked Pat what to do and he said, "I don't want anything to do with it, you can sit there and do that. That's you."

'It was difficult to feed them on a dollar a day. We had lots of salads and a hot meal in the evening. They were working all day so they were ready for it.

'I tried to place the itinerary for the students in the early evenings so that they could watch the professionals working later.

'Then Ballet Theatre arrived. I forget how many of them there were, thirty or something. Nijinska came up with her husband and daughter to start work on her new productions to be ready for Mexico in September. Can you imagine trying to control that lot?

'Fokine was about to arrive and start work with me but I thought, Oh no, not yet. So we dissuaded him, thank God. We didn't start the new work, *Bluebeard*, till Mexico.

'When you think of that enormous company! There wouldn't have been one but for Kapp and me doing the juggling.'

Neither Alicia nor Dolin shirked the physical labour of running the place. They cleaned and swept, Alicia wearing trousers which, although worn in Hollywood by Marlene Dietrich, were still ahead of fashion.

On Freddie Franklin's birthday they celebrated with a square dance, the fiddle played by the famous 'caller' Sammy Spring. In a photograph of the occasion they look as if they are having a good time.

Alicia gave master classes, exhibitions and rehearsed the ballets for Mexico. She and Dolin gave an outdoor performance of a piece entitled 'The Sylphide and the Scotsman', a *pas de deux* they had choreographed, she in her *Les Sylphides* costume and he in kilt and tam-o'-shanter.

There is a photograph of Alicia and Dolin in which she is poised on one toe on a tree-stump in an arabesque. Dolin supports her, his arm outstretched and parallel to hers. He is stripped to the waist and she wears a swimsuit.

Agnes de Mille arrived one weekend. It was two years before she was to achieve international recognition for her choreography for *Oklahoma*. She was to dance an item from her concert repertoire entitled 'Degas Study: Stage Fright'. She recalled the occasion in her book *Portrait Gallery*.

'I arrived on a rainy night to find matters in considerable turmoil. There were tales of Markova hurrying from several classes in tears, Baronova was crying down the road in a neighbouring farmhouse, everybody rushed around very busy with housekeeping and rehearsal chores, stopping only to snarl at one another. I was assigned to a dormitory with Lucia Chase who wasn't crying that summer, [and] Nina Stroganova who was . . .

'When I arrived at "Jacob's Pillow" Markova had been closeted upstairs for two days and showed no sign of coming down although the weekend performances were imminent. Passing across the upper hall I peered unkindly through the half-open door. She lay in Ted Shawn's great double bed stretched like a Rachel on her death couch, the dark silken locks unmoving against the waxen shoulders, her eyes neither open nor shut, sealed in misery . . . the little head remained unmoving against its pillow. I watched for some time in fascinated shame. Tears trickled down her cheeks in an unending stream. In an adjacent room another lady devotee of Dolin's lay ill and weeping. Most great male dance stars, I have noticed, seem to have one or more of these dedicated followers trailing after them asking and getting absolutely nothing except the privilege of attending to mail, shopping a little, keeping a list of the star's social engagements and waiting hand and foot on the brilliant centre of their attention. Sometimes they are paid as secretaries and sometimes they foot their own bills.

'Downstairs the new master of "Jacob's Pillow" sat at dinner, the *hoi polloi*, the *corps de ballet* and friends ate in a kind of barracks but I, as a guest artist, was entitled to a place on the host's right.

'"Rooms full of weeping women," he said, spooning up his soup vigorously. "I wish they'd either get well or . . ."

'"Or what, Pat?" I said.

'"Or, well, now look here, ducky, the house is getting positively soppy with tears. What good does it do them to go on like this? I must say I think they rather enjoy it. I really do. But I certainly don't. For one thing the weather's too damp."

'"I think Alicia is not enjoying herself."

'"Then why doesn't she stop? Women are too preposterously silly." He called to the cook. "Send the trout to Madame Markova."

'This was promptly returned untouched . . .

'Alicia continued crying until it was nearly performance time and active measures had to be taken. An old friend and balletomane, a father and head of a household and thus someone used to family tantrums, advanced into the chamber of melancholy, pulled her from the bed and shook her until her teeth rattled. "Alicia," he said. "If you don't start getting ready for this afternoon's performance I'm going to turn you over my knee."

'She whimpered and started to pick at her make-up. He left her to the care of assistants who, scared to death and speechless, rushed to propel her through the preparations. She was supported across the yard to the theatre, the porches still dripped with summer rain . . .

'Alicia leaned in her dressing gown against a dank post, her acolyte waited round-eyed beside her with a tray of powder, hairpins and mirror. I was about to do a comedy dance and stopped to say that I hoped Alicia felt better. She gave me a graveyard smile and looked west to the Berkshires. Paddy Barker, her assistant, shook her head with the air of a nurse who knows the end is inevitable but hopes it will be quick.

'When I left the stage Alicia was in her skirt and trying out the points of her slippers; her breath still came unevenly from crying. Below-stairs when I changed I listened to the music from the Prelude from *Les Sylphides* and felt the slight jarring of the floor overhead from the great soft descents. At the conclusion there was a full six seconds of silence and then tumult. Several girls drifted below and stood dazed.

'"What happened?" I asked. They sat unable to continue with their changes. It seemed Markova had never before approached the beauty of her performance that afternoon.

'I hastened to offer my congratulations. Alicia was bouncing around upstairs in the farmhouse clad in a darling dressing gown and as happy as Christmas morning. Purged, delivered, vindicated.

'She had tied a bow in her hair.

'"It was rather good, you know," she said to me with brilliant eyes, "I can't say I was too displeased."

'"The girls said it was transcendent." She put her head on one side and considered.

'"It was all right," she said, then she scampered off down the hall to visit the other invalid's room whence presently came peals of girlish giggles. They sent down for enormous trays of food.

'I do not know why she carried on this way. I do know that she had only one concern in life: to dance better and better and better. This was all she did. She did not interest herself in one other thing.'

Such was the success of the festival that an official festival committee was formed with Reginald Wright as its first president.

Before proceeding to Mexico, Ballet Theatre returned to New York for a couple of weeks to rehearse its repertoire.

Alicia consulted her doctor. Although she can get depressed, if there is a reason for it, the bout graphically described by Agnes de Mille had been severe. She felt run-down.

He examined her and Alicia recalls him asking, 'What have you done to yourself? It's holiday time in the summer and you're going to start a new season. Now, take a week off.' He gave her a bottle of vitamin syrup telling her, 'You just need building up.'

It was more than that. The pressure of 'Jacob's Pillow' had been immense. She had no husband and no family and had to bear it alone. Dolin was there but, as always, whatever comfort he gave was paid for in terms of aggravation.

Ballet Theatre undertook a season at the Palacio de Bellas Artes, Mexico City. The atmosphere was hard-working and creative, and several new ballets were tested out on the Mexicans before making their all-important New York debut with Ballet Theatre.

Among these was Fokine's *Bluebeard*, to music by Offenbach and Antal Dorati. Dorati was Musical Director of the Ballet Theatre and a great asset. His opinions were eagerly sought and he put much hard, and original, thought into what he did. He was as vital to Ballet Theatre as Constant Lambert had been to Sadler's Wells.

Bluebeard, with décor by Marcel Vertès, was premiered on 27 October 1941.

One of the reasons Alicia had joined Ballet Theatre was to work with Fokine. He was a god and she had danced his ballets with reverence. Diaghileff had stressed to her that certain sections in certain ballets should be danced in a particular way for no other reason than that Fokine had wanted them like that.

Their first meeting was in New York prior to the 1941 season. She found him difficult and he could be sarcastic. He had argued with Diaghileff over Diaghileff's obsession with Nijinsky and his determination to build his choreographic career. It had been years ago but the hurt still rankled.

Alicia was desperate to learn from Fokine, and he had plenty to teach her, so she was determined to get on with him. It was not always easy and there were times when she bit her tongue. She cringed when he was sarcastic to other dancers.

Before she left for Mexico she had worked with him on a new production of *Les Sylphides*. On their first day of rehearsals Fokine sat in the empty studio and commanded her, 'Show me what you have.'

She asked which opening variation he would prefer to see as she knew all three, so he told her to dance them all. She did so. Without commenting, he sent for her partner, George Skibine, to dance the *pas de deux* with her. Skibine was just twenty-one, an extremely talented and dedicated dancer. He had formerly worked at the Bal Tabarin as a can-can dancer, which needs enormous skill.

He danced the *pas de deux* with her and Fokine was silent. His face registered nothing. Then he contemptuously asked, 'So this is *Les Sylphides*?'

She replied it was as she had learned it with Diaghileff.

'It is not really *Sylphides*,' he told her.

She asked him to teach her what was *Sylphides*.

'From the next rehearsal he did exactly that,' she wrote in *Markova Remembers*, 'instructing me in every nuance of timing, phrasing, musical understanding.'

Until that time Alicia had never really enjoyed the ballet, although she had danced it many times and seen several great dancers in it, including Karsavina.

He made her relearn all three variations, then told her which he preferred. He explained that his choreography was different from Petipa's. He wanted curves as opposed to straight lines. He told her to leave the stage as if she were reaching for the moon, urging her 'Reach! reach!'

'He taught me,' she continues in *Markova Remembers*, 'that you have to pass completely beyond technique – even throw it away . . . Everything has to be sustained, floating. No effort must be seen, ever . . . there is no beginning or end to movements – they melt away like sound on the air . . .'

An incident in rehearsal stuck in her mind. She had always danced a certain movement looking at the floor, as she had been taught to do and as she had seen other ballerinas do. Fokine asked if she had lost something. He told her she must look at her partner, then the *corps de ballet*. Suddenly the whole thing made sense to her and she found, for the first time, that she was enjoying the work.

She also worked with Fokine on *Bluebeard*. Despite the title this was a comedy, and she was cast as Princess Hermilia to George Skibine's Prince Sapphire. Dolin was Bluebeard and, in addition to Baronova, the cast also included Jerome Robbins.

The New York debut of *Bluebeard* took place on 12 November 1941 at the 44th Street Theater. Fokine decided he would play Alicia contrary to type. For her finale she performed a high-kicking can-can dance, holding her skirt up French-style and including thirty-two lightning-speed *relevés* on *pointe*, a doubleturn mid-air and a balance on *pointe*. She ended a Tarantella flat on her back with her legs kicking in the air.

This was heavy-going and she was permanently bruised. She had to stuff her tutu with padding for protection. But, for all the comedy, Fokine had included a beautiful *pas de deux*.

She also danced *Giselle* with Dolin at the 44th Street Theater on 27 November 1941. The company was not at the Met as the opera season was still in full swing. The production was new to her and had been devised earlier, by Dolin, for Ballet Theatre.

This was an uncompromising *Giselle*. The sets were black on white, which suggested old lithographs. She spoke with the designer, Lucinda Ballard, who created a shocking pink costume for her for the first act. It was a revolutionary production aimed at a younger audience.

Alicia made the headdress for the second act herself, a phantom thing fashioned from fish-bones which she had daubed with luminous paint. When the lights hit it it shone like an aura. She had done the same thing for her first *Giselle* with the Vic-Wells.

According to Arthur Todd, writing in *Dance and Dancers* in 1955, 'The great Markova boom did not really get underway until 1941 then . . . she became a star with Ballet Theatre . . . All of us will always remember those wonderful years in the early 40s when Markova was dancing *Giselle* . . . On those nights the house was always sold out to capacity and the atmosphere electric. I well remember one of these evenings when there were 36 curtain calls for Markova.'

Jerome Robbins was part of the company then. He went on to choreograph many hit shows including *The King and I*, *Gipsy* and *West Side Story*.

Rumours were circulating that Alicia believed she was in touch with the spirit of Pavlova. Agnes de Mille recalls how Robbins would station himself in the wings to watch while Alicia danced. In *Portrait Gallery* she writes:

'But he was impious. As she came off stage, with slightly heightened breathing demanding powder and a towel, he asked pertly, "How's the spirit doing, Alicia? Are you in tune tonight?"

'"Not bad, ducky, really not bad," she twinkled. "The last bit was pretty good." Then she was off in a *pas de bourrée* too rapid for the naked eye to follow. She minded his joking not a bit.'

Alicia recalls, 'Jerry and I were great friends. He used to call himself my "official catcher". He was always in the wings when

I did *Giselle*. There was one point when my veil had to be whisked away, to create a magical effect, and it had a piece of tape attached to it which could be jerked from the wings. It needed someone reliable to do it at the right time. Jerry always did it.'

Alicia was never under the delusion that she was in touch with Pavlova. Pavlova was an inspiration but never a spirit guide.

'I admired her and she was my ideal,' she says. 'But you must remember I never started out wanting to be a ballerina. My mother took me to see her on film when I was eight but it never entered my head that I would like to do that. People said all sorts of things because I resembled her and my mother told me that when she was carrying me she did think that it would be wonderful if I could dance just a little like Pavlova but, even knowing that, it didn't influence me. I had qualities she never had and her temperament was different, she couldn't have danced all those modern and humorous roles I did. A great lady and a superb dancer but we were different.'

According to Agnes de Mille, Alicia insisted that her costumes be cleaned before every performance. This was unusual as costumes in most companies were passed from dancer to dancer and only cleaned when filthy.

In *Portrait Gallery* Miss de Mille relates an occasion when ballerina Nora Kaye discovered, during a performance, that her change of costume was missing. She was informed that Markova had visited the theatre that afternoon and had sent it to be cleaned. Markova was wearing it herself later in the week. Miss de Mille was with Miss Kaye when she received this sobering news and recalls, 'Miss Kaye's face was, as they say, "a study".'

On her first Ballet Russe tour Alicia had danced Fokine's *L'Epreuve d'Amour*. It was one of the ballets whose scenery now reposed on the sea-bed at Cannes. This prevented her from ever dancing it again.

Another of Fokine's works was a *pas de seul* lasting less than three minutes. *The Dying Swan* had been Pavlova's *pièce de résistance* and every dancer of note had viewed it as Pavlova's personal property.

Now that Pavlova was dead Fokine tried to persuade Alicia to revive it. In this he was backed by Sol Hurok who was convinced of its box-office potential.

Alicia did not want to dance it at first. The public still identified it with Pavlova and she felt it was too soon. She thought she might be considered erring in taste.

But Hurok and Fokine persevered. For three weeks, before the

Ballet Theatre left for its tour, she worked solidly on the one piece, Fokine constantly coaching her and Hurok paying for his time. Fokine modified the choreography, where he felt appropriate, to suit Alicia's particular talents.

With his encouragement she first danced it at the Boston Opera House on 23 January 1942, the anniversary of Pavlova's death. The programme pointed out that she danced it as a tribute to Pavlova. The audience loved it and from then on it became one of her most requested items. She danced it all over the world. Fokine died less than a year later. But at least he saw his *The Dying Swan* performed again.

The original *The Dying Swan* had first been danced by Pavlova in a St Petersburg gala in 1907. Set to Saint-Saëns's woundingly beautiful 'The Swan' cello melody from *The Carnival of Animals*, it depicts a dying swan struggling for life. It became instantly identified with Pavlova, and a fragment of her sublime performance is preserved on an old film. It is the most famous ballet solo in the world. To many people it is the epitome of ballet.

Although the fact that Pavlova gave the debut performance of *The Dying Swan* is well documented, it has been disputed by ballerina Lydia Kyasht, who was born in St Petersburg, had a career at the Marynsky, and then came to London where she took over from Adeline Genée as prima ballerina at London's Empire Theatre.

She maintained constantly, emphatically and until her dying day, that she had been the first to perform *The Dying Swan*. She swore that she had danced it at the Dvorianskoe Sobranie at a charity to raise money for wounded soldiers long before Pavlova had danced it.

Stranger travesties of truth have happened. Whatever the truth of the matter, Fokine said he wrote it for Pavlova and he should know.

There have been other versions – there is no copyright on a title – but the only two versions to have been choreographed by Fokine were Pavlova's and Markova's.

While in Los Angeles with Ballet Theatre Alicia played at the massive open-air Hollywood Bowl, the first of many appearances there.

A fellow member of the Ballet Russe de Monte Carlo, Tula Finklea, was to follow her to to Hollywood where, in 1943, she forsook traditional ballet, changed her name to Cyd Charisse, appeared in her first feature film, *Mission to Moscow*, and became a film star.

Alicia recalls, 'She was really too tall for a ballerina. In those days we were all much smaller. But she was so beautiful everybody was enamoured. That was why she went into the movies and all that ballet training was a wonderful background. We kept in touch and the last time I saw her was when she was in *Charley Girl* in London.'

Thirty-five thousand turned up for Alicia's Hollywood Bowl appearance. She shared the largest attendance record with Toscanini. 'I couldn't believe that opening night of *Giselle*,' she says. 'They came to me backstage and said, "Look through the peephole, look who's sitting there." There was Charlie Chaplin, Paulette Goddard, Jesse Lasky and Eleanor Powell, who sent me a wonderful basket of flowers, and I don't know who else. It was packed with stars. I was flattered, of course.

'Huge auditoria don't bother me. It was the same with the Albert Hall, I loved dancing there. I'm a strange person. I'd be knotted inside until my first appearance. Everyone thought I was so cool they never knew the agonies I went through. But once I was out there I forgot everybody and just became whatever I was meant to be on stage. Once I could make contact with the audience I didn't have to worry.

'When I think back to the different places I've danced in, from the Ballet Club which had a stage the size of an average room to a record attendance of thirty-five thousand at the Hollywood Bowl! The bigger the audience the more I thought, How wonderful it would be if I could make them happy and satisfied.

'It's no more difficult projecting to a big audience than to a small one – it's the same whatever the size. I was very adaptable and practical which, of course, isn't supposed to go with what I've been on stage. I think I got that from Daddy who was an engineer. It makes life interesting.'

In April 1942, while she was dancing *Giselle* at the Met, Alicia learnt that Spessivtseva had been committed to an asylum in Poughkeepsie, New York State. Her sensitivity, which had enabled her to dance sublimely, had to be paid for. She had become unable to separate reality from fantasy.

Poughkeepsie was about seventy miles away and Alicia took the train to visit her. As it was Easter she bought her a pot of lilies. Spessivtseva had periods of lucidity and would see visitors with whom she associated happy times.

She chatted warmly with Alicia but was horrified when she discovered she was due to dance *Giselle* the following evening. As far as Spessivtseva was concerned Alicia should have been in bed resting.

In the summer of 1942 she was back in Mexico City working

with Massine on his *Don Domingo* and with Dolin on his *Romantic Age*. Fokine was working on *Helen of Troy*.

Fokine and Massine headed a group of choreographers and designers including Dolin, Antony Tudor and Jerome Robbins who were creating new ballets for the forthcoming New York season. Antal Dorati was the conductor.

Before all this activity, which she thrived on, Alicia was able to take a couple of short holidays, one in Guadalajara and another in Acapulco, then a little fishing village with few visitors. There, happy as a lark, she frolicked in the sea, reed-thin in her two-piece bathing suit, with Robbins and Dolin.

In addition to *Don Domingo*, and other ballets, she was working with Massine on *Aleko*, set to Tchaikovsky's music and Marc Chagall's décor, which was premiered in Mexico City on 8 September 1942 and in which she was partnered by Skibine and Hugh Laing. Tudor played her father. She was the sultry gipsy Zemphira.

Chagall designed her costumes, one of which contained a spectacular heart, which he hand-painted on the fabric himself. For the rest of his life, whenever he wrote to Alicia, he signed his letters with a heart with his name inside. Perhaps he was in love with her.

She was also working with Antony Tudor on *Romeo and Juliet*, in which Romeo would be Hugh Laing. Laing was a Barbados born-dancer who had come to America with Tudor and for whom Tudor designed most of his ballets. He had seen Alicia and Laing together in *Lilac Garden* and thought they would be the perfect Romeo and Juliet. Tudor was Tybalt.

Earlier, in New York, Fokine had promised Alicia that he would create a *Romeo and Juliet* ballet for her, for Ballet Theatre, but he did not care for the Prokofiev score and it never came to pass. Later, Tudor suggested that he do it for her. He did not like the Prokofiev music either. It was Antal Dorati who suggested the Delius version which he then arranged for Tudor.

Salvador Dali was approached to design the sets and, in time, submitted his ideas. These were unsuitable, particularly the balcony scene which featured a giant set of false teeth held up by crutches. Eugene Berman was next approached and his Botticelli-influenced designs were perfect.

Tudor conceived Juliet as around thirteen years old. Alicia was thirty-two; quite an acting feat was required. Her only assistance was a red wig.

When the company left Mexico for their pre-New York tour,

Romeo and Juliet was constantly rehearsed. Alicia worked on it in waiting rooms during the delays between trains. 'It could be one in the morning and we'd be waiting for a train. Massine and Tudor would say, "Come and rehearse."'

Tudor has been described as 'the choreographer of human sorrow' for his ability to imbue his dances with a depth of psychology startling at the time. He advised her to re-read the play and immerse herself in the part. 'My inspiration for Juliet was Peggy Ashcroft. I'd seen her do it in the 1930s at the New Theatre season when Gielgud and Olivier alternated as Romeo. She was wonderful.'

The ballet was not finished when the company arrived in New York. It was incomplete when the season opened and remained incomplete four days before it was due to be premiered.

Alicia had a full season. In addition to *Romeo and Juliet* she was dancing *Aleko, Giselle, Don Domingo* and *The Romantic Age*. Whenever she was not on stage she was rehearsing in the vast rehearsal room, the same size as the stage, in the roof of the Met.

She slept in her dressing room to save time travelling, and she and Tudor often worked all night. Someone would bring her orange juice, honey and vitamin pills in the morning. She was also taking daily lessons from Vincenzo Celli.

Hurok was concerned that she would make herself ill and, when rehearsals had gone on till past five one morning, he insisted on taking the whole cast out for a meal to Lindy's, where he stoked them up with smoked sturgeon, raw onions and rye bread.

Then he persuaded Alicia to go back to her hotel and rest. She went to bed at 7 a.m. but was up two hours later and back rehearsing at the Met.

The first night was 6 April 1943. The house had been sold out for weeks in advance. Alicia was also scheduled to dance a matinée that day of *Princess Aurora*, but withdrew from this. Nora Kaye was substituted. It was one of the few occasions when Alicia did not fulfil her advertised obligations.

That afternoon she relaxed as best she could. She took a yellow cab and drove round Central Park with the windows open, breathing in air that seemed fresh after the rehearsal room. She then went to bed and had a meal before returning to the Opera House.

As it was, the ballet remained unfinished on opening night. 'We brought the curtain down at a crucial moment – which was very exciting,' said Tudor.*

* Quoted in *The Last Impresario*.

Even in its unfinished state it turned out to be one of Alicia's greatest successes. She was praised as much for her acting as her dancing, so much so that drama students were sent in parties to watch her.

No Met season would have been complete without her *Giselle*. The trusty Dolin was Albrecht. Experienced as they were in their roles the performance did not lack spontaneity.

Trouble came before her first entrance, which is through a cottage door upon which Albrecht knocks.

Dolin knocked and the audience waited expectantly. She did not appear. Then the whole cottage shook as though caught in an earth tremor.

What had happened was that she had been unable to open the door, a nightmare come true. A helpful stage hand had noticed before curtain-up that the door had a tendency to swing open. He had taken a nail and improvised a hinge which would keep it closed. He had not told Alicia what he had done.

Dolin guessed she was locked in and hissed, 'Stop shaking the house down, ducky! I'll come round and help let you out!'*

He left the stage – leaving the audience puzzled as to why he had knocked on the door and walked away – but before he could get to her Alicia had rushed round to the wings and made her entrance, skipping on as though she were coming through the garden. The audience greeted her in silence, not sure who she was.

The spotlight managed to find her and she blinked in its light, unsure what to do. Her moves were off schedule now. So were Dolin's, who came running on from the wings on the opposite side from which he had disappeared. Before they could pull themselves together they were taken off guard by a round of applause. The audience had suddenly recognized Markova.

Afterwards she threw an un-Markova-like tantrum. But, after some time, when she had accepted that the stage hand had acted for the best of motives, she saw the funny side. But from then on she always checked the cottage door before a performance – every time.

Such was the demand for tickets for *Giselle* that the Met put on extra performances. Later she and Dolin gave a concert at the massive Lewisohn Stadium to an outdoor audience of twenty-four thousand. This was the largest audience any ballet performance had ever had. The intimacy still came across; had a pin been dropped in that massive arena, immediately after the performance, it would have been heard.

She and Dolin took part in some experimental dry runs of *Giselle*

---

* *Markova Remembers.*

for NBC Television. Television was constantly developing and new techniques had to be learnt. After they had danced, tenor Giovanni Martinelli made an appearance to represent opera.

Meanwhile, Alicia developed a bad eye. Due to the arduousness of the *Romeo and Juliet* rehearsals conjunctivitis set in. She wore a patch in the daytime but this would not do for a performance. As she could not put make-up on the bad eye there were difficulties in *Aleko*, in which she was dark-skinned. She had to appear with one eye naked. As she put it, 'the effect on the audience was as if I had a massive squint . . . I looked a bit like Carmen Amaya, she had a squint.' Signora Amaya, whom Alicia knew, was a fiery Spanish gipsy dancer, the top of the tree in her field.

Sir Thomas Beecham was in New York while Alicia was dancing *Romeo and Juliet*. As he was an expert on Delius he was invited to guest-conduct some performances. It seemed appropriate. *Romeo and Juliet* was a British ballet with British dancers; why not invite this most British of conductors? Beecham adored Delius and luxuriantly slowed the tempo. It caused quite a stir.

'Some dancers would find it difficult,' says Alicia. 'But I didn't mind; in fact, I thought it was wonderful. Not Mr Hurok, though, we were always into overtime.'

The folk of the orchestra were always delighted when it was a Beecham night as they could be sure it would overrun and they would be paid accordingly. But it was not so good for Hugh Laing. 'I think I'm going to die,' he moaned to Alicia one night as he held her aloft for what seemed for ever.

Soprano Maggie Teyte came to several performances. She suggested Tudor should choreograph *Pelléas and Mélisande* for Alicia, Laing and Pat. Dame Maggie, the possessor of one of the most hauntingly limpid voices the world had ever known, had sung *Pelléas and Mélisande* many times and had been closely associated with Debussy.

The inevitable tour followed New York. Many of the venues were, again, one-night stands in places where a ballet had never been mounted before.

By now unions had become more organized and the company only performed six evenings a week as opposed to seven. But they were often travelling on the seventh day.

None of the team forgot those hardships and Dolin recounted some in his biography of Alicia. 'One December morning, at three o'clock to be exact, I recall a group of the world's greatest dancers waiting for a bus to take them to Miami twelve hours away. Alicia was stretched out on the pavement with three overcoats . . . as her mattress, and her own hatbox as a pillow . . .'

They were in Chicago around Christmas time and, as the box office could be expected to be low at the time of year, Hurok gave the company a week off, as a holiday, and to get themselves sorted out for Christmas.

When in Chicago Alicia and Danilova would sometimes share lessons with Laurent Novikoff, ballet master at the Met, who also had a studio in Chicago. A former Bolshoi soloist, he had been another of Pavlova's partners.

Laundry was a problem on tour and sometimes, when there was a long train journey, the toilets would be full of drying underwear and tights.

Massine distanced himself from the troupe when travelling, rather as Diaghileff had done with the Ballet Russe. He liked his comfort and travelled by limousine and trailer. His chauffeur prepared meals for him.

Sometimes he would allow Alicia to use the trailer as a dressing room, if conditions were cramped. He did this in the town of Eugene, Oregon, on a blizzard-driven night when the company was appearing at the school hall. She was dancing the second act of *Swan Lake* and Massine was appearing later in the programme in his own *Gaité Parisienne*.

His trailer was parked right outside the stage door and while Alicia stood in tutu, awaiting her cue, he tucked into a large meal. Massine always ate before dancing which, to put it mildly, was unusual, but he claimed the food gave him stamina. As she made her entrance the smell of the food wafted on to the stage with her.

Now and then the dancers got a night off. On one such occasion, in Texas, Alicia and Youskevitch went to the pictures while Danilova and Freddie Franklin danced *Coppélia*.

Always, in these situations, they had to warm up, then wait until the show was taking place before leaving the theatre. They had to tell the company manager where they were going. Like doctors, they were on constant call. It was as well they were on this particular night.

They were enjoying the film as 'tourists' – a term the cast applied to dancers who went on the town on a night off – when the manager called them to the foyer. Both Franklin and Danilova had food poisoning. They had completed two acts but were unable to finish. Alicia and Youskevitch had to take over.

Fortunately, the cinema was near the theatre. They were thrown on with no time to make up, and Alicia did not have the right shoes. But they completed the performance.

Baths were at a premium. When the company was in a town 'The Army Game' was played again. Alicia and Danilova would take a suite for a day, at a low rate, and each have a long soak. A maid would be tipped to bring extra towels. Then, one by one, friends would come up and have a bath. The hot water ran continuously.

In one town where they were appearing at a cinema the set could not be erected until the film had finished. The ballet was due to start at eight and at least an hour of preparation was required if the curtain was to go up on time. But at seven the audience was still watching the film.

The company manager, in panic, instructed that the film be stopped. He then went in front of the audience and pleaded with them to leave in order that the ballet could take place. To his fury he found he was addressing his own dancers.

17

The Billy Rose Revue

While on the West Coast in 1943 Alicia was rehearsing Massine's *Mam'zelle Angot*, which she was to premiere at the Met, when she wrenched a muscle in her side. She keeled over in a faint. She had, as usual, been overworking. Massine's choreography was so demanding that she had to perform a backbend in mid-air while Eglevsky turned with her. It was that which had caused the problem.

She was helped home but there was no time to rest. That same evening she was appearing at the Hollywood Bowl in *Aleko* in front of a capacity audience of over thirty thousand. There was no question of cancellation.

She danced and very nearly got through but, towards the end, the pain flared up again and she once more collapsed on stage.

Hugh Laing was her partner and he carried her off. The audience were thrilled at the drama of it all.

The show had to go on and Muriel Bentley finished the performance. She did not have to do a great deal more than walk on and get stabbed. This was normally the climax of the ballet but, that night, it seemed anticlimatic after Alicia's real-life drama.

Alicia was taken to her hotel, by ambulance, in great pain. At first she thought it was appendicitis but the doctor diagnosed nothing more serious than a pulled muscle, which is very serious for a dancer. He strapped her in plaster and told her that the only cure was prolonged rest.

She remained in Hollywood while the company moved on.

La Argentinita, the famous Spanish dancer, together with her sister, Pilar Lopez, also a celebrated dancer, were also Hurok artists, guesting with the company at the bigger venues in New York and Los Angeles. As they did not have to tour they, and their Spanish maid, came round and looked after Alicia. Poor Argentinita was to die just two years later at the age of fifty. She had started at six and literally danced herself into the grave.

As soon as possible, Alicia returned to New York, where she took her apartment at the Windsor and convalesced until the opening of the Met season.

It was not long enough.

She danced the second act of *Swan Lake*, with Dolin, and during the second night, when he lifted her in the famous *adagio*, the pain shot through her again. She collapsed for the third time.

This time she had a hernia and surgery was required. It is unusual for female dancers to get hernias; they happen more frequently to the men who have to do the lifts.

It was mid-season and she felt she was letting the company down, even though it was through no fault of her own. She spent the two days prior to her operation teaching *The Romantic Age*, which was the new ballet, and *Giselle* to Cuban dancer Alicia Alonso, who was taking over.

After her operation the surgeon told her there was a risk she might never dance again. She must rest, this time for months. There was no alternative.

She remained in hospital for a couple of weeks then moved to the Windsor where she stayed in her room for three months, living on room service. It was lonely and she was frightened.

She tortured herself with the dreadful thought that she might, indeed, never dance again. Then what would she do? How could she earn her living?

Friends came and kept her up to date with the gossip and news. Sometimes they brought food and wine which they ate squatting on the bed.

A regular visitor was her friend Vincenzo Celli. Celli had been a leading dancer with La Scala until a hernia had ruined his dancing career. So he had every sympathy with Alicia.

Celli, and his wife, were friends of Toscanini's, and sometimes had Sunday lunch with the maestro. Toscanini, of course, knew Alicia as she had often gone to rehearsals for his NBC programmes.

One Sunday, when Celli told him of Alicia's trouble, he sent him round with a ginger kitten for her, 'to keep you company'. He knew she liked cats. 'And he did keep me company,' says Alicia. She called him Bambi.

She had known Celli since 1925 when they had been in Monte Carlo and he had been struck with this 'mere child dancing major roles with a skill beyond her years'.* He had been studying privately with Cecchetti who had passed much of his knowledge on to him. Alicia and Celli had resumed contact in 1938 when she had been in New York dancing with the Ballet Russe.

She had taken a company class with Celli, and it had not taken him long to discover her little ways. 'I remember that class to this day, filled as it was with famous stars and all happily working together. The attention had to be general and impersonal as the lesson was limited as to time.

'I was about to call on Markova to demonstrate . . . when I discovered she had disappeared, but well mannered as she instinctively is, she afterwards called me and explained her abrupt disappearance. She had an aversion to large company classes and made arrangements to study with me privately.'*

As Wendy Toye noted during the Markova/Dolin days, few saw Markova practise.

She saw Celli whenever she was in New York and took classes from him. On the road it was difficult for her to practise and faults could creep in. Celli ironed them out.

'A renewed vitality must be kept alive through continuous vibration like a rare Stradivarius,' he wrote. 'The body must be kept in tune in order to function at the highest summit of its capabilities. One could buy a Stradivarius but a dancer's body must be created. Sacrifice and a conformity to an ideal Markova carries in herself and this no teacher has taught her.

'A young flippant dancer once breezed into a rehearsal and, heading towards Markova, exclaimed, "Do you remember me? I danced for you last year when I was a student." "How nice," Markova replied. "As you see, I am still a student."*

Cecchetti had coached Pavlova. Celli had been with the great man on the occasion of Pavlova's Italian debut. They had gone to her dressing room afterwards. 'She had had an overwhelming triumph,' Celli recalled. 'But the eagle eye of the master had caught some flaws of execution, perhaps invisible to others. I was shocked to hear him greet her with, "Anna, I am sorry, but you will never

* *Dance and Dancers*, December 1955.

amount to anything." This was in 1928, just a short time before her untimely death.'*

Celli did his best to spur Alicia on to recovery. 'I knew that if I could get her interested in her lessons and back to her world she would dance again,'* he wrote.

Dolin came to see her regularly and, when on tour, phoned every night after the curtain came down.

Fortunately she was still being paid as Hurok had insured her, as he had all the principals. After some discussion, Lucia Chase of Ballet Theatre and Hurok made up her wages between them. Even so, it was expensive living in the hotel twenty-four hours a day, and when the company went on tour without her, as it had to do, she fell into a black depression.

She told Dolin, over the phone, that she felt she had reached the top of the tree only to have the branch break under her. Normally she is comfortable with her own company but, in her depressed condition, the long lonely hours were bad for her.

The newspapers did nothing to lift her spirits. They printed all the rumours that were circulating to the effect that she might never dance again.

As the time passed Celli persuaded her to try a few steps in the hotel room. She was tottery but managed, and they decided it would be a good thing if she returned to the studios for classes.

Meanwhile, while convalescing, she had been approached by Billy Rose – arch showman, songwriter, club owner and sometime husband of Ziegfeld's leading lady, Fanny Brice – who wanted her to appear in a new Broadway show he was putting on, *The Seven Lively Arts,* a showcase for top artists in varying fields. Rose had the Midas touch; he wore 'big time' like a cloak.

He had never seen a ballet, but he had met Agnes de Mille at a party. She had just had her own stupendous success with the choreography for the new hit show *Oklahoma!* With his new show in mind, he asked her who was the best dancer in the world and she, loyal to the core, answered without a second's hesitation, 'Markova'.

After swearing to Rose that she would say nothing to Alicia about his idea, she phoned her and warned her to expect his call.

It had duly arrived and she had met him and listened to his offer. Never hasty to make decisions, she said she would think about it. She did not want to sever her ties with Ballet Theatre so, if she did the Rose show, things had to be worked out amicably.

* *Dance and Dancers*, December 1955.

She was not, however, given the chance to be amicable. She and Rose had met a few times in restaurants and soon the gossip columns were full of speculation that she was to join him.

Ballet Theatre, which she had been at pains not to offend, served her with an injunction forbidding her to appear in the show. As she had not yet agreed to do so she responded through her lawyer.

The case came to arbitration and she attended with her representative. During the proceedings it came out that not only had she sustained her injury while dancing for Ballet Theatre but, prior to that, she had been dancing not only her full repertoire but the repertoire of another dancer who had been ill. And for no extra payment.

Also, she was physically incapable of dancing for anyone in her present condition. As soon as she was able she had every intention of honouring her remaining contract with Ballet Theatre. 'All this went on while I was trying to convalesce,' she recalls.

The arbitration went in her favour and Alicia was free to sign with Rose. But she still had not quite made up her mind to do so. More important to her than the arbitration was to discover exactly what she could now do. Would she be able to restore her full capabilities?

She went to Celli's studio for classes. But as soon as she walked in the door she nearly turned tail and fled. A reception committee of photo-journalists was lined up, cameras at the ready, waiting to snap her as she started practising.

She was visibly shaken. She tried a few warm-up exercises but was distressed as the cameras rose at the ready. Celli banished everyone from the room.

She continued to practise and, in January 1944, after a fretful Christmas, she was able to rejoin Ballet Theatre on the West Coast. Before leaving New York she ensured that Bambi had a good home by leaving him with her lawyer, David Holtzman. He looked after many British stars and Dolin had recommended him to her; he had met him through Noël Coward. 'You'll need someone to look after you,' Dolin had told her. 'Particularly with Hurok.'

Her doctor stipulated that she limit herself to just one performance a week, not the eight or more she had undertaken before. She resumed dancing with *Romeo and Juliet*, and it seemed more than enough at present. She prayed she would be able to get through that.

Rose would ring her every night, keeping in her good books, just before curtain-up, and the call-boy would holler from the phone, 'Long-distance call for Miss Markova! Mr Rose calling from New

York for Miss Markova.' Everyone heard and everyone knew of the arbitration. If she had been the revengeful sort she could have taken ironic satisfaction from that. No one could say a word as she had permission from the courts to appear with Billy Rose should she choose. But a few faces were red.

She was coping but still weak. A residency in New York would be better than another grinding tour. Her health was her paramount concern. 'If I signed with Rose I would be staying in New York and I wouldn't have to cope with the big ballets, which would be easier. It would give me a chance to recoup. The most important thing for me was to get back to dancing properly. I signed for Rose although he had never seen me dance.'

Rose had already signed up Beatrice Lillie, comedian Bert Lahr, and Benny Goodman. There was another pretty young girl in the cast in a small part who went on a few years later to captivate London when she starred in *Annie Get Your Gun*. This was Dolores Gray.

Rose did not carp about expenses and had bought the Ziegfeld theatre for the show, former home of Florenz Ziegfeld's fabulous Follies. He restored it so that the original Dali murals glittered like new.

Alicia and Rose got on well and she would sometimes spend weekends with him, and his wife. He explained his ideas to her. She had never heard of such luxury. She was to be installed on her own floor at the theatre in a suite with private dressing and bathrooms, all gleaming with white and pink décor by Dorothy Hammerstein. A painting of a pair of ballet shoes would adorn her door.

Rose wanted Alicia to dance a fifteen-minute version of *Giselle* in the show but she baulked at that. The ballet meant too much to her to prune it so drastically.

Just as Rose had asked Agnes de Mille who was the best dancer in the world he now asked Alicia who was the best composer. She told him Stravinsky, and Rose commissioned him to write a piece that was eventually entitled 'Scènes de Ballet'.

Stravinsky was now based in Hollywood, married to Vera Sondeikina who had fitted Alicia's *Rossignol* costume in Monte Carlo. As Alicia was in Los Angeles at the time, this meant that she could have meetings with Stravinsky to discuss the music, but she had to catch him in the right mood. Radio was the rage and programmes were sweeping America. Stravinsky was caught up in it and liked nothing better than to tune in.

Alicia considers his finished score 'the masterpiece we know today and I am most proud that it should have been created for me, at my suggestion'.* Dolin was not so enthusiastic and described it as 'music that turned out to be more than unsuitable for the revue and to which I valiantly and most unsuccessfully tried to choreograph and to show Alicia to her best advantage. Its only merit was it was short and Alicia danced in it.'†

She and Dolin appeared at a Sunday concert at the Hollywood Canteen, founded by Bette Davis to entertain servicemen, as America had now joined the war. Artists gave their services free, served the men doughnuts and coffee and sometimes danced with them. It was a terrific morale booster. Only a lady as commanding as Miss Davis could have got such an enterprise off the ground.

At a later Canteen concert in which she and Dolin took part they were joined by Heifetz, Melchior, Helen Traubel and Rubinstein. To Rubinstein's accompaniment she and Dolin performed the Grande Valse from *Les Sylphides*. 'The organizers had taken a huge hangar for the concert. They realized that certain of the men enjoyed classical music and dancing. As Pat lifted me I could see hundreds of men lying on stretchers. We were at one end, with Rubinstein on the grand piano and Heifetz on his fiddle. Believe me, that hangar could have been filled twice over.' The stretcher cases came from the nearby military hospital in San Diego.

When the war was over she, and presumably Dolin, received signed certificates from Miss Davis thanking them for their work. She treasures hers.

She and Dolin appeared in a film while in Hollywood – *A Song for Miss Julie*. They played Valentine Day characters who came to life.

She was back in New York for the Met season and was to open with *Giselle*, with Dolin, on Easter Sunday, 1944. This was her first classic since the hernia and she was terrified. She relentlessly practised to get into peak condition.

Those who believed Markova never suffered from stage fright would have thought differently if they had seen her in her dressing room that night. She knew that everyone was eager to see if she could still make the grade. Among the audience was an eagle-eyed Sol Hurok, avid to see how his precious investment would handle her Met return. Billy Rose was also there; it would be the first time he had seen her dance. Everyone knew of her accident and curiosity was intense.

* *Markova Remembers.*
† *Markova: Her Life and Art.*

There was an added pressure in that the Ballet Russe, who were in competition, decided to open in New York on the same night as her much-advertised return. Hurok was using her to fend off the rivals and judging by the packed house his strategy had paid off. Newspaper critics spent a frustrating evening dashing between the two performances.

Dolin called in as she was making up, to wish her luck, and found a trembling little figure who told him she was physically sick with nerves.

A New York audience can be the hardest in the world. The British will make allowances for an out-of-sorts favourite, even cheering a poor performance if they feel the artist has done her best, but Americans judge a performer by what they get on the night.

She was so petrified on her initial appearance that her face was too rigid to smile. Even so, she left the stage after her first scene to a standing ovation. It continued throughout the ballet. Whenever she danced the audience shouted its encouragement.

Some artists claim applause should be restricted to the end of a performance. Not Alicia. She was always delighted when the public applauded, be it in the middle of a performance, after a *pas de seul* or wherever. That night each burst of applause inspired her. As she put it in Dolin's biography of her, 'I have no patience with dancers who pretend to dislike applause breaking out during the action of a ballet. If they feel that way about it, they should never appear in a theatre.'

The cheers at the end nearly raised the roof and she was presented with bouquet after bouquet.

Crowds were waiting for her at the stage door and she appeared, serene and happy. She went home secure in the knowledge that she had retained her status. Said the *New York Herald Tribune*:

'A trustworthy spy of mine reported that Markova far exceeded any of her previous performances, and that she received at the end the greatest ovation ever heard at the Met . . .'

Billy Rose saw Dolin partner her and invited him to join the cast as well, as Alicia's partner. In his writings, Dolin says he was reluctant to join *The Seven Lively Arts*. In fact, he jumped at the chance. He, like everyone else, was tired of the constant touring and welcomed a residency in New York for a while. He also welcomed the comparatively high money and the chance of starring on Broadway.

The show opened in autumn 1944 for a two-week try-out in Philadelphia before transferring to Broadway, where it played

Sugar Plum Fairy on tour in America, 1947. (© Maurice Seymour)

In Florence being fitted for
shoes by Salvatore Ferragamo.
She loved his designs so much
she had them in every colour,
1951.

Alicia and Miskovitch in "Les
Sylphides" in TV Studio, 1954.

Alicia with Ram Gopal in
"Radha Krishna", spring 1960.

Official Metropolitan Opera
House portrait of Alicia, 1963.
(© Louis Melancon)

HM The Queen, Margot Fonteyn, Marie Rambert, Alicia and Arnold Haskell. At the official opening of the Royal Academy of Dancing's premises in Battersea. Fonteyn was President and the three Vice-Presidents were Dame Marie Rambert, Alicia and Haskell. (© Donald Southern)

Receiving Doctorate of Music from University of East Anglia, 1982. Gown designed by Cecil Beaton. (© Eastern Daily Press)

ABOVE LEFT Greeting Sir Frederick Ashton in New York, 1970, at the Dance Magazine Awards. Ted Shawn is behind Alicia. (© V. Sladon)

LEFT Alicia and Erik Bruhn together for a talk at the London Ballet Circle, 1982.

Alicia on her 80th birthday.
(© Barry Swaebe)

BELOW LEFT Alicia presenting
Dame Ninette de Valois with
"Evening Standard" Ballet
Award.

BELOW Alicia with 1994
"Evening Standard" Ballet
award at the Savoy Hotel,
1995.

Alicia teaching Iohna Loots, of the Balanchine Ballet, the role of the Nightingale. 1995. (© Tiddy Maitland)

twice daily for six months. That was success in those days. Alicia opened the second half with the Stravinsky ballet.

With the exception of the ballet music, the score was by Cole Porter and, in the finale, she and Dolin danced to his music.

Porter lived at the Waldorf Towers and, before opening, Alicia had gone there to see him and discuss the finale. He suggested 'Night and Day' but Alicia thought this unsuitable as it had been 'used so much. In the end Cole had the idea of using something he had done in Hollywood, which he thought would be right. It turned out to be an orchestral arrangement of "Easy to Love". It had been done in the style of "The Dance of the Hours" and it was perfect.' She and Dolin choreographed it between them, something they often did.

Before her entrance Alicia would warm up in the foyer outside her dressing room, using the banister as a barre. This, of course, was her own private area, as all the principals had their own dressing rooms on their own floors. Goodman must have pressed the wrong button one day, for out he stepped with his clarinet under his arm.

'He asked me what I was doing and I told him I was warming up. "I do that too," he said. But he called it "tuning up". "Maybe we could tune up together?" After that, not always but sometimes, the lift doors would open and out he would come and play for me while I warmed up.'

He usually played Mozart for her. Word spread around the company and it was suggested that they might include the routine in the show. Neither of them wanted that; it was just a pleasant way of getting ready.

Stravinsky had composed a melody for Alicia and Dolin's *pas de deux* which was played on a trumpet. The morning after the first performance Dolin sent him a telegram. 'Ballet great success but if you would allow a violin to play *pas de deux* instead of trumpet it would be a triumph.' Stravinsky replied: 'Satisfied with great success.'* The *Seven Lively Arts* gave Alicia a Broadway audience she would never have had had she remained strictly within the confines of Ballet Theatre.

Sunday was her day off but, now that her strength was improving, she sometimes gave extra performances for Ballet Theatre at the Met, and for the Theater Benevolent Fund. She also danced a jitterbug with a serviceman at the Stage Door Canteen, the New York equivalent of the Hollywood Canteen. Her partner was one

* Account taken from *Balanchine* by Bernard Taper, Macmillan, 1960.

'Killer Joe', a coastguard who had earned his nickname because of the enthusiasm with which he danced and swung his partners around. When Alicia finished with him he was mopping up buckets of sweat – his, not hers.

Meanwhile, back in Britain, Eileen and the girls had moved to a flat in Blackpool. Alicia's Marble Arch flat had been bombed. They salvaged what they could and joined Vivienne in the relative safety of Blackpool, where Vivienne had been sent by the Civil Service.

Flats were hard to come by, even in Blackpool, but Eileen's bubbling personality helped them through. 'Leave it to me,' she told the girls as she left them outside the estate agent's office. 'She came back jangling the keys,' recalls Doris.

In addition to money, Alicia sent them food and clothing parcels as not much was available at home. Donna Lasky, the daughter-in-law of the great Hollywood pioneer producer, Jesse Lasky, was a friend of Alicia's, having met her in Britain during the Markova-Dolin days. She once sent Alicia's sister Doris an outfit as a present. 'I was the best-dressed girl in Blackpool,' Doris recalls. 'Alicia used to send lipstick and nail polish and things like that which you couldn't get here.'

Others also received parcels. Fonteyn had ribbons for her ballet shoes, which were unobtainable at home. Food parcels were sent to de Valois, Cyril Beaumont, Arnold Haskell, Fred Ashton and Philip Richardson of the *Dancing Times*.

Alicia used to organize collections at Ballet Theatre. 'I used to go round the company and I had boxes, one would say "Shoes" another "Sweaters" and so on. Word came through of the scarcities and I used to do what I could. I heard that onions and lemons were unobtainable in England so I bought some to send. I got some old sweaters. You had to be careful as new things could be pinched, after all nothing was available and the temptation must have been strong, and I stuffed the sleeves with lemons and onions and labelled the parcel "Unsolicited gift". I made the parcel look very scruffy, so as not to attract attention, and hoped it got through.'

The Seven Lively Arts ran through until the spring of 1945. That spring Alicia was photographed by Carl van Vechten, in colour, in the countryside in brilliant sunshine, in her *Giselle* costume, hugging a lamb which was wearing a blue blow. It was real Hollywood schmaltz and looked wonderful.

As soon as the show finished Alicia, Dolin, Bea Lillie and Freddie Franklin took a holiday on the coast in California.

While they were frolicking on the beach, Dolin, out of boredom and to prove how good a dancer he was, challenged Alicia to perform sixteen *entrechats* without stopping. Freddie Franklin recalls it.

'"I bet you can't do them," he said to her. This is on the beach, on the sand. So Alicia got herself together and did sixteen beautiful *entrechats*. Then she said, "Now, Patty, dear, it's your turn." But he wouldn't do it. Then he said to me, "I bet you can't do as many cartwheels as I can," and I said, "All right, Pat, go ahead." When it was my turn I saved my energy and did more. He was furious and said we'd have to do it all over again and I would have to go first this time. But I said no. He was terrible like that.

'Then we went into the water and Bea Lillie couldn't swim and was terrified. She used to call me Frank. "Frank!" she'd holler when a wave came. "Lift me!" Well, I wasn't very good in the water either and I'd be frantic with her on my shoulders yelling. The antics were marvellous."

New Yorker magazine wrote an article on Alicia stating that she followed every performance with steak and double-frosted chocolate sundaes. It was the truth. She used up so many calories during a performance that afterwards she sometimes weighed two pounds less than when she'd started.

Agnes de Mille writes: 'I have seen Alicia stripped, she has no body at all. She has no bust, no stomach, no hips, no buttocks. She had two long supple arms and two long, strong legs joined by a device that contained, in the most compact manner possible, enough viscera to keep her locomotive. She was utterly feminine but as incorporeal as a dryad. Her slenderness, her lack of unneeded flesh, was a rebuke to anything gross in the world.'*

She fought all through her career to keep her weight up. The target was seven stones, if she could attain that she was happy, but she was often less, sometimes considerably so. She ate sweet things all the time. When in London she would add a Guinness to her diet.

New York Times critic John Martin adored Alicia. One day he surpassed even himself in enthusiasm. Agnes de Mille was appearing with Alicia at the time:

'Martin . . . dared to risk his very considerable reputation by writing, "Markova is not only the greatest ballerina in the world today, but very possibly the greatest that ever lived." A claim impossible to substantiate but eye-catching.

'I happened to be backstage the day after Martin's incredible

---

* *Portrait Gallery.*

pronouncement was printed. In my minor way I was going through the process of warming up, quieting down and cutting off from daily life. I passed Alicia's room. She was standing alone, rubbing the toe of her slipper with a piece of gauze soaked in benzine.

'"Alicia," I said, slipping on to her sofa. "Tell me something, as one woman to another, how does it feel to read in a newspaper a statement like Martin's, 'the greatest ballet dancer of all time'?"

'"That's very well and good," said Alicia, placing the slipper precisely beside its fellow, drawing her silk dressing gown up neatly, and sitting down with crossed ankles. "It's easy to write something like that, but it's I who have to live up to it. What am I to do the next day, I ask you? I said to Celli, I must work all the harder. I mean, ducky, the audience is going to expect something after reading that bit. It will be hard lines if I let them down. There's always the next performance to think of, that's what I said to Celli."

'Alicia had at the time reached the age, not a great one, when in the days of Russia's imperial ballet the stars were forcibly retired and pensioned. But she was dancing better than ever, with virtuosity and an enormous brilliance of dynamics and power. Instead of slacking off with the years she seemed to be attaining greater and greater physical and emotional strength, and achieving subtler and more exquisite refinements of style. Building her reputation had been hard: maintaining it was harder.'*

Alicia's one extravagance was designer clothes. She spent money on her outfits and was always stylishly turned out, her face immaculately made up.

Dolin still held court in his dressing room afterwards, but if there were people to be wined and dined he made sure Alicia was with him. To all appearances they were a married couple and Alicia always picked up her half of the tab. Which was only right and proper.

But he was not always right and proper. His attitude sometimes drove Agnes de Mille mad. In *Portrait Gallery* she writes of a night in 1944 when Dolin had danced in Los Angeles at the premiere of her ballet *Tally-Ho!* Miss de Mille, who herself had danced in the performance, was in his dressing room.

'[He was] talking his way through cold cream and towels. His dressing room had the air of a levee but he usually remembered to point out the quiet little figure, already cleaned up and dressed impeccably, sitting in attentive silence. He was very grand at these

* *Portrait Gallery.*

seances, lounging about in his expensive dressing gown, he was ducal, even royal, languidly receiving homage and never rising. At one interview I stood in his dressing room for ten minutes discussing problems about the current production . . . there was much about his performance that distressed me. Elsa Maxwell was in the other chair but he didn't bother to introduce us. He also didn't bother to offer me a seat. At the end of the interview I said quietly, "You must excuse me for not removing my hat." And I left the room.'*

'Oh, the characters we had then,' laughs Alicia when reading that account. 'They were wonderful.'

Miss de Mille added, concerning Alicia, 'The fact that she rarely took time to comment does not mean that much passed her unremarked.'

* *Portrait Gallery.*

18

The Tropics

Alicia was soon back on tour with Ballet Theatre. Once again she endured the rigours of one-night stands. The six-month stay with *The Seven Lively Arts* seemed like heaven in comparison. By now she had regained her full strength and it seemed that nothing could stop her. She had altered various details of her productions. Since she had recovered from the hernia she felt differently about certain things. It was like a new start.

War ended in 1945 but Alicia stayed in America fulfilling continuous contracts. She was so busy that there were occasions when she left the theatre in full make-up and could only take it off when she arrived at her destination for another performance. By now she was using aeroplanes. It was the only way she could get everything done.

There were changes in Hurok's loyalties. He still represented Alicia but had left Ballet Theatre to represent Colonel de Basil's 'Original Ballet Russe'.

Towards the end of 1945 Ballet Theatre mounted a new production of Stravinsky's *The Firebird*, to open in New York, under the supervision of Adolph Bolm who had danced in the original production. Alicia was to be the Firebird, Dolin the Prince, and Marc Chagall the designer.

Bolm had studied under Karsavina and Legat, had been a member of the Marynsky and had toured with Pavlova. In 1909, during the Diaghileff season, he had electrified Paris, as a dancer, with his portrayal of The Warrior in Fokine's 'Polovtsian Dances'. He had joined Ballet Theatre in 1939 where he had made a success of choreographing Prokofiev's *Peter and the Wolf*. He ended his days choreographing for the movies.

The Firebird is a collection of Russian fairy tales telling of a prince who captures a magical Firebird. It is one of the most successful ballets of the twentieth century and has frequently been revived since Diaghileff first presented it in 1910.

Alicia's costume was designed by Marc Chagall. In order for Chagall to create the Firebird costume Alicia had to stand still in all-over tights while he drew the design on her body, rather as Matisse had done for *Le Rouge and le Noir*. Under his direction, costumier Edith Lutyens cut out pieces of coloured net while he pinned them to her.

She wore a beaked headdress made from bird of paradise feathers. To enhance the effect of a bird she wore brown body make-up smeared with oil over which buckets of gold dust had, literally, been thrown. This stuck to the oil and caused a brilliant effect when hit by the lights.

Removing the gold dust caused problems. It had to be scrubbed off and only came away with difficulty. There was no way she could get rid of it all in her dressing room. This did not matter in New York where she could put on a sweater covering her sparkling arms, go out for a meal and then soak in a bath when she got home. But when the ballet eventually went on tour there was no time for a bath before moving to the next venue. She had to try to sleep in transit, on buses and planes, covered in the irritating stuff.

Travelling through North and South Dakota by train on one such tour she had the added misery of a bad cold. As she shivered in the compartment Bolm came in carrying some cans of baby food he had bought for her at a recent stop. He heated these in a pan of boiling water from the dining car. She felt better afterwards. After that, baby food was added to her essentials for a tour, together with the first-aid box and mink coat.

A mink coat was the stamp of success in the 1940s and no star could be without one. Mink is hard-wearing and stands ill usage. Alicia's coat served her as a blanket, mattress and pillow on many occasions. Then, after a shake, it could be worn properly and she would look like the front page of *Vogue*.

Although Balanchine had created ballets for Alicia, there were some that got away and were given to other dancers. One such was *Night Shadow*, based on music from Bellini's *La Sonnambula*, arranged and with additional music by Vittorio Rieti. Rieti had approached Alicia with the idea.

Unfortunately, contractual difficulties arose and Alicia was unable to do it. It was eventually premiered in 1946 by the Ballet Russe de Monte Carlo with Danilova, Maria Tallchief, and Freddie Franklin. When Alicia talks about it she mimes someone creeping about holding a candleholder. 'That could have been me,' she says.

In the spring of 1946 Eileen was able to make the trip to America to see Alicia. They had not seen each other for seven years. 'I was so happy to see Mother, and she had a marvellous time in New York. Fortunately she came in time for the Met spring season so she saw me in *Firebird*, *Romeo and Juliet* and *Giselle*.'

Eileen had a wonderful time, sitting in a box when Alicia danced. She stayed six months and was also able to see Alicia premiere *Camille* at the Met before going home. This was a new ballet choreographed by John Taras to Schubert's music. It had been one of the first offers Hurok had made Alicia after he had joined Colonel de Basil. It was a lavish production with designs and costumes by Cecil Beaton and sponsored by Elizabeth Arden.

'I was the first dancer to have *La Dame aux Camélias* choreographed for me. Nowadays people tend to remember the Fonteyn, Nureyev, Ashton version but this was before that. It was an arrangement suggested by George Balanchine, Taras had worked with him a lot. Beaton's costumes were fabulous. I was photographed in the country scene and that, for the photographer, won nearly every award.'

Alicia and Dolin re-formed the Markova-Dolin Company, still represented by Hurok to whom they were under contract. This meant she was dancing the big ballets with the Ballet Russe and, in between, touring with Dolin. The troupe also included John Taras, who was choreographer and ballet master, Eglevsky, Rosella Hightower and George Skibine. Handsome Skibine had just been demobilized from the army. He had been Alicia's partner in *Aleko* and *Bluebeard* and other Ballet Theatre productions both in Mexico and New York. Fokine had first put them together.

In Chicago Dolin went down with a strained knee which prevented him from dancing. It must have been severe as Dolin rarely took time off. Albrecht was danced at short notice by Skibine.

He had already danced Hilarion and brought something entirely new to the role. The luckless Hilarion was usually portrayed as a homely type. In the early *Giselles* he had red hair and a beard, the antithesis of Albrecht. Skibine brought a dignity to the role and received warm notices for it. As Alicia says, 'Not until the Bolshoi

Ballet came to Western Europe did we see again a Hilarion who drew such sympathy.'

In 1947 Alicia appeared in Jerome Robbins's *Pas de Trois* with Eglevsky and Dolin. This was another non-*pointe* work she was glad to add to her repertoire as it gave her a break from constantly being on her toes.

After this Hurok had arranged a tour for the Markova-Dolin Company of Central and South American and Caribbean states, including Guatemala, El Salvador, Mexico, Costa Rica, Colombia, Venezuela and Cuba. Flying was the only way to cover the distances involved and they travelled by Pan American.

Some of the cities in which Alicia performed were at high altitudes and she suffered breathing difficulties. There was also violence in the streets, much of it caused by the rapid change of political factions.

In Bogotá her performances were cancelled owing to a revolution. The British Consulate advised her to stay in the hotel, telling her 'there's going to be a shooting today.'* Sometimes she was glad they were travelling by plane, if only for the quick getaways.

The French music-hall star Alice Delysia, a friend of Alicia and Dolin, had married a government minister and lived in Nicaragua. Although there was political unrest in the country, things could be dull on the social front and she invited Dolin and Alicia to lunch.

Unfortunately it was cancelled as their plane could not land owing to another revolution that had immobilized the airport. Alicia wrote, 'So we missed luncheon and the possibility of a bullet in the hors d'oeuvre.'*

The pilots, who regularly dropped and picked them up, were able to keep them abreast of the news of the outside world by giving them the newspapers. 'The boys would do a quick head count, just to make sure we were still all there.' They also brought them bottles of milk which were gratefully accepted as to drink the local product was to invite convulsions.

In Cuba Alicia danced on the worst stage she had ever danced on in her life. It was so buckled by heat that it had corrugated into waves. She could not dance on *pointe* and for the only time in her life she danced *Les Sylphides* off-*pointe*.

The Dying Swan has to be danced on *pointe*. There was no way Alicia could do that on the stage as it was, so she persuaded the stage manager to nail a piece of lino across an area to which she would restrict herself.

* *Markova Remembers.*

This was fitted after *Les Sylphides*, while the audience remained in the auditorium. They sang while the carpenters hammered it home.

Fortunately the lino was flat enough for Alicia to dance on *pointe*, although she could still feel the bumps underneath. Nevertheless she cast her spell and the audience were enraptured.

That year she and Dolin returned to Mexico to support the institution of a national ballet company. Doris had now joined her as Eileen had returned to Britain after her triumphant stay. Doris had bidden the Windmill farewell by now: Mexico City did not particularly agree with her owing to its altitude, and she developed hives.

In Mexico, they introduced another *Camille*, a new production they had choreographed themselves.

The local Mexican dancers, who augmented the *corps de ballet*, loved it. They also loved Alicia. So much so that, on her last night when she was dancing *Giselle*, they went souvenir hunting.

She had just finished the mad scene. Her hair was dishevelled and she was rushing to her dressing room to scrub off the dirt from the stage before changing for the second act.

A group of Mexicans were waiting and rushed at her with scissors, snipping off locks to remember her by. She feared she might have to finish the ballet bald-headed.

Fortunately Doris fended them off. But they went only after Alicia promised she would give each one a personal memento after the performance.

She kept her word and every dancer left with something – a powder puff, comb or hairnet. She was touched – and pleased to still have, more or less, a full head of hair.

Before leaving Mexico she and Dolin received news from England. A letter was forwarded to them from David Webster, General Administrator of the Royal Opera House, Covent Garden. The Opera House had served as a dance hall during the war but had now reopened in its proper function. Webster invited Alicia and Dolin to dance with the Sadler's Wells Company. De Valois seconded Webster's offer.

They had received other offers to dance in Britain since the war had ended but Alicia felt they should not return until something special was on the cards. Dolin had itchy feet and would have accepted earlier commercial engagements, but since the offers included Alicia he could not do much about it without her agreement. But Covent Garden was special and, this time, the idea of returning appealed to her as much as to him.

Meanwhile they were under contract to Hurok, and in the autumn of 1947 the Markova-Dolin Company started another tour. They were at the San Francisco Opera House in November, where they danced *Giselle* with the San Francisco Civic Ballet. This was their first *Giselle* with a civic company.

They continued touring until the spring.

In New York Constance Collier invited Alicia to tea. Charlie Chaplin was coming and, knowing Alicia was in town, had asked Miss Collier to invite her. If all three of them happened to be in New York at the same time they invariably got together. 'Constance would ring and say, "Charlie's coming in, he wants to know if you're free."'

On this occasion Alicia took Doris with her, not telling her whom she going to meet. 'I thought, I won't say anything, she'll die,' says Alicia. She got virtually a command performance as Chaplin leapt on the table at one point and demonstrated what he had in mind for his next project. Doris still sighs over that afternoon.

Another time at tea Miss Collier introduced her to a shy young actress. This was Marilyn Monroe, aged twenty-nine. She told Alicia she was keen to learn Shakespeare and was having lessons with Miss Collier. Alicia was struck by how unhappy she seemed.

In the meantime she and Dolin accepted the Covent Garden offer. But she could do nothing about it for a while as she was off on a tour of the Philippines – the first artist to tour the Philippines since 1936 – prefaced by appearances in Honolulu.

In Hololulu she was awakened by a shriek in the middle of the night. It was from Doris in the next room. At first Alicia thought she was being murdered. When she got there she found her sister pointing with a trembling finger at a large spider on her wall. 'Get rid of it,' she gasped.

Alicia got a tumbler and a card and removed the insect, then went back to bed. 'It was either spiders or mosquitoes. I was always to the rescue.'

The heat was so intense in Honolulu that her feet swelled and her shoes were too tight. As there were no ballet shops in Hawaii she had to get through a performance in too-tight shoes, which was agony.

She put through a panic call to Capezio, her ballet shoe-makers in New York, to fly over a dozen pairs at a size larger than usual. She also needed new block shoes as the heat had melted the blocks in her existing ones. They were a soggy mess by the time the performance was finished. 'I always wore a very soft *pointe*, they all knew, and I ordered some one inch longer and stronger. We christened them my "tropical shoes" and whenever I wanted them in the future, I just said my "tropical shoes" and they knew what I meant.'

Due to the route, it took four days to fly from Hawaii to the Philippines. In order that she could sleep, a mattress was laid on the floor of the plane. Years of touring had taught her to sleep anywhere, whatever the discomfort. She was like a cat curled up in the fuselage. The plane was unpressurized and the heat overpowering. There were five of them in the cabin – Alicia, Dolin, Doris, their pianist and her new manager, Alfred Katz. They existed on chicken salad, the only meal the airline could supply.

Dolin noted: 'We travelled thousands of miles by air, becoming the most widely travelled dancers in the world, with more flying hours to our credit than any other members of our profession.'

On that long flight, as Alicia slept in the aisle, Dolin wrote that he had time to analyse his feelings for her. He had known her for years and travelled thousands of miles with her under severe conditions but still he did not understand her. He loved her, in his way, but she was a sphinx, even to him.

Each time a relationship threatened to form with anybody she dissolved it, he reflected.

'I do everything single-mindedly,' says Alicia. 'And if I were to go in for marriage and a family then I would give up dancing. My family would be all. As a dancer how could I ask anyone I loved to put up with my life? It wouldn't be fair. There are times when I regret it now. Sometimes I think I should have married – I nearly did four times – but it wasn't to be. I suppose I really am one of those people married to their careers. But there have been times when I have been very lonely with no one to turn to.'

In 1960 she told journalist Sally Vincent: 'It is not merely that I am a ballerina. I am a woman in a profession – and any woman in any profession has a problem with her relationship with men. A man, for some reason, is frightened of a capable woman . . . Men see me dancing and they see someone ethereal and fragile. They just do not know what to make of me.'

Dolin wondered, as he had before, if she found the career worth all the effort. He was happy enough with his lot. He liked being the centre of attention. He was able to attract people to his aura and that seemed satisfaction enough. But Alicia was different.

He had plenty of time for thought as the plane had to touch down several times to refuel. They were shocked by the devastation the Japanese had wreaked during the war. Conditions were primitive and the places full of military personnel. At one stop there was no fresh water and they had to drink tinned tomato juice. As it was tinned they knew it would be free of harmful germs.

Alicia arrived in Manila as fresh as anyone and, again, was shocked by what she found. It was rubble. Soldiers were everywhere. The blinding sun highlighted every detail. The road from the airport had disappeared and the route was marked by empty petrol cans.

Only half of their hotel was standing, the other half having been demolished by air raids. A notice at reception read 'Park Your Firearms Here'. There had been a gun fight in the foyer the night before. She was taken to her room, several storeys above ground level, and as she was walking towards it she opened a door in the corridor. There was a sheer drop and she stared into nothing. Had she walked through she would have plummeted to the ground.

Walking was painful as she had a septic toe and the heat aggravated it. She tried to disguise her pain, but feared she might be unable to dance after all the travelling. Even to put on a ballet shoe was agony. 'The American army came to my rescue. They were wonderful. Their doctor came to the hotel, took a look at it and gave me some wonderful ointment for it, which had been prepared for all the poor, marching people. For ages they gave me a supply of this. That was the first time they came to my rescue – then their doctor used to inject me with liver extract, anything to get through the performances in that heat.'

The President died as soon as they arrived. Alicia learnt the news at seven the next morning. 'I like to sleep late, especially on performance day, and I was woken by the phone. It was Katz. He said, "I'm sorry to wake you but the performance will have to be postponed. All performances have been cancelled. News has just come through that the President has died." I said, "Thank God," and went back to sleep. The President had saved my performance. I know it's terrible to say and, of course, I was very sorry.'

They started their tour of the islands instead, flying in a military plane with spine-crippling metal bucket seats. 'It was one hundred and twenty degrees in the shade and the plane had been standing on the runway. I was just wearing a cotton dress. I sat on the seat and it was like sitting on a lighted gas ring. I jumped up and yelled.'

Their first performance was on Cebu. They looked out of the window and there was no sign of a living soul nor anywhere to dance. Why, they asked themselves, were they there? Katz supplied the answer. He had booked them.

They were taken away and, eventually, found themselves in an open-air theatre. Alicia's dressing room was a tent. 'Filipino women were sitting on the stage, sewing sacks together. They were making the scenery for us. They had nothing, nothing at all. The army had given them a pile of sacks, which was all they had, and they were opening them up and sewing them together to make a backing for us. There were tuberoses everywhere, their smell was overpowering, they were growing wild and the women were picking them and sewing them on to the sacks.'

People began arriving and they eventually played to a packed auditorium.

'We opened with *Les Sylphides* and when Pat lifted me I could smell the roses, they were wonderful. There were also two large urns full of them on the side of the stage. When you think what those people had been through and what they did for us, putting their minds and imaginations to work. I was really touched.'

Alicia always travelled with her own gels (colour filters), so her lighting cues would be right. Doris was in charge of the lighting and explained to the stage hands that these had to be fitted over the lights and changed at various points during the dances.

She wasted her time. The first change came and stayed. The stage hands, who were really just untrained boys, abandoned the lights when the dancing started. They watched in fascination, forgetting what they were supposed to be doing. Normally Alicia would have been livid at such inefficiency. That night she didn't say a word. She could see the Filipinos had suffered enough during the war. She was humbly glad to be there entertaining them and grateful for her lot in life.

Her feet had swollen again, but she did the best she could. 'Ballet was never meant for the tropics,' she moaned to Dolin as they danced.

Their reception was tumultuous. They were the first escape from harshness the Filipinos had experienced for years. The children had never seen anything like them, and stared wide-eyed.

While they had been on the islands there had been a frantic search in Manila for a piano. They were to appear in the ruined opera house and there was no accompaniment. When one was found it was out of tune but it had to do; there was no one to tune it.

The evening was so hot that Alicia's hands were too sweaty to grip Dolin. She had to turn her back to the audience for a moment to wipe them on her tutu. The house was packed. Hundreds were turned away.

They decided to give an additional concert with all tickets at $1 each, so that everyone could afford to get in. There was such a stampede for tickets that the opera house could not accommodate the demand, so they agreed to appear in the baseball stadium.

A scratch orchestra was assembled for this occasion which turned out to be the remnants of the Manila Symphony Orchestra. The instruments were barely usable. Both Alicia and Dolin donated any profits from the evening to a fund for the orchestra to buy new instruments. They danced for nothing.

Members of the US Army, who were stationed nearby, trained searchlights on them as they danced and, in order to provide electricity, the main grid of the island was diverted.

At a gardenia-festooned presentation ceremony before leaving Alicia was given two dresses in national costume and a string of pearls which, as Dolin put it, 'the Japanese had missed in their looting expeditions'. She did not want to take the pearls but could not insult her guests by refusing. They had, literally, nothing else to offer.

But she and Dolin gave something in return. Before leaving Manila they visited the leading ballet teacher and gave a crash course. This was priceless as there was no one to teach anything.

She lost a lot of weight on that tour and returned to New York weighing just over six stones.

'I was skin and bone,' she says.

19

Home Again

Alicia had never had roots, even as a child. She accepted her gipsy status unquestioningly. It was part of the price she paid to be true to Diaghileff, as was the lack of a husband and children.

But she had missed England and her family and longed to return. She was delighted to be dancing in London, 'particularly with Sadler's Wells, a company where I had been very happy'. The repertoire for the return had been quickly agreed. 'Ninette had sent me a Christmas card and scribbled some suggestions on it. I ticked off what I thought appropriate. We both knew each other so that was all right. That was how things were done then, it's very different today.' Among the chosen repertoire were *Giselle*, *Swan Lake*, *Les Sylphides*, *Sleeping Beauty* and *Job*. David Webster had come to New York to see them and had finalized the details.

By Hurok's lights Alicia had gone mad. The money was derisory in contrast to what they had been earning – she was now on a weekly guarantee of $1,000 with Hurok, and that was just the basic minimum. She was still the highest-paid ballerina in the world. 'But Mr Hurok made demands. We thought we could budget comfortably on that sort of money, but then we were expected to provide a group of so many dancers, costumes and orchestral arrangements. See how much of a thousand dollars is left after that.'

Against the Covent Garden invitation Hurok had come up with the offer of another tour at money that would have been pure fantasy to de Valois. 'But there was another point. I saw my doctor and he said, "Are you crazy?" Well, I thought, I don't consider myself crazy. "Are you trying to be the richest girl in the cemetery?" he asked me. "That's what you'll be if you accept these offers from Mr Hurok. You're not a machine."'

Dolin felt the same way. He had written to Irving Deakin, an associate of Hurok's, on 16 January 1948: 'We simply cannot go on with these frightful tours, and have told Sol plainly.'*

It had been almost ten years since Alicia had danced at home. She was now thirty-eight. As Agnes de Mille pointed out, in the Imperial system under which she had been trained, she would now have been retired and on a pension. The ten years between twenty-eight and thirty-eight are crucial in a dancer's life; after that the vitality of youth has to be replaced by experience.

Dolin arranged to fly home but Alicia, still scrawny from the Philippines tour, took the *Queen Elizabeth*. The journey would take six days and she booked a state room and stayed in it the whole time. The rumour that she was on board spread round the ship but no one saw her. 'I used those six days to sleep and try to gain a little weight. I'd lived mostly on mashed bananas in the Philippines, they were in skins so I knew they were safe, you daren't touch a salad or anything like that. I used to look at myself each day in the mirror and think, I'll be a skeleton when I dance at Covent Garden. It was very worrying.'

A cable reached her from de Valois. Could she, in addition to the agreed performances, take part in the Ballet's Benevolent Fund Gala to be held at Covent Garden in the presence of Queen Elizabeth (now the Queen Mother) and Princess Margaret? It would mean appearing earlier than she anticipated; in fact, the day after the *Queen Elizabeth* docked at Southampton. She cabled her acceptance. Dolin, who was in London by now, received the same request and he, too, accepted.

The ship docked late at night, leaving no time for rehearsals. She was thankful that Dolin was her partner.

Doris was with her and arranged for the transportation of her costumes to the opera house and dealt with Customs while Alicia sped by car through the night to the Savoy Hotel, where she had reserved accommodation.

She had hoped to stay at the Savoy for the duration of her visit but this was not possible. Owing to postwar restrictions guests were only allowed to stay at any one hotel for five consecutive nights. So she was constantly shifting from hotel to hotel. 'It was like another tour and everything was still rationed. I must have got

* Quoted in *The Last Impresario*.

to the Savoy about two or three in the morning and I remember room service was a cup of tea and some biscuits, that was all they had. So I had that and I was on Covent Garden stage at ten the next morning. I was in my street clothes, just to meet Ninette and everyone. It was very emotional. It was very emotional just being at Covent Garden. But I was swaying, I still had sea legs.'

She also met Vivienne and Bunny whom she had not seen for a decade. Vivienne was still a civil servant. When Doris and Bunny had been unable to get dancing work during the war it had been Vivienne's salary which had helped keep them going. Bunny had given up dancing to marry and now had a daughter, Susie. Susie and Alicia took to each other straight away and remain close.

Much later, when Alicia arranged for Susie to study ballet at a dancing school, there was a face-to-face confrontation when she had to tell her ballerina aunt that she felt she would never be able to dance like her. 'I don't expect you to dance like me,' Alicia told her. 'Just do the best you can.' But Susie felt she was not cut out to be a dancer and left. That was fine by Alicia; she'd given her her chance.

Everything was ready on time at the Opera House the next day, except for the Queen and Princess Margaret. The Princess had measles which prevented her appearing and, as it was infectious, the Queen had also cancelled.

Alicia was far from at her best. She still felt groggy and she and Dolin were introducing to British audiences the difficult *pas de deux* from *Don Quixote*. She could feel the rolling of the boat with every step.

The audience assumed that this was now the way Markova danced and, according to Dolin, whispers went round that she was finished. This was not the glorious homecoming she had planned. It was a depressing evening.

She was to open the first of her Covent Garden engagements proper on 7 June 1948 with Sadler's Wells' new production of *Giselle*.

There was enormous curiosity and press speculation and Alicia was flattered when she heard that Dame Adeline Genée was in the audience. Whatever the shortcomings of *Don Quixote*, there was no lack of anticipation in the house that evening.

Her stomach was knotted with nerves as she waited behind the door upon which Albrecht would soon knock. She reflected on the number of times she had been knotted with nerves while waiting behind Giselle's front door. 'But I was prepared this time. For *Don Quixote* I had had no time; now I was ready.'

Even so, when she stepped on stage she was terrified. Then the deafening applause almost rocked her; it was like an earthquake. If she had had doubts about her welcome they were laid to rest.

At the end of the performance she was, again, deafened by cheers. Had the gallery been less sturdily constructed it might have crashed down from the impact of patrons stamping their feet.

Her family were in the audience, Eileen about to throw up with excitement and Bunny sobbing. It was unnoticed among the general euphoria, shared by the press.

'Markova gave us a Giselle whose quality has not been seen in London for ten years.' – *Daily Telegraph*

'To see her floating about the stage is to believe in the gift of levitation . . .' *The Times*

'Seen again in *Giselle* after more than ten years were Markova and Dolin a disappointment to the critical gallery? . . . No. They gave a tremendous performance.' Richard Buckle, *Observer*

'Markova's Giselle is still one of the great balletic charact-erisations within living memory . . . The simplicity of the mad scene heightens the pathos, while the second act trans-figures her into a vision as ethereal as any lithograph of Grisi or Taglioni. A pure inner flame burns throughout, so that we are ever conscious of the tragic Giselle rather than the expert ballerina. Though Giselle is a character created by a choreographer, and not by a dramatist, she is, when danced by Markova, as real to us as Juliet or Ophelia.' – *Theatre World*

Beryl Grey was Queen of the Wilis; it was the first time she had seen Alicia dance. 'I think she was the best Giselle I have ever seen, there was never a dancer like her.'

Alicia was also to dance *Swan Lake* and *Sleeping Beauty* at the Garden. *Sleeping Beauty* was new territory for her. She had never danced it.

This aristocratic ballet, with choreography by Petipa and music by Tchaikovsky, had been premiered at the Marynsky in 1890 where it had been judged the epitome of Imperial achievement. Cecchetti had been among the cast.

Unfortunately it is expensive to produce and, without the Tsar's fortune to back it, full-length versions were rare. Pavlova danced a drastically shortened adaptation in New York in 1916.

Diaghileff had introduced the ballet to the British, under its alternative name, *The Sleeping Princess*, in 1921 when he had brought it to London. But for an attack of diphtheria Alicia would have been in it as Princess Dewdrop. She was now twenty-seven years older and had the leading role to learn.

Sergeyev was again in charge of production. *The Sleeping Beauty* had been in the Sadler's Wells repertoire since 1939 when he had revived it with the help of his Stepanov notes. After this a more lavish version had been mounted when the company had transferred to Covent Garden in 1946.

Dolin knew that Alicia was a quick learner but even he was astonished by how swiftly she learnt the role. She already knew the Rose *adagio* and part of the second and last acts which she had danced in recitals, and she learnt the rest in a fortnight. As Dolin put it: 'It was an amazing feat, and I doubt whether it has ever been equalled by any other ballerina.'*

There was great interest in Markova among the other dancers. Most of them had not seen her dance; if they had, it had been years ago when they had been children. She was something of an enigma, someone about whom they had heard reports and the legend that she never practised.

Moira Shearer, who later had a successful career doubling as a ballerina and film star,† was appearing herself with Sadler's Wells at the time. She was one of the few who had seen Alicia dance before.

'It was long before the war when she was with the Ballet Russe at the old Alhambra. I was training with Nicolai Legat. I saw her dance a solo in *Carnaval* and I'll never forget it. I've never seen such lightness and speed, it was marvellous. And she was so tiny, very small indeed.

'She was much older when she came back to Covent Garden for *The Sleeping Beauty* and at rehearsals as many of us as could crowded into the wings watching. She seemed to walk through everything and we thought, Well, that's all right, that's the way you do it, that's how you rehearse.

---

* *Markova: Her Life and Art.*
† Her most famous film is the highly acclaimed *The Red Shoes* (1948), in which she starred with Helpmann, Ashton, Massine and Ludmilla Tcherina; she also featured in *The Tales of Hoffmann* (1951), as did Helpmann, Ashton, Massine, Tcherina and Dolin; and Terence Rattigan's *The Man Who Loved Redheads* (1955), plus others.

'On the performance night we were all crowded in the wings again. She was as light as thistledown. Afterwards there wasn't a bead of perspiration on her brow.

'The audience loved her and I've never heard a reception like it. I marvelled at the wonderful way she did everything. That is real artistry.

'Markova was possessed of a great self-knowledge and was wonderfully clever. Pavlova was similar and had divided her career into three stages. When she was young she had wonderful leaps and elevation. Through the years that began to lessen so she concentrated on her quick footwork. In the third part of her career she became much slower and specialized in her superb balance. She could stand on one *pointe* for ever. Alicia had something of the same.

'In *Sleeping Beauty* she had dressing room five, it was the star room and I was next door in dressing room four. I remember calling in before the performance to have a bit of a natter and to wish her luck. I was astounded at the good order there, it was remarkable. Her make-up table was arranged as though she were a surgeon about to perform an operation. I expected to see scalpels there. Everything was meticulous. She even had a little Wili's cushion on her chair.'

Alicia still had commitments in the United States and could only stay in London for the season. She returned to the Met where she guested at the tenth anniversary of the Ballet Russe de Monte Carlo, in which Danilova also danced. From then on it was constant touring. In one week alone she appeared at Madison Square Garden, New York, and the Hollywood Bowl, California. There were also appearances in Montreal where she was heralded into a baseball stadium by a regiment of Mounties.

She loved dancing in huge stadiums; she was one of the few artists who found the Albert Hall 'very comfortable. I adored the Albert Hall since I first danced there when I was twelve years old and I still adore it.'

Arenas in London did not come much bigger than the Empress Hall. On a freezing night in January 1949, with the co-operation of impresario Tom Arnold who had also been involved with the Hippodrome *Mother Goose*, she and Dolin opened for five consecutive evenings appearing in front of an average nightly audience of seven thousand.

In order to publicize the event her promoters earmarked a large budget for advertising and her name was plastered on posters all over London, even on the sides of buses.

It was freezing at the Empress Hall as it was normally an ice rink and a floor had been laid over the ice to accommodate them. She rehearsed covered in woollies and had no voice for the entire run owing to laryngitis.

All five nights were packed out, which caused a rethink among the management as to the sort of people to whom ballet appealed. There had always been diehard fans who had packed the gallery, but ballet was branded as the province of the rich. This reputation was now in doubt.

They gave a concert repertoire of excerpts from *Swan Lake*, *The Nutcracker* and *Les Sylphides*. Contemporary ballet was represented by, among other things, a melancholy variation created for her by Nijinska called 'Autumn' – no one could dance with such melancholy as Markova when she had a mind to – the variation from Ashton's *Les Rendezvous*, which they were taking with them on a planned trip to South Africa, and, of course, *The Dying Swan*.

In February 1949 Alicia and Pat returned to America for a Puerto Rican concert tour. She had danced there before under Hurok's auspices. There were also appearances at New York's City Center with the Ballet Russe. In addition to her usual repertoire of *Giselle*, *Swan Lake* and *Nutcracker*, she danced Massine's *Seventh Symphony* and *Le Rouge et le Noir*. The city, under a pall of snow, was magical, a Disney fantasy. But she did not have long to savour its beauty.

Under the auspices of impresario Alex Chernievsky, in negotiation with Alfred Katz and the South African Theatres management, she and Dolin were booked for a tour of South Africa and Kenya, starting in March 1949 in Johannesburg.

Alicia persuaded the reluctant South African bookers to allow her to fly via London so she could spend a few days with Eileen. This did not go down too well as she was wanted as soon as possible, but she insisted on it. For some reason she particularly wanted to see Eileen; she did not know why herself. 'I know I was being difficult but I just wanted to see her. I get these psychic things from time to time.'

She took her to Covent Garden, where Danilova and Freddie Franklin were dancing *Coppélia* as guests of Sadler's Wells. They all went to dinner afterwards at the Savoy, where Alicia and Pat were staying. 'I had no home at the time so I based myself there. It was near Covent Garden and the theatres and they took good care of me.'

It was not a late night as her flight was leaving at six the next morning. After dinner she told Eileen that she intended to buy her a cottage near Brighton, nothing grand but a place to live, where she could always find her. 'It would have been a home for her and a bolt-hole for me.' She thought she could buy this with the help of her South African earnings. Sadly, it was the last time she was to see her mother.

She also had a meeting with Tom Arnold about another arena performance.

In South Africa the demand for tickets was overwhelming. The twelve recitals for which they had initially been booked were increased to forty-eight, including extra performances in Port Elizabeth, Durban, Pretoria, East London, Bloemfontein, Bulawayo, and Salisbury. They gave six additional performances in Johannesburg alone.

Her repertoire now included an additional piece called 'Blue Mountain Ballads', based on Tennessee Williams' poems. The choreography was by Donald Saddler.

Such was the clamour for autographs after performances that it sometimes took her two hours to get away from the theatre.

Although she did not like doing so, she had intended to confine herself to giving excerpts from *Giselle*, as it seemed there were insufficient facilities to stage it fully. But while in Johannesburg she realized that it might be possible to give it in its entirety at the Alhambra Theatre. The stage was big enough and they were promised an orchestra. She cabled New York for her first-act costume to be air-freighted across. Dolin set to work on staging, improvising scenery and costumes.

In order to flesh out the ballet they recruited dancers from Cape Town University Ballet and the South African National Ballet, usually rivals but who pulled together for this venture. 'They had to, there was no other way. We gathered them all together and told them, "You can't be pulling against each other if we're to do this."'

They put straight actors into the roles of Hilarion and Giselle's mother.

There was not much time available but she and Dolin spent hours of what time there was coaching the cast. It was the first time *Giselle* had been seen in its entirety in South Africa.

Soon after this they were invited to be guests of honour at a tribal war dance ceremony at the Rand mine. It went on for five hours. 'When the Zulus stamp the whole earth shakes, it's fantastic.'

Soon after the start of the tour, while Alicia was still in Johannesburg, Eileen died. She had been living with the Crewleys in Brighton and had come to London for a day trip. She had contacted Vivian Van Damm, a family-oriented man, and he had invited her to lunch at the Windmill.

Unfortunately the lift was not working that day and she had to walk up several flights of stairs. She made it to Van Damm's office but suddenly felt unwell. She had always had high blood pressure and her heart gave out. Van Damm sent for an ambulance which rushed her to Charing Cross Hospital. She died soon after arrival. It was as sudden as that.

Doris was in Paris at the time, working for dancer Katherine Dunham, but Vivienne was contacted in Blackpool. She in turn contacted Bunny and they met in London. When they arrived at the hospital the sister told them it had been a massive stroke, adding, 'You should be so pleased she's dead, otherwise she would have been paralysed.'

Vivienne cabled the grim news to Alicia. It arrived on a day she was due to dance. As always art took precedence over personal feelings. It was up to her to pull herself together and give a performance.

She writes in *Giselle and I*: 'Looking back on such experiences, I sometimes wonder about their influence upon me. The artist whose work lies in the theatre is always compelled to throw a bridge across gaps opened by private grief, and this must sometimes be done with what seems like inhuman swiftness. Yet, long afterwards, it may be seen that such griefs are distilled into the art itself, and help purify it.'

With the performance out of the way her feelings took over and she felt unable to face the fans waiting outside.

Dolin was a tower of strength. He had known Eileen for years, and he consoled Alicia before she left to sign autographs at the stage door. She masked her emotions, something she had to do all her life, and was the chic ballerina when leaving. For once, however, she did not attend the reception afterwards, and it took her a few days to pull herself together. Owing to the demands of their programmes they could not perform every day.

In critical triumph they progressed to Lourenço Marques where the stage was so rotten that a leg of the piano crashed through it. The hole remained, gaping at them, as she and Dolin worked around it. As there were just the two of them on stage they were able to adapt the choreography accordingly.

After the performance the manager came to thank Alicia for the performance. 'I did say to him, "I want you to promise me that you'll have your stage properly repaired before you have your next dancers here. It must be put in order." He looked at me very seriously and said, "Yes, I know, but I must tell you the last dancer we had here was Anna Pavlova in 1924."'

Alicia is not given to dictatorial outbursts and had not summoned the manager. Had he not approached her nothing would have been said about the stage. She has, however, had the odd burst of temperament. 'I once had a tantrum with Alfred Katz. I looked around for something to throw at him and all I could find was a box of Kleenex, so I threw that. Well, that wasn't going to hurt anyone, was it? We all roared with laughter. After that, if there was any trouble he would say to me, "Where's the Kleenex?"'

They returned to London in August. The original tour, scheduled for a month, had stretched to three months.

She moved back into the Savoy, now her home, and then went to visit Eileen's grave at the Jewish Cemetery in Rottingdean. As Eileen had been living in Brighton when she died she was buried in Sussex. Dolin went with her.

It was a glorious afternoon as they stood and looked at the grave. Alicia had hoped she would be able to spend more time with her mother in her planned Sussex cottage. As it was, she was grateful she had had the premonition urging her to see her before leaving for South Africa. It had been Alicia's career that had kept them apart, constantly demanding that she travel. Nothing could be done about that now.

Later, when Pat's mother died, she was buried in the non-Jewish cemetery next door, just the other side of the hedge from Eileen. 'I remember, it must have been twenty years ago now, I went to see Mother's grave. By then we had moved Daddy next to her so they were together.

'I used to hop on a train at Victoria, buy some flowers, take a taxi to the cemetery, get the taxi to wait then hop on the train back. I went one Saturday and, of course, that's the Jewish sabbath so the cemetery was closed.

'I told the driver to drive to the next cemetery. I found Mrs Kay's grave (when Pat eventually died he was buried next to her) and knew Mother was buried just the other side of her. So I crawled through the hedge and paid my respects, left the flowers, then crawled back and came home.'

She and Dolin had to embark on a new season of arena ballet from 27 August to 1 September 1949, this time at Harringay, later best known as a dog track but which then also featured boxing matches and horses. The smell of horses permeated everything.

Dolin was not in a good state at the time. Prior to the performance he was in hospital recovering from a savage attack. He and Alicia had been on holiday in the South of France. She had left to come home while he had stayed on, and he had been attacked and viciously beaten. Alicia thought they should cancel but he would not hear of it. Battered as he was, his face particularly, he was determined to dance.

A full production of *Giselle* was to be included in the repertoire, at her request, although others felt it too intimate for a stadium. She would not be dissuaded and told them she felt she could 'get it across'.

She had learnt through the years the problems of facing a huge audience in the round. More projection was needed. 'This projection must have more power from within, rather than from enlarged and exaggerated physical gestures and grimaces,' she says. Being in the round meant that she could be viewed from every angle; there was no way she could relax by turning her back to the audience for even a second.

Scenery was rudimentary – cut-out cottages for Act One and just a gravestone and cross for Act Two. Other effects were achieved by lighting and music. The Ballet Rambert provided the *corps* and all the other roles.

They were billed unequivocally as 'The World's Greatest Ballet Stars'. The London Symphony Orchestra was conducted by Anatole Fistoulari, who had conducted Alicia years ago with the Ballet Russe. Tickets ranged from 2s 6d to 12s 6d. This was a bargain; the profits came from the huge number of tickets sold.

There was uproar from some of the snobs. An article in the *Manchester Guardian* expressed disapproval, the critic clearly never having recovered from the sight of Markova in *Mother Goose*, something he mentioned he still deplored. Always her champion, Dolin picked up his pen and flattened the man.

As with the Empress Hall, the stadium was packed. This was not the Opera House crowd, cramming into the crush bar in the interval; these were hard-working people with little money to waste. They smoked, ate sweets during the performance and, in the interval, queued for hot dogs, orange squash and cups of tea. There was no sense of grandeur; it was the sheer talent of the performance that kept them glued to their seats.

Beryl Grey called round to see Alicia after one arena performance and was full of admiration for how she had ensured her comfort backstage and made a nest for herself. 'There was not much in the way of luxury,' she recalled. 'But Alicia had got someone to get some tables and chairs from somewhere, and, I think, some curtains and had done the place up as nicely as she could. She also managed to scrounge a sagging old couch and made herself comfortable on that. She greeted us rather like a queen, stretched out on that couch. You forgot the surroundings, it was just like being received in Buckingham Palace. She always created this aura of serenity.'

20

Festival Ballet

Alicia and Dolin followed the Harringay performances by a trip to Paris where they were booked for *Giselle* at the Empire Theatre with the Grand Ballet du Marquis de Cuevas.

The Marquis was a Chilean impresario who had married a Rockefeller heiress. He had taken over and renamed the Nouveau Ballet de Monte Carlo where Nijinska was ballet mistress. It was the first European company to have a large contingent of American dancers and its first Paris season, in 1947, marked the beginning of an extensive touring programme.

The company relied heavily on the drawing power of guest stars. Later, in 1961, when Nureyev had defected to the West, it was the first company to offer him refuge.

The Paris venture was not as successful as Harringay. For a start, when they arrived in Paris, in the late afternoon, they discovered there had been a mix-up and no hotel accommodation had been booked. There were four of them: Alicia and Pat, Doris and Benn Toff, who was impresario Julian Braunsweg's administrator and a wizard at designing and mounting scenery. He had been invaluable to them when on the road with the Markova-Dolin Company.

Paris, still reeling from the onslaught of the war and enduring food rationing, was packed out and there was no accommodation to be had. Eventually one room was secured for all four of them. They had something to eat, then sat up all night in their clothes.

On the second day there was supposed to be an orchestral rehearsal with the company, which they had not yet met, preparatory to a performance on the third day.

The electricity went off at breakfast. Paris was susceptible to electricity blackouts at that time. There would be no rehearsal. 'That was when I said to Pat, "I'm sorry, no performance, either." I did a Callas for the first and only time in my life. We called a press conference for noon and I said to the reporters, "I wouldn't insult you all by giving a slipshod performance. It's too important to me and you're too important to me." They agreed. Then we had something to eat and caught the plane back to London. I hadn't danced in Paris since my Diaghileff days. It was to be my Paris debut of *Giselle* and I wanted it to be right.'

That autumn, while Alicia was in London, the Sadler's Wells Ballet opened the Met season in New York with *Sleeping Beauty* starring Margot Fonteyn. This was the first time the ballet had been danced in America and Sadler's Wells were taking a risk on an unknown quantity. Fonteyn was petrified: 'I started an attack of stage fright which must have been the longest in history.'* The press did not reassure her, yelling for her to 'show a little more leg', while she attempted to look as 'disdainful' as possible.

The premiere took place on a sweltering October night and it was a gala occasion. Danilova was there, among other ballet stars, with Freddie Franklin. The terrified Fonteyn stepped on to the stage and received, as Franklin put it, 'very nice applause. But by the time she had finished the Rose *adagio* the place was in uproar.' She herself described her reception as 'incredible'. She was a hit. The *Daily Express* commented:

'Margot may be the biggest ballet sensation in America since that other English ballerina Alicia Markova.'

Little Peggy Hookham had made her mark.

Shortly after Alicia had returned from South Africa she had moved into a spacious mansion flat in Knightsbridge, a stone's throw from Harrods. Vivienne was working back in London by now, and moved in with her, as did Doris.

Doris and Vivienne would be there more than Alicia as she was still regularly commuting to and from America with Pat. One of the inducements for Alicia of taking on the flat was that it had previously been occupied by Americans and had central heating, something not many London flats had in those days. Her years in America had taught her to appreciate such refinements.

By Christmas Moey had moved in, too. Moey was Alicia's new cat, a tabby kitten she had picked up in Brighton on a trip to Eileen's grave. She knew the manager of the Metropole Hotel in Brighton,

---

* *Margot Fonteyn.*

from her Monte Carlo days when he had been there too, and had called in for tea. He introduced her to his two little daughters.

The family cat had given birth and a home was needed for one of the kittens. 'Mr Haskell says you like kittens,' one of the girls had said to Alicia. Arnold Haskell, who also knew the manager, had told him Alicia was coming. 'Yes, I do,' she responded. 'Would you like one?' the girl had asked. The upshot was that she brought Moey home with her on the Pullman, where he slid around on the table all the way to Victoria.

At that time he wasn't named. She called him Moey because Bunny's daughter, Susie, who was about three then, had an imaginary friend called Moey. Alicia thought she would materialize Moey for her.

Moey, like all cats, developed his own personality. He became an Alma Cogan fan. Miss Cogan became a huge star in the 1950s and whenever she was singing on television he would rush to the set and stand gawping at her, enraptured. 'He adored Alma Cogan,' says Alicia.

Moey seemed to know when Alicia was returning from her travels and would become excited, leaping around the hall in a frenzy. He once in his excitement knocked down one of the three plaster geese that were hanging there.

Moey's predecessor had been Tinker, who had lived with Alicia in the Marble Arch flat before the war. With the money she had made from *Mother Goose* she had bought a little piano, the first of the miniature pianos. 'There were only two in the country, the little Princesses had one and Selfridges the other. I always had a vase of flowers on it and Tinker would nip all the heads off. I'd come back and there were just the stalks.'

He got away with murder. In those days Madame Manya would come to fit Alicia for her new tutus, gorgeous confections which Alicia forbade anyone to touch, keeping them in their boxes until they went to the theatre for performances.

'One day, Manya had fitted me, and put the box in the hall to go to the theatre. When the taxi came she lifted the box and it weighed two tons. Tinker had crept in and gone to sleep there. The trouble was that his bed was an old tutu so he thought this was his too.' Normally she would have been upset by this breach of protocol but, as it was Tinker, he was forgiven. 'We've learnt a valuable lesson,' she told the distraught Manya. 'From now on we must keep the lids on.' They were tied on after that.

Dolin called round to see her during that first Christmas in Knightsbridge. While he was there, a piece of music to which they had danced came over the radio. Alicia leapt up and danced to it on the carpet. She was move-perfect. Dolin, again, marvelled at her phenomenal memory. He had a pretty good memory himself but, as he acknowledged, not in her league.

Beryl Grey also visited her in Knightsbridge. She was having doubts about her future at Covent Garden and needed to talk things over with someone who understood the problems.

'She was very kind,' recalls Beryl. 'She gave me sound advice that was based on her years as a top dancer. I'll always be grateful.'

Whatever the problem, it has long been resolved. Alicia remembers the meeting but will not say what they discussed; she gave her word and that is still binding. The passing of a mere half-century is irrelevant.

Around this time Alicia and Dolin, under the auspices of Julian Braunsweg, formed a small company, to tour Britain giving gala concert evenings.

Among the dancers was a troupe of teenage students from the Arts Educational School, thirteen girls and two boys, almost ready to embark on their own careers.

Comedian Leslie Crowther was at the school and, unlikely as it sounds, he appeared with Alicia in *Swan Lake* as Von Rothbart, the Owl Magician and wicked uncle of Odette.

'It happened at the point of the ballet where I . . . had to lure Odette away from the Prince, interrupting their *pas de deux*. No one had told me that my musical cue was the reprise of the passage of music in question. So when it played for the first time onto the boards I pounced. The audience must have been puzzled to see a somewhat uncomfortable wicked uncle hovering in the background, turning the passionate *pas de deux* into a *ménage-à-trois*. With consummate artistry Dolin, abandoning a surprised Markova, *grand-jetéd* sideways towards me, hissed, "Get off the bloody stage," and rejoined his partner. Needing no second prompt, I fluttered off stage as I fondly imagined an owl would do, to find the *corps de ballet* splitting their tutus laughing.'*

For a while that anecdote was part of Leslie's cabaret act.

Alicia was not as perturbed by Crowther's misdemeanour as some might expect. Malcolm Goddard, then one of the pupil dancers, remarks: 'None of the books I've read on her show her humour. Maybe she shows it more now as the pressure's off her a bit, but it's something I've noticed through the years. It first came to my notice when I was doing a *pas de trois* with her, and Dolin,

---

* *The Bonus of Laughter,* by Leslie Crowther, Hodder and Stoughton, 1994.

in *Where the Rainbow Ends* at the Festival Hall. Dolin was St George and, I think, she was the Spirit of the Lake.

'My partner and I were downstage when she came and leapt into our arms. We had to rush backwards with her while she maintained her position.

'Well, we rushed her so fast that when we came to put her down her instep hit the ground. She stood there in this wonderful shape shaking with laughter. That was the first time I realized there was a sense of humour there. I expected to be blasted off the stage instead of which she was hooting with laughter. The audience couldn't see it, of course, but it was quite clear to me. I thought she would have been angry but she wasn't at all.'

Early in 1950 Alicia and Dolin undertook a tour of the Caribbean, which took in Jamaica, Cuba and Puerto Rico, returning to London in the spring, when they resumed touring.

The small company led to the creation of another company, which remained under the representation of Julian Braunsweg. He was a Polish director of vast experience who had managed the Russian Romantic Ballet in Berlin in the 1920s and went on to manage Karsavina and Argentina. He had also advised Pavlova on the running of her various companies. Another of ballet's eccentrics, he was only eclipsed in flair by Diaghileff and Sol Hurok. There were times when he pawned his wife's jewellery to keep the show on the road and, once, had hidden under his desk when a debt collector called.

The heart of the new company consisted of Alicia and Dolin, who was Artistic Director, plus soloists John Gilpin and Nathalie Krassovska. The *corps* came largely from pupils from the Arts Educational School.

The brilliant and youthful Gilpin was a great asset. Although only twenty, he had already created roles in Howard's *The Sailor's Return* and Ashton's *Le Rêve de Leonore*. He was to stay with the company for nearly fifteen years. Dolin was smitten by him.

Nathalie Krassovska had a classic Russian pedigree in that her mother had been a Diaghileff dancer and she had studied with Preobrajenska and Legat and partnered Lifar. She was to stay with the company for nine years.

Among the guest dancers were Danilova, Massine, David Lichine, Mia Slavenska, former Baby Ballerina Tatiana Riabouchinska, and the Yugoslav Milorad Miskovitch. Miskovitch was later to become Alicia's partner but, at that time, he mostly partnered Slavenska.

The emphasis was on nineteenth-century classics and twentieth-century masterpieces. 'Britain didn't go much for the really new things,' says Alicia. 'Both *La Chatte* and *Le Rossignol* went down better on the Continent.' Alicia had a vast repertoire – classics, new works and jazz – which was why it was so difficult to replace her when she left Sadler's Wells. Eventually it took four people to do what she did.

The repertoire included *Petrushka, Giselle, Beau Danube, Nutcracker,* the second act of *Swan Lake, Les Sylphides,* plus new works, including *Pas de Quatre,* some of which had first been performed that season.

While the company was being set up Alicia established certain points. 'We'd had so many companies before and I was coming up for forty and I'd been working since I was ten, so I wasn't keen to have too much responsibility. But I wanted two new productions, *Giselle* and *The Nutcracker.*

'Most importantly I wanted the Stoll Theatre to be our home. I knew the theatre and it had an enormous rehearsal room on the roof, could accommodate a full orchestra and had dressing rooms for a company which would be spending its life there, all day and most days.'

London's Stoll Theatre became the home of the new company and a gala opening was scheduled for 25 October 1950, preceded by a tour.

It was a busy time for Alicia. She was in the midst of another tour to be followed by concert appearances with a symphony orchestra and Dolin at the Albert Hall.

The Albert Hall performances never took place. She went down with acute appendicitis in June, in Manchester, and was rushed to hospital.

She was operated on at St John and St Elizabeth's Hospital in London's Hampstead. Edna, her dresser, visited her and found her a bright and good patient, doing what her doctors ordered. 'I was always a good patient because I wanted a good recovery. I wanted to get out as soon as possible and back to what I should be doing.'

She was anxious the press did not discover she was ill, which had always been the case. She wanted to be dancing again as soon as possible and did not want stories of her illness putting people off buying tickets. The staff looked after her well. 'The sister was wonderful. Talk about a sense of humour.'

While she lay in her hospital room she settled on a name for the new company.

The whole world was talking about the forthcoming Festival of Britain, due to open on the South Bank in 1951. Plans of the site had appeared in the press, plus artists' impressions of the shortly-to-be-constructed Royal Festival Hall and the towering Skylon, a unique and beautiful abstract talon of sculpture, which would float in the sky eternally pointing to heaven, and be seen from miles around. Unfortunately it was bulldozed down shortly after the Festival closed under orders from Winston Churchill.

As Alicia read about these plans for the Festival the name came to her. The new company would be the Festival Ballet. 'I knew we would be ambassadors, visiting foreign countries, and that they would understand what the Festival of Britain meant.'

As soon as she was able to leave hospital Alicia went to Monte Carlo, with Vivienne, to convalesce. She stayed at the lovely Hôtel de Paris where many people knew her. Monte Carlo was still quiet then.

The Festival Ballet made its debut at the King's Theatre, Southsea. Alicia was not well enough to dance but motored down and sat in a box on opening night. She rallied enough to dance in Edinburgh where a member of the audience gave her a sprig of white heather for good luck, which she still has. Edinburgh had always been a lucky city for Alicia, ever since the days she had danced in it for Diaghileff.

Opening night at the Stoll drew ever nearer.

Braunsweg walked in on a band-call at the Stoll one day and stood stock-still in amazement. The *corps* were sweating through their moves in practice clothes. Alicia, in the midst, was wearing a mink coat and high-heeled shoes. In an unhurried manner she would say which moves she would make before strolling to another spot and checking her timings with the conductor.

Braunsweg had worked with the most famous names in ballet and had never seen another ballerina, not even Pavlova, rehearse in a mink coat. He never forgot the sight and wrote about it in his book *Ballet Scandals.**

Malcolm Goddard, by now a member of the Festival Ballet, was one of that sweating *corps* and recalls the incident.

'A critic, when reviewing Braunsweg's book, said that such a thing was totally unbelievable and could not have happened, but I can assure you it did, I was there. Those shoes were black suede with very high heels, she loved them and she loved that mink, too, which she rarely took off. The rest of us were in practice clothes, as we had to be, but Alicia was in high heels and a mink. I saw it.'

* Allen and Unwin.

277

'I was cold,' says Alicia.

On opening night, which heralded a three-month season, she danced *The Nutcracker* in its two-act version, including the Snow Queen scene. She was the first dancer since Pavlova to include that scene. Hurok had insisted on it in America where it had been built on Eglevsky. Dolin then learnt it, as had Youskevitch.

The new *Giselle* was premiered on 2 November. Goddard was Hilarion and recalls a performance during which the theatre heating system developed an airlock. 'She was dying away on stage at the time, and this thing kept exploding, it sounded like rifle shots in the auditorium. There was not a murmur from her, not at the time nor afterwards. If she mentioned it to the management I never heard about it. There was never any foot stamping from her.'

'I was dead before I fell, so I couldn't make any reaction,' says Alicia. 'Then I had a quick change. I never wasted time.'

In December 1950, while the Stoll season was in full swing, she agreed to make a film of *Giselle*, commissioned for American television, with Dolin as Albrecht and Goddard as Hilarion, 'wearing my Errol Flynn hat,' he says. There would be a commentary by Jack Buchanan, and the London Symphony Orchestra would be pre-recorded and conducted by Malcolm Sargent. She spent a day with Sargent beforehand discussing her tempi.

No one was paid; it was all done for love of the art. It was after the war and no one had any money. Naturally, if the film had taken off, they would all have benefited and everyone was happy to settle on that basis.

This would not be the full ballet but a version abridged to two thirteen-minute segments with a break in between. Alicia wanted it to be in colour but this was ruled too expensive.

She was not happy about the abridgement but realized the film would provide some record of her creation, something she wanted.

It took a week to shoot the film at the Riverside Studios, Hammersmith, and this had to be done between Stoll commitments. She, and the rest of the team, got up at five on the freezing mornings, and a car took her to the studio.

Among the camera crew was Terence Young, one of Hollywood's most sought-after cinematographers, and Nicholas Roeg, who went on to win fame as cinematographer on *Far from the Madding Crowd* and director of many films including the acclaimed *Don't Look Now*.

She danced all day, then the car returned to take her to the Stoll for the evening performance.

It was exhausting and, as soon as filming ended, she went down with gastric flu and spent a week in bed. A columnist wrote that she was calling out in delirium in the belief that she was still under arc lights.

She denies that. 'It takes more than that to knock me out. I think I was born under two stars – one practical and the other fantasy. With those two you can have a very interesting life.'

The film was worth the strain. For all its shortness it gives the essence of her Giselle. It was shown in London cinemas in 1952 and still pops up from time to time, all over the world. Only recently Alicia had a letter from someone who had seen it in the Australian outback.

For a souvenir she gave Goddard a pair of her ballet slippers which she autographed. He was amazed that the satin on the blocks was barely marked.

'And we were dancing on wooden floors,' he says. 'Not the beautiful floors of today. One of the things you notice when you see the film is her extraordinary speed. I've never seen anybody exit in the second act of *Giselle* so fast, and with all that intricate footwork.

'I learned economy on stage from Alicia. When she was learning anything she pared it down to basics. Nothing was wasted and no movement unnecessary. I was lucky to have spent time with her, and Dolin too. He could be selfish off stage but on stage he was most unselfish. He always said to me, "Your duty is to present the lady, and make her look as good as you can."'

The first foreign booking for the Festival Ballet came from Monte Carlo in the spring of 1951. After this the company name was to change to London's Festival Ballet; it later became London Festival Ballet. Alicia was to dance *Giselle* with Dolin and Malcolm Goddard and, while there, take part in a charity gala during which she danced a solo.

The bill included several music-hall acts and Goddard was talking to her after the performance. 'Isn't it typical,' he moaned. 'They put you on after a variety act. You'd think it would be better arranged; they always put dancers on after the comic.'

'She was wearing a magnificent ermine stole at the time,' he recalled. 'She stroked this, looked at me and remarked, "I got this for following George Lacy twice daily at the Hippodrome."'

The Paris critics flocked to Monte Carlo to see *Giselle*. It was the first time they had seen her in the role as she had quit her earlier Paris booking with the Marquis de Cuevas. After the performance

Prince Rainier presented her with a gold commemorative medal to mark the Festival's first appearance in Monte Carlo.

Back in Britain the Festival continued to tour. In Sheffield they played the town hall which had two enormous stone lions on stage which could not be moved. A compromise was reached when they were draped in black and the choreography altered so that the dancers moved round them.

There were so many autograph hunters waiting outside that mounted police had to be called before Alicia could leave. That often happened during the tour.

In Manchester they played Belle Vue circus. There were no dressing rooms so the company had to improvise. Dolin changed in the elephant house. The stage area had a tin roof and the rain pelted down so hard none of the dancers could properly hear the orchestral beat.

'That was when Benn Toff was so wonderful,' remembers Alicia. 'When we were setting up the concert tours I said, "I don't mind dancing in those places but how are we going to do it?" They were town halls, boxing rings, sporting arenas, huge movie houses, anywhere we could accommodate the people. But they didn't have theatrical facilities, how were we going to manage? With a *corps* of a dozen we could hardly climb up ladders to the performance places.

'When you have problems you sit down and discuss them and Benn came up with the idea of designing a portable stage which was mostly scaffolding. It couldn't take too long to construct and dismantle as we were always moving on. He became in charge of production, with Doris, and we were able to carry our own floor which would be laid over whatever was there. Benn would secure things for all of us. That was his big contribution to Festival Ballet and I would like it recognized.'

Despite all the stress of the tours no one ever heard Alicia swear. The most that came out was 'dash' or, under extreme provocation, 'God Almighty'. Dolin could let rip with the best but Alicia has never sworn.

By now Alicia and Goddard had become friends, but he remembers how awed he was by her at first.

'She was always the *grande dame* to the company, it was really forelock-pulling time. In those days the hierarchy of theatrical behaviour was different. There were no first names addressed to the principals and, when I spoke to her, I always called her "Miss Markova". It wasn't servile, it was respect. There was a slight aloofness at first, which I now know was shyness.

'I had been in the company about eighteen months before I went out with her. I wouldn't have wanted to go out with her before then, I would have been out of my depth.'

'He was just a student, then,' she says. 'But if anyone was talented both Pat and I thought it was up to us to take them to eat afterwards and talk about things. We did that with all our people.'

During one London run the conductor was Robert Zeller. He was an American who had worked with Alicia during her American days; they were old friends. Alicia, Goddard, Doris and Zeller would make up a foursome for dinner, then go back to Alicia's flat afterwards. Goddard remembers those gatherings with affection.

'Usually, at about two in the morning, Alicia would kick off her shoes and show us how all the variations in the ballets should be done. Not performance-wise but what they should hold. She told me, "All these solos should contain these steps, they're like the arias in opera." They were not her steps but those she had learned from the Russian legends during her Diaghileff days. "They are tests," she went on, "and if you can't do them you shouldn't be in ballet." It was a fantastic experience.'

He never discussed romance with her and she never mentioned it to anyone else that he was aware of. 'I wouldn't expect her to tell me anything like that,' he says. 'And I wouldn't dream of asking. But if you are an artist it's very difficult to sustain a relationship with someone. Pretty soon they realize that they play a pretty poor second to the career. Maybe nothing else has been necessary for Alicia. I think, for her, it has been totally fulfilling.'

In 1951 London was overflowing with tourists who had come to the outrageously successful Festival of Britain. The Festival Hall was now built, its Skylon stabbing the sky, magnificently protective above it. Crowds flocked to the South Bank by road, railway and river. Buses were packed, Waterloo Station was jammed, and river buses churned along the Thames. Across the water could be heard the yells from Battersea Park fairground and its piped music wafted for miles.

Things felt good to Alicia, too, at the Stoll. Business was booming and *Giselle* continued to be her triumph. Already the critics had lavished praise on her in 1951; she had been variously described as 'a wisp of vapour', 'skimming like a dragonfly', 'clothed in the secrets of dew and mist', and, from Cyril Beaumont, '. . . it is difficult to believe the tarlatan skirt enfolds a living woman.' Her explanation for her effect of lightness was 'due to one hundred per cent exhausting muscular control' and 'my good steak every day'.

In those days she used to have red meat and a Guinness after every performance. Nowadays she does not eat red meat.

'When I stopped dancing my whole digestion changed. One period in New York I used to eat steak tartare a lot. Mary Martin was on Broadway, doing *Peter Pan*, and we used to sometimes eat together. The waiter brought me steak tartare and she said, "What's that?" I said, "You should be having it with all your flying." And she did.

'The very first time I had raw meat was when I was working on my first full-length *Swan Lake* at Sadler's Wells in 1934. Dame Adeline Genée had asked Dame Ninette how I was getting on.

'One day there was a little parcel for me at the stage door, left by Dame Adeline. It was a jar of what looked like ointment. There was a note saying that her aunts and uncles had given her this when they were training her to build stamina. She said she called it "rat poison". It was concentrated raw meat. Years ago they used to give it to boxers, it strengthens you and you don't get flab. It was what she was brought up on.

'So when I saw steak tartare in New York I thought it must be similar to the "rat poison". I used to say to Mary Martin, "What would we do without our rat poison?"'

For all her success in *Giselle* Alicia did not monopolize the role and several guest ballerinas were invited to dance it during the season.

Booking them was Pat's responsibility as he was Artistic Director. His status was important to both of them. By now, Alicia was the bigger box-office draw and for him to be Artistic Director somehow balanced things out. It was a job he did well.

This helped keep them on an even keel. She was happy to lead the company and dance. But whatever titles they held, they discussed everything between them. Now and then a dancer would come to Alicia with a problem which she could have solved but she would always refer the person to Dolin. He would then invariably ask her advice.

Liberace was in town, about to open at the Café de Paris. Dolin came into the Stoll and told Alicia that he had invited them to his opening night. Since the cabaret didn't start until getting on for midnight there was plenty of time to get there after curtain-down at the Stoll.

She was photographed with Liberace in his dressing room after his performance and when the photographers and press had gone they settled down to 'catch up on things'. His act had been honed since they had seen it in Chicago. He captivated London as he captivated the world right until the end of his life, virtually dying on stage.

Young John Gilpin was also captivating audiences and during this season he danced Albrecht to Alicia's Giselle.

'I didn't want to do it. I admired John very much and we got on, but for me it was like dancing with my son, we weren't right for each other in *Giselle*. He was perfect in *The Blue Bird* with me. That was pure dance. He was small and technically perfect, just what was needed, speed and sparkle. That we enjoyed together but not *Giselle*. I danced less with him than any other partner.'

Finishing the Stoll season in the summer, the Festival Ballet moved to Golders Green in the autumn, for a week at the Hippodrome, followed by another week in Glasgow. There malignant fate sat by and smiled.

'We were opening with *Nutcracker*. There was always a one-act overture ballet beforehand and this was to be danced by Gilpin, but he hadn't turned up. Pat was in a bit of a state as he had to arrange things. He couldn't dance as he was partnering me in *Nutcracker*. He had to make an announcement to the audience.

'I went on the stage, behind the curtain, to warm up. I'd done my barre and I was jumping when a board gave way and I wrenched my foot, breaking the ligaments in two places, although I didn't know that then.

'Had it not been for Pat having to make that announcement I wouldn't have danced, but I thought I can't go to him now, in the midst of all his trouble, and say I'm not dancing, what will he do? So I didn't say anything and thought I'd try to do it. I might have to change a few things when I'm alone but I'll try to manage the *pas de deux* with Pat. So I didn't say anything to him.

'After the performance about six of us went to dinner. The pain in my foot was terrible but I still didn't say anything as Pat was worried about John.

'But as I got up I saw my foot had swollen. It was like an elephant's foot. Everyone looked at me so I told them what had happened.

'I was taken to hospital at about one in the morning and X-rayed. Next morning I got on the phone to Bill Tucker, my foot specialist, and he told me to get to him as soon as possible.'

Meanwhile Ashton was developing a new ballet for her on the Marguerite theme, and she started to work on it with him while having treatment with Tucker. Her priority was to get fit for the Festival Ballet Monte Carlo Christmas season.

She had treatment with Tucker every day and he did what he

could. Although she was not happy about her foot she flew to Monte Carlo and danced *The Nutcracker* on opening night.

Dolin, who was to have partnered her, arrived late from New York and was too tired to dance, so Gilpin partnered her. She danced the Snow Scene then, in the interval, sent for Dolin, who was out front. She told him she would have to cut the Sugar Plum Fairy. She would try to get through the *pas de deux* but the Fairy would be impossible.

She left Monte Carlo the next day in agony having worsened her injury. Bill Tucker told her she must not dance for six months: 'We tried it both ways, firstly with treatment and dancing and that didn't work, so Bill told me, "It's the other alternative. You'd better have six months off. You need a real rest."'

She went, with Doris, to stay with Eleanor Peters in California. Mrs Peters was a follower of the ballet and Alicia had met her when she was dancing in Seattle. 'She had a beautiful house in Sherman Oaks with servants and guest suites and a pool. It had formerly belonged to Jack Oakie.* All her family followed the ballet, and she had always given a big party for the company.'

Dame Judith Anderson used to come for lunch and Roger Moore would sit by her pool at times, as did Jarmila Novotna. Leslie Caron was also a regular and she and Alicia would chat about ballet while washing up, Leslie washing, Alicia drying. No one put such a sheen on a glass as Alicia. She was famed for it.

There, in the sunshine, she healed. And thought about what to do next.

---

* Former vaudevillian who became a comic in films. Famous for his startled 'double take'.

21

The Romantic Erik Bruhn

Alicia remained in California through the spring of 1952, making regular trips to New York to see her foot specialist. He was confident that the injury would mend but she had her days of doubting.

She is not a natural depressive but, if there is something to worry about, can suffer agonizing bouts as she had at 'Jacob's Pillow' in 1941. This was happening now. She fretted over the problem from every angle and, at times, thought the blackest.

But things did improve and she, and Doris, moved to New York where, as soon as she knew it was safe to do so, she resumed practice with Vincenzo Celli. As before he stressed to her the need to work, to be relentless in her desire to come back as strong as ever. He gave her back her enthusiasm.

Her first booking, when she began dancing again, was from the Teatro Colón, Buenos Aires, where she was to appear in a new production of *Swan Lake*, followed by a series of recitals, with the Polish Roman Jasinsky.

She had danced with Jasinsky during the Ballet Russe season at City Center in New York in 1939. 'Pat partnered me in the classical ballets but Roman partnered me in *Le Rouge et le Noir*.'

Doris was going with her and, about a week before they were due to depart, they heard rumours that Argentina's First Lady, Eva Perón, was unwell. She died on 26 July 1952. The beautiful Evita was revered as a goddess and the country was plunged into two weeks mourning. All theatrical performances were postponed.

Owing to the political situation in Argentina they were warned by the American embassy before leaving that, whatever happened, they were not to complain but to accept everything.

When they eventually arrived at Buenos Aires airport, after the mourning period, Alicia was intercepted by officials and taken to a chapel, stacked with roses, and told she was there to pay her respects to 'Our Lady' – Evita.

Next day, when she arrived at the theatre for rehearsal, she was escorted to an improvised chapel which, again, was crammed with flowers. Again she was given the opportunity of paying her respects to Evita. All personnel, when entering or leaving the theatre, were expected to pay obeisance to Evita.

As this was a new production of *Swan Lake* a new set had been designed. This was revealed to them as Alicia and Doris sat in the stalls during a rehearsal. The castle was a replica of Windsor Castle. 'They thought I would feel at home with an English version.'

'She was terrific,' says Doris. 'When the theatre people came along she said it was marvellous.'

The invisible Evita continued to make her presence felt. Robert Zeller, when conducting rehearsals, found he had only a handful of musicians instead of the full orchestra; the balance had been requisitioned to play at a mass for Evita. There were many masses, all over the city, and it was a similar pattern throughout. 'They were either playing mass during rehearsals or had rehearsed but were playing mass during the performance.'

Alicia received her customary bouquets after each show and was surprised, and displeased, after the first performance, when she saw her dresser disappearing with most of the flowers.

When she asked what was going on the dresser explained that there was a flower tax. A proportion of all flowers had to be given to Evita in her chapel. Alicia requested that she at least be given the cards so she would know whom to thank.

At rehearsal, on the day before her last performance, she bade the stage manager goodbye, saying she would see him the next night.

'Tomorrow morning, at nine o'clock,' he told her.

Who, she wondered, had called a rehearsal at nine on the morning of her farewell performance?

She discovered it was not a rehearsal but a performance for the 'syndicate', the trade union workers. Unpaid. It was the only time in her life she has given a performance at nine in the morning.

Security was often an issue in the precarious governmental climate, as they had discovered at their hotel on the day of their arrival.

Alicia had a suite and Doris had an adjoining room with bath. Soon after her arrival, Alicia was due at a press conference and photocall, to be held in the hotel. She had travelled from a sweltering New York through an even more sweltering Rio and then on to a cool Argentina. She wanted to change into a cocktail dress and one of the big hats that smart ladies wore then.

Doris came to Alicia's room to help her get ready, leaving her opened case on the bed in her room. Suddenly a valet and maid appeared, unbidden, from Doris's room. They explained they were available if required and left, again, through Doris's room.

When Doris returned she discovered that her case had been rifled and her handbag was missing.

Things had been as bad during the performances. 'There was a wide corridor in the theatre with the dressing rooms leading off it. You had to lock your room when leaving for the stage and lodge your key with a security lady who sat at a desk in the corridor. I never had any valuable jewellery anyway – why tempt people while travelling? – so I was never worried by things being stolen.

'But after the performance Bob Zeller was talking loudly in the corridor. Everything of value had been stolen, passport, money, the lot, despite the fact he had locked his door. It was only later I realized he had been travelling on an American passport – we had had visas.'

Leaving Argentina was not without its problems, either. Doris and Alicia were assembled at the airport at about five in the morning, when they were told there would be a delay as one passenger had not shown up. There were repeated calls over the tannoys for a Miss Knownas who failed to identify herself. The passengers protested at the delay and no one knew who Miss Knownas was.

Finally a harassed official came over with the lady's passport, which she had registered before her disappearance. The mystery was solved. It was Doris. Her passport identity was given as 'Doris Marks also known as Doris Barry'. With their imperfect grasp of English the authorities had taken the words KNOWN AS as Doris's surname. Alicia still sometimes calls her Miss Knownas.

They had to land for a scheduled stop in Rio. When taking off again there was a false start; just before lift-off, the plane jerked to a halt, giving the passengers a terrible jolt.

Doris felt a stabbing pain in her abdomen. She was in agony. It turned out to be an attack of appendicitis. It was so bad that Alicia insisted her doctor be radioed in New York (where she was due to start rehearsals for her forthcoming Met season) to stand by with an ambulance for her.

In New York, while Doris was rushed off, Alicia had to sort out their luggage and get it transported to the Windsor Hotel. 'You were supposed to be looking after me,' Alicia says to Doris. 'And I ended up sorting everything out for you.'

Doris was operated on and Alicia visited her every day in hospital.

In New York she fulfilled a booking from Ballet Theatre to guest during its autumn Met season and then tour. Since her foot had stood up to the Buenos Aires engagement she knew she could sustain the tour. She was never sure, after an accident or illness, whether or not her stamina would be impaired.

By now her relationship with Dolin and London's Festival Ballet was frosty. While convalescing in California she had been offered lots of work, plus television engagements. These had been widely reported in the press and had come to the attention of Pat and Braunsweg.

They thought she was using her injury as an excuse not to dance with them, but to stay in America. She had had no contract with the Festival Ballet and was actually at liberty to do what she wanted, but it was a question of loyalty. In fact, she had been unable to dance at all, 'since that awful performance in Monte Carlo until Buenos Aires'.

Meanwhile, Pat and Braunsweg, for all their affrontedness, were not averse to utilizing the costumes and musical arrangements she had lodged with the company.

Ballet Theatre had a policy of employing American dancers and not relying on foreigners, but Alicia had danced with them so many times she was not regarded as a foreigner, more as a friend.

Youskevitch was her partner and they opened in *Giselle* on 26 September 1952. This was a stark production with harsh sets and costumes. There was nothing stark about her reception: she had not appeared at the Met for four years and, as one journalist put it, her ovation was so long 'it must have been heard at the Battery, down on the harbour.'

Doris was, by now, out of hospital but still weak. Alicia moved her into the Windsor where she would be comfortable and could be looked after by room service.

She now had to tour America and Canada and sent an SOS for Vivienne to join her. Vivienne did not need asking twice and joyfully looked forward to the adventure. She was not disappointed.

In Chicago a potential disaster struck. Alicia missed her timing, in *Giselle* of all ballets, and sailed straight through Youskevitch's arms on to the floor, landing in a snowstorm of tulle. Youskevitch's face was, as Miss de Mille might have put it, 'a study'.

The impromptu dive had been accomplished so artistically that most of the audience did not realize it was an accident, so she held back the nervous giggles, bent back one leg, and got up and resumed the ballet. It was only later that she realized she had badly bruised her hip. But she could dance with that.

Critic Arthur Todd saw her Chicago *Giselle* and, some years later, wrote that he remembered the traffic being 'tied up for blocks around the opera house'.*

During another performance of Giselle a further accident took place. She was alone centre-stage in arabesque, her hands raised in prayer. As she posed motionless on one foot the audience were silent. 'For any dancer it can be a tricky moment. You have to hold your balance, not wobble, and it's utterly noiseless.' Suddenly one of the vast electric bulbs overhead exploded, with a sound like a bomb detonating, and she, and the stage, were covered with lethal splinters of glass. The whole audience gasped out loud.

She maintained her balance but the rest of the performance was spent dodging the fragments. The *corps* and poor Youskevitch had a terrible time. He later picked glass from all over his body.

One evening, Vivienne was standing in the wings watching Alicia, and noticed a nail sticking out of the woodwork. Someone had already snagged a costume on it and it was in danger of tearing more. She took a hammer, which was lying nearby, and put the nail to rights.

To her horror a union representative told her she could cause a strike. It was not her job to bang in nails, officials were employed to do that. He was not joking. She explained that she was ignorant of protocol and offered to return the nail to its original position, terrified she had jeopardized the performance.

At the reception afterwards she saw the official and made it her business to charm him. He was charmed; he not only forgave her but asked her out.

In Canada, after another performance, Alicia found an income tax inspector waiting for her in her dressing room. 'I found this very nice gentleman waiting for me, Vivienne had shown him in. He had watched the performance and was interested.'

He was also interested in tax demands being met. She was not behind with taxes but was scheduled to leave Canada for America

* *Dance and Dancers*, 1955.

the next day. The vigilant officer was ensuring tax was paid before she left.

If there were tax problems, and there were bound to be from time to time, she would explain her situation in person. When in New York she had to go to the Bowery to settle her tax, usually on the spot, to 'that horrible place', as Doris calls it.

At one meeting Alicia explained: '"I'm willing to pay but can I do it in instalments? If you let me go on the tour then I can pay you off so much a month." They were delightful. I gained two members for the audience that day. They became balletomanes but they wouldn't have been if I hadn't gone there personally.'

That year, 1952, she appeared at Ted Shawn's Theater, dancing solos. He summed up the essence of her art as 'chaste'. 'She was his favourite among favourite ballerinas,' wrote Anthony Fay in the Massachusetts *Sunday Republican*.

Early in 1953 Alicia left for a London season at Covent Garden to guest with Sadler's Wells. Included in her repertoire were Act Two of *Swan Lake* and *Les Sylphides*, which she danced with John Field. She would also dance *Giselle* with Michael Somes, the company's leading male star. Her opening night was 16 March.

On Good Friday, *Les Sylphides* was televised by the BBC. Cyril Beaumont was involved and Tamara Karsavina, then aged sixty-eight, invited to advise. Lydia Sokolova staged the *corps de ballet* and was delighted to be part of things, and Svetlana Beriosova and Soviet-born Violetta Elvin, two of the brightest young dancers of the time, were among the principals.

By now Alicia was so immersed in the role that she was able to write in *Giselle and I*: 'Giselle had now outgrown mere dancing, and through her, I could do what I had always dreamed about and worked for – use the magic of the ballet to open doors upon life itself.'

She got on well with her niece, Susie, Bunny's daughter, who by now was six. Alicia liked being an aunt and would sometimes take Susie with her to her dressing room after she had watched the matinée. She would sit quietly on a chair and meet the procession of visitors that Alicia always received.

'Do you know all these people?' she once asked Alicia.

'Not all of them.'

There was no time for Susie to wonder why her aunt received a stream of strangers. They had to move out. The opera was on that night and Aida needed her dressing room.

Susie still remembers those dressing-room sessions. 'I was always told to sit quietly, but I knew how to behave. I was struck, even then, by how calm she always looked despite all the curtain calls. And I'll never forget all those flowers; sometimes the baskets were larger than her. Now and then she would allow me to go on the stage and present flowers to her.

'She was my very own Sugar Plum Fairy. There was a cupboard in her room and she used to say, "Let's see what the Sugar Plum Fairy has brought you," and she would give me something. At Christmas there was always an extra present from the Sugar Plum Fairy.'

The Sugar Plum Fairy still buys presents. Alicia says, 'I saw a little pair of shoes in a shop window and I thought they would be perfect for one of the Espinosa children [the famous family of dancers of Spanish origin]. I had them wrapped and gave them, not from me, but from the Sugar Plum Fairy.'

'It became difficult a bit later, when I was at the Arts Educational School,' Susie continues. 'I was studying ballet and theatre but I never felt I got credit for what I did. I was always being compared to her. People would say, "Oh, she only got that because of her aunt."

'I'm a social worker now, and I think she might have made quite a good mother. She's always got time for children and never talks down to them. But I don't know how she'd get on alone with a child all the time, that might be different. She is a good aunt, she's been wonderful to me. I talk to her on the phone at least once a week.'

That May Alicia interrupted her Covent Garden season for an appearance in Paris with Ballet Theatre where, with Youskevitch, she finally gave the city her *Giselle* at the huge Palais de Chaillot. From then on Paris was at her feet.

She returned to London and resumed her season. Usually she would arrive home after midnight, put her flowers in water, and sleep for twelve hours at a stretch. 'I do that whenever possible, not just after a ballet. That's never any trouble.' Moey would make himself at home next to her on the bed. She was asleep long before him.

That June, Sandor Gorlinsky, her new representative, organized a series of English concerts for her and Somes. She introduced audiences to her new solo, 'Bolero 1830', which she performed in a crimson and gold costume. This had been created for her by Ana Ricarda, a pupil of both Celli and Argentina. Her dances usually had a Spanish flavour. Alicia was delighted to have something else not on *pointe*.

Ana, a sometime member of the Grand Ballet du Marquis de

Cuevas, was an old friend. She had taken Alicia to tea at the Russian Tearoom virtually on her first day in New York. Alicia had never forgotten her kindness and repaid her throughout the years. She gave her private lessons. They also shared many one-night stands on tour and had a similar appetite. Alicia remembers them ordering meals when they were together in Texas. 'Prawn cocktail, T-bone steak and French fries and apple pie and cream.' When Doris was in America, and needed accommodation, she would sometimes stay with Ana's mother.

The next few years were spent in a turmoil of travel. Alicia crossed the Altantic three times one summer and spent more time on aeroplanes than she did on stage.

She went to New York after the Covent Garden run and, while there, appeared on television's top-rating peak-time *Your Show of Shows* which starred comedians Sid Caesar and Imogene Coca. She danced the prelude from *Les Sylphides* followed by the *pas de deux* with the show's choreographer, James Starbuck. She had met Starbuck during her days with the Ballet Russe in America when he had been a member of the company.

This was the first time *Les Sylphides* had been seen on American television. Men in tights were not considered suitable for family viewing then. 'We've got to try to get to that audience,' Alicia told Starbuck. 'So Jimmy dressed as a poet in romantic pants and shirt.'

Alicia was not just dancing, she was introducing the various items. 'It was the first time anyone in America had heard my voice. Can you imagine how nerve-racking that was? We would have a run-through on the day before the show then do it, on a Saturday, "live".' For the finale she changed into a 'glamour' dress.

Among the writers for *Your Show of Shows* were Mel Brooks, Woody Allen and Neil Simon. 'Can you imagine the cost of that line-up now?' she asks.

She was in Paris for the autumn of 1953 for a season at the Théâtre de l'Empire with the Grand Ballet du Marquis de Cuevas. Nijinska was now attached to the company as ballet mistress and George Skibine was principal male dancer.

She enjoyed working with Skibine – their theatrical chemistry always worked – but was unhappy about the production of *Giselle*. The scenery had, long ago, been based on Benois' designs but was now shabby, a 'museum piece' as far as she was concerned.

Such was her success that her scheduled two *Giselle*s were increased to three, although this meant cancelling another advertised programme featuring other artists.

Unfortunately Skibine strained his back before they could dance their final *Giselle* and his place was taken by Vladimir Skouratoff.

While in Paris she danced for President Auriol at the Palais d'Orsay at one of the grand charity balls, attended by many dignitaries. The President had wanted to see her *Giselle* but had been unable to attend so had specially requested that she dance at the ball. She received two decorations for her trouble.

She was soon back in America, at the Met, for the New Year's Eve gala performance of the operetta *Die Fledermaus*. A ballet was created for Alicia by Zachary Solov to the music of Strauss's 'Acceleration Waltz'.

She had a devoted fan in Tony, the Met's stage doorkeeper. He always slipped round to the front to watch her dance and wrote poems to her, which he left in her dressing room. One line read, 'She danced the heartbeat of the world.' During the war he had left her little presents of fruit, which was hard to come by.

Around that time she appeared on another *Your Show of Shows* where she danced *The Dying Swan*. She was juggling her career with Met appearances, guest appearances and television.

She then flew back to London for a season at the Stoll with the Grand Ballet du Marquis de Cuevas. She had a repertoire with so many companies that she was able to step straight off an aeroplane and dance. Before starting with the Marquis she slept for an uninterrupted twenty-four hours.

In addition to her usual repertoire she was to dance Dolin's *Pas de Quatre*, and to promote this she danced an excerpt on television.

It was a bitter winter and frozen fog hung over the Stoll. The heating system was never reliable, as evinced by its explosion during her Festival performance of *Giselle*. Now, when it was most needed, it failed completely. The dressing rooms were Siberian cells and the stage a fridge. It was worse for the audience than for the dancers. Some sat wrapped in travelling-rugs.

This was the production of *Giselle* on which Alicia was not keen, so she was delighted to learn that, somewhere, in transit, the tomb had been lost. 'It wasn't a tomb,' she says. 'It was a covered orange box.'

Designer Bernard Daydé, who was in charge of production and a fan of hers, made her a new tomb, full of foliage and reeds, which was much better. She gave him an autographed ballet slipper. Later she was to thank him even more by inviting him to design at the Met. The press carried photographs of Daydé measuring Alicia for her new tomb.

The tomb cheered her up but she decided to beef up the

lighting as well and spent hours with the electricians making suggestions.

No sooner had the applause for her performance died down than she was back in America for performances with the Royal Winnipeg Ballet, in Washington, DC, in addition to Met performances.

She returned to Britain to start a concert tour, booked by Gorlinsky, with Yugoslav dancer Milorad Miskovitch. This had been her idea and she had spent much time working out the music and repertoire.

She and Miskovitch toured England, Scotland and Wales, for six weeks, accompanied by two pianos, except for an appearance at the Royal Albert Hall on 15 April 1954 where they were accompanied by a symphony orchestra. In addition to her repertoire Alicia was also responsible for costumes, stage effects and musical arrangements.

She danced *L'Après-midi d'un Faune*, choreography by Nijinsky, music by Debussy, for the first time during this tour, although this was primarily a vehicle for Miskovitch. 'He was a wonderful classical partner but I needed something to show off his individual talents. I had *The Dying Swan*. So I said, "I'll play the nymph and support you in *L'Après-midi*."

'I asked Sokolova if she thought we could adapt it for just the two of us and she said, "Why not?" She had been one of the nymphs when Nijinsky had danced it, so she worked on it.'

As always, Alicia received dozens of guests after each performance. A colourful fan arrived in Edinburgh.

'I had my robe on and was sitting there receiving. Suddenly this scruffy sort of man, all whiskers, burst his way in and pushed past everyone – they were all dressed up, of course – and grabbed my hand and gasped, "Thank you, thank you, thank you," and I thought, Oh, he's enjoyed the performance. But he said, "You know, I came here this evening with the most terrible headache, I was going crazy, and now it's gone. Thank you, you're better than aspirin," and out he went.'

Ram Gopal came to one of her performances in London and told her again how much he wanted to dance with her.

She returned to Edinburgh that summer where she opened the Diaghileff Exhibition to mark the twenty-fifth anniversary of the death of the great man. She later closed it in London.

She and Miskovitch then made appearances in Paris before opening the Nervi Festival in Italy.

The setting was idyllic, on the sea front backed by countryside. There was a rail track behind but performances were scheduled so that the rail services would not interrupt. That, at least, was the theory. 'During the rehearsals an elderly gentleman came to play the celeste for the Sugar Plum Fairy. I think he worked in a bookshop. The rhythm was not quite right. Milorad and I were sitting on the stage and did not say a word. The conductor broke us for lunch and stayed to work with him.

'During the performance I couldn't believe it when, just as I started the Sugar Plum Fairy, a rogue goods train came puffing down the track. I couldn't hear a thing. So for once I counted the beats and carried on. When it came to the part where the orchestra joins in I looked at the conductor and saw he'd raised his baton for the beat. By that time the train had passed and it seemed all right.

'Afterwards I asked the conductor if the celeste player had got it right and he said, "We'll never know, none of us, we'll never know."'

Miskovitch had to honour bookings in Japan after Nervi, but Alicia went on to Lisbon where she was partnered by Alexis Rassine, who had to be coached in *L'Après-midi* as he had not danced it before.

After that, with Miskovitch, she made appearances in America, including Hollywood's open-air Greek Theater. They stayed with Eleanor Peters while in California.

She was back in London, at the Royal Festival Hall, for the Christmas ballet, *Where the Rainbow Ends*, choreographed by former child progidy John Taras. Both Dolin and Goddard appeared with her.

During this run she was visited in her dressing room by Ninette de Valois. There were blizzard conditions and no public transport was running. The doughty Ninette had staggered through the elements on foot, across Waterloo Bridge from Covent Garden, to the Festival Hall.

She was in trouble and wanted a favour. She had had Fonteyn down for the imminent 1955 Covent Garden season but Fonteyn had just told Ninette that she would be unable to do it. She was getting married. Despite the trouble this would cause Ninette, she had congratulated both Fonteyn and her fiancé separately. She had seen Tito Arias in the foyer of the Opera House and told him, 'I'm so happy to hear the news. Margot needs an anchor.' 'Damn it, madame, I'm not an anchor,' he had replied.*

De Valois urgently needed a replacement for Fonteyn and wondered if Alicia could step into the breach? She would have,

* *Margot Fonteyn.*

and willingly, but was committed to the Met. 'It was the one time I couldn't help her out.'

For her Met season she was to dance in a new production of Gluck's opera *Orfeo*, conducted by Pierre 'Papa' Monteux, where she performed the 'Dance of the Blessed Spirits' to choreography by Zachary Solov, ballet master at the Met and a former Preobrajenska pupil, like so many others with whom she had worked.

She scooped the reviews in *Orfeo* but this caused no ill-feeling among the singers. 'They were wonderful to me. They used to send me flowers and buy me presents.' Rise Stevens was Orfeo and Hilde Gueden Euridice. The director was Herbert Graf. 'I always adored working with him, and Papa Monteux.'

She was to dance in *Orfeo* at the Met again, both in 1957 and 1958. 'It gave me the opportunity of dancing to music I love very much, especially the clear flute melody of "The Dance of the Blessed Spirits". The essence of this act is timeless, far above hurry and anxiety of any kind.'

She stayed in New York for the 1955 New York season with Ballet Theatre.

Such was the demand for tickets for *Giselle* that it was decided to give an extra matinée performance on Easter Sunday. Unfortunately Youskevitch was dancing that evening in a different programme and felt, reasonably enough, that he could not give two performances in one day.

She did not have to look far for a substitute. Erik Bruhn was dancing with the company. He was a twenty-seven-year-old blond Dane who, that season, had already partnered Alicia to great success in *Les Sylphides*.

He had not danced Albrecht but told Alicia he 'would be very happy to learn'. He had just four days to do so and was, as he later admitted, terrified of partnering the great Markova in this ballet she had so made her own.

She took him through the role. 'I knew he was right, anybody would have. I said to Lucia Chase [director of Ballet Theatre], "If he's willing to work then so am I," and it worked for both of us. He was a romantic dancer and it suited his training. Even so, there was such a short time for him to learn the part that it was a surprise to both of us that it worked quite as well as it did.'

Bruhn looked, as Alicia says, 'the absolutely number-one *danseur noble*'. Albrecht had always been dark in New York, and Youskevitch, who had been dancing the part, was also dark. To have a blond Albrecht would defy tradition so he was kitted out with a wig.

Dolin was passing through New York at the time and good-naturedly spent half an hour or so giving Bruhn some tips on the second act. Half an hour with Dolin was worth a day with anyone else.

Alicia and Bruhn not only worked together as a dancing team, they blended as personalities. They never lost contact. Years later, when Bruhn and Nureyev lived together, he still wrote to her, sometimes outlining some of the problems of their relationship.

Word got out that Markova was to dance with a new partner at short notice and *Dance* magazine took an exclusive set of photographs of her coaching him.

It was no novelty for Alicia to coach partners. She had regularly done so, and she had worked out variations for Miskovitch for their concert tour.

On show day the excitement in the auditorium grew with the performance. The audience broke into waves of applause and, at the end, it seemed it would never stop. The experienced Alicia had sensed what was happening during the performance but to the young man it was all a haze until that final, deafening crescendo of applause. Commented the press:

'The two artists saw the work eye to eye, played together with a beautiful rapport and developed the dramatic theme with power and an irresistible poignance.' – John Martin, *New York Times*

'She gave him all her experience, and between them they shaped such a performance as only they themselves, dancing again in this ballet, will be able to match and surpass perhaps in our time.' – *Dance News* (New York)

That particular *Giselle* is now ballet legend. As recently as 1993 Peter Watson wrote in his biography of Nureyev*: 'He [Bruhn] danced with all the major ballerinas . . . but his greatest success came as Albrecht in *Giselle*, opposite Alicia Markova in 1955 at the Metropolitan Opera House in New York. The critics went overboard that night, all agreeing for once that this was a performance that made history. From that day, Bruhn was regarded as the best male dancer, certainly in the West.'

It was not the first time in ballet history that an older woman has inspired a young man, nor would it be the last. In 1961 Fonteyn was

* *Nureyev*, Hodder and Stoughton, 1994.

on the brink of retirement when the young Nureyev came crashing through the international barriers defecting, more or less, straight into her arms. Their partnership extended her career by years. 'She had always told me she wanted to retire at forty,' Alicia recalls. 'She liked the sun and swimming, things ballerinas aren't supposed to do. When she went to live in Panama I thought, Well, at least you've got the sun. It was not the same, though.'

Alicia met Nureyev several times and had seen his first performance in the West with the Marquis de Cuevas' company in Paris. If she was in the vicinity when he was dancing, she always saw his performances.

But she felt an uneasiness on his part when they were together. 'I don't know if it was because of Erik,' she says. She thought, perhaps, that Nureyev's influence on Bruhn's later career was not always to the good. 'Or perhaps it was because of Margot.' By then the Nureyev–Fonteyn partnership was in full swing.

Alicia feels that a partnership between her and Nureyev would never have been feasible. 'I don't think it would have worked. For a start there was the age difference. I was more or less giving up when he came on the scene. Remember Margot was nine years younger than me. People thought there was a big gap between them, what would another nine years have done? And I don't think our temperaments would have been right together. There was, more or less, the same difference in ages between Erik and me as there was between Rudi and Margot.'

As a result of Alicia and Bruhn's triumph they were invited to Copenhagen that autumn to perform *Giselle* with the Royal Danish Ballet.

She had also been booked for the first week of October to open the Paris season for the Grand Ballet du Marquis de Cuevas with Taglioni's *La Sylphide*.

After the Bruhn Met matinée Alicia returned to London. She had never danced *La Sylphide* and tried to contact the Marquis's producer/choreographer, Harald Lander. 'He was supposed to teach me what to do but I could never get hold of him and the date was getting nearer. Meanwhile the Royal Danish Ballet was in Edinburgh. Erik was with them, dancing James in *La Sylphide*. I phoned him: "What can I do?" I asked. "Lander doesn't exist." "The only thing I can suggest is to get yourself here," he said. "There are two performances tomorrow, matinée and evening. I'll make you a reservation at the hotel." I had to rush up to Edinburgh and saw both performances.'

While she was with Bruhn some BBC Television executives

approached them and arranged for them to appear on television, in London, in Act Two of *Giselle*, before they left to dance it in Denmark. They were supported by the Ballet Rambert and full orchestra. Alicia also took part in the popular music quiz *Music for You*.

In Copenhagen she fretted about Erik's health. He had lost a lot of weight. 'I would say to him, "Are you eating?" As soon as rehearsals broke I'd say, "Come on, let's go to the canteen." Later he became so ill, poor man. He was never very strong, even when we worked together. I put it down to nerves. Every night he had terrible attacks of nerves.'

Copenhagen had *Giselle* in its repertoire, but it was not a good production, consequently it had never been a favourite among audiences. There were gaps in the second act as the full score was still a comparative rarity. The BBC, who had so recently televised Act Two, possessed the complete score and, at Alicia's suggestion, someone got on to the Corporation and the music was air-freighted to Copenhagen.

Bruhn had worn a dark wig as Albrecht in America but, in Denmark, many men were blond, so he did not bother with the wig. Alicia preferred it that way. She never wore a wig herself in the role; she had a horror of it falling off in the mad scene.

Alicia took numerous solo curtains, then broke with Opera House tradition by taking Bruhn by the hand and leading him on. The audience cheered even louder.

They appeared on Danish television in a special arrangement from Act Two.

Bruhn asked her to stay in Denmark and introduce him to the ballet hierarchy there – he was not the star then that he was to become. But she had to leave for Paris and *La Sylphide* and was still concerned about the part.

Hans Brenaa was the authority and was in Copenhagen. Erik got in touch with him. Brenaa coached her while Erik partnered her in his role as James. 'I put their *Giselle* right for them and Brenaa and Erik prepared me for *La Sylphide*. Afterwards Erik told me that his regret was that he would not be able to dance it with me in Paris.' She was partnered, in Paris, by Monte Carlo-born Serge Golovine.

She danced *Giselle*, with Skibine, but the performance was eclipsed by *La Sylphide*. It was the talking point of the season.

That spring she appeared in a season at La Scala, Milan, where she danced *Aurora's Wedding*. The bill also included a new Visconti-produced ballet by Massine, who was there seeing it through, and appearances by the Spanish dancer Antonio and his company. Antonio was then at the height of his fame.

Preparations for La Scala were delayed and the booking was extended. Alicia was worried as she had to leave, shortly, for appearances in Rio.

'I told Sandor [Gorlinsky] I didn't think I'd be able to fulfil all the Milan bookings but he told me not to worry. In addition to La Scala I was booked at a smaller theatre nearby, the Piccola Scala, for two performances of my concert repertoire, for which I had already been paid.

'I did the La Scala performances but then I had to leave for Rio and could not fit in the Piccola Scala. I explained things to the management and they told me, "Don't worry, you will come back, do them when you can." Well, to this day, I still owe Piccola Scala two performances.'

22

Sell-Out in Israel

Alicia was due in Brazil in June to give a season at Rio's Teatro Municipal, followed by appearances in São Paulo. She arrived, with Doris, and the temperature was sweltering, it was 100°F in the shade. She had last been there in 1940, fifteen years previously, with the Ballet Russe, and had fond memories of going to clubs then and listening to the exciting samba rhythms of Xavier Cugat.

As before she was struck by the beauty of the place, particularly the profuse, savage flowers, among them the brilliant orchids of which she received basketfuls after her performances.

Rehearsals were problematical from the start – there was no air conditioning in the theatre and the heat was appalling. No one had thought to order orchestral parts for *Giselle*.

She remembered that there was a score in Paris. Paris was contacted but, it seemed, the music had disappeared after her performance. The Brazilian Ambassador in Paris was contacted and a member of his staff detailed to find it. He eventually did so and arranged for it to be couriered to Rio. But this had taken time and it did not arrive until performance day. The musicians had an extremely lengthy rehearsal. 'It was a matter of getting the show on, and in that heat!'

Albrecht was Belgium-born Oleg Briansky, former principal dancer with the London Festival Ballet. The rest of the dancers were Brazilian. The ballet mistress, Tatiana Leskova, previously a member of the de Basil company, had prepared them as much as possible before her arrival. They were keen and eager to please.

They did please her, as did Briansky, and she pleased the

audience, taking over twenty curtain calls. There was a wonderful atmosphere in the theatre and the season was already sold out. She looked forward to a trouble-free run – and should have known better.

After the euphoria of the first night she went out for a celebratory dinner and ate curried shrimps. Not the wisest choice in the tropics.

She went down with ptomaine poisoning and was unable to leave her hotel room for six days. As she could not bear light she lay in darkness, the curtains shutting out the glaring sun. The very thought of food made her want to vomit. She could not take even a sip of water.

'I had awful pains and sickness. I told Doris to get on to the British Embassy at once. She came back, the Ambassador was away, on holiday in England to escape the heat. So I told her to get on to the American Embassy. They understood immediately and sent a doctor, he was a Brazilian, a wonderful doctor, and he had just come back from America so he knew who I was and understood the situation.

'I was getting delirious by this time and he said I couldn't be moved to hospital and would have to be treated in the room. He got a nurse and she moved in and I was put on a drip. It was that that saved me.'

Her response was instantaneous. The nourishment coursing through her body rallied her. She got better by the hour. Doris was called in from her room next door and instead of seeing the corpse she half expected, found her sister peacefully sleeping, the colour returning to her face, and the fever lessening.

But the poison had taken its toll and she was weak. Her doctor insisted she postpone her appearances. She took some days off then resumed her run.

She was summoned to the President's box after her final Rio performance. There she removed both shoes, autographed them, and presented one apiece to the President's daughters. They had seen all her performances. She left the box barefooted and walked straight into a horde of company dancers, each wanting a souvenir. As had happened in Mexico, hands snatched what they could.

From Rio she fulfilled her São Paulo booking where a huge audience awaited her.

She left Brazil exhausted.

A trip to Israel had to be postponed as she was simply not up to it. This was a bitter disappointment as, being Jewish, she had been particularly looking forward to dancing for the Israelis.

She went to St Tropez and stayed with choreographer Ruth Page, resting as much as possible but at the same time studying Miss Page's *The Merry Widow* which she was to dance in Chicago that November.

She also managed to appear at the International Eisteddfod in Llangollen, Wales, that summer, with the Ballet Rambert, before an audience of eight thousand. She had been hoping to dance *Giselle*, with Miskovitch, but was not well enough for that. 'The doctors told me I had managed to get through Rio and had wisely cancelled Israel but I just could not do *Giselle*. The programmes I used to carry were two hours long. I came to an arrangement with Mim Rambert and instead of *Giselle* I did *Les Sylphides* with Miskovitch, and *The Dying Swan*.' She also partnered Miskovitch in *L'Après-midi d'un Faune*.

The setting was beautiful, the stage banked by thousands of flowers from local gardens.

On 16 November 1955 she was at the Chicago Opera House in Ruth Page's *The Merry Widow*, to inaugurate the Chicago Opera Ballet.

Sonia, the widow, was a sophisticated fireball, crackling with colour. Her costumes included a flame gown and black lace outfit climaxed by a rose-bedecked picture hat. The *Widow* transferred to Broadway, where it ran through Christmas. The marquee bore Alicia's name in huge letters.

The Chicago Opera Ballet later changed its name to Ruth Page's Ballet. Under this banner, Alicia also appeared in another of Miss Page's creations in Chicago, *Revanche*, set to Verdi's music and based on *Il Trovatore*.

In 1956 the Bolshoi Ballet came to Covent Garden with their *Giselle*, starring the distinguished Soviet dancer Galina Ulanova. At that time the two greatest Giselles were considered to be Alicia and Ulanova. Alicia loved it and saw it several times. 'What struck me was the wonderful discipline and schooling of the artists from the example of Ulanova throughout the whole company.'

Also that year she and Miskovitch appeared on BBC TV in a biographical programme on Pavlova. Actors portrayed the action while she danced Pavlova. 'I had to learn all Pavlova's dances for that.'

In the autumn she appeared in Madrid with Spanish dancer Pilar Lopez's company. Pilar Lopez was the sister of La Argentinita who had been so kind to Alicia when she had been taken ill at the Hollywood Bowl. She danced *The Dying Swan* and the Prelude from *Les Sylphides*.

She was in New York for Thanksgiving where she took part in a special television show which starred the popular Danish pianist-comedian Victor Borge, for many years an international TV favourite.

Borge wanted to play the first movement of Beethoven's 'Moonlight Sonata' straight, but his producers were worried the piece was too long to be played uninterrupted. 'I'd already met him and admired him – he was so funny – but I was told that for the show something visual was needed while he played. He left it to me to do whatever I wanted, so I choreographed a piece. It was the first time I had choreographed for television. It was just a one-off, but the big thing on Thanksgiving night.'

At Christmas she was again in *Where the Rainbow Ends*, in London, this time at the Coliseum.

In the new year, 1957, she flew to Brussels for television appearances with Miskovitch and the Ballet Rambert. This was to be followed by further television appearances in Wiesbaden. Beryl Grey was also a part of the company. Miss Grey's husband, Sven, who was a Swedish osteopath, travelled with them.

In Brussels they had lunch at the British Embassy before the performance, then travelled by chauffeured cars to Wiesbaden via the autobahn. Alicia's car contained Madame Rambert and Doris.

'I was getting rather hungry,' says Alicia. 'And I kept saying to Mim there must be somewhere we can pull over, just a coffee and a sandwich will do. The only place we could find was a truck drivers' stop and it must have been one in the morning by then.

'I'd come straight from the performance so I had rather a lot of make-up on and, being the star, my mink coat. Well, you can imagine the looks we got at this truck stop. Doris, the Duchess, didn't care for it at all. I didn't mind. Through the years I've learnt not to worry if people look, or say things, when you're hungry.

'We then got back in the car and asked the driver how much farther it was and he said it would take another hour. Then the car started to swerve, our dear driver was falling asleep. Mim spoke German, so we put her in the front seat to talk to the driver and keep him awake. Well, one hour turned into two hours, then three, and still we never got there. So we had to stop, again for food and black coffee and, again, there was the reception committee.

'Back on the road all we could see were hundreds of trucks passing us. We couldn't go too fast in case the driver fell asleep again. I couldn't drive and neither could Mim or Doris, so we only had him. We eventually arrived about 7 a.m. People think when you're booked for a performance that's all there is to it, they don't realize what else is involved.'

She was involved that year in her final appearance, although she was unaware of it then, at 'Jacob's Pillow'. According to the Massachusetts *Sunday Republican* she was 'winning cheers and bouquets'.

She was in New York in the early spring for guest appearances. As was the Royal Ballet, formerly Sadler's Wells Ballet, with Dame Ninette, for a season at the Met.

'Dame Ninette had booked me for guest appearances at Covent Garden in May. We'd agreed on the dates but the problem came up as to who was to partner me. Michael Somes, who had partnered me before, was in Australia with Fonteyn. Ninette suggested either Bruhn, Skibine or Briansky, she admired them all and knew they'd been successful partners for me.

'I told her that, of course, I would be happy with them but that I didn't think it was fair to the members of the company. She really didn't see any of the younger members as a partner, she wasn't sure, but she said she'd leave it to me.

'I'd been looking at the company, as I always did, and said to her, "How about David Blair as Albrecht and Philip Chatfield for the last act of *Sleeping Beauty* and *Les Sylphides?*" She said it was OK with her if I felt I could get them ready.

'The next problem was that David Blair was going straight to La Scala, Milan, from the Met, only coming back to London in time for the performances, so I said, "If he's in New York and I'm in New York why can't we start working here?"

'So, we rehearsed in New York, and David went to La Scala and we remet in London.'

Alicia remained loyal to her fans and could spend up to two hours in her dressing room after a show seeing people. Susie was sometimes with her but was used to it by now.

She cut the Taglioni Cake in the Green Room. The prima ballerina always has to make the first cut. The Taglioni Cake has become a ritual, invented by Cyril Beaumont. He was a collector of Taglioni memorabilia and the cake was baked to a favourite recipe of hers.

On opening nights, instead of sending Alicia flowers, Beaumont would give her something of Taglioni's. For her opening *Giselle*, upon her return from America, he had given her a spool of blue silk (Taglioni had been an embroiderer), telling her to put a piece in her ballet shoe for luck.

When the curtain came down after her last performance that

season, on 22 June 1957, the applause was deafening. De Valois had guessed that it would be and had asked Alicia to prepare a few appropriate words to be spoken from the stage.

With the poise of the veteran performer, she stepped from amidst her flowers and instantly hushed the mighty house by raising a finger to her lips. To an appreciative silence she began her speech. 'Giselle and I have travelled many thousands of miles together . . .' She had them in the palm of her hand. What a difference from the first time she had been asked to address an audience and could barely muster a sentence.

Public speaking was to play an important part in the years to come, but it was not a natural skill, like dancing. It was something she mastered only with effort.

It was a special evening in another way, too, for David Blair. He had been married that morning to dancer Maryon Lane. Before leaving for their honeymoon they called at Markova's dressing room with a bottle of champagne, and asked her to drink a toast with them.

She was touched. The three of them sat together and she toasted the young newlyweds. She was forty-seven, a middle-aged leading lady still in costume and make-up, the perfume of expensive flowers permeating the room and the cheers for her performance still echoing.

They were two talented kids who would never reach her artistic stature. They slipped through the stage door virtually unnoticed while she attended a queue of autograph hunters.

The Blairs went off to start married life while she went home alone. 'They went off to their bliss and I went off to eat.' She wished them all the luck in the world.

She always remembered a quip from one of the Covent Garden stage hands, made during her performance that last night. In order to rise from her grave she had to step into a little manually operated lift which brought her through a trapdoor to the stage floor. As she stepped into the lift that night, the essence of the supernatural, the man working it had called out, 'The last jet to Wililand'. It had amused her.

That year Alicia appeared on ITV's top-rating *Sunday Night at the London Palladium* where she danced the Snowflake Scene from *The Nutcracker* with Miskovitch.

She also appeared in the 1957 Royal Variety Performance with Tommy Steele. Although she was not in a sketch with Steele, he posed with her for promotion photographs, he with his guitar and she, apparently, dancing to it. 'No one ever thought they would see us together,' she says. 'Tommy was marvellous to his dancers in his shows.' Afterwards she was presented to the Queen, something that was to happen several times in the future.

She appeared in many of the big Palladium variety shows during the next few years, many of them televised, and enjoyed working with some of the biggest names in light entertainment, among them Tommy Trinder, Harry Secombe, Bruce Forsyth and Jimmy Tarbuck. 'If ever we were working in the same building I'd always call in to say hello.'

One of her favourite television appearances was on *The Frankie Howerd Show*, transmitted 'live' from the BBC Wood Green Empire.

'The whole idea was that Frankie and I would dance in *Les Sylphides*. He told the audience that he'd seen me dance and that he was sure he could dance too – you know how he carried on. He said, "I've asked Markova and she said she'd come along." Then he disappeared to get into his tights. He came back with them all baggy, he looked so funny.

'Then I came on in a dressing gown, to warm up, and he told me, "I'm all ready but what can I do about these wrinkles in my tights?" So I told him he'd have to get a belt.

'He went off to get one and I removed the dressing gown and stood in costume. The conductor asked me where my partner was and I said, "He's gone to get dressed." He said, "We can't wait, don't you have an understudy?" So I said "yes" and my partner came on and we danced the *pas de deux* – perfectly with the orchestra.

'When it was over His Lordship came on, all ready to go. I said, "We've done it, we couldn't wait for you. But at least you know how to put on tights now." It was hilarious because you never knew what he would come out with. After that if we ever met we'd always chat.'

In 1958 she took part in a benefit gala at the Coliseum on behalf of the Royal Academy of Dancing where she was presented to Princess Margaret. The Spanish dancer Antonio, with whom she had recently appeared at La Scala, was also on the bill. She had known Antonio since her first trip to Rio during the war.

'Massine and Hurok were always on the look-out for new talent wherever we went. We'd been rehearsing and Massine asked me what I was doing that night. He'd heard of two wonderful young Spanish dancers who were appearing in a nightclub, did I want to see them with him? I said I'd love to go. Hurok went, too, there were about six of us in all. One of the dancers was Antonio and the other Rosario. He was about fourteen and she was sixteen, I think. I know they were marvellous.

'The Copacabana had wonderful supper shows. It was the place to be then, like the Lido in Paris. I saw Carmen Miranda there in cabaret. We'd dance till five in the morning. When I did my *Desert Island Discs* I chose one of Xavier Cugat's records from those days. I brought a few home with me and I've still got them.'

That year she danced *Giselle* in London, Paris and New York. While at the Met, during the opera season, she danced in *Orfeo* again. In one way it was a sad year as Constance Collier died. Alicia went to her funeral.

'It was about ten in the morning and all the theatre world was there. I was delayed by traffic and everyone had gone up to the service by the time I got there. I saw a big freight lift nearby, full of furniture, and I asked the men in it if they could take me up.

'Another little lady came by then. She had a woolly hat pulled down over her hair and dark glasses, very simply dressed. I was in my mink coat. She said to me, "Are you going to the service?" I said yes and the men said, "Well, both of you get in and we'll take you up."

'She stood next to me and said, in a little voice, "It's Marilyn, do you remember me?" I said, "Of course I do." "Can I come with you?" she asked.

'When the funeral was over all the grand people were leaving in their limousines. Elizabeth Arden saw me and came over and asked if she could give me a lift, "if you don't mind dropping me off at a meeting first, then my chauffeur can take you wherever you want to go." Then she looked at me and said, "And your friend?" She had no idea who she was.

'Oh dear, I thought. Do I say who it is or better not? Better not at the moment. The way Marilyn had got herself up I sensed she did not want that. "Bring her along, too." Elizabeth said.

'That was the last time I saw Marilyn Monroe.'

Alicia flew back to London for a season of Italian opera at the Theatre Royal, Drury Lane. She was to appear in Bizet's *The Pearl Fishers* and Rossini's *William Tell*. In both operas she choreographed the ballet sections herself.

She had researched into *William Tell* in New York and discovered that, over a century earlier, Rossini had inserted special music into the opera for Taglioni but the choreography had been lost. She had to create something new.

'In those days ballet in opera was a major event. In 1847, the year of Taglioni's retirement, Jenny Lind made her London debut and after that opera moved into the ascendant and ballet into the decline as far as western Europe was concerned. But in Russia it was different and events were taking place which led to even greater glories in dance and the emergence of the Diaghileff ballet and Anna Pavlova.

'I set about creating for *William Tell* a ballet that would grow out of the action instead of merely providing a diversion. Taglioni's dance had been called "La Tyrolienne" so I decided the dance should be in Tyrolean rhythm and I modelled my costume on prints of the time. But I did not want this to be old-fashioned, it had to be in keeping with the style of the romantic ballet yet new and applicable to today.'

Alicia discovered that Rossini had meant his *William Tell* ballet to be danced to music from a chorus, so she arranged it that way at Drury Lane.

In addition to dancing with a *corps* she needed a partner. As the ballet was in the Danish Bournonville style she wanted someone who was familiar with that mode of dancing. Børge Ralov was engaged.

The Danish Mr Ralov, former leading male dancer with the Royal Danish Ballet, was the man who could have changed Alicia's life, and had wanted to.

In 1932, when she had danced at the Royal Theatre, Copenhagen, Ralov had been principal dancer with the Danes, and had fallen head over heels in love with her. He had wanted to marry her and said so to Eileen. He later met Doris and Vivienne, in England, and told them so, too. But Alicia did not love him and had turned him down – affectionately but, nevertheless, firmly.

'If I had married him I would have had Danish citizenship. I would probably have danced with the Royal Danish Ballet and been a Danish ballerina now.'

Ralov had recovered from his broken heart and was on his second marriage by this time. 'He went on marrying,' says Alicia. 'I think there was another one, too.'

Madame Manya made her costumes for her.

The *William Tell* dances were so successful that she performed them in recital at the Festival Hall and a couple of times on television, once on *Sunday Night at the London Palladium* where she was partnered by Skouratoff with whom she had danced during her season with the Grand Ballet du Marquis de Cuevas, and another time at a prestigious BBC gala from the Wood Lane studios, in which Maria Callas also took part.

In Bizet's *The Pearl Fishers*, for which no ballet had been written, she was a temple priestess and created a dance modelled on classic Indian movement to the music from the prelude of the last scene. She came down the temple steps, 'the calm before the storm'.

With the help of Arnold Haskell she contacted an Indian girl student, who was studying in Britain, who advised her on make-up, hair and costume. 'I knew that in India things must be done in a certain way and I didn't want to do the wrong thing.' She wore a costume of burgundy and gold.

While in *The Pearl Fishers* she was invited to Buckingham Palace to receive her CBE (Commander of the British Empire) for her services to ballet. This was an enormous thrill for her, and just as much so for her family and immediate colleagues. Edna, her dresser, was utterly delighted and pinned the notification on Alicia's mirror and was photographed in front of it.

Then followed an international tour with London's Festival Ballet. One of the highlights of this, for her, was that she would finally be able to dance in Israel. The British government was involved in this tour and the Festival was very much an ambassador of things British.

She had not danced with the Festival since 1952 and the reunion could have been tricky. There had been some resentment when she had remained in America after her foot injury and then gone on to Argentina. Some had thought she had elected to stay in America rather than return to the Festival.

She had, however, remained in contact with Pat, and they soon picked up their relationship. They had shared too much for a company squabble to make a lasting difference. But they had not danced together for seven years and he was now fifty-four, an advanced age for a dancer.

They opened in Paris at the Théâtre des Nations, formerly the Sarah Bernhardt Theatre, where Alicia had Bernhardt's original dressing room.

She danced two *Giselles*, one with Gilpin and the other with Pat. 'As usual, with no rehearsal,' she says.

Charlie Chaplin was in the audience, with his current wife, Oona O'Neill, playwright Eugene O'Neill's daughter. Alicia had met Oona in America, through Constance Collier, as, indeed, she had met Chaplin.

Chaplin told her she had inspired him to write his film *Limelight*, which had appeared in 1952, in which he played a broken-down comic saved by a ballerina. The beautiful Claire Bloom had acted the ballerina but he had wanted Alicia for the dancing sequence. Unfortunately, engagements with Sol Hurok had prevented this.

From Paris they moved to Nice, for a single performance, then to the San Carlo Theatre, Lisbon.

She was presented with a silver bowl by the director of the Lisbon theatre.

After Lisbon they had to travel to Marseilles for an overnight stay, then catch a boat to take them, together with scenery and costumes, to Israel. Alicia was feeling far from well at the time as she had caught a fierce bronchial cold.

There was a problem in Marseilles and they were not allowed to leave as planned, but forced to stay over for nearly a week. The ship went without them. Alicia remembers that the hotel, which no one liked, was full of foreign correspondents. Then ace correspondent Randolph Churchill arrived. 'Something's up,' Pat told her.

After a week of hanging around Marseilles it was clear they were never going to make Israel on time by boat. The week was miserable in that Alicia didn't dare go out as the port seemed full of gangsters.

Eventually seats were secured for them on El Al, the Israeli airline. Doctors were treating her cold and she was advised not to fly in her condition. But there was no option if she wanted to dance in Israel.

They were taken to the airport where they waited for what seemed like hours. No food or refreshment of any kind was available. They were amused for a while when a plane landed and dozens of men disembarked in robes, each carrying a kettle. They whiled away the time wondering what purpose the kettles served.

Their arrival in Israel marked the celebrations of the tenth anniversary of its creation and they were officially welcomed by the British Ambassador.

Her first performance was to be *Giselle* at the Mann Auditorium in Tel Aviv. Although she had never set foot in the building she felt she knew it well as she had danced at so many charities in New York to contribute to funds for its construction.

She was a friend of Freddie Mann, after whom it was named, who had looked after her at many of her American stadium appearances. In the future, after she had retired, she would sometimes see him and his wife at the Hôtel de Paris in Monte Carlo.

But the Mann Auditorium was a concert hall and unable to support scenery, so she could not dance *Giselle*. This caused grave disappointment as it had been sold out weeks in advance. She substituted concert items which were well received but could not compensate for the loss of *Giselle*.

She was tempted to put on an improvised version, without scenery, but decided against it. She wanted her Israeli *Giselle* to be as excellent as possible.

The next venue was Haifa and the site was the movie theatre where, again, the stage was unsuitable for *Giselle*, being too small.

Something had to be done otherwise *Giselle* might never be seen in Israel. The Festival management entered into negotiations with the authorities to improvise an auditorium on the beach, with the sea behind, facing the newly erected blocks of high-rise flats. The setting was like the Nervi Festival but without the railway line.

The Haifa authorities pointed out that there would be difficulties. For dressing rooms they would have to manage with a series of little tents. Old carpets could be laid over the grass to protect ballet shoes.

Evening came and the stars appeared. Everything looked beautiful, magical even.

The audience began to arrive in lorries, buses and various other forms of transport.

Behind the scenes things were not so fairy-tale. As often happened in warm climates, Alicia's make-up was full of insects. Someone yelled that scorpions were about. The odd scream rent the air.

When she made her entrance she found the stage splintery and unyielding, making it difficult for her to prepare for leaps. Some flowers had been arranged as scenery and, while she danced, she could see large spiders making for them. Flying insects descended in droves, drawn by the lights; a fence at the back of the stage heaved with them. God forbid she should brush past it.

Although an amazing ten thousand tickets had been sold the actual audience was nearer thirty thousand. Hundreds of vehicles were parked on the hills above the stage and the balconies of the tower blocks were crammed with spectators getting a free show. Braunsweg nearly went mad with the knowledge that he could not charge them.

Unsurprisingly, Alicia's death leap at the end of Act One was not executed as skilfully as usual. She landed heavily on the stage and knocked herself out cold. As she says, it 'carried full conviction'. Applause erupted all around.

She was carried, senseless, off stage and put in her tent where she gradually came to. Still groggy, she changed costume, cleaned herself up, took a drink of water then danced the second act. As a child she had been considered delicate.

News of her Haifa success spread. Promoters in Tel Aviv felt they had been short-changed and asked her to think again about giving *Giselle* there. She agreed and gave her last performance in Israel at the Ramat Gan stadium, in the suburbs.

From Israel Alicia continued to Geneva then Munich. When she had arrived in Israel she had been suffering from a heavy cold. Dolin had been anxious about her; she had not been well at all. Now, owing to the clear air of Israel, she felt fine.

She was, though, worried about her Munich performance. Apart from her television appearance in Wiesbaden she had avoided performing in Germany since the war. She was concerned that there might be anti-Jewish feeling. The audience, in fact, was magnificent, as were the critics.

The tour ended in July when she returned to London for four *Giselles*, partnered by Briansky, at the Festival Hall, now the home of the London Festival Ballet. Said *The Times*: 'In the First Act her mime and general sense of drama carried with it a thousand small subtleties culled from a life-time's experience . . . Yet again she defied the force of gravity and floated through the second act . . .'

From London it was New York and the Met where she danced *Giselle* with Bruhn for Ballet Theatre. John Martin wrote in the *New York Times*: 'By now Markova could dance *Giselle* in her sleep, but what is so notable is that she never does. She is as fresh, as sensitive, as creatively alert, as if she had never done it before. But what a wealth of background she has accumulated for it . . .'

She also took part in the opera season at the Met, where she danced in *Orfeo*. Mid-season she was urgently contacted by Sol Hurok. He was in trouble. Could she immediately dance two performances of *Swan Lake* in Havana, Cuba? She left almost at once.

Revolution was in the air and her iron nerve was called upon when she heard Castro announce over the radio, 'Tonight we take Havana.' Fortunately, that night the only things taken were the curtain calls.

Then it was back to the Met. 'That season I alternated between Rudolph Bing and Fidel Castro.'

In some of the photographs of her, elegantly dressed, embarking or alighting from aircraft, she is seen with cuddly toys under her arm. These were presents for her new nephew Nigel, Susie's brother.

When Nigel grew up, he once stayed with her overnight when he was in London for a job interview. In the morning he was about to leave for the interview when she noticed a button missing from his mackintosh and insisted on sewing it on before he left.

Alicia is always immaculately turned out when in public. It is her trademark. She also likes things neat at home; the place is full of documents and paraphernalia, the equipment of a full career, but everything is orderly. She will not go to bed at night unless the cushions are plumped up, fresh for the morning. 'She's a perfectionist,' sighs Doris. 'They're not easy to live with.'

Just as Alicia felt a special link with Israel because her father was Jewish, so she felt an affinity with Ireland as her mother was Irish. Yet she had never danced there.

The chance came in 1959 when she was offered the opportunity to appear at the Dublin International Arts Festival guesting with the London Festival Ballet.

She had a friend in Dublin. Cecil Beaton was also at the Festival and met her at the airport, clasping her in camera-catching theatrical embrace, his coat flung over his shoulders.

Beaton never missed a chance of being seen with Alicia. During the run of *Camille*, in 1946, he had attended the opening performance with Greta Garbo and taken a curtain call with the cast afterwards. Garbo, left unattended in her stall, had been furious. 'Why did you have to do that?' she had demanded. 'You had made your contribution up there, why show yourself to everybody? Really, you shouldn't associate with ingenues.'*

Garbo must have been unusually tetchy that night, probably because she had been temporarily abandoned and was frightened someone might talk to her. She knew, and quite liked, Alicia, as much as liked anyone. They had met when Alicia was in the *Seven Lively Arts* on Broadway. She had been invited to a dinner party and Garbo had been there. Alicia would now and then bump into Garbo going into or leaving the hairdressers, which was situated in the building where Garbo lived. On these occasions they did not speak, but Garbo would nod in recognition, which was more than she usually did to most people.

Marie Taglioni had danced in Dublin and had given one of her ballet shoes to an admirer who now passed this on to Alicia; she had read that Alicia had played Taglioni in *Pas de Quatre*. Alicia tried the shoe on and it fitted perfectly. 'It was a strange feeling.'

Although she had no idea of it at the time, that was to be the last time she danced *Giselle*. 'It was the first time I'd danced it in Ireland and the last time ever.'

---

* *Loving Garbo* by Hugo Vickers, Jonathan Cape, 1994.

23

Ram Gopal

Alicia was back at the Palladium in 1959 in the glittering 'Night of 100 Stars'. She danced the Taglioni variation from *Pas de Quatre* in the first half then changed into an evening frock and took part in a sketch with Bob Hope and Laurence Olivier in the second half. 'They asked me if I would be a sport. Bob was centre-stage and then Larry and I danced on from the wings. Larry was so nervous. "I'm the world's worst dancer," he told me. We danced up to Bob who tapped me on the shoulder to cut in. But instead of dancing with me he danced off with Larry.'

The previous year, in New York, she had received a call from BBC Television. Her former dresser Morty, Edna's mother, had been discovered by a *This Is Your Life* researcher. She was to be honoured as the subject of a show. Could Alicia appear?

She could not make it in person as she was dancing at the Met but she agreed to film a tribute at the BBC studio in New York. She was regularly asked to contribute to *This Is Your Life* and always did so if she could.

Morty's show was live and the public saw Alicia flashed up on their screens at home, in black dress and pearls. Morty chatted to her image, not realizing that Alicia had filmed the piece.

In 1959 Alicia herself was the subject of *This Is Your Life*. She was, as is the policy of the show, in ignorance of what was about to happen until Eamon Andrews surprised her. Doris had been the initial contact, providing the names and whereabouts of the guests. She nearly had a breakdown trying to keep the secret from Alicia who always seemed to be in the room every time a member of the team rang.

Among the guests were Jessie Matthews, who filmed from Australia, Marie Rambert, who told of Alicia's relish for steak and kidney puddings, Serge Lifar, who burst on with the force of a volcano and nearly hugged her to death (she was clearly delighted to see him, all thoughts of their problematical *Giselle* forgotten), and the show was topped by Fonteyn who told how Alicia was 'both my inspiration and my despair'.

Fonteyn nearly did not make the show. She would not leave home until she had seen the show start. For some reason she was terrified, at that time, of being the subject herself and thought Alicia might have been in on a ruse to ensnare her. Later, when she lived in Panama, she changed her mind and would have been delighted to have been a subject.

As noted, Dolin was conspicuous by his absence. He was disgruntled that Alicia was being honoured rather than he.

Ram Gopal and Alicia finally danced together in the spring of 1960 in London.

The ballet was *Radha Krishna*, a Hindu love story, the 'Ballet of Krishna'.

Gopal now lives in Fulham amid a shower of Indian artefacts, paintings and bronzes, many depicting him in classical poses. Flowers are everywhere and in pride of place is Annette Rowden's magnificent bronze head of Alicia.

Now seventy-five and frail, he is still exquisite, the physique tiny, the face delicate. He dresses in gold, silk and a bejewelled turban. Rings glitter from every finger of his perfect hands. Any room he enters is filled with his presence.

He recalls an occasion when Alicia had been dancing *Giselle* at the Met in 1953. He had presented her with a garland of marigolds, the flower associated with goddesses, and told her, 'I have never seen a *Giselle* to remotely equal yours.'

In 1994, when Alicia was coming up for her eighty-fourth birthday, Gopal commented: 'I saw her a few weeks ago, she looks about thirty to me.' Apart from being a great artist he is clearly a gentleman.

In 1960 Gopal was preparing for a London season. He suggested to Alicia that she join him; it was time they danced together. They appeared at the Prince's Theatre from 7 to 19 March, billed as 'Ram Gopal and his Indian Company with Markova as a Special Guest'.

Eastern dances have fascinated many artists. Pavlova had visited

India in the 1920s and been impressed by the Ajanta Frescoes, hence her ballet bearing their name. She had also danced *Radha Krishna* with the great Udai Shankar. 'If she was able to do it, so can you,' Gopal had told Alicia. Nijinsky, too, had given a number of interpretations of Indian dancing, notably *The Blue God* which Gopal had originally wanted to dance with Alicia.

In order to dance with Gopal she had to learn a whole new dance grammar.

'I coached her in my special choreography,' Gopal remembers. 'I taught her many Indian movements and she learned quickly. I concentrated on her beautiful hands; she was very expressive. She had a great aptitude to learn. Madame Manya made her costumes but I chose the materials for her in Indian shops in London.

'She gave the impression she was weightless, like a lotus blossom. When we danced together there was a deep sympathy and she exceeded what I had expected of her. We danced to the orchestra I had brought from India, it was pure Indian music but she didn't seem to find it difficult.'*

'I worked through the dances daily,' Alicia recalls. 'I thought if I'm going to do it then I'm going to do it correctly. It's a language. This is a fish . . .' She makes the movements with her hands then she laughs. 'It's thirty years since I've done this and I still remember it.

'It was difficult, anything new is difficult, but it was compensated by the welcome I got. It took me two hours to make up each night, because there was a complete body make-up as well as the face. Before I got in every day Ram would burn incense to perfume my room. Then on matinée days everyone in the company would eat a huge meal. I didn't have to be a sylph rising from the ground this time so I ate it as well. As a company they really embraced me and brought me into their community. They were lovely to me.'

Doris and Malcolm Goddard went to the first night and afterwards joined Alicia and Gopal for a celebratory meal at the Dorchester.

The *Dancing Times* commented:

'When Ram Gopal told this Western cynic that Alicia Markova had learned the dance of Radha so quickly and magnificently that she must have danced it in another incarnation his words fell on unbelieving ears. Yet when I saw the Radha/Krishna love poem danced by these two great dancers from different hemispheres I could see what he meant . . . Markova accomplished

* 1994 interview with Ram Gopal.

all the sensuous arm movements and highly stylised gestures with immaculate perfection and a rhythm as oriental as any I have seen. Pale and Eastern in appearance in her white and flowing garment she has fully assimilated the feeling as well as the exterior pattern of this exotic dance form . . .'

That August Alicia and Gopal appeared together at the Edinburgh Festival.

Alicia was due in New York that autumn for a season with Ballet Theatre to dance with Bruhn but had to cancel due to ill-health. She had severe colitis and was treated at the London Clinic. She was coming up for fifty and her body was undergoing a change. 'I was coming into a tricky period, although I'd tried to ignore everything and carry on.'

Owing to the enforced inactivity she was able to work on an autobiographical book about her experiences on the road with *Giselle*. It was entitled *Giselle and I* and published by Barrie and Rockliff. It is dedicated to 'Serafine Astafieva, My First Great Teacher'.

Giselle and I came about because she was frustrated by people telling her what she had danced, and how she had danced it, when clearly their memories were defective. 'People would come to me and say, "You wore a pink dress," when it had been blue, or, "I saw you dance so and so in Birmingham," when it had been Glasgow, so I decided to write a book and put the record straight.'

She also became a radio presenter for a thirteen-part BBC series, *Markova's Ballet Call*. The programmes were talks based on her career, illustrated by music from ballets in which she had appeared.

'The BBC sent round stacks of records and I would go through them and choose what I wanted. I had worked with most of the conductors anyway. When that was done I'd write my script. Then I used to go into my little booth at Broadcasting House to do it. I've always enjoyed broadcasting and never been frightened of microphones. I think I got used to them when I was doing all those one-night stands. No sooner would I get off a plane, or train, than there would be a reporter, from a radio or television station, pointing a microphone at me, asking my opinion on everything.'

Later that year, when she felt better, she received a call from Dolin, who was working in the Newcastle area. He wanted her to partner him in a television transmission for Tyne Tees Television. 'It'll only take you three days,' he told her. 'A day to get here on the train, a day to do it and then a day to get back home.'

The piece was being directed by Keith Beckett, a dancer who

had been with her in the London Festival Ballet and had made a great success with *Petrushka*. He was now a television producer.

'At first *Les Sylphides* was mentioned,' she recalls. 'But then I said to Pat, "What about *La Sylphide*?" It had never been done on television. They only wanted about five minutes, so we did the opening of the ballet. It was not too demanding for him, he was seated throughout most of it, it would not be anything that would worry him and he would look wonderful. I knew it would be right for us.'

It was the last time they danced together although they had not planned it that way. 'But I had a feeling about it,' she says. 'When you've got to that stage you know each other pretty well.'

In 1961 she intended to extend her Metropolitan career or, as critic Henry Fielding wrote with, as it turned out, foresight: 'Markova Builds a New Career at 51'. It was not a new career but an extension of things in which she had always been interested. She was to dance the Blessed Spirit in Gluck's opera *Orfeo*, as well as provide the choreography and direct the entire opera.

'This is the first time, I believe, anyone has combined these three functions in opera,' Fielding continued. 'This unusual appearance at, I am assured, an unusual fee . . . may signal a new phase in Markova's dazzling career. In future we may see less of her in her usual role of star dancer and more as the organizing brain behind ballet and opera. I shall be the last to suggest that Markova's dancing days are over, she has only just returned from another tour with the Festival Ballet, but at 51, though she looks 20 years younger, she may well think of turning more to the less physically exhausting role of choreographer and producer.'*

It may have been less physically exhausting but was not mentally so. She was working several hours a day on *Orfeo*. Unfortunately, her directorial debut did not come about.

In 1962 she appeared at the Festival Hall with the London Festival Ballet at its Birthday Gala. She partnered Miskovitch in *L'Après-midi d'un Faune*, not the greatest vehicle for a ballerina.

'It was my final performance,' she says. 'I didn't know that when I danced.'

* *Daily Herald.*

24

Retirement

Alicia's bout of colitis had taken a lot out of her. She had also had severe shingles, one of the reasons why she had undertaken the radio shows while recuperating. Then, in 1962, she had her tonsils out. The operation was exceptionally unpleasant as it often is for adults. Before that she had been plagued with several bouts of tonsillitis. 'The surgeon told me that I had to promise not to dance for six months, to take six months off. If I did this he could guarantee me "another ten good years". So I thought to myself, Well, it must be done.

'After the six months I started training again. One day I looked at myself in the mirror and thought, What are you doing? You're fifty-one and not getting any younger. Are you crazy? You've had a fabulous career and enjoyed it. You've just been advised to take it easy, now you're going to compete against yourself. It's silly.

'I completed my training until I was in dancing form again, but I still spent a lot of time thinking about things. The colitis had been one warning, the shingles another, and then the tonsillitis.

'Christmas came and went and I was going away on New Year's Day, 1963, for a holiday in America. I was going to New York first, then on to Florida.

'I was at Heathrow and there was thick snow all around. The press boys came up to me and asked if I had any New Year's resolutions. In those days whenever I went to the airport the press always turned out.

'I don't know what possessed me but I said, "Yes, I won't dance in public again." Before I took off there were about fifty pressmen representing various countries asking me questions. When I arrived in New York *Time* magazine was there asking if it was true I'd retired. I said it was.'

Her retirement was a surprise to Doris. She was at home when the phone rang and the press asked her about it. It was the first she had heard: 'It would have been nice to have been told,' she says.

'They asked me what I was going to do and I really hadn't made up my mind,' continues Alicia. 'So I said I was going on holiday. I hadn't planned to make the announcement but I had been thinking about it for months, ever since the operation. I hadn't discussed it with anyone, it was entirely my decision. I never gave a farewell performance, I didn't want to. I wanted to avoid it, in fact, I didn't think I could take it. I think my nerves would have got the better of me there. I wanted people to remember me as they had last seen me.

'It was a difficult decision but I've made difficult decisions all my life. I knew it would change many things for many people. It had been a difficult decision in the early 1930s when Massine had asked me to join the Monte Carlo company and I had stayed with the Wells. I didn't dance outside Britain for eight years and that had been a deliberate policy. It had also been a difficult decision when I decided to go to America. But I always made difficult decisions and always by myself.'

Newspapers all over the world were full of Markova's retirement. She stuck to her decision and there were no Adeline Genée-style 'celebrity' one-off come-backs. Bing was permanently trying to persuade her to make appearances in operas or ballet, 'if only for the opening night,' but she would not. She never danced in public again.

'It is painful to think she will dance no more,' wrote critic R. B. Marriott. 'We have, however, glorious memories of her and the woman herself, still only 52, happily among us.'

Others tried to persuade her to rethink. Edna, her dresser, was one. 'I could never understand why she retired the way she did,' she says. 'I still don't understand. She could have had lots of retirements and lots of come-backs. I thought it was a shame. I did tell her I thought she was wrong but she just smiled.'

Freddie Franklin was also surprised. 'I don't know why she did it. She could easily have carried on – and to make her last appearance in *Faune*. Why that? Why not something on *pointe*, something spectacular? I've never known why she chose that particular ballet.'

'I chose it because I didn't feel I was up to anything else,' she says. 'Maybe I did make mistakes, according to other people, but then I sit down and think, Well, maybe they wouldn't have been able to achieve what I did.

De Valois has not spent the years wondering why Alicia retired when she did. 'She made the decision, she obviously thought it was right.' Unequivocal to the end. 'She knows me very well,' says Alicia.

Alicia knows exactly why she retired. 'I was fifty-two and certain things would have to be replaced, or changed, if I continued. Things would have to be whittled away. I didn't want that.'

Two years later, she told journalist Jane Gaskell, 'It was hard to decide on retirement and I felt a waste of emptiness myself afterwards.'

She was used to a certain financial level by now, plus the intoxication of performances. That would all pale. She had sacrificed romance and family for the dance. It was her legacy from Diaghileff. Now the price had to be paid.

What is left for an ex-dancer?

She became a director of ballet. She had not planned it, not even turned it over in her mind.

Two days after her retirement, while in New York, she received a phone call from Rudolph Bing. He told her the Met was having a dress rehearsal of a new production of *La Sonnambula* starring Joan Sutherland. Alicia was a friend of Sutherland's; they had met some years previously in Paris when Alicia had been dancing there and La Sutherland singing. Bing wondered if she might like to come to the rehearsal to see her 'and other old friends'.

These included nearly everyone who worked there. She had played the Met more or less consistently since her first appearance in 1938 – 'it was my home'.

Among the friends was Antony Tudor, who had choreographed *Romeo and Juliet* for her and was now Director of the Metropolitan Opera Ballet School. He was organizing educational programmes for the Met and currently working on two projects, the *pas de deux* from *Les Sylphides* and the Rose *adagio* from *Sleeping Beauty*.

Tudor said he knew she was on holiday but could she, before she started, stage these for the Met educational programme?

'So I said yes,' says Alicia. 'The production side had always interested me. I signed up with the Met and staged them for them. It was a very happy time.' So happy that when she had finished the dancers presented a petition to Bing stating they wanted her to stay on as Director of the Opera Ballet and become responsible for the dances and 'movement' in the operatic repertoire. Tudor had no objections.

'So I had a meeting with Bing,' continues Alicia, 'and he told me, "If you accept this post things will be entirely different from when you were a dancer. You will be management now, not an artist. You'll be administrating and dealing with things you've never had to be responsible for before. It will be difficult and maybe not very nice at times. You had everybody falling over themselves to help you before but if you join the other side you'll get all the complaints. You may find that everybody may not be so pleasant to you. But, if you're willing, we'd love to have you." So I said I'd try.'

She had not planned to work again. She told journalist Catharine Brewster, 'When I said . . . I was retiring, I meant completely. I came to New York for a month's vacation, found myself signed for a lecture tour and to direct the Metropolitan Opera Ballet.'

The lecture tour was organized by agents Colston Leigh and was entitled 'My Life in Ballet', into which she could weave all her experiences and anecdotes. She ended up lecturing in many states. It became a career in itself.

It was agreed she would start her new position at the Met in August. Before that she became consultant with the Florida Palm Beach Ballet.

In June she came back to New York, *en route* for London, to make arrangements for her stay at the Met. While there she received a phone call from Doris in London.

Doris would open mail for Alicia, while she was away, and deal with it if she could. She was ringing about a letter Alicia had received. She was cagey about its contents and Alicia asked her if she was feeling all right. The letter was from 'a very important person', she told Alicia. 'I think she needs a reply as soon as possible. I think she wants to promote you.'

'You enjoyed her Christmas performance,' Doris went on, still cagey. 'You thought she was a very good DAME. Do you understand, she wants to promote you?' The penny finally dropped.

Alicia was to be made DBE, a Dame of the British Empire. It was still confidential and, in those days, international telephone calls were made via operators and Doris was being careful in case anyone was listening in,

Alicia received her DBE from the Queen and, while in London, also received the Royal Academy of Dancing's Coronation Award, which was presented to her by Margot Fonteyn.

She returned to New York, appropriately, on the *Queen Elizabeth* and checked in at the Windsor, where she had a suite. It was full of flowers from wellwishers who congratulated her on her DBE, welcomed her to New York and wished her well for the Met season. It was a lovely, warm return. But other visitors were waiting for her, too, and they did not wish her well.

'At about five in the afternoon I went downstairs to say hello to Benny, the porter, get the evening paper and get something to eat at the delicatessen just round the corner. Before that I'd given the valet some clothes to press for me.

'When I came back I put the key in the door, opened it and saw the dresses hanging, pressed, on the back of a door. I closed the front door and double-locked it. This was years ago but even then things were happening in New York that are only just beginning to happen over here.

'I saw some flowers that had not been there when I had left, so I thought the porter must have brought them up and went to see who they were from. As I leant forward I felt something sticking in my back.

'I straightened up and there was a man with a gun in my back. Out of the bedroom came a second man and he had a knife which he held at my stomach. Both were big and both had handkerchiefs over their faces. I don't stand an earthly, I thought. "Take anything you want," I said. There was a trunk in the room with all my furs.

'The man with the knife went to the Venetian blinds and cut the cord from them. Next thing, they threw me on to the bed, face down on the pillow so I couldn't see what was happening, and tied my wrists and feet behind me. Later, the doctor told me they had tied them so tight that it had stopped my circulation and I passed out. My wrists were swollen for ages afterwards. They thought I'd had a heart attack and went.

'God knows how long I was out. When I came to I stayed where I was in case they were still there. Then I thought, I can't stay like this, and I managed to knock the telephone receiver off its cradle. I could hear the operator saying, "Hello? hello?"

'Talk about gymnastics. I had to get my head near the receiver and I said, "Quick, I've been held up."'

The intruders were never caught. Later, staff remembered two well-dressed men arriving with a bouquet. They did not ask for her but got into the lift. No one took any notice – flowers were always arriving for her. There was no sign of a break-in and Alicia is convinced it was an inside job.

She had stayed at the Windsor, on and off, for over twenty years and had felt secure there. After that she wanted to move. She was later introduced to a property millionaire who owned the Town House. 'I took his advice and moved in. I was there for six years on a special deal.'

At the Met she was in charge of movement on stage for the singers, and worked with many international names including Sutherland, Pavarotti and, also, Domingo. She became particularly fond of the two tenors; they were both keen on sport, as is she, and she was able to talk their language.

Her interest in sport, and athletics, is not casual. She loves horseracing – her enthusiasm was sparked in the 1930s when she and Lilian Baylis were first taken to the races by a member of the Sainsbury family. She never misses the Grand National on television and, while working on this book, a section had to be postponed while she watched the 1995 Grand National, rejoicing in Jenny Pitman's win.

Neither does she miss an important tennis, football or rugby match. She is a fan of the superb Linford Christie and will speak at length of his relationship with his coach Ron Roddan. 'That is how it should be, it's the sort of relationship I try to encourage.'

Although the singers at the Met could sing better than anyone in the world, stage movement was another matter. 'I was able to be helpful,' she says.

The first Met operas on which she worked choreographically were *Manon*, starring Anna Moffo and conducted by Thomas Schippers, and Birgit Nilsson's *Aida*, conducted by Solti. The down-to-earth Nilsson and Alicia got on well. Both operas were part of the 1963/4 season. In addition to helping the singers, she coached the opera ballet up to her own 'exacting standards' as Catharine Brewster put it, supervised the choreography and rehearsed the dancers and the ballet recitals that were given outside the opera house. 'Discipline, the training for an object of beauty, can only be attained by hard work,' she said. 'Breathing, posture, co-ordination of mind and body, it gives one confidence . . .'

'She is very proud of her slender feet and legs,' continues Miss Brewster, 'which show nothing of years of hard muscular work. "Proper ballet training," she said firmly, "should never result in bulging muscles. Serenity is shutting doors in one's mind and relaxing. That's the secret of beauty and a beautiful life."'

Her life took another course. She stayed at the Met from 1963 to 1969, but it was to be ten years before she moved permanently back to London. Her actual retirement had lasted two days.

She was involved with the production of twenty-five operas each season. For *Manon* she had choreographed a new ballet and for *Aida,* which was a big, new production, she had engaged the services of choreographer Katherine Dunham.

As the Met was an American company she was keen to promote American talent, hence Chicago-born Miss Dunham's appointment. She felt the Met had relied too strongly on Continental artists in the past. She was thrilled with the success of *Aida* and, even now, will excitedly pore over the colour photographs of the production.

'Morale has been high around the Met since the announcement of Dame Alicia's appointment,' proclaimed the *New York Times.* 'It is one of the greatest things that has happened to our ballet in many years,' seconded John Gutman, the Met's Assistant Manager. Gutman became her administrator for ballet: 'He was marvellous.'

'I'd always enjoyed opera,' says Alicia, 'and I was in the same opera house in which I had spent so much of my career. The Met was home to me. I was in touch with the same orchestras, the electricians who had lit me, all the same people. I loved being in my office and to be able to hear the singers. I enjoyed being able to listen to those full orchestras with great maestros. I'd worked with them all, and knew them all.

'Although it was different, it wasn't a difficult transition, and the decision hadn't been forced on me. If it had been I might have felt differently. I didn't have to take the job and I decided to do so under my own volition. I realize now how important that was.

'I had enjoyed my career, and now I enjoyed being around other people who were having wonderful careers.'

She confided her 'beauty secrets' to the press, at the request of Catharine Brewster. This boiled down to '"sleep well, eat well and gets lots of fresh air," says Dame Alicia, her great dark eyes shining. "Sleep is the most important, the greatest luxury today." To watch Alicia Markova is to watch a poem in motion . . . a testament to the fact that beauty is really total.'

Alicia exploded with laughter when she recently read the last review. 'Those articles used to be syndicated – you gave the one interview and it was syndicated to millions. It turned up all over the country.'

While in England she had had a hand in the production of a long-playing record set. It had been successfully released in Britain and now came out in America.

She had seen Joan Sutherland sing both at Covent Garden and in Paris and, in keeping with the rest of the world, had been thrilled by her voice.

Sutherland, with her conductor husband, Richard Bonyng, used to come to the Knightsbridge flat to visit Alicia. On one particular birthday of Alicia's they had come with Ted Shawn, formerly of 'Jacob's Pillow', who was passing through London at the time.

Decca had released an immensely successful two-volume LP set of Sutherland entitled *The Art of the Prima Donna*, with the orchestra conducted by Francesco Molinari-Pradelli. They now planned another two-volume set to be entitled *The Art of the Prima Ballerina*, with the orchestra to be conducted by Bonyng.

This was an important venture for him. His wife had soared to fame as the world's greatest coloratura. Her records billed her as 'The Voice of the Century' and it was no exaggeration.

Much of her success was due to the coaching she had received from her husband. He had nurtured her unique upper register and agility which had shot her to fame. Decca was now keen to consolidate Bonyng's reputation as a conductor.

'He wanted the interpretations for the new album to emphasize a dancer's viewpoint rather than a musician's,' says Alicia. Ballet records were often useless to dancers as the tempi were too rigid. He asked Alicia to advise him.

She did more than that. Her scores were marked with her tempi and she had always travelled with them. She went through these with Bonyng, pointing out the reasons for her various timings, tapping them out to him on the table. She then assisted with the sleeve notes and pictures.

Walter Terry wrote in the *Sun Herald Tribune*:

'Music You Can See: Yes, that is the very special characteristic of a new album *The Art of the Prima Ballerina* . . . Dame Alicia Markova selected and supervised this ballet music as a tribute to the art of the ballerina and chiefly the romantic age of ballet. Why is it music that invites you to see? Because the album's 12 ballet music pieces are played at dance tempi. This is unusual; for example, there must be at least 20 *Swan Lake* albums and the tempo employed for Odette's coda in Act II is so fast that not even a ballerina being given a hot foot could do it.

'Dame Alicia has changed all this. The retards, the accelerandos, required by the dancer are present and so, also, are the dynamic intensities. For here, in this remarkable and delightful album, are mirrored in sound the motor rhythms, and they are different from plain metric beats, of dance gesture, delicacies, muscular bravura, movement, climaxes.

'Among the excerpts from *Giselle* we hear the music for the ethereal lifts in Act II as Albrecht lifts Giselle in increasingly higher arcs above his head. The music slows accordingly to accommodate the all important aspect of this ballet, the movement, and we can see it, perhaps Markova herself, supported by Dolin or Bruhn, seemingly to soar unaided, dressed in a mist of white in the eerie woodland . . .

'The album, which has a glorious cover colour photo of Markova as Taglioni in *Pas de Quatre*, also includes a 10 page booklet of comments by Dame Alicia and her collaborator. Reproductions of lithographs of Taglioni . . . and the other greats of the romantic age and photos of Pavlova, Spessivtzeva, Karsavina, Danilova and of course Markova, who has often been called the greatest Giselle of our era, and the reincarnation of Taglioni.'

At the end of her first season Alicia set about nurturing the Metropolitan Ballet Company. Her auditions for dancers became an annual event. As there were so many applicants each was given a number which was called out to summon them in. She auditioned for hours at a time and the only sign of impatience she betrayed was if someone forgot their number. 'You must try to remember,' she told one girl. 'I want to see how you think as well as how you dance.'

One dance group lost the beat during a waltz and she interrupted, 'I'm not really getting what I asked for, you are missing the rhythm. Just an ordinary glissade, it's very simple.'*

She was no despot. She comforted one nervous dancer who was struggling to count bars while an inexperienced pianist distorted the rhythm. The girl asked her for the exact count and Alicia candidly told her, 'I never count, I just go by the music,' – advice Stravinsky had given her when she had been fourteen.

She held auditions in the roof studio of the Met. On one day alone she saw 231 aspirants. Out of these she shortlisted five boys and twenty girls and from these she finally chose three boys and six girls who joined the *corps de ballet*.

In April 1964 she appeared at the Opera Club ball and was photographed by the *New York Times* with Blanche Thebom, the American mezzo of Swedish extraction. Miss Thebom was wearing a diamond stud signifying a Swedish royal honour. Alicia's bosom glittered with the sparkling rosette, cross and star of the DBE. She often did not dance at balls. As she put it, 'Men are often afraid to ask a ballerina to dance.'

* *New York Times.*

That year she also contributed a filmed tribute to Dame Ninette de Valois whose turn had come as the latest *This Is Your Life* subject. Among Dame Ninette's guests were Adeline Genée, Helpmann, Fonteyn and Nureyev.

For the 1964/5 season Alicia worked, among other operas, on *Turandot, Aida, La Forza del Destino* and *Salome*. In *Salome* she coached Birgit Nilsson in the Dance of the Seven Veils. 'She was covered the whole time. She had black fishnet tights and wore a wig made of black cock feathers. Those productions were marvellous, each one was like a Broadway show.'

As ballet director Alicia had the choice of either staging the ballets herself or selecting suitable choreographers. She announced to the press she was eagerly searching for new choreographical talent.

With the dancers she took three rehearsals a week, establishing a consistent company style.

If the dancers were late they were fined by their union. This had nothing to do with her. When she had been touring America, before unions, she had thought they would be a good thing and had campaigned for them. Now, as director, she was to see another side of things.

She was also involved with the Met's educational programme, which meant working with aspiring dancers.

'Metropolitan Opera, variable haven for dance . . .' wrote Doris Hering in *Dance* magazine. 'Will the coming year and Alicia Markova change the picture? . . . in the excerpts from *Les Sylphides* and the Rose Adagio, girls who had previously seemed rather nondescript suddenly were attractive with clearly defined features and a sense of their own presence. The boys too had begun to take on more authority.

'What was the source of this difference?-It was Alicia Markova. She had not only been staging the classic excerpts, she had worked diligently on grooming and on deportment . . .

'She had her first strong inkling of success when she arrived for the performance that we attended and found three girls diligently trying to clean a spot from a fourth girl's costume. To her this meant that they were beginning to be proud not only of themselves but of each other. The dancers were developing company awareness.'

She went on an audition tour for new dancers, which was her own idea. She held these in 'a firm but friendly way', according to the *New York Times*, who sent a journalist to cover the event.

Smart in veiled hat, grey dress and earrings, she was flanked by John Gutman and her ballet mistress, Audrey Keane. She asked the dancers for *pliés, bourrées* and *entrechats*. She tapped her foot, occasionally snapped her fingers or waved her hand and sometimes even stood and gestured. If the dancers did not understand what was required of them she raised a leg, pointed a toe or lifted a hand to explain.

She was able to time her holidays for June, when the Met went on tour. She would spend three weeks in London, seeing her sisters but staying at the Carlton Towers Hotel which offered a special rate to Met employees. That way she did not upset Doris and Vivienne's routine, as they now shared the Knightsbridge flat. She would always visit Ascot during that time. 'Ascot is a must for me,' she told the *Daily Sketch*. 'I always like a little gamble though I never seem to win.'

Ascot was in June, and that month she heard the shocking news that Roberto Arias, Fonteyn's politically minded husband, was critically ill after an assassination attempt. He recovered but was left paralysed for the rest of his life. Fonteyn had to remain in England at the time; she was dancing in Bath.

'I know something of the agony Margot has endured,' Alicia told the *Daily Sketch*. 'Many years ago, in South Africa, a huge audience awaited me. My beloved mother was dying. I had to go on – so many people depend on you. You think of the public who have made you, the company and the traditions of the theatre and you think of the one you love who also needs you and you pray for a miracle.'

After her three weeks in London Alicia would spend another three weeks in the South of France before returning to New York for the 1964/5 season. In addition to the other operas, she now assisted Zachary Solov, who was creating new dances for *Samson and Delilah*. Even if she had wanted a dancing come-back now there was no time for it, although Bing was still trying to persuade her. He had wanted her to lead a polonaise with Solov in *Eugene Onegin*: 'Zach would love it!'

Opening night for the season was 12 October, with Sutherland's *Lucia di Lammermoor*, which Alicia had choreographed. After the show, television's chat-show king, Johnny Carson, hosted a supper for baritone Robert Merrill who was celebrating his twenty years at the Met. The wall-to-wall celebrities included Eva Gabor, Alan J. Lerner, Rudi Vallee and Alicia.

On 16 November the Met was to present her staging of *Les Sylphides* which was to share the bill with Donizetti's *Don Pasquale*. This would be the first ballet production the Met company had produced under its own steam. There was great curiosity about it.

'Now comes the Met Opera with . . . a mystery figure and a possible source of strong directorial strength in Dame Alicia Markova,' wrote Allen Hughes in the *New York Times*. 'And make no mistake about it, she is the significant figure in the Met venture.

'Except for George Balanchine she has, by virtue of her performing career, more artistic stature and authority than any other individual in charge of a ballet company in this country. Because she is a real lady, smooth, chic and soft spoken, it will be easy to assume she might lack the determination and strength required to command a company. This could prove to be one of the most fallacious balletic assumptions of the century. In conversations this writer has had with her last year, Dame Alicia indicated that the hand in that velvet glove was made of durable, if unusually attractive, steel.

'She did not dream up the idea of doing *Les Sylphides* one day last week . . . she began rehearsing dancers in it more than a year ago. Because she is a perfectionist, is rightfully proud of her past achievements, and is determined that her reputation should not be tarnished by present carelessness, it can be assumed that she would not allow her company to be exposed in so delicate a work as *Les Sylphides* if she did not think it was ready.

'It is possible, therefore, that Dame Alicia could pull off the ballet coup of the year, if not the decade, by proving that the Met ballet can dance infinitely better than anyone else has dreamed it could.

'If she does this, and if the production of *Les Sylphides* becomes a ballet to see this season, Dame Alicia may well find herself in a position to have her way in the ballet world wherever, and however, she wants it.

'Lovely ladies have rattled empires in times past and Dame Alicia may be just the one to rattle a few right now.'

By 22 November Hughes had seen *Les Sylphides*:

'MARKOVA GIVES MET NEW VERVE: There is a new spirit at the Met Opera that has nothing to do with singers, musicians, stage hands, directors and others connected directly with opera – and everything to do with ballet. It is a surge of morale and unlike anything the Met has known for years and rests squarely on the shoulders of the new *Les Sylphides* . . . all doubts vanished when the work was unveiled, the November 13 unveiling was brilliant. The audience applauded wildly, the critics praised it and Dame Alicia smiled . . . The work itself was certainly no novelty but the performance was nothing short of revelatory . . .'

Alicia's new life did not lack incident. The Met quickly realized the value of her name and were not slow to put her on view.

That Christmas she directed the ballet for the Macy Thanksgiving Day Float. This meant an outdoor rehearsal at midnight in the freezing New York winter. She insulated herself with trousers, overcoat and fur hat.

The following year, on her annual holiday in the South of France, she teamed up with Dolin, Milorad Miskovitch and Hollywood movie star Greer Garson, who was also there on holiday.

She had known Garson since her days in Hollywood. The British-born star of *Mrs Miniver* had lived with her mother and used to give traditional Sunday lunches to which Alicia and Pat would go.

In 1965 Alicia took part in a charity lunch at the Plaza Hotel, with comedy pianist Victor Borge, with whom she had appeared on television. She was presented to Princess Benedikte of Denmark.

Alicia had forged several links with Denmark over the years. She had danced there with de Valois in the early 1930s at the beginning of her Sadler's Wells career, had appeared with the Royal Danish Ballet, and had had several Danish partners including Erik Bruhn.

She was to continue her Danish links. The Royal Danish Ballet were in New York for a season and Alicia met star dancer Flemming Flindt. She had known him when he had danced with the Festival Ballet. Flindt mentioned that he was interested in choreography and, liking what she heard, she brought him to the Met for their production of *Faust*.

Hans Brenaa was also with the Royal Danish Ballet and he came to the Met to work on Bournonville's *La Ventana*. The company worked for weeks to perfect the Bournonville style.

Later Alicia was to work with another star Danish dancer, Peter Schaufuss.

The Metropolitan Opera Ballet gave a season at the Lewisohn Stadium and Alicia arranged the programme. She had had personal experience of dancing at the stadium, which stood her in good stead. She worked with Fokine's son, Vitale. It poured with rain on the day of the dress rehearsal.

Vitale managed the Fokine estate and also acted as ballet master. 'I had done *Les Sylphides* which showed off my girls,' says Alicia 'and now my boys were coming up so I wanted *Prince Igor* for them.'

In addition to *Les Sylphides* and the *pas de deux* from *The Blue Bird*, the stadium programme included *La Ventana* and Bartok's

The Miraculous Mandarin. 'It was the most modern of works and had won prizes in Paris. I persuaded Bing to bring it over. I must say he was very supportive.'

Alicia was able to keep in contact with friends and was delighted to meet up with Balanchine again. It was over thirty-five years since they had worked on *Le Chant du Rossignol* together. Then he had been a refugee eager to prove himself, now he was one of the most prestigious choreographers in the world, eagerly sought after by, among others, Nureyev – on whom he was not keen. 'Balanchine was never one for showmen, he preferred to be very quiet, which was why he was not keen on Pat in those early days. He was not very pleased when I went off with him. But he needed Pat's advice, and he took it.'

The Met's production of *The Magic Flute* was designed by Marc Chagall, he who had designed her heart-shaped *Aleko* costume. She was photographed with him, in profile, her hair entirely covered her handsome nose.

Unlike Maria Callas, and other artists whose feuds with Rudolph Bing are legendary, Alicia got on with him. 'He was a genius,' she says. 'He could be difficult, I suppose, but not with me. Somehow we understood each other.

'We used to have planning meetings each week, and the heads of each department would sit round a huge table. Lighting, Technical, Orchestral, you name it. Naturally, I was there for Dance.

'Bing was always there. He was the first in the building at eight every morning and the last one out at midnight. That's why his reign was so memorable.

'The long hours didn't bother me, I was used to them, it was the way I'd been trained. Maybe that's why we understood each other.

'Bing had to deal with fourteen unions in that house. In an ordinary working week we had a performance every evening and a matinée on Saturday so that was a repertoire of seven performance each week.

'What people don't always realize now, when I attend meetings all over the world, is that I've encountered most of the technical problems before. I'll say, "Just a moment, we had that problem thirty years ago at the Met, here's how we solved it." They usually change the subject.

'I had to learn about union liaison and that was totally different to anything I'd been used to before. When we were coming up for the ballet evening, which was the first one I became involved with, it was agreed I could have the stage to myself, with the company, for the ballet rehearsal. So, at the meeting, I asked how many hours I was allowed.

'The usual thing happened, you know, the head of this department makes requests and the head of that department insists on certain things. My ballet mistress was with me and she said we couldn't fit in all we had to do in the short time allotted.

'But I said we'd manage with what we'd been given. Then I asked about the time I had been allocated for lighting.

'Rudi, the electrician, whom I'd known for years, and who had always lit me, asked me what I needed. When I explained he told me he wouldn't be able to let me have the full lighting plan until the orchestral rehearsal, and that would be too late. I didn't want to be too demanding as the Met had never done a company ballet evening before and they might have said, "Let's not bother," so I didn't say too much.

'Bing asked, "Do we get a full dress rehearsal?" I said, "Yes, but I need the stage before that. I'd like costumes with piano before." For the operas we used to have a week on stage with a piano, then costumes, and finally the orchestra alone for the singers, so I wasn't being unreasonable.

'Well, the performance date got nearer and I had no lighting rehearsals and then something went wrong with another production, as it always does, so they grabbed my time. I received a memo about the lighting from Rudi – everything we did had to be reported on memos, I'd never seen so many in my life, and all with numerous copies. I'd never had to deal with that sort of thing before and it drove me crazy.

'When I was with Pat I was accustomed to saying, "We'll do this, then I'll go there," and we'd work things out like that. Now I was informed this was not the way things were done at the Met, there had to be a memo about everything. Dated, in triplicate, and with the time on it.

'So how do you think we worked it out? Rudi was a friend and he knew I wouldn't insist on going through the official channels otherwise we'd never get anything done. He said to me, "The rehearsal starts at ten, but if you can manage it I'll order coffee and Danish for nine in my office." That was where we worked out the lighting plots, all unofficially. We couldn't have done it officially, there was no time.

'I arrived at nine and his secretary had the coffee and Danish ready. We did *Sylphides* first. He'd lit me in *Sylphides*, in all my performances over how many years? I said, "Right, Rudi, will you give me what you used to give me when I was on? Over to you."

'"That's fine," he said, and that had taken all of five minutes. Then there was the new work we were doing, Tudor's *Echoing of Trumpets*. This was its first American production. It's about war, very modern, a complete contrast to *Les Sylphides*.

'The Met was doing *Fidelio* at the time and I said to Rudi, "Can you give me what you're doing for the prison scene in *Fidelio*, that looks about right." That took another five minutes.

'We were also doing *The Blue Bird* which Rudi knew well; he'd lit me in that many times, too, so he had the plot for that as well. We were closing with *Samson and Delilah*, the big Bacchanale, which we'd lifted out of the opera so that was already there.

'We were there for about half an hour then sat and enjoyed our coffee and Danish. After that we went down to the stage for the rehearsal. Bing was there with his entourage plus four assistant managers and secretaries. So were the orchestra and conductor, whom I knew well.

'I got my megaphone, that place was so big I needed it, particularly if there was music playing. I always had my megaphone, Bing had bought it for me, the management insisted I have it as I never shouted.

'If we had a big opera, and the ballet were in it, and it had to be choreographed, with everyone on stage, I would be in charge of four hundred people. I had forty-five dancers alone, plus the chorus. It makes me laugh now, when I'm in a rehearsal studio and someone will say to me, "Do you really think we could manage all that?"

'We didn't mention the meeting, because it was unofficial. We'd have been blacked if anyone had found out. The rehearsal started on time at ten and we were through without overtime, which was very important to the management.

'At the end of it Bing said, "That was very good but I'm a little bit puzzled." He was always very English and used to wear a bowler hat and carry a rolled umbrella. "How did you get all that done?"

'"Everybody's been most co-operative," I said. "All departments have been wonderful."

'"Yes," he answered. "So I've heard, that's already come through to me. I'm very pleased."

'So we all went for lunch and as we walked across the stage, Rudi was there and Bing said to him, "You know, I don't usually say anything to you but I'm really surprised it's all worked out so well because it's our very first ballet evening."

'"Actually, Mr Bing," Rudi said (everyone called him 'Mr Bing', later he was 'Sir Rudolph'), "Dame Alicia knew exactly what she wanted."

'There had been new décor for *Les Sylphides* but that did not cause problems as, again, the designer, Rolf Gerard, was an old friend. There was no money and no time, there never was, and the only way things could be worked out was through friendship.

'Rolf had done the *The Merry Widow* for me in 1955, now he was resident designer at the Met. I told him, "I don't want just black curtains and I don't want the usual park that everyone has. I want something a bit more modern, magical." People forget the theatre is about illusion, getting away from problems. When you know somebody you can talk directly to them. He told me not to worry.

'He worked that out by taking his whole department to the bar across the way, and buying them drinks. Then he told them what he wanted. They came up with the most lovely thing I've ever seen.

'But there were still union rules and we had to be careful. I was aware of that.

'I soon developed a system. I think it was on the first day of my new position that somebody came in with a complaint. I sat on the chair and listened then said, "Go over there, that's the line for complaints, you queue up over there." And we laughed, and after that I always used to say to Audrey, "Send them down the complaints line." We had a good relationship, you have to get on with people, understand their problems and work them out. I've always believed in that.

'Now and then, if there was a problem I couldn't work out, Audrey would send me home to take a bath. I'd forget about the problem while I was soaking, then the answer would come to me. I'd go back knowing what to do.

'I was three years as director in the old house and another three years when we moved to the new house at the Lincoln Center.'

In 1966 the old Metropolitan Opera House was demolished and a new one built in the new Lincoln Center. It was part of a complex that also housed the New York City Opera and the Beaumont Theater.

Alicia danced on the stage of the old Met during the last performance. The Bolshoi Ballet were dancing, under Hurok's representation. After the performance, as many dancers as could be assembled whom he had represented and who had danced at the Met danced a polonaise set by Yuri Grigorovich.

Dressed in her evening frock, she led the cavalcade with Jerome Robbins and Danilova. It was positively the last time she danced on stage, and that was only as a tribute to Hurok and to mark the end of an era.

A vast area was demolished to make way for the new complex and a prestigious stone-laying ceremony took place, attended by President Eisenhower and representatives from the various fields of art, such as Sam Wanamaker and Leonard Bernstein.

'I was invited to the ceremony,' remembers Alicia. 'The area was flattened, it was just like being in a prairie. They had a model of what the finished complex would look like.

'It was a perishing cold day and limousines brought us to the site. I was told to dress in my second-act costume from *Giselle* and I was freezing. I stayed in the limousine until the last minute and then rushed out to be photographed with everyone. I was standing next to Martha Graham, who was representing modern dance. She was wearing a dress with long sleeves so she was covered but I had nothing on, really, just my wisps of tulle. They took a bit of time setting up the shots and Martha said to me, "It's all very well us doing this, but if you don't get inside soon, Alicia, you'll get pneumonia and die. You won't be here when it's built."

'As soon as I got back to my hotel I had a hot bath and then I remembered from the old Russian company when Chura had said, "Take a little tot of vodka," so I did. I survived. I was expecting to go down with an awful chill but I didn't.'

She was presented with a 'lovely souvenir of the old Met'. Kirsten Flagstad and Alicia had shared the same dressing room in the old building. Flagstad had had it during the opera season and Alicia for the ballet. Certain effects of the old building were auctioned and writer Arthur Todd bought the doorknob and gave it to her. She also has a piece of the famous golden curtain which a stage hand cut off and gave her on that last night.

She had her office in the new building furnished to her own specification as much as possible. There was a blue carpet and she went to Bloomingdale's garden department and bought lots of spring-coloured cushions to cheer up the functional furniture. The fabric featured red geraniums, blue cornflowers and the like. 'No natural flower could survive in the air-conditioned atmosphere. What's it going to do to us humans? I thought?' She also bought a range of brightly coloured artificial flowers. Her DBE citation hung from a wall and a picture of Diaghileff was on the window ledge.

Her office overlooked the Beaumont Theater and an area dominated by a vast Henry Moore sculpture of a figure in a pool. A monumental and serious work of art, it had cost a fortune.

'The trouble they had with that sculpture. According to regulations the pool had to be only so many inches deep. First of all it leaked so everyone in the Beaumont had the leakage.

'The kids discovered the Henry Moore, and it was fabulous for climbing on and sliding down into the water. I would look out of my window and think, If Henry Moore could see the pleasure that he's given to those kids. It was wonderful.'

One night she unexpectedly came across Bing prowling the corridors. 'It was late and I was coming up to my office with Audrey. We got out of the lift and all the lights were blazing. Then Bing came along and I wondered what on earth he was doing there as his office was on the other side. He was as taken aback to see us as we were to see him. He'd just had a meeting with the board and, I think, had had a roasting about the electricity bill. He obviously thought we didn't need all those lights, and was going round turning them off.'

She was at dinner one evening and among the guests were columnist Leonard Lyons and his son, and composer Marvin Hamlisch, who was working on his musical *Chorus Line*. Lyons Junior told her he was a football player and his team were losing. She gave him some tips on how she kept fit. Lyons' team won their next match. 'I don't say anything, but perhaps I made him think a little,' she says, sounding rather like Dame Edna Everage.

Colston Leigh booked her for lectures in the Met breaks. In one season alone these lectures took her as far apart as Virginia and both North and South Carolina. She took in colleges, clubs and women's societies. In all lectures she paid generous tribute to Diaghileff.

Her talks were largely anecdotal, and she would say, 'People seem to imagine us as puppets. Surprise is sometimes voiced that we even have a sense of humour – this is the most important thing in life for me. Without it I would have been dead years ago.' After her talk she invited questions. She flew to the venue, stayed overnight, and dined with the organizers, which was what they really wanted, then flew back.

One of her lectures was to be at the University of Cincinnati College-Conservatory of Music. She had danced many times in Cincinnati during her touring days. Unfortunately she was unable to fulfil the booking owing to two bad falls she sustained while rehearsing at the Met. These brought a darker and more ominous shading to her reign.

The first occurred on 1 July 1966 in the corridor of the Opera House in the Lincoln Center. 'We'd just finished rehearsal and I was going to lunch with Antony Tudor. It was summer and I was getting the ballet company together for an outside performance at the Lewisohn Stadium.

'Antony came to pick me up and we were walking down the corridor which was uncarpeted. The lights weren't on, as the full company had not yet moved in. I didn't see a metal plate on the floor, I think it was the cover for the fire hydrant, and my heel caught on it and threw me on the concrete.

'It flashed through my mind that Hurok had always wanted me to have my nose bobbed. I was about to flatten it.* I turned my head but I hit my front teeth and fractured a cheekbone, broke two ribs and my patella went. I was a real mess. I was just wearing a cotton dress so there was nothing to protect me.

'The President of Israel was a guest at the Symphony Hall at the time so everything was cordoned off for security. People came but I lay for nearly two hours before an ambulance could get to me.

'I was a week in hospital and two months at home with a nurse. Altogether I was four months off work.

'I always believe in having the best opinions and I phoned London soon after the accident and spoke to Bill Tucker, the orthopaedic specialist and a good friend of mine. I had been to him in England when I had injured myself in Glasgow with the Festival Ballet. He told me not to fly home and gave me the name of a specialist in New York whom he considered the best knee man in the world. I was lucky because he was in New York at the time.

'I still ran things at the Met. Audrey and Harry Jones, my assistant, would come to visit me and I would tell them what to do. But I was saved by a wonderful nurse, Doris. She was a black girl from Georgia, where her family owned peach orchards.

'I'd been having agency nurses until then and they were always changing. Eventually Doris came and when she first arrived I thought, Here's another one. But she was so interested in what I did, I thought, This can't be true.

'One day the phone went and Bing made an appointment to come round to see me. It must have been an emergency because he never came to see me, I always saw him at the opera house. "Is that *the* Mr Bing?" Doris asked. "Yes," I said. "How do you know him?" "I adore opera," she said. "And I'm in the choir." This is heaven, I thought. For the next couple of hours she was walking on air at the thought of meeting Mr Bing.

---

* Pat and Ashton also urged her to have it bobbed. 'I'm a coward,' she told them. 'Everyone has their noses bobbed,' Pat told her. "At that time I had fantastic balance, so I said, "How do I know my balance won't go, I'm not risking it."'

'Before he arrived I said, "Tell me, Doris, you're a temp, do you have another case waiting? I really need someone to stay with me until I'm better. Would that interest you?"

'"You'd be giving me the greatest thing in life," she answered.

'To this day, I believe that that wonderful nurse brought me through that terrible time. She had a completely new outlook, which was so good for me. She'd say, "We'll have coffee at eleven because at twelve we must watch *Sesame Street*." I said, "What's that?" That's how I learnt about *Sesame Street*. I'd always been in the theatre, I didn't know it. We watched all the quiz shows and learnt things from them. She was so good for me.

'Antony Tudor had sent me a crate of individual bottles of wine, instead of flowers, and we'd have these with our meals. Doris would cook for us on the little electric stove in the apartment. She'd choose the wine.

'After the nightmare, and the constant change of nurses, and me still in a state of shock, she was a godsend.'

Alicia went back to the Met in November to work on the Christmas production of *Die Fledermaus*. She was using a stick. and had to have her leg raised on a chair, when sitting. Doris stayed with her until after Christmas. Then Alicia went on a cruise.

The second accident happened in March 1968. She was still walking with a stick.

'I was about to go out with Bing to see some production. It was just after lunch and I was going to meet him in his office. The floor was still not carpeted and it was very cold. I was dressed in boots, fur coat and fur hat. Fortunately I had all those clothes on and they helped protect me.

'My knee just gave way. I fell on the concrete and fractured a collar-bone and my cheek again and my left ankle. The pain was terrible. Someone must have told Bing because he was suddenly there with Mary, the Met nurse.

'I was rushed in an ambulance to Casualty at the Roosevelt Hospital, which was almost next door. I was there for nearly seven weeks.'

She decided to sue and, eventually, her case came to the Supreme Court. 'Needless to say, I lost.' She was considerably out of pocket as the expenses were down to her.

While she was in hospital people rallied round. The doorman of the Town House, where she was staying, came to see her every day, bringing the mail and messages.

When she left hospital her sister Bunny spent two weeks, staying in her apartment with her. Doris could not come over as she was by now working with Hughie Green on television's *Opportunity Knocks* show and in the middle of production. When Bunny went Vivienne arrived and they went for a holiday to Palm Beach. It was out of season and quiet, which was exactly what Alicia wanted.

When she returned to the Met she worked on Cilèa's *Adrienne Lecouvreur*, which was the gala opening for the 1968/9 season. This was predominantly a vehicle for the magnificent soprano Renata Tebaldi and the also magnificent but highly strung tenor Franco Corelli.

There were unscheduled dramas in this piece. At remarkably short notice Corelli was indisposed. Bing put out an SOS to everyone he knew for a replacement tenor. This was not easy as *Adrienne* is not frequently performed and, therefore, not in every tenor's repertoire.

Finally a young Spanish tenor was located who was guesting at the New York City Opera. He had recently been working in Israel. There was no time for him to prepare but he knew the opera. This was Placido Domingo. He and Alicia hit it off at once, but then 'Everyone adored him,' she says.

For all the excitement Domingo brought to the Met there was further unhappiness in 1969. With the multitude of powerful unions, and management regulations, the place was a powder keg, ready to explode at any second over any trifling matter. It erupted that year – there was a strike after which Bing ordered a lock-out. This was to last for nine months during which no work could be done.

In December 1969 Alicia had her knee operated on in New York. As she couldn't travel she stayed there over Christmas and Vivienne came over to join her. She resigned from the Met.

Her knee still did not seem to have the mobility for which she had hoped, so she contacted Bill Tucker. He and his wife had a holiday home in Bermuda and he told her to get on a plane and come over. He would take a look at the knee and, at the same time, the rest and warm climate would do her good.

She arrived in Bermuda in March 1970. She had been there twenty-four years earlier, in 1946, for a holiday between tours in America, when she had rented a cottage at Cambridge Beaches. This time she stayed at the Elbow Beach Surf Hotel. The Bermuda *Mid-Ocean News* trumpeted her visit from its front page: 'The Great Markova Visits Here to Recover from a Knee Injury'.

She spoke to the press, enthusiastically extolling the new young talent in England, 'like Antoinette Sibley and Merle Park'. She was persuaded to give a lecture at Hamilton City Hall.

She returned to New York and reminded her agents, Colston Leigh, that she still owed a lecture to the University of Cincinnati College-Conservatory of Music, the home of the Cincinnati Ballet.

'They had been so good about the cancellation. So I explained that they would have to meet me at the airport with a wheelchair but if they didn't mind that then it wouldn't interfere with my talk. They told me that if I could just get there they'd take good care of me.'

She stayed for a few days and, while there, David McLain, head of the dance division, asked her to return in the fall and join the faculty as Distinguished Lecturer on Ballet. She accepted his invitation.

She returned to London that summer, still walking with a stick, arriving just in time to catch the last day of the Kirov Ballet who were playing the Festival Hall. It was the day after Natalia Makarova (a member of the Kirov) decided to stay in the West, although there was a vain attempt in some quarters to suppress this news at the time. Alicia was invited by the Kirov's Natalia Dudinskaya to a matinée.

Dudinskaya was keen for Alicia to see twenty-two-year-old Mikhail Baryshnikov, who was dancing with the company. Unfortunately he was not due to dance that day but Dudinskaya wanted Alicia's opinion of him so, after the matinée, she enticed Alicia to stay for the evening performance and plied her with champagne and smoked salmon (an old Soviet custom). An emissary was sent to inform Baryshnikov he was dancing that night.

Dudinskaya, married to dancer/choreographer Konstantin Sergeyev, had been a magnificent dancer herself, whose technique is described by the *Concise Oxford Dictionary of Ballet* as 'stupendous'. She danced all the traditional roles and created some Soviet ones, including Chaboukiani's *Laurencia*. After her retirement she became ballet mistress at the Kirov. She danced in two major Soviet films and was awarded the Stalin Prize no less than four times and, in 1973, was to receive the Order of the Red Banner.

Baryshnikov arrived on time.

'Baryshnikov was dancing the Vestris* Variation,' recalls Alicia. 'Pat was the first to dance it when we were doing our concert programmes in America. Celli had arranged it for him, to Rossini

* Vestris was a famous dancer.

music. He wore the costume of the period, based on the lithograph of Vestris, and used a lot of the steps of the period. He was wonderful in it. He would do that and I would do *The Dying Swan*. We did it in all the arena performances.

'Dudinskaya wanted to know how Baryshnikov's version compared to Pat's, as the Kirov had their own version, and she also wanted me to see this brilliant young man. I sat with Sergeyev. I met Baryshnikov afterwards but he just bowed. I don't know whether he could speak English but he was not allowed to mix. At the time they were very protective.'

Four years later Baryshnikov defected to Canada and, systematically, proceeded to set the world on fire. There had not been such an inferno since Nureyev.

Alicia joined the University of Cincinnati College-Conservatory of Music in the autumn of 1970, to start the third phase of her life. 'I had spent six years at the Met finding out what opera was about, now I was going to find out about the academic world.'

The university had presented her with its Award of Distinction when she had lectured there in the spring: 'In recognition of her major influence on the development of international ballet in the twentieth century.' She had replied, 'I can think of nothing nicer than receiving an award like this for something that one has really enjoyed doing.' In return she presented to the university a crown that she had worn in *Sleeping Beauty*.

She staged Dolin's *Pas de Quatre* for the Cincinnati Civic Ballet, a semi-professional group, and became affiliated with the company which was about to turn professional.

She remained a year as a lecturer then was made a Professor of Ballet and Performing Arts. Again she worked with singers. 'I knew what the Met required for auditions. I told them, "They don't just stand and sing now, they have to move while singing, run up and down ramps and up stairs."'

Initially she had been invited to give just a single lecture each week, if that was all she felt she wanted to do. 'In the end I gave three classes a week and a talk, I never called it a lecture.' She was giving classes mostly to young dancers. She enjoys young people. Later, in Yorkshire, she was to work with children and liked that too.

There were excellent facilities at the university, including a new pavilion with a dance studio about to be completed.

Alicia did not travel to the university in the customary professorial manner. 'Those who know and work with Markova say the great ballerina behaves like a queen and is treated like a queen,' wrote the Cincinnati *Courier-Journal*. 'She is chauffeured from her hotel to classes ... Markova is always impeccably groomed. Her dark hair is neatly coiffed. She uses eye-liner to frame her expressive brown eyes. And she wears beautiful clothes. "Diaghileff brought us up to believe that one should always present the best of oneself, yet not be a slave to fashion," she said.

She became a supporter, almost a coach, of the Cincinnati basketball team. She watched all their matches with the Dean and his wife and the directors in their box. She knew most of the team. 'They knew I was interested,' she says.

One day, when she was taking some of the girls for a lesson, she was asked if she would object if some of their boyfriends sat in. These were members of the basketball team. She had no objection and they sat in the visitors' gallery.

'Afterwards the boys told me they'd like to come again,' she recalls. 'I said that was fine, just let me know. One of them then said, "To be honest, we wondered if you would give us a special class? We were watching you teach jumping. Maybe you could help us with our jumps?"

'"I've done something like that in New York," I answered, thinking of Leonard Lyons' son. "Yes, OK, I accept you."

'When you jump in basketball you can't be prepared, you have to be ready to jump at any moment. That was the training I gave them. I was taught, in the old school of ballet, to learn to jump without preparation, it's not done like that today, I'm always asking them why they're labouring. You must always be ready for it, transfer your weight without letting anyone see what you're doing. The good thing was they had height.'

She did not confine her sporting advice to basketball; she also encompassed boat racing.

She was staying, on holiday, in Henley with Bunny at the time. Another of Bunny's guests was the Oxford rowing coach Dan Topolski. He, and the members of his team, wanted to lose weight but keep up their strength. Alicia recommended her own way of eating. 'It is a matter of when and how much. You have to find out what suits you best. The whole point is to find out how you behave. Some people need a big meal to function, others function best with the meal afterwards. Massine needed a meal before a performance but if I had an evening performance I had my big meal lunchtime then waited until after the performance and had another one about midnight, with a glass of wine. You have to find out for yourself how you function.'

The Cincinnati tenure was not without drama.

'One day there was a student uprising and I was in the midst of it. The students lay down in the drive but never stopped me from going in. "I'm not going to teach," I told them. "But some of my personal things are in there and I want to do some writing. I shan't be long. If you want to lie out here in the drive that's OK by me."

'"We won't be in class tomorrow," they told me. "We're marching in protest."

'"If that's what you've chosen to do, that's fine," I told them. "But I think you might do more good by turning up for class."'

When things had settled down a new professor arrived and the staff went to the President's office to welcome him. It was Neil Armstrong, the first man on the moon. 'He was not a great conversationalist,' recalls Alicia. 'But when I was introduced to him as Professor of Ballet he joked to me, "My little dance on the moon wasn't so good."'

There were, during these years, sporadic appearances in Britain. One of these was in 1972 when she appeared on Scottish Television to give a master class on *Giselle* with the Scottish Ballet Theatre Company.

A preview of the recording was given at the Theatre Royal in Glasgow, and Alicia was presented with a bouquet by nine-year-old Fiona Busby, a third-year ballet student. But when Fiona came face to face with the *grande dame*, towering over her in high heels, hat and mink, she stood, covered in confusion, lost for words and about to burst into tears. Alicia well understood that feeling. She knelt down and cuddled her, then picked her up in her arms. Fiona was soon smiling again.

Before leaving, Alicia gave her some advice on dancing. 'Work hard, have confidence, then work even harder.'*

She also coached the Royal Ballet, formerly Sadler's Wells, in *Les Sylphides* in a season entitled 'Ballet For All'.

In 1973 ballerina Nadia Nerina organized a seventieth birthday party in London, at the Ritz, for Arnold Haskell. Alicia should have been in Cincinnati but was in London at the time recovering from another operation. When she had flown in from Cincinnati she had had a fierce abdominal pain. She was admitted to the London Clinic to have a gall bladder operation.

In addition to Alicia, among Haskell's ballet guests were Alicia Alonso, de Valois, Lifar and Galina Ulanova.

After the death of his first wife, Vera, some people had thought

---

* *Scottish Daily Express.*

that Alicia and Haskell might marry, bearing in mind their mutual interest in ballet. She dismisses this. 'How could that be? I'd known him since I was ten. He and his mother had been at my very first season in Monte Carlo when I was with Diaghileff. I was like his sister. His mother had always wanted a daughter and I was like a daughter to her and a sister to him. It never entered my head. I was at the Met when Vera died and I got the message that he was coming to see me. I consoled him as best I could but there was never any thought of marriage.'

Haskell did, in fact, marry into the Marks family. He married Vivienne and became Alicia's brother-in-law. Vivienne and Haskell were devoted to each other and happy together until his death.

In 1974, after four happy years at Cincinnati, Alicia felt she had to take stock of her life. She was sixty-four and still a gipsy. If she was going to stay at the university and continue to teach then she would have to settle down. She was asked if she was going to take tenure:

'Most people accept a position then settle down in the university for life but I didn't want that. Homes and apartments are for families with children and people who need schools for them. But I wasn't a family, I couldn't put roots down. I didn't want to start thinking along those lines. I decided I wanted to spend more time with my sisters, in my own country; after all, I was born in London. I first went to America in 1938 and stayed for ten years. I went back in 1963 and spent another ten years there. I'd done the job I came to do in Cincinnati, it was time to go. I just felt I wanted to come home and see my family. So I decided to come back.'

Earlier, in 1971, the *Courier-Journal* had noted: 'It's doubtful that she'll settle in Cincinnati forever. She misses her nieces and nephews in England. "They're growing up and I'm missing it. I don't want them not to know me."'

She had left her mark on Cincinnati. When she had joined the university she had told David McLain: 'Are you sure you really want this heritage, this tradition that goes directly back to the old Russian school? A lot of companies are abandoning it today, feeling that it's dated.'* McLain had assured her that he did. That was precisely what she had given him.

* *The Enquirer* magazine.

25

Indian Summer

In London Alicia moved into the Knightsbridge flat, with Doris, and was treated like minor royalty. She was invited on to the boards of ballet schools, companies and organizations and accepted nearly all of them. She was, and still is, a part of any major ballet occasion. Sometimes she would invite her sisters as guests, and it was not uncommon to see the four Marks girls at a table together. His 'Little Women', as Arnold Haskell called them. Sadly Bunny has since died of leukaemia.

Alicia is a straight-speaking adjudicator. She sits apart, her face betraying no strain, just as when she was dancing. She is motionless throughout the performances, concentrating. The only movement that might take place is when she reaches for her glasses, slung round her neck on a chain, and places them on her nose. She cannot help but be conscious that, frequently, the eyes of the audience flick from the dancers to her. With her Diaghileff training, her introduction of new ballets and her trailblazing tours, she is a colossus, towering in a flat world of sameness.

Her comments are straight from the shoulder, which is not that common now when sensibilities are taken into consideration and no one wants to hurt anyone. She, of course, evolved from a school where the maestro flung his cane if anything was wrong. She does not use a stick now and, even if she did, it would remain in her hand. Neither does she say anything unkind. Some criticism, however, may be implied by what she does not say.

She does not waste time on unjustified praise. If she likes a dancer she says so, clearly, telling the rest, perhaps, that they might have to work harder. Even if the dancers are tots she takes it all very seriously and treats them like young adults.

In 1975 Robert Helpmann asked Alicia for her help. He was involved with a production of *Les Sylphides* at the Sydney Opera House where he was a co-director of the Australian Ballet. There were certain design difficulties about which he was concerned. She agreed to go to Sydney as a consultant. She was delighted to be packing her case again.

She had never been to Australia but made up for this by staying a couple of months. In addition to putting on the production, for which she suggested an Australian designer in order to give it 'its own feeling', she gave talks, lectures, tuition and master classes both in Sydney and Melbourne.

Merce Cunningham was also in Australia with his company, due to open with his new 'contemporary ballet'. The day before her Melbourne departure, his management rang her and invited her to the opening of the first night, which was the next evening.

She explained that she was about to embark for Melbourne first thing in the morning but was nevertheless persuaded, without much difficulty, to attend.

Merce needed all the support he could get. A former member of the Martha Graham company, he is prominent in the field of *avant-garde* dance. Audiences have frequently been perplexed by his works.

'I first met Merce in New York,' she recalls. 'I've known him for years, since he started, really. He was way ahead of his time by any standards and to the Australians he was really new. He always came to my performances when he could and I did the same for him. People sometimes asked me why, because his productions were so different from mine, but I said he seems a nice gentleman and we have things to talk about and discuss, artistically.

'I read somewhere, around his seventy-fifth birthday, that he is the greatest choreographer in the world today. I wouldn't necessarily agree with that, but he is certainly interesting.'

Her own seventieth birthday was marked by a performance by the Royal Ballet at Covent Garden. She took her place in the royal box and the General Director, John Tooley, placed a printed notification of the occasion in the programme, together with the best wishes of the Opera House.

A month later she was present at another celebration – the thirtieth anniversary of the founding, by she, Dolin and Braunsweg, of the Festival Ballet.

In 1981 she appeared on her own peak-time television series

when the BBC starred her in *Markova Master Classes*. Knowledge-able and assured, she coached dancers Margaret Barbieri and David Ashmole.

That year marked the ninetieth birthday of soprano Dame Eva Turner. A gala was held at the Royal Opera House and, preceding that, a tea in the royal box. The Dame's special guests for this were Sir Michael Tippett, Sir Geraint Evans, Lord Miles and Alicia.

That was the occasion when Alicia was due to speak, but was stricken by laryngitis. John Tooley caused laughter by announcing that this was the first time he had had to apologize for the absence of a ballerina on stage owing to laryngitis.

The Royal Ballet School gave a week's season at Covent Garden in 1982. Among the ballets presented were Peter Wright's *Giselle* for which Alicia had coached the dancers.

In 1983, while she and Ashton happened to be in New York at the same time, Makarova – now a Broadway star – opened in *On Your Toes*, the musical that contains Balanchine's spectacular 'Slaughter on Tenth Avenue'. She and Freddie attended and created quite a stir among the smart audience.

That year she flew to Houston, Texas, to take part with Dolin in a tribute gala to the 'Ballet Russe de Monte Carlo Stars'. It was the last time they appeared on a stage together. Among others assembled for the occasion were Freddie Franklin, Igor Youskevitch, Nathalie Krassovska, Mia Slavenska and Irina Baronova.

In December 1985 she appeared on Yorkshire Television's pres-tigious and star-studded *Royal Celebration of Youth*, recorded in the presence of the Queen. Among the wall-to-wall celebrities were Sebastian Coe, of whom she was a great fan and with whom she managed to have a few words, Dame Vera Lynn, Cilla Black, David Frost, Terry Waite, and the young Rory Bremner.

Each established artist presented a younger talent. Alicia pres-ented Katherine Healy, who was dancing with the London Festival Ballet but about to finish with them the following month after, as she put it, 'my stormy 14 month stint as one of Peter Schaufuss' "baby ballerinas".'*

Alicia was in the audience for her last night, and came round to her dressing room afterwards to comfort her. She told her, 'I understand, I remember what it was like.'

'I remembered in that moment, with a jolt, that she was the first notable baby ballerina in this century,'† recalls Miss Healy.

* *Dance Now.*
† *Dance Now.*

On her seventy-fifth birthday the Royal Ballet dedicated its opening performance of Peter Wright's *Giselle* to Alicia. Critic Clement Crisp applauded this tribute and described her as '. . . one of the greatest Giselles of this century, her interpretation . . . [is] acknowledged as a supreme example of the ballerina's art.'

In an article in the *Financial Times* on 7 December 1985, Crisp wrote:

'With a phenomenal memory for style and step, Markova is a balletic treasure house. It is this richness of her experience which seems to me typical of the assets wasted by our national ballet. It should be an accepted fact of British dance that great artists hand on their wealth of understanding about technique, and the implications of their roles, so that young aspirants may comprehend the vital aesthetic and technical life of the repertory. They would thus learn of the traditions, of the subtleties as well as the practicalities, of performance, of pacing and shaping and interpretation, that their mentor has gained through long theatrical experience, and has garnered in their turn from instruction and coaching by their forebears.

'It is this chain of interpretation that brings continuity of wisdom, and richness of meaning, to every major role . . . A vital substructure of Soviet ballet is the transmission of knowledge from one generation of artists to another through extended coaching . . . it was a tradition of the Imperial ballet, too . . .

'Dame Alicia Markova can speak of working as a very young dancer on the *Swan Lake adagio* with Mathilde Kschessinska, the first Russian Odette . . . and successor to Legnani, the role's creator at the Marynsky. She has worked with Fokine, Nijinska, Massine . . . But will any of our aspirant ballerinas speak, in years to come, of learning with Markova about the roles she so illuminated? Will they, in their turn, be able to pass on the received wisdom not just of their own careers but also of so grand a preceptress? . . .

'Our national ballet can claim parentage with the old Russian ballet through its canon of classics bequeathed by Nicholas Sergeyev. It would do well to consider that there are obligations owed to these ballets – as to the native Ashton repertory – concerning text and style, which are implicit in this priceless inheritance and this irreplaceable link with the past.'

By now Alicia was President of the English National Ballet, whose headquarters, Markova House, was named after her. 'I think Americans think I own the place,' she said recently. She is Governor of the Royal School of Ballet where she has taught for twenty years, and has been Professor and Lecturer for the Yorkshire

Ballet Seminars since 1975. Her portrait hangs in Sadler's Wells in a position of honour.

Alicia's eightieth birthday was celebrated on 4 December 1990 by a gala in her honour at Sadler's Wells, the proceeds to go to the Dance Teachers' Benevolent Fund. There had been another gala in her honour in Manchester, the previous week, in the presence of the Princess of Wales in aid of a leukaemia charity. She was particularly moved that night as it was not long since she had lost Bunny to leukaemia.

Few of those taking part in the gala could have seen her dance but many of the audience had, and some had even danced with her. Among the ballets presented were several she had performed, including *Les Rendezvous*, the ensemble dances contributed by pupils from the Royal Ballet School which, as *The Times* critic John Percival noted, provided 'an apt reminder that Markova is a great teacher, who has devoted the last quarter of a century, since she has stopped performing, to handing on the tradition which she first absorbed as a 14 year old prodigy in Diaghileff's company'.

The Nutcracker was also acknowledged. 'Nobody, I think, can ever have made more of *The Nutcracker* than did Markova and . . . Dolin,' wrote Percival. Andria Hall danced the Sugar Plum Fairy, having been coached in the part by Alicia.

Balanchine, her first choreographer, was represented by Merrill Ashley and Adam Lüders from New York City Ballet who danced a duet from *Chaconne*, its first performance in Britain.

There were also *Le Spectre de la Rose* and excerpts from *Swan Lake* and *Giselle*. Dolin's *Pas de Quatre* was included. 'Many present must have seen her in their mind's eye,' Percival wrote, 'still soaring miraculously across the stage, still finding absolute perfection of shape, nuance and timing in every move, and still effortlessly exerting the charm with which nature blessed her.'

She was interviewed by Ray Connolly of *The Times* and Peter Brinson for the *Independent*'s 'The Sunday Review'.

Brinson started his piece: 'She sits in her Knightsbridge flat, upright, no wrinkles, hair grey in a sort of bouffant style which she says is how it has grown from the dark classical style of her dancing days, severe, drawn tight and parted down the middle. Even now, her body speaks more than her voice. Pauses between words are filled with shrugs, gestures, eye contacts. For a person so English in lifestyle, she is Italian in body language: words are extra.'

That year her dressing room was recreated at the Theatre Museum, Covent Garden, to illustrate the degree of preparation she put into her appearances, notably at a time when artists did their own make-up. In addition to the dressing room she donated many wigs, costumes and trunks as a gift to the nation.

In 1990 it was forty years since Alicia, Dolin and Julian Braunsweg had founded the Festival Ballet. It has changed its name several times and is now the English National Ballet.

A fund-raising gala was held at the Royal Albert Hall, where Alicia had first appeared when she was twelve, a far cry from the King's Theatre, Southsea where the Festival Ballet started. Then she had been unable to dance owing to appendicitis; now she was guest of honour.

Both Dolin and Braunsweg are dead. She must have remembered her continuous spats with the egomaniacal Dolin, whose energy and devotion to her had proved such a pillar of support over the years and who, in her way, she truly loved. Perhaps she thought, too, of how Braunsweg had pawned his wife's gems to keep things going and had even hidden under his desk when the debt collectors called. She had a lot to reflect on. 'Oh, they were characters, then.'

The Festival Ballet has suffered any number of setbacks through the years, helped frequently by Alicia's audience-pulling power. She was still adding her support.

In August 1992 Alicia staged *Les Sylphides* for the ENB's final programme of the summer season. Billed as 'A Tribute to Mikhail Fokine', it marked the fiftieth anniversary of his death. Clement Crisp was there and did not enjoy the evening, describing it as '. . . the spirit of the choreographer invoked and then given a thorough pasting'. He continued in his review for the *Financial Times*:

'The honourable exception is Dame Alicia Markova's staging of *Les Sylphides*. Markova learned the ballet from Fokine. He coached her in all three ballerina roles, recognizing in her exquisite style the essential Romantic image that lies at the heart of this ravishing and difficult work. In her several productions, Markova has sought to pass on the physical nuance and musical finesse that Fokine demanded and which, in her own interpretations, she so beautifully displayed . . . the ENB cast tried hard to seize the dreams and drifting magic of the text: the fascination was in seeing how moments of Markova's own style – sweetly floating, so musically subtle – surfaced amid the dutiful performance, like happy memories.'

In the November of that year Alicia was at the Russian Embassy where Queen Anne Marie of the Hellenes was a guest, surrounded by KGB colonels, as she hosted a gala in honour of Cecchetti, now lauded by the *Evening Standard* as 'Inventor of The Method on which all modern ballet is based'.

In January 1995 she spent several days filming for Russian television recalling, for Russian audiences, Pavlova, Spessivtseva and Diaghileff.

The following week she was at Markova House, recreating her role from *Le Chant du Rossignol* for the video archives of New York's George Balanchine Foundation.

It had suddenly been realized that the choreography would be lost but for her. No one was aware of any records of it. It was getting on for seventy years since she had danced it but her memory was as sharp as ever.

Sitting in the Wedgwood-style studio, Alicia recounted her memories of the role, and of Balanchine, Matisse and Stravinsky. She had worked on the part with all three. When the CD of the music was played she knew exactly where she wanted to go. She also remembered the orchestration. 'That should have been two trumpets,' she said at once when a particular passage was played.

She coached nineteen-year-old dancer Iohna Loots in the role. Gliding around the hall, her fur over her shoulders much as Julian Braunsweg must have seen her in the *Giselle* rehearsal (although it is now fake fur), she put the young dancer through her moves. She would point a toe, make a gesture with her arm, tilt her head. It was unmistakably Markova. The speed, lightness and poetry were still there. It seemed as if she could have taken a leap at any time.

To the American crew, and its co-ordinator, former Balanchine dancer Nancy Reynolds, she was a legend. They were visibly in awe. And she was awesome.

'Life just flowed over Balanchine,' Nancy said nervously as she eyed Markova on the floor. 'Nothing existed to him but his work, domestic things, bills, nothing else existed . . . I hope this is the passage she wanted.'

It was not and Alicia's quiet voice cut across as she pointed it out. There was silence in the room, then the engineer operating the CD player tried to explain the difficulties of cueing it up. The Dame was unimpressed.

'I can't hear you, speak up,' she interrupted. He started to stutter.

In the car taking her back to Knightsbridge, she was still full of the work. 'If I hadn't agreed to do it, they would have lost the ballet,' she said.

Knightsbridge is not what it was when she had moved in, and to get to her flat it is now necessary to circumnavigate a network of one-way roads. 'Balanchine would have loved this,' she joked as the car wormed its way past the Berkeley Hotel into the complicated web of traffic lights and turns.

Knightsbridge was an icy wind-tunnel but she got out of the car, stood at the door of her block and talked of Balanchine and *Le Rossignol*, impervious to the fact that the car could be clamped at any moment. It was late at night and she had been working all evening but still she wanted to talk.

Balanchine had created *Le Rossignol* for her and it had taken its shape because of her and what she could do. Now at eighty-four, she was passing it on to a new generation.

'My life has turned full circle,' she said.

Afterword by Markova

I was not born with a desire to dance. I had a natural facility for it but did not realize this until I went for training to cure my flat feet and knock-knees. Had I had straight legs I might never have danced. Then I was taught by Diaghileff that ballet is for life and I wanted only to dance.

I suppose I wanted to get married in my early life but it never happened. I think you could say that I'm one of those people who were married to their careers. It depends on the person; maybe I was that sort of person.

I'm a perfectionist and perfectionists are difficult to live with. Doris will tell you that. Perhaps at the time I didn't realize I was that sort of person. Whatever I undertake I always want to do it well, whether it's the lead in a great classical ballet or cooking a meal. For me the career was enough. Actually, people used to fall in love with me all the time.

I just want to be myself. I don't think I've ever been tough or ruthless – determined, yes, and I know I'm obstinate. But I don't believe you have to raise your voice and yell to make people do things. If anyone yelled at me it would paralyse me and I wouldn't be able to do anything at all. It's best to be straightforward and simple, treat people like human beings. You need to have respect for people; if you treat them like idiots they behave like idiots.

There have been times when I have wanted to creep away and lose it all, to be ordinary. But how can you be a wife and a dancer? Men are afraid of a woman who is alive and with her own personal instinct.

When work gets too hard I think longingly of peace and quiet and a place of my own. I will have that one day but I have never planned and I am not going to plan now. I have knowledge and it would be stupid of me to just sit on it and take it with me.

Sometimes when I am on a jet travelling around the world I am lonely but one cannot do everything, or have everything, in this life. I have no complaints. I'm grateful every day for what I have.

I think God meant me to dance and he meant me to work hard at it.

Index

Index